FAMILY
ACADEMY OF MISFITS BOOK 3

BEA PAIGE

This book is dedicated to my family. You know who you are.

Bea xx

"To do a great right, you may do a little wrong; and you may take any means which the end to be attained will justify."

— **Charles Dickens,** *Oliver Twist*

PLAYLIST

It is no secret that I listen to music whilst I write. Some authors like to write in utter silence, I'm not one of them. Music is my muse. I have been known to write, listen to music and sing all at the same time! Oftentimes music will inspire an idea and it's no different for this series. Delinquent (book one of Academy of Misfits) was inspired by Billie Eilish's Bad Guy. This playlist has grown somewhat since Delinquent and Reject, so why not check it out!

Listen to the full playlist on Spotify <u>HERE</u>

PROLOGUE

F amily.

A word that means so much to so many.

A word that, for a long time, I never really understood.

I had a mum, yes. A junkie mum who gave birth to me. She was my flesh and blood, and I'd loved her. *We'd* loved her, my brothers and me.

But it wasn't enough.

She tried to be who we needed, but in the end she gave us up because life was just too hard, and she was too weak to fight.

She left us alone.

She cast us adrift with no anchor to keep us safe, with no notion of what it means to be part of a family filled with warmth, love and security. And just like the last stuttering beat of her heart, that dream of family was snuffed out entirely when my baby brothers were taken from my arms, screaming for their mum, and for *me*.

I mourned the loss of my family that day. I mourned the loss for weeks, months, years after her death. I never really got over it. Instead, I became secretly infatuated with the man whose blood runs through my veins. The man my mum had loved. The man that had caused my mum's addiction, who broke her heart.

The man I now know to be the King.

The same man who bore a son as evil and as hateful as him.

The same man who uses kids to do his dirty work, to sell drugs and to inflict fear.

The same man who traffics girls for sex.

The same man who ordered the kidnapping of my friend.

The same man who *kills*.

He's my father and Monk is my brother, but neither are my family.

We might share the same genes but that means nothing to me. That doesn't make them family and it never will.

When my mum died and my brothers were taken from me, I never believed I'd find a family to call my own. But I did. Tracy became my surrogate mum. Bray, another little brother. Eastern remained my best friend but then became so much more.

Then later, I found more family in the most unlikely of places and now I understand what the word truly means. Family is about the people you *choose* to open your heart to, the people you can count on to have your back, to be by your side when shit gets tough. Family are the people who support you when you can't hold yourself upright. Family are the actions of people who will do anything to prove you mean as much to them as they mean to you. Family are the ones who laugh with you, who fight for you, who fucking cry with you. Family are the people who break down your barriers, who embrace your scars and aren't disgusted by them. Family are the ones who anchor you whilst the storm fucking rages, whilst the world around you crumbles to dust. They're the ones who stitch together your battered and broken heart, making it beat again. They're the ones who make you strong.

And now that I have a family, I will fight tooth and nail to keep them safe even if that means going up against my father and his son.

He might be the King. He might own a lot of people. But he'll never own me and he sure as fuck won't destroy what I've fought so hard to keep.

"Asia, you ready?" Ford asks me, drawing me back into the moment.

I grit my teeth and nod my head, ignoring the bead of sweat that falls down my spine, reminding me of the fear and danger we're all in. "I'm ready."

He glances at the rest of the guys, a determined set to his jaw. "We finish this tonight. No one fucks with our family and gets away with it."

Stepping forward, he holds his arm out, his hand fisted. Eastern doesn't hesitate, he places his palm over Ford's closed fist and grips it tightly, a fierce look passes between them. So much has changed these past few months since I joined Oceanside and despite the dangerous situation we're in, my heart swells with admiration, with joy at the loyalty they share now.

Next to place his hand into the circle is Camden. His split knuckles are still weeping, and beneath the swelling of his face I catch the darkness in his gaze and the need for revenge.

"You up for this, Cam?" Ford asks, concerned. The last few months have brought us closer, bound us together in an unbreakable unit. Camden gives Ford a look that cuts his question dead.

"No motherfucker is going to stop me, and if I should die tonight I will spend all of eternity making sure that cunt wished he'd never been born."

Ford nods, grimacing. We exchange looks. Both of us are fearful for him. If we survive tonight, it'll take Camden a long time to recover. Perhaps he never will. Either way, we'll be right there by his side ready to catch him when he breaks, and he will break. We all will eventually.

Sonny flicks his gaze to mine and for a moment I can't breathe. He says so much without saying anything at all.

"Sonny?" I question. Being here is hard for him, not because he doesn't want to fight, but because he's afraid of what will happen if he does.

"I'm here. I've got your back. Let's do this," Sonny says just as fiercely, placing his own hand over the others. I hope he survives this. I need him to.

"Asia?" Eastern prompts, his gold-flecked brown eyes more tumultuous than I've ever seen before. I know he wishes I wasn't here. I know he wishes I'd stayed behind. That I was safe. They all do. But this is my family too. This is my fight as much as theirs, more so perhaps.

"This is where I belong. I'm ready," I repeat, cupping their hands between mine and pushing away the pain I feel inside. I grip their hands tightly. "It's time for payback. It's time for retribution."

Around us the air crackles with tension and the humming need for vengeance.

The King might be my father, Monk my brother, but they're *not* my family.

These boys are. No, correction, these *men* are.

And we're here to fight.

ONE

One month earlier.

"**W**hat is it, Asia?" Camden asks, gently grasping hold of the paper. I let it slide from between my fingers, unable to react.

It can't be true.

It can't.

I stumble a little, my knees sagging. Eastern hauls me upright, pulling me into his side as we all listen to Camden read the note out loud. Every word slashes against my skin, widening the cuts they've already made, scarring me deeper than a knife ever could.

"You're his *daughter?*" Camden accuses, his hand dropping, the note fluttering to the floor. In my peripheral vision I see Sonny crouch down, reaching for the piece of paper, but my attention is fixed on Camden.

"I…"

"This is bullshit, of course she isn't. There's no fucking way!" Eastern snaps, hauling me closer, crushing me against him as if that alone can protect me from the truth. I can barely stand upright, let alone form any words to protest as vehemently.

He's my father.

Monk's my brother.

They have Pink.

"We don't know anything for certain," Hudson says, but I can tell he doesn't believe his words any more than I do.

He gives me a sorrowful look and there's something about that which makes this so much worse. If it's true and I am the King's daughter, then his blood runs in my veins.

"Him...?"

My voice trails off as I try to wrap my head around the news. The room seems to expand then shrink and I feel strange in my skin all of a sudden, like I don't belong. A dull pain begins to thud in my head, a feeling that has become familiar lately. I reach for my temple trying to rub away the oncoming migraine and the weird feeling inside.

"This is bullshit," Eastern repeats as my mind races with questions.

Do I look like him? I know I've got my mother's olive skin and dark hair, but my nose is a completely different shape to hers and my lips are fuller. And what about Monk? He's my half-brother. Did he know I was his sister when I started Oceanside Academy? Had he known when he'd hunted me down with his wolves? Was it when I hit him, intent on hurting him as much as he hurt me? When I beat him in the fight, did he know who I was then? Or was it after? Is that why he accepted me into the HH crew? Is that why he took Pink because he knows what she means to me and he wants revenge? All these thoughts flit like angry ravens trapped inside my head, their claws and beaks tearing at my flesh and bones, reaching inside for my DNA, searching for the truth.

I want answers, I want to understand.

But there's not one person in this room who can tell me. The only man who can give me what I need is the arsehole who'd rather kidnap my friend and use her against me to get what he wants, than to actually act like a father should. Well, fuck him and fuck his shitty son too. Fuck them both…

"*Fuck…They've got Pink.*" I shake my head, trying to rid myself of the feeling that somehow I'm responsible for all this.

"None of this makes any sense. How could Monk walk out of Oceanside with Pink? Tell me *how* the fuck that happened!" Eastern snaps, his anger drawing everything back into sharp reality. He's glaring at Frank who clears his throat with a loud cough, sending my scattered thoughts into chaos. I shake my head trying to focus on what he's saying.

"…One of the kids set a fire in the rec room in the main building. Both Buddy and I went to deal with it… Monk must've made his escape with Pink whilst we were distracted."

"So you were tricked by a bunch of fucking teenagers? Is that what you're saying?" Ford asks, his voice is cold, deadly in its calmness as he approaches us. "I thought you were an ex-marine or something? Aren't you supposed to be the best of the fucking best?" He barks out a laugh. "No match for a bunch of street kids, eh?"

"We underestimated them. We made a mistake not checking on everyone after the fire had been put out. For what it's worth, I'm sorry."

"Fuck your apologies. Fuck you all. Pink is in the hands of that little prick and his bastard dad because you couldn't see past a simple distraction trick. Fucking *idiots*," Eastern seethes.

Frank flinches. "It was a mistake. One that won't happen again."

"Damn fucking right it won't if I have anything to say about it," Camden says stepping forward and smashing his fist into Frank's cheek before anyone can stop him. "That's for fucking up!" he roars, spittle flying from his mouth in anger.

Frank doesn't retaliate. He simply rubs at his cheek and nods his head, accepting Camden's form of punishment. Beside him Hudson grits his jaw and I can hear Cal swearing under his breath, but neither make a move to step in.

"I'll do everything I can to help get her back," Frank responds with a clipped tone, before turning on his heel and striding from the room, his large muscles bunching with stress as he walks away.

"What a useless fucking dick," Eastern snaps.

"Enough! Frank is a soldier who's seen and done shit that warrants your respect," Cal says, moving to stand beside Hudson now. He clasps him on the shoulder in solidarity seeing as all the hate and blame is aimed at them both now that Frank has left the room.

"Respect? You're fucking kidding, right?" Ford growls this time.

"He fucked up. You said your piece," Hudson says, looking between Ford and Eastern, "And you dealt a blow," he snaps, glaring at Camden. "That's enough. Now we need to work on figuring this shit out."

"I'll tell you what needs to happen. You need to get the fuck out!" Eastern continues, dropping his arm from around my back and stepping towards Cal and Hudson.

"Hey, *hey*!" Sonny says, stepping between them and placing his hand flat against Eastern's chest. "It ain't their fault."

"Yeah, then who's fault is it? Because it sure as fuck isn't Asia's," Eastern bites out.

He's breathing hard, his nostrils flaring. Sonny winces. Right now he's stuck between supporting us and defending his foster family, trying to bridge the gap that's forming.

"I know but fighting amongst ourselves isn't helping the situation." Sonny catches my gaze and frowns. He knows just as well as I that our tenuous bond is in danger of breaking if we don't fix this somehow. All I know is that this is all happening because of me.

"But it is my fault, Eastern. He's *my* father," I hush out.

"No, Asia. No!" Eastern insists, turning to grasp me by the shoulders. "You don't know he's your dad, and even if he is, *none* of this is your fault."

"Mum refused to speak of him," I mutter, words falling from my lips like broken dreams shattered by ugly reality. "She made up all those stories, Eastern. She made me long for a man who wasn't real. She turned him into a fantasy, a fairytale, because she *knew* the truth of his identity was too ugly. The King *is* my father. I know it."

My head falls forward, the weight of this revelation heavy on my shoulders. All those questions my mum evaded over the years. All those leads that had turned into dead ends. I'd searched high and low, but it was as though my dad didn't want to be found. Now I know why. It all makes sense. I'm an illegitimate child born to a heroin addict. Of course he walked away from that, from me. Pain and confusion lacerate my heart, making it a bleeding pulpy mess. Why didn't he want me...?

What am I thinking? Why do I even care? I *don't* want that man as my father. Gritting my teeth, I push down all the confusing feelings inside of me. He's taken Pink. He's threatened her life. He's hurt so many people. I could *never* love a man like that.

"We don't know if he's your father for sure," Sonny says, frowning. "Just because that little prick has left a note saying it's true, doesn't mean that it is."

"Sonny's got a point," Ford agrees. In two steps he's beside me, twining his fingers with mine. I grip hold of his hand, squeezing tightly.

"You're right, we don't know for certain." Hudson scrapes a hand over his face. He looks haggard, even more so now than yesterday. He glances at Cal, a look passing between them.

"He's my dad. *I* know it," I glance back over at Camden who looks as pained as I feel. My dad and his mum… *Oh, god…* Camden's mum. In all of this I've failed to remember his mum and the danger she's in. I'm such a selfish bitch. "Your mum," I whisper, locking eyes with him.

Like a wrecking ball, those two words barrel into the room knocking us all sideways with the impact. Camden stumbles, shock littering his features, reflecting my own. Sonny grabs his arm, hauling him upright. The fear in his eyes makes my heart vibrate like the delicate wings of a butterfly. I struggle for breath as darkness swims at the corners of my vision and my head pounds, threatening oblivion.

"I need to call her… Fuck! I need to see if she's okay," Camden rambles looking frantic, unhinged even, as he pats the back pockets of his jeans searching for his mobile phone. "Where the fuck is it?" He rushes to the bed he was sleeping in, throwing the duvet on the floor in search of it. When he doesn't find it immediately, he starts ripping the room apart. Kate's cry of fear snaps me into action.

"Camden, let me help you find your phone," I say, pulling my hand free from Ford's grasp and shrugging free from Eastern's hold. I can do this. I need to focus on helping him find his phone as much for my peace of mind as his. I approach him slowly as he rips up the room around us.

"Where the fuck is it?!" he roars, pulling cushions off the bed and ripping the drawers from the bedside cabinet. They crash to the floor, making me jump.

"Camden, please, let me help you," I beg, holding my hands out to him. I approach him slowly, just like that time on the beach. He's so full of fear for his mum that he might just lash out like a wild animal that's injured and cornered. When my fingers meet his back, he stills, trembling with anxiety. I rest the flat of my hand against him hoping it's enough to comfort him, then take a deep breath and turn to face Hudson.

"We need a minute. Can you take Kate and leave us for a bit?"

Hudson meets my gaze and nods. "Sonny, bring Kate. Ford, you should come too. Grim wants to talk to you."

Both Sonny and Ford look at me, waiting for my approval. I nod tightly. "It's okay, just go."

"You sure? I can stay," Sonny says, glancing warily at Camden who still has his back to them all.

"I'll stay," Eastern replies, squeezing him on the shoulder.

"Watch him," Sonny mouths to Eastern, looking pointedly at Camden.

"You got it."

As the others file out of the room, Ford strides over to me, cups my cheek with his hand and presses a hot kiss against my mouth.

"This isn't on you. Do you hear me?" he says fiercely, his grey-green eyes flashing with sincerity. When I don't answer, his hand slides from my cheek and wraps around the back of my head as he presses his forehead against mine.

"This *isn't* on you…"

He knows what's deep in my heart. I blame myself. The King is my dad and he took Pink to get to me, after all. I want to collapse into his arms, needing to feed off his strength, but he moves away before I can. It's intentional, he's forcing me to be strong. To find that strength within myself.

"Do you hear me, Asia?" he repeats, taking another step away from me.

"I hear you," I whisper, nodding tightly and straightening my spine. A look passes between us, a look that tells me Ford will never let me crumble. He'll be the one to keep me strong even when I feel weak.

His gaze moves to Camden, boring into his back. "You are not your father, Asia, just like I'm not my parents. This *isn't* on you and anyone who believes it is needs their head fucking tested."

Beside me, Camden falls to his knees. Ford hesitates, but I shake my head.

"Go."

When the door shuts, clicking softly, I exchange worried looks with Eastern before crouching down beside Camden. He's curled over, clutching the back of his head as though he's trying to shut the world out. Eastern approaches us both but remains at the foot of the bed when I hold my hand up for him to stop.

"Camden, let me help you find your phone..."

"What's the point? If the King knows about the deal you made with Crown then she's already dead." His voice cracks, despair leaching into his voice as my own heart crumbles to dust.

TWO

I stare at Camden's trembling shoulders hating the world, hating Monk, hating the King. But most of all hating myself.

Somehow I need to fix this.

"She's dead..." he cries out, convinced the King has killed his mum.

"You don't know that yet. We don't know *anything* yet. All we have is this note that Monk wrote, that's it," I say, sliding my arm around his shoulder. I'm not sure who I'm trying to convince more, him or me.

Camden tenses under my touch as though it bothers him. I swallow the bile rising up my throat, forcing myself to be strong. I don't think I can deal with him pushing me away, not after how far we've come. "Don't talk like that. Let's find your phone and call your mum, yeah?"

As if on cue, a phone starts ringing or rather the sound of Drake singing *Back to Back* draws all of our attention to the gap beneath Camden's bed. He reaches out and after a moment pulls back, his phone clutched in his shaking hand. He looks at the screen, worry tight around his mouth. He answers, pressing the speaker button, then covers his mouth with his finger. My heart kicks up a notch as I glance at Eastern.

"Camden, how's your weekend away with those bunch of pricks?"

Monk's laughter escapes the mouthpiece and it takes all I have not to snatch the phone from Camden's hand and rip into the cocky little shit. Eastern slides off the bed and crawls on his hands and knees towards me. He wraps his arm around my shoulder, hugging me to his side tightly. He knows I'm close to blowing my shit. I grab hold of his thigh, my fingers digging into his jeans.

"What do you *want*, Monk?" Camden asks.

His voice is calm. If I didn't know any better I would think he wasn't at all bothered about his mum's safety. Yet, the naked fear in his eyes shows me he most definitely is.

"Things are about to get very interesting and you, dickhead, are on the shit list. Oh, the trouble you've caused."

"What are you talking about, Monk?" Camden's hands are shaking as he looks at us both.

"You really don't know?"

"Know *what*, Monk?"

"This is fucking priceless."

I can hear the glee in Monk's voice. The little prick is loving this.

"Monk, stop fucking around and tell me what you're talking about. I've had a shit fucking time stuck with these arseholes. I don't need your bullshit as well," Camden says, keeping up the pretence that we're still enemies.

"I thought you enjoyed Asia's company... pretty little thing, ain't she?"

Camden's nostrils flare, rage flashing in his eyes. "She's mine, Monk, so I suggest you back the fuck off." He's playing the part of overprotective boyfriend well, that part *isn't* put on for Monk's benefit.

"Oh, I don't want her like *that*." Monk laughs, the sound of his voice sending another bout of rage rippling over my skin, not to mention nausea rising up my throat. "Besides, I've got a new plaything... she's looks so pretty in *pink*."

His voice trails off and I hear a muffled cry in the background that has me screaming with rage into Eastern's palm that has suddenly covered my mouth. Camden moves away from us quickly. Trying to get some distance between us and the whimpering noises I'm now making.

"What the fuck was that?" Monk snarls, hearing my outburst.

"The fucking TV. Look, I'm losing patience, Monk. Fucking say what you want to say or get off the damn line," Camden snaps.

"Just trying to make conversation..."

"Monk!" Camden growls.

He chuckles then finally says what we've all been waiting to hear. "Our little smart-mouthed gang member is my *sister*, Camden. You've been fucking the King's daughter and he ain't happy. Not one little bit."

"You're full of shit," Camden immediately responds, faking his disbelief.

"Nah, I'm not. Looks like the King has a thing for skanky-arse heroin addicts. Asia's the product of a nasty little fuck."

I pull against Eastern's hold, wanting to reach into Camden's phone and yank that motherfucker out by his neck, but Camden flashes me a warning glare. Gritting his teeth, he waits for Monk to fill the silence.

"But that's not the best of it, *boss*," Monk boasts gleefully, the sarcasm thick and heavy. "I get to have some fun whilst the King decides how to play this..."

"What are you talking about?" Camden snaps, his anxiety making itself known.

"Surely you've heard by now?"

"Heard what?"

"You know how this works. The King needs to get Asia in line. There's really only one way to do that."

"What. The. Fuck. Do. You. Mean. Monk?" Camden repeats, needing to hear him say the words. To spell it out.

Monk laughs, the sound ripping at my skin until I swear I'm just a fucking skeleton bleached white by the sun.

"Pink is *my* plaything now, just like your mum remains the King's... Let's just hope Asia does what Daddy Dearest wants otherwise Pink will be carted off to some distant land to become some sick fuck's sex toy and your mum will find her new home ten feet under the dirt."

"You bastard," Camden snarls into the mouthpiece. "If you do anything to hurt either of them..."

"You'll what? Cry into your fucking pillow?" Monk responds cruelly. "Listen up, arsehole, and pay fucking attention. In a few days we'll send word to you and my pretty little sister. As long as you *both* do as you're told, Pink and your precious mum will remain alive. You fuck up, they're dead..."

"How do I know that they're not dead already? Why the fuck should I trust you?"

Monk falls silent, there's a moment of muffled talking then a second later a sob fills the air. "Camden, is that you?"

Pink's quaking voice sounds through the loudspeaker. I have to press Eastern's hands harder against my mouth to stop myself from calling out to her.

"There we go," Monk sneers. I picture his twisted features and rage burns inside, focusing me, forcing me to be strong.

"And Mum?" Camden questions.

"I thought you might ask that..." There's more silence, a longer stretch this time. Then a soft voice fills the air.

"I'm here, love."

"Mum?" Camden's voice cracks.

"I'll take care of her, okay? Just don't-"

There's the loud crack of skin meeting skin, and a low moan that sounds far too female to be Monk's. Camden's body goes rigid with rage. The veins in his forearm pop beneath the skin like angry snakes beaten out of the grass.

"You fucking cunt," Camden roars.

Monk chuckles in response. "Be a *love* and do as you're fucking told. You'll be hearing from us soon."

The phone clicks off and I force Eastern's hand away, launching at the mattress and punching it until I run out of steam and fall backwards on my arse. Frustrated tears fall hot and heavy down my cheeks.

"Asia, look at me," Camden urges, crouching down in front of me. When I fail to follow his gentle command, he grasps my face in his large hands and lifts my head up. "He doesn't know, Asia. The King doesn't know about your deal with Crown."

I shake my head, wild thoughts ripping through my mind at the thought of Pink, prisoner to that sick twisted bastard Monk and his father, *our* father. I know what Monk did to Ruby. I know what he's capable of. He just hit Camden's mum, for fuck's sake.

"He's going to hurt her just like he hurts your mum!" I pant, frustration and despair clawing at my fraying strength as I grip hold of his wrists, squeezing tightly.

"No! The King will never allow him free rein over Pink. He trusted me with the crew and not Monk. Why? Because we all know that he's too much of a live wire. That speaks volumes."

"Not anymore. You heard what Monk said. You heard what he *did*. He has them both."

Doubt crosses Camden's features, but he forces it away. "He'll pay for striking my mum, for scaring Pink," he growls before dragging in a breath and letting it out slow and steady. "But so long as they're alive there's hope. The King doesn't know. We have a chance to set things straight," he repeats, making sure I understand.

"If that's true, then *why* take Pink?"

"Like Monk said, to get you in hand. As long as they have her, you'll do anything. He has plans for you, I just don't understand what that is right now."

"Jesus fucking Christ," Eastern exclaims. "I don't like this one bit."

"Neither do I..." Camden replies, glancing at Eastern before meeting my gaze once more. "Believe me, I want to fucking rip the world apart so I can find them both, but we have to be smart. We need to wait and see what he wants."

"And in the meantime, Monk gets to beat on Pink?" I accuse, feeling hopeless.

"He may be acting the big man now but trust me on this, the King won't let him fuck this up. They die, he loses control over us."

"I'm not talking about Monk killing Pink... She doesn't deserve to be his fucking punching bag. Maybe we should just try and find them now."

"If I thought the right thing to do would be to go looking for them now then I'd be the first to suggest it."

"But we're not going to, are we?"

Camden shakes his head. "I swear to you, Asia, we *will* get them back, but we have to wait. We have to see what the King wants," he says fiercely, twining his fingers in my hair and tugging on the strands.

"I hate to admit it, but Camden's right, Asia," Eastern agrees. He gently pulls me free from Camden's hold and folds me into his lap. "We'll figure this out. I promise."

But their reassurances and promises aren't enough. I'm deaf to them because all I can hear is Pink's frightened voice. All I can see are Monk's words scrawled across that tatty piece of paper. All I know is that my father isn't the hero of this story, he's the villain and he's got Pink.

THREE

I must've passed out, or fallen asleep or something, because I awake with a groggy head wrapped up in Eastern's arms on the double bed. He's spooning me from behind, his arm folded around my waist. We're alone, the curtains drawn against the bright winter's day. I shift in his arms a little trying to slide out from his hold. Everything comes rushing back and my head pounds. These fucking migraines are ridiculous.

"Hey, you're awake," he murmurs gently.

"Fuck, what happened? What time is it?"

"Just past three pm. You kind of zoned out a bit…"

"My head," I mutter.

"Migraine?" he asks me, loosening his arms a little, allowing me to shift in his hold. I turn to face him lifting my hand so I can massage my temple.

"You worried me there for a bit."

"Yeah, I've been having them for a while now. They're doing my head in. I can't believe I blacked out."

"It's all the stress. You haven't had an episode like this since you were a kid. How long have they been back?"

"A few weeks."

"We need to fix you up with some medication. All this stress ain't good for you."

"I don't care about that, Eastern. I care about Pink, about Camden's mum. What the fuck are we going to do?"

"Right now, you need to look after yourself."

I open my mouth to protest, but he presses a warm finger against my lips. "Shh, the guys are downstairs trying to figure shit out. Let them. You need a minute. This isn't something you have to carry alone. We're all here for *you* now. You don't have to fight the world alone anymore."

"Is Camden with them?"

"Yeah, do you need me to get him?"

"Not right now. If I'm being honest, I'm not sure I can face him. I need to get my head straight first."

"Okay, whatever you need. I got you."

He gives me a tentative smile, one that doesn't reach his eyes. He's worried just as much as I am but he's trying to be there for me. Eastern has always been that person who has stood by me when everyone else had given up. He's my best friend and so much more now.

"Why do we always have to fight so fucking hard?" I mutter, trying and failing to hold onto the rising despair that threatens to break me. A warm tear rolls down my cheek and I move to swipe it away, but he gets there first.

"Because this is what we do."

"I'm tired of it, Eastern. I don't even know who I am anymore," I admit. That weird sensation of not being right in my skin creeping over me again. One minute I'm Asia Chen, the next I'm the King's daughter. Right now, I don't want to be either. I just want a normal life, with normal first world problems and not this shit hanging over me.

"You're Asia, you're the strongest person I know. Don't stop fighting," he murmurs. The warmth of his fingers trail across my cheek as he captures another tear that breaks free. "But if you need to break every now and then, then *I got you*," he repeats fiercely.

His words echo those I spoke to Camden on the beach not that long ago. We all need someone we feel safe enough to break down in front of. Eastern's that person for me.

"What do you think he wants? I'm pretty sure it's not a Sunday stroll in the park so he can get to know me after all these years," I say bitterly.

"I don't know, but given it's the King, it can't be good."

"Fuck, Eastern…" I'm so close to crumpling and letting everything go, that I have to bite down on the inside of my cheek to stop myself from losing my shit completely.

"Come here," he mutters, his voice hoarse with emotion.

I scoot closer, wrapping my arms around his back and pressing my face into the crook of his neck, breathing in his scent of apples and smoke. It's familiar and comforting. I clutch onto him, onto the one person who's been a constant in my life. His hands smooth down my back in firm but gentle strokes and I find a little peace in his arms, enough to settle my crushing thoughts and calm my soul for a little while at least.

"Do you remember that time Old Man Joe gave me a hiding because I broke into his shed and nicked his clapped-out tandem bike so we could go ride around the estate like a couple of idiots?" he asks after a while, taking me back to a time that seemed so much easier in comparison.

"Of course, I remember. Best day of my life," I mutter into his neck, my lips whispering against his skin as his pulse beats against my lips. We were ten, mischievous and bored. School was out for the summer and we'd been hanging out at the park trying to make use of the one broken swing and a rusty climbing frame for fun. When

Eastern disappeared for ten minutes and returned with the bike, I'd literally screamed with delight, almost knocking him off it in my excitement.

"I got into so much trouble for that," he says, the vibrations of his laugh rumbling against my chest.

"God, your mum hit the roof when she'd found out what you'd done. I think that's the only time I'd ever seen her whack you upside the head," I say, pulling back slightly so I can look at him, remembering the skinny, dirty knee boy he once was. When he smiles, grinning with amusement, I'm reminded that he is no longer that boy, but a man. I swallow hard.

"Fuck, I remember. That bloody hurt."

We both laugh at the memory, settling my sudden nervousness in his presence. I'm pretty sure he had a ringing ear for two full weeks after, as well as a bruised ego given the whole estate had watched Tracy give him a piece of her mind. I'd felt his embarrassment and shame as though it were my own, but I'd also felt jealous. Jealous that he had someone who cared enough to be angry. My own mum was too high to even know where I was, let alone able to summon enough energy to give me a hiding too.

"Yeah, but that wasn't the funniest part because once she'd finished with you she gave Old Man Joe a mouthful for hitting you. Pretty sure I learnt several new swear words that day. At one point I thought he was gonna keel over and die."

"Yeah, me too." Eastern grins, making my own lips curl up into another smile.

"We had fun back then, didn't we?"

"Yeah, loads... but there was a lot of crap times too. You went through more than most."

Eastern sighs heavily, his grin falling. I see another memory form in his eyes, and I know exactly what he's thinking about. "You were so strong that day. Stronger than I could ever have been in the same situation."

"I wasn't, Eastern. It broke me, seeing her like that."

"You held onto her as though your love could wake her up... I'll never forget it."

"I wish you would. I wish *I* could," I mumble, dropping my gaze from his.

We've never really talked about that time, but I know Eastern is just as affected by my mum's death as I am. He was the one who found me clinging to her body, begging her to wake up. He'd come by to give me my birthday present but instead had to raise the alarm, and whilst Tracy called the ambulance, it was his arms my brothers and I fell into and didn't leave until the police forced us apart.

Always him. Always Eastern.

"You've lived through so much shit, Asia. Too much..."

"Please," I hush out, shaking my head. "I don't want to think about mum right now or that shitty day. Not today, Eastern. Talk about something else."

"Okay," he murmurs, feathering his fingertips against my skin and wiping away another tear I hadn't realised had fallen. He presses the wet tear against his mouth, his tongue licking it away. Something about that has my heart squeezing with pain and my thighs clenching with desire, two opposing forces pulling me in different directions.

It's funny how that works... I mean, in times of great distress the natural human reaction is to seek out comfort, warmth, *sex*. A coping mechanism I suppose. Somehow I need to cope with this situation better than I am... I need to forget for a moment. Maybe it's a selfish wish given the circumstances, but that's what I need. I need to forget, and I can't think of anyone better to lose myself with than Eastern. I love him. It's that simple.

"Eastern…" I begin, trying to form the words I need to make him understand.

I'm acutely aware of his hot stare, of the way his fingers are smoothing over my hair, of his warm breaths feathering over my skin. The tightness in my chest is a powerful ache that reminds me of all the things I've lost and what I have right here in front of me.

"Eastern… I need," I try again, but his finger presses against my lips making my words dissolve on my tongue. The look of love in his eyes has my heart expanding.

"I'm *so* proud of you, Asia. Of the woman you've become." He laughs to himself a little at how that sounds. "You must think I'm an idiot."

"I don't," I hush out, meeting his gaze, getting trapped there.

"We don't often get compliments being the way we are, and you deserve so much praise."

"You mean being *delinquents*?"

"Yeah, I suppose. Thing is, you're so much more than that shitty fucking label, Asia. You're artistic, so fucking talented. You're brave, strong. You don't take any shit and you stand up for the ones you love regardless of the repercussions. You, Asia, are a fucking beautiful human being. You always have been."

I laugh awkwardly, not used to getting compliments, and especially not used to this electric charge between us. It's grown in intensity of late. I mean, last night was fucking awesome, but that was lust. This, right now, is more. This is love. When I look into Eastern's eyes, I know he feels it too.

"Thank you for being so…"

"What, Asia?" he smiles gently, understanding that it's hard for me to really tell him how I feel.

"...so fucking amazing. You mean *everything* to me, Eastern. I could never have gotten through all the shit growing up without you. I'm sorry for the way it has been between us recently. It's always been just us and I know that this has been hard on you... accepting them." My hand reaches up and cups his face, my fingertips feathering over his skin.

"I know that. I know you and I can take all of this because I know it makes you happy, and when you're happy, I'm happy. Besides, those arseholes aren't that bad..."

"Yeah, they're good guys... when they're not being arseholes," I respond, and we both laugh then fall silent for a while, content on just holding one another.

"That week when Old Man Joe gave me a beating and mum grounded me..." His voice trails off as his gaze flicks from my eyes to my lips and back again. I suck my lip ring between my teeth as his focus zeros in on my mouth, his pupils widening.

"What?"

"That was the first time I realised I loved you. Not the best friend kind of love, but something more. I wanted to kiss you so bad that week. I almost did so many times, but I never quite plucked up the courage." He shakes his head, smiling ruefully as his fingers run up and down the bare skin of my arm, scattering goosebumps over my skin.

"And now?" I ask gently, my heart squeezing so hard that I think for a moment it's about to burst. It's been through a lot these past twenty-four hours.

"And now what?" he asks, tipping his head to the side as he regards me.

"Do you have the courage to kiss me just like you kissed me last night? Like you wanted to back then?"

Eastern laughs. "Back then I would've been happy with a quick kiss on the lips. Last night was something different too. Don't get me wrong, it was fucking amazing but right now, this," he says, a frown creasing his forehead as he tries to explain how he's feeling. "...This is *more*."

"I know." He's right, it is. It's so much more. "Eastern, I need..."

He shifts closer, pulling my body against his length, understanding what I need even when I can't form the words to tell him. I feel his arousal between us, and the thick, heavy feeling of lust wrapped up in years and years of friendship and love.

I need to forget about my father.

I need to forget about Monk.

I need to feel something other than pain and disappointment.

I need Eastern inside of me because he's the only one who can heal me right now.

My best friend. The boy I love.

In this moment, no one else will do.

FOUR

"W hat do you need, Asia?" he asks softly, drawing me back into the moment with him.

"I *need* you... I always have even when I convinced myself I didn't," I admit.

Eastern smiles tentatively, his thumb skating over my bottom lip. "If I start, I might not be able to stop."

"I don't want you to stop. I want you to start and never end. Don't let me go, Eastern. Don't let me fucking go..." I choke out, feeling more vulnerable than I ever have before.

"Never," he responds, leaning closer, his soft breaths feathering over my skin. "I'll never let you go, Asia. *Never.*" His chest is heaving as his fingers slide into my hair and his mouth hovers over mine. "I've thought about this moment for so long." His face screws up with concern, and I can feel him pulling back despite the need in his eyes, in mine.

"You're vulnerable, I don't want to take advantage..."

"Eastern."

"Yes?"

"Shut the hell up and kiss me..."

He grins, closing the gap half a second later. When his mouth meets mine, I let out a moan. A deep satisfied moan as I melt against his body. This feels right, so right.

I fucking love this boy.

He's home.

He's my past, my present and my future.

He's mine and right now I need to be his.

Eastern pulls me closer on the bed, his leg hooking over my hip as his kiss deepens, his tongue meeting my own in languid strokes. The surety of his hold has me searching for the warmth of his skin. I need to feel him, touch the hard plains of his muscles. We've grown up together, fought each other's battles, had each other's backs and now I want nothing more than to lose myself in his hold, to love him as much as he loves me. I need him to anchor me when I feel so cast adrift.

Eastern's fingers curl tighter in my hair as his arm slides around my back and he clutches my arse forcefully. I feel his erection between us as his hips roll against mine and his tongue seeks out the warmth of my mouth.

"Asia. I'm so damn hot for you," he hushes out, his lips and teeth grazing against my chin now, tracing my jaw line as he gently twists my head to the side. "You might have to remind me to breathe, because I swear you make me breathless…"

I giggle at his crappy sex talk, but inside I'm melting into a puddle of mushy, loved-up goo. So perhaps it isn't so crappy after all.

"Breathe," I remind him before sliding my tongue over the shell of his ear making him jerk in my arms.

"Fuck, Asia, you wouldn't believe the dirty thoughts I've had about you."

His body shudders as I nip his earlobe, the warmth that radiates between us growing intense.

"Do you like that?" I tease, loving how his cock hardens further with my words and my touch.

"You're not doing a very good job at helping me not to die, Asia," he laughs, a deep groan rises up his throat when my hand reaches between us and cups his cock.

"I need to feel you against my skin," I say sharply, wanting all the barriers between us to be gone. My fingertips itch to feel him so I move them away from the heat of his cock and slide up and under his t-shirt. I press the flat of my hands against the smooth muscle of his stomach as his mouth finds mine again and he kisses me harder. My fingers spread out over his chest finding a smattering of hair that I want to rub my cheek against, that I want to kiss.

"Take it off. Take it all off," I pant, my hands reluctantly leaving his skin to find the hem of his shirt as I help him rip it off his head allowing me a brief moment to touch and taste him. My tongue licks over his skin. Finding his nipple, I bite gently.

"Fuck, Asia," he growls, leaping off the bed so he can remove his jeans. He yanks them off, not taking his eyes off me. My eyes flick to his tight boxer shorts and the thick length of him.

Oh. My. Fuck.

He grins. "Now you."

Sitting up, I remove my clothes quickly, leaving on my knickers and bra. Eastern drags in a sharp breath as he takes in my pebbled nipples and the strip of hair that I know he can see through my lacy underwear.

"Fuck me," he mutters.

"I thought you'd never ask," I joke, my cheeks instantly flushing when he slides off his boxer shorts and his cock jerks free. He's big, wide. The tip is angry and red. I have the sudden urge to take him in my mouth, to taste him on my tongue. Before he can make the next move, I get up on my hands and knees and crawl towards him. "Don't move," I say.

He lets out a stream of curse words as I sit before him on the edge of the bed and reach for his cock, grasping the base and wrapping my lips around the tip.

"Asia," he moans, his hips jerking as I take him as far as I can into my mouth. He tastes like he smells, and I hum, my mouth vibrating around him. A feeling of power washing over me.

"If I stop breathing, don't forget to give me mouth to mouth," he manages to utter before grasping the back of my head with his hand and rocking his hips gently. He's holding back, afraid of hurting me, but his moans of ecstasy spur me on. Grasping his arse with my free hand, I squeeze, hollowing out my cheeks then suck, drawing him deeper into my mouth as my tongue flattens against the underside of his dick, feeling the pulse beat in the thick vein that runs there. I lick him, my saliva making him slick. He jerks again, his glutes tightening, and I taste pre-cum on my tongue. His taste makes *me* wet. I feel the dampness flood my knickers.

"Stop, Asia. Fuck me, you've got to stop before I come," he grinds out, placing his hands on my shoulders and pushing me back gently. I let him go with a gentle pop of my lips and look up at him as his dick bobs between us, glistening. He brushes his fingers over my forehead, moving my hair out of the way with gentle fingers, then he backs off and picks up his jeans, searching in the pocket. A second later he pulls out his wallet, and a condom tucked away inside. It's so cliché that I can't help but tease him.

"Are you always this prepared?" I ask him, pressing my thighs together to try and ease the throb there.

"I've always been hopeful," he admits with a cute smirk and a shrug of his shoulders. Then he's serious. "Last chance to back out."

"I never back out. I never back down. You should know that by now, Eastern. Besides, I started this. I want this. I want you. Always. Forever. Now."

My body heats as he tears the condom wrapper open with his teeth and rolls it over his length. When our eyes meet again, I swallow hard.

Eastern bites down on his lip.

"Lie down, Asia. Let me love you," he hushes out, stalking towards me.

I shuffle backwards resting against the headboard as I watch him crawl up the bed, his arm muscles bunching as he moves, his cock swaying beneath him. He straddles my legs, reaching for my hips as he pulls me down the bed so I'm flat on my back. Before I can even think about how turned on I am, he reaches behind my back, unclasps my bra and pulls it off in one quick movement.

"Asia, you're fucking beautiful."

He leans over, his chocolate-brown hair whispering across my skin as he takes my nipple into his mouth and sucks hard. I jerk, my back arching beneath his touch as his fingers slide up my sides and clasp my breasts. He shifts, settling between my legs until his tongue slides up my hot skin, scorching over my collarbone and the length of my arched neck until he licks the seam on my lips, parting them, and plunders the depths of my open mouth.

His kisses become less gentle and more intense, more needful, greedy, and in response to this sudden change my nails scorch a trail down his back, marking him with pink streaks, just like his lips and his fingers mark me. When he pushes my knickers aside and slides his fingers over my slit, parting the skin and seeking out the spot I so desperately want him to touch, my hips buck pressing against his hand.

"Eastern, please."

It's such a feral need, this feeling inside. It's something that takes over me in the moment. It's raw, desperate somehow. I want to absorb his love. I want to blot out everything else that hurts and only feel him deep inside me. I want him to fill up the ache in my chest with something I can hold onto. I want more.

His fingers dip inside, his thumb circles my clit teasing me, making me hot, frustrated.

"No, Eastern. Please, fuck me," I hush out, panting with desperate need.

"Asia, we'll have plenty of time to fuck," he whispers, pushing up on his elbows and cupping my head between his hands. His thumbs press into my cheeks, gently smoothing away the tension I hold in my face. "Right now, I'm going to love you."

When he enters me in a slow, deliberate move I can't help but pull his face to mine, my fingers digging into his scalp. We kiss softly as he settles within me, filling me up with every inch. As my body adjusts, the slight sharp sting of pain easing into bliss, I lift my legs and wrap them around his arse.

"Oh God, Eastern," I cry out, my body arching as he moves within me, knowing instinctively what I need. He rocks into me, this man I love. This boy who I've always known will care for me. My best friend, my heart, my home. He moves steadily, with purpose, with determination to get me off, to make me forget about everything I've learned today, if only for a little while.

We clutch at each other, lips glistening with passion, fingers burning with desire, skin flashing with a heat that rushes over us both incinerating every past hurt to dust and dissolving painful memories until they are insignificant in the moment.

Our skin is slick, our kisses burn. They mark; they imprint a lifetime of friendship across our skin, tattooing our love for each other in breathless moans and whispers of forever. Our lips stay fused together as we move in harmony chasing the orgasm that is building between us, expanding and growing, evolving words into actions, promises into reality.

"Will you chase me?" I ask.

"Always," Eastern assures me, thrusting one last time.

His back arches and my eyes slam shut as we come together, two best friends who've found home in each other's hearts, words of love ringing in our ears.

FIVE

Reality is female. It has to be, because it's a right bitch.

When Eastern and I finally head downstairs and into the living room where everyone is waiting, reality slaps me in the face.

Hard.

One moment I'm making love to my best friend and the next I'm faced with Kate's haunted, pale face and the varying shades of concern on everyone else's. I haven't even given Kate a second thought since she left the room. I pushed her out of my head to save my sanity, not able to take on anyone else's pain. Now that I'm faced with her, I feel like a piece of shit. Swallowing, we exchange glances and my first thought is to apologise to her, to hug her and reassure her that everything is going to be okay. Only I can't, because that would be a fucking lie. Over the years, so many people have promised me the same and never once did those promises come true.

"Your mum's a heroin addict... but everything will be okay."

"We're putting you in care... but everything will be okay."

"Your brothers won't be living with you anymore... but everything will be okay."

"Your dad's a fucking criminal… but everything will be okay."

It's bullshit.

I'd rather be prepared for the worst than be given false hope with a lie. So, all I can do is apologise. "I'm sorry, Kate. I needed to sort my head out."

She nods tightly, a wobbly smile forming on her lips. "Of course you did. I understand."

On the other side of the room Mr Carmichael watches me. He's not his usual put together self. In fact, sleep seems to have bypassed him completely. He looks rough as shit. Good.

"Mr Carmichael," I sneer, unable to help myself. What the fuck was he doing when all the shit went down? He's got a lot to answer for.

"Asia," he nods, wincing a little. "I'm…"

"Come in, we've a lot to sort out before you head back to Oceanside," Hudson interrupts, waving us into the room.

Eastern squeezes my hand pulling me towards the sofa. Just like yesterday all the adults are on one side of the room, Ford, Camden, Kate and now us, on the other. There's an invisible line separating us and the only person who seems to be straddling that line is Sonny. He's perched on a footstool, his broken arm back in a sling, watching us closely. He looks stressed, so much more so than yesterday. It's clear he's been mediating between the two sides. Trying to bridge the gap that's forming, just like I knew he would. I give him a shaky smile, grateful for him. For holding everything together.

"You okay?" he asks.

"I will be." *When I've killed the King*, I think.

I sit between Kate and Ford, Eastern resting at our feet. Kate picks at her nails nervously and I grab her hand, holding it in mine. She lets out a shaky breath, then sits up a little straighter.

On the opposite end of the sofa Camden has his bare feet pulled up onto the seat cushion, and even though there's only a small space between us, the gap feels wider than it should. His body language is a little closed off, defensive, and when I catch his gaze I can't help but notice how his eyes narrow at the flush that shines on Eastern's cheeks, probably on mine too.

"Feeling better?" he asks me, his voice gruff.

"I am," I state, not allowing myself to feel guilty about the fact Eastern and I just had sex. I won't. Camden nods, a muscle in his jaw ticking. Knowing him the way I do, I'm sure he's finding it hard not to go all domineering on my arse. He's a contradiction, swerving between possessive and giving. The two sides of his personality warring constantly.

"I'd like to say it's good to see you, Asia, but under the circumstances that doesn't seem appropriate," Mr Carmichael says, and even though he doesn't apologise outright I know he's sorry too. I see just how much in his eyes. They're very expressive, even when he has his game face on, but I can't acknowledge his silent apology because I'm angry. At him, at the King, at the whole fucking world right about now. The anger I'd managed to suppress in Eastern's arms comes hurtling back full force.

"Camden told us you weren't feeling well. Do we need to call you a doctor?"

"No," I immediately snap. "Just a migraine. I'm fine."

"Asia, I'm responsible for your wellbeing..." Mr Carmichael insists.

Kate snorts. "Like you were for Pink's?"

"I deserve that."

No one corrects him.

"Want to fill us in on what you've been discussing?" Eastern asks, ignoring Mr Carmichael's attempt to steer the conversation in another direction.

"Grim has made some calls. She believes she might know where they've taken Pink and Camden's mum," Hudson explains, glancing at Grim.

I stiffen. "Where?"

Ford rests his hand on my thigh and squeezes. Giving me his support and his strength, without allowing me to feel weak. I'm grateful for it. With Eastern I can be vulnerable, with Ford he gives me what I need to fight. A little bit of his iron-clad resolve seeps into me.

"*Where?*" I repeat.

Grim locks eyes with me whilst everyone else in the room waits for her to elaborate. "I'm not one hundred percent certain. It's a hunch. One thing I do know for sure is that neither Pink nor Camden's mum are at the spa in Hastings. My girls haven't seen or heard anything about them being brought there."

"And?" Eastern butts in.

"And the King is extremely possessive to the point of obsession. Cam filled us in about the phone call from Monk. No matter what we think about his relationship with Cam's mum, if she's with Pink, then the King will be close by. Which makes this all the more difficult." She sighs, pulling on her cigarette deeply. Behind her Louisa coughs, wafting the air about her face. The woman's pregnant, she doesn't need Grim puffing like a chimney around her. I would've said as much if Louisa hadn't excused herself at that moment. She leaves the room with Max, but not before giving me a gentle smile.

"I want to talk with you in a little bit. Come find me in the kitchen when you're done here, okay?"

"Okay," I respond, briefly wondering about what she wants to say to me before turning my attention back to Grim. "Well, fucking spit it out. What does your hunch tell you?"

"The King has many places of residence dotted about the country that he likes to stay at depending on his mood and business dealings, but there is one place that he uses as a hideaway that he believes is a long-held secret. It's not."

"Grim has built up a lot of acquaintances over the years, and a lot of respect. People trust her, and with trust comes information," Bryce explains, butting in.

"Oh my fucking God, will you just tell me where they are!" I snap, my patience ending.

"There's a small island off the coast of Kent. Barely any residents bar a handful of tenants. He has a private home there. A small castle converted into a *palace fit for a King...*" she explains with more than a heavy dose of sarcasm.

"Fit for an arsehole more like," Camden growls.

"And, you think he's taken them there because...?" I insist.

"It seems the logical choice. The King believes he's safe there, but I happen to know someone who has a vested interest in the King and his actions."

"Who?" Camden asks Grim.

"A woman called Ma Silva. She was a very good friend of my grandfather's once upon a time. She'll tell me if my hunch is right and he's suddenly got a couple of new house guests." "Who the fuck is Ma Silva and how does she know the King?" Eastern asks, before the rest of us can.

"She's his godmother, and she happens to own most of the island his *palace* is located on."

"His godmother?" I ask incredulously, drawing my eyebrows together in a frown.

"Yes."

Camden shifts on the sofa, swinging his feet to the floor. "Why the fuck would his godmother help *us*?"

"Because she owes me and because she knows he's not a good man."

"And if your hunch is right, and he's keeping them there, what then?"

"Then we send someone to watch, and we wait to see what he wants from you, Asia."

"Fucking perfect," I mumble.

Grim stands and walks towards the French doors that open out to the garden. She unlocks the door and flicks her cigarette butt out before turning back to face us.

"I know it might not seem like it, but we have the upper hand because we have knowledge, and that is very powerful."

"But that's only if your hunch is correct, right?" I insist. "If you're wrong and they're not being held there, then what?"

"Then we do more investigating," Cal says, flipping off his phone that he's been using to send text messages the whole time we've been talking. "We'll find them. Whatever it takes. It'll be…"

"Don't. Don't you dare say it'll be okay. We all know that's bullshit."

"Asia, Cal is doing his best," Mr Carmichael begins.

I whip my head around and glare at him. "His best ain't good enough. You know as well as I do that when it comes to people like Monk, like the *King*," I spit, refusing to call him my father, "that we have to fight fire with fire."

Letting go of Kate's hand, I stand. Eastern stands too, moving towards me, but despite my need to collapse into his arms and beg him to take the pain away, I reach for Ford instead. He gets up, his fingers twining with mine, holding me tight. I need his strength and he has it in abundance. "I want them dead! Nothing else is good enough."

The room stills. Even Grim's eyes widen before she grits her jaw and nods with understanding. "We all do. But that ain't gonna happen. At least, not whilst he's still got the people you love. We get them out and then you get to deal with the King. You have my word."

"Grim!" Hudson warns. "She's just a kid. You can't offer her vengeance like it's a fucking sweet."

"Asia's been screwed over enough. If she wants revenge, who am I to say she can't have it?"

"Now hold on a minute," Mr Carmichael says, stepping in. "Asia isn't going to be killing anyone."

A look passes between Grim and Mr Carmichael, one I can't interpret. I laugh bitterly. "But here's the thing, Mr Carmichael, I'm not sure I see any other alternative. Tell me, did you have one when you put that man who killed your brother into a wheelchair?" I cock my head, narrowing my eyes at him. When he opens his mouth to respond, I wave my hand in the air. "Actually, don't answer that because I'm pretty sure you didn't have to fuck that guy up like you did. Your alternative was to walk away except you *didn't*. I'm not walking away from this."

"I don't want that for you," Mr Carmichael responds.

"Fuck what you want!" I snap back.

"*We* don't want that for you," Bryce says this time, concern filling his eyes.

"You don't know me. Why would you even care?" I accuse, the kid within me who's never had anyone looking out for her, or even considering her wellbeing, raises its ugly head.

"Because I know what it's like to have a father who's evil. I know what it's like to have a father who hurts the people you love just so he can hurt you more. And I know what it's like to have a mother who's weak, putting her own needs first. I understand your anger, your pain. I really fucking do. But I also know that revenge is only sweet when you don't fuck your own life up to get it. You're just a kid and murdering someone isn't what we want for you."

"It doesn't matter what you want. I might be *just* a kid in your eyes, but I know how this works. Even if we do manage to get Pink and

Camden's mum out unharmed, he will hunt us all down. He won't let this go. I don't even know the man, but I know that much."

"Asia's right. He will." Camden gets to his feet too, determination set in his jaw. His hands are balled into fists and the tension between us all grows. "But for once I agree with Mr Carmichael, and with you, Bryce," he says, shocking me. Camden's piercing topaz eyes bore into mine as he continues. "You're not a murderer, Asia."

Sonny scrapes a hand over his face. "We won't let you ruin your life."

I shake my head. "You see something that isn't there. You saw how I was with Monk. I'm capable of hurting people."

"Asia, knocking someone out and ending someone's life are two very different things," Eastern says, the love he feels for me softening his gaze.

"You think I couldn't do it? You think I couldn't kill that bastard for what he's done?" I seethe.

"No one here doubts that you could do it, Asia, but that doesn't mean *you* should," Hudson sighs.

"I'm just as fucked up as the rest of you."

"You're wrong. I see what's within you and it's so fucking *good*. Why do you think we're all so drawn to you, Asia?" Camden responds, angrily. "It isn't just because you're strong, brave, and fucking beautiful, it's because despite all the crap life has thrown at you, you still have a conscience, a sense of right and wrong. You protect the ones you love. Nothing you do is selfish."

"Killing the King *is* protecting the ones I love," I argue with him.

Bryce shakes his head. "No, it isn't. That's called revenge and it will ruin you."

"None of that matters now."

"Yes, it fucking does. It matters. *You* matter to us," Sonny insists.

"I won't let him change you into someone you don't recognise,"

Camden continues, not taking his eyes off me for one second. "I lost who I was because of *him* and I'm finding my way back to that person because of *you*."

"I agree," Ford says, breaking his silence. "The payment is too high. You kill him, you'll lose a piece of yourself and we all want you whole, Asia, because you're the only person who makes us feel the same way."

I turn to look at Ford. "So what do we do then? Beg the King to give Pink back, to release Camden's mum and hope that he finds it in his heart to do that? Don't make me laugh." I can't help snapping, immediately regretting my sharpness given he is being so… sweet. It must've taken a lot to say what he just did, to bare a piece of himself like that. He winces, hurt flashing briefly across his gaze before he shuts it down quickly.

"No. We play the long game," Camden says, drawing my attention back to him. "Grim will confirm Mum and Pink's whereabouts. Then we wait for his instructions."

"And then?"

"And then when he least expects it, we finish him. *I* will finish him. I'm already tarnished, Asia. I've already done so many bad things in his name, things even you aren't aware of. But this one last bad thing, I'll do it, so you don't have to."

With that, Camden turns on his heel and strides from the room, leaving me more heartbroken than when I'd entered it. Thing is, they may believe I'm good, salvageable, worthy of their protection, but I know better. The King's blood runs through my veins after all.

I'll be the one to kill him.

SIX

"Hey Asia, Sonny, pull up a seat and help yourself. Where are the others?" Louisa asks, looking up at us over the mound of sandwiches she's been making. Behind her, Max is washing up some utensils. He gives us a wink as we take a seat at the kitchen island before wiping his hands and hugging Louisa from behind. They're so at ease with each other, relaxed. When he presses a kiss against her cheek, she leans into him and smiles softly.

"Ford's talking to Grim. Eastern and Kate have gone to find Camden," Sonny explains as he reaches for a sandwich and takes a bite, humming with appreciation.

"You talked things through? What's been decided?" Max asks, releasing Louisa and busying himself by putting away what he's just washed up.

"I'm going to kill the King," I say with a shrug. I've already gotten used to the idea. I'm going to do it regardless of how anyone feels.

Max stills and Louisa frowns. Clearly neither of them thinks it's a good idea either.

"No, you're not," Sonny says, forgetting his sandwich and reaching for my hand. "You heard what Camden said."

"You think I'm going to let Camden take the fall for me? No fucking way."

"Asia," Sonny pleads, refusing to let my hand go when I try to remove it from his grasp.

"No, Sonny! I'm going to kill that arsehole and probably his bastard son too. He'll wish he'd never fucked with my mum, with any of us." I snatch my hand away, my anger rising once more. I'd suppressed it in the room with Eastern, allowing his love to soothe me, to soften my sharpened edges. But now, it's coming back full force and I can feel every part of me hardening, readying myself for what I have to do. The walls are going back up, shielding me from harm.

"Asia, please. This isn't you." Sonny attempts to give me a one-armed hug. I can hear the concern in his voice, see it in his eyes, but right now I can't acknowledge it. I can't. I have to be tough. The people I care about have been threatened and I'm done with it.

"I have to do this," I say, shrugging out of his hold and pushing him gently away from me. If I let him comfort me I'll lose it. I won't have the strength to be the person I need to be.

"Sonny, come with me?" Max asks, looking between us. He knows I need to gather myself, either that or he's concerned for Sonny's state of mind given he's looking at me with so much anguish. Selfishly I want the smiles back, the dimples, but I know the only way that will happen is if I back down, and I can't. The horrible truth is, none of us will be happy if the King remains alive. That just enrages me further. How dare that man fuck with our lives. How dare he!

"No, I'm staying. Someone needs to make Asia see sense," he snaps.

But it's Louisa who doesn't give him a choice. "Go with Max. Asia and I need to talk. Right now you need to give her some space. Go!" she orders.

Surprisingly he does as she asks but not before addressing me.

"Any one of us would step in and kill that rotten bastard for you, Asia. *Any* one of us. Thing is I don't want to lose them either. We might have only made that pact last night, but I won't let what we have be destroyed. You might think you're alone, but we proved to you last night that you're not. I will remind you every day that we're here, that we've got your back…"

"Then have my back with this."

"I *do* but I draw the line at murder. No one's killing the King. He'll be brought to justice and we'll live our lives together whilst he and his bastard son rot in prison."

"It's a pretty notion, Sonny. But you know as well as I do that being locked up in prison won't stop them. Death is the *only* way. I have to kill him."

"Jesus, fuck! Can you even hear yourself, Asia? Think about what you're saying." His baby blue eyes are wild with concern and fear, not for the King, nor Monk, or himself. But fear for me. It makes my mouth go dry and my resolve wanes.

"Just go," I say, turning my back on him as Max walks him out of the kitchen. My heart hurts, not because of what I have to do, but because Sonny just looked at me like he doesn't know who I am. I drop my head, trying to will myself not to fucking break down again.

Louisa sighs heavily, sitting down next to me. She rests her hand over mine, and holds it, not saying a word. Eventually, I look up at her.

"You're tough, Sonny wasn't wrong about that," she says, her gaze searching my face. "But I see what you're doing."

"And what's that?"

"Pushing them away just when you need them the most. A natural reaction given the circumstances, especially for someone who's always had to look after herself."

"I suppose you're going to tell me that's what it was like for you.

You were alone, looking after number one. Pushing everyone away. I bet your mother was an addict too, yeah?" I scoff, wincing internally at how fucking ungrateful I sound.

"She was, actually. Drink killed her. Well, liver failure did, but it was the booze she drunk in copious amounts that took her from me way before she died physically. So yeah, I get where you're coming from more than most."

"I'm sorry," I mutter.

"Me too."

For a while we just sit. Silence gapes between us but weirdly I don't feel any distance or animosity, just understanding. She's allowing me a moment to just be. To breathe, to settle my thoughts.

"When my friend Nisha was kidnapped, I wanted to tear the world apart..."

"Your friend was kidnapped too? Am I like living your life or something?" I respond wryly.

She laughs a little, even though neither of us think it's particularly funny. "She was. Someone wanted money and they used her to try and get it."

"What happened?"

"I trusted the people I care about to help me. Those people were Hudson, Bryce, Max and Cal. Believe me, I wanted more than anything to murder the man who took her. Thing is, he nearly murdered me and if it wasn't for my men, he would've raped me before he did."

"What happened to your friend?" I ask, meeting her gaze.

It softens, her eyes filling with love. "She survived her ordeal, married Cal. They're my family now too. I'm lucky. I'm lucky to have found my family, to have a family of my own. I nearly destroyed that by running from them when I should've stayed. I ran because that's what you do when you feel alone and always have to take care of number one. I pushed them away. Fortunately for me, they wouldn't let me go."

"I don't mean to push them away," I admit, feeling torn up inside. "I just can't see them hurt." Not more than an hour ago I was clutching onto Eastern like he was my lifeline. The thought of hurting him ruins me, but the thought of the King doing the same enrages me more.

"I know you don't. Thing is, sometimes we have to just take a leap of faith and believe that things will work out the way they're supposed to in the end."

"Don't tell me everything will be okay..."

"I'm not telling you that. I won't. You and I both know that there's a good chance people are going to get hurt. There's a good chance people that *I* love are going to get hurt. But I trust in those same people to make this right."

"That's easier said than done. Your father isn't a fucking demented criminal. He has to die. It's the only way. You must see that."

"Maybe that's true, but you don't have to be the person to kill him. You are not alone anymore. There are so many people here for you, Asia. My family are here, your boys are here, Mr Carmichael, Frank, Grim. *I'm* here. You aren't responsible for any of this and you're certainly not responsible for sorting this mess out. From what I can gather, the King has many enemies. Powerful ones, with their own agendas. The harsh truth is, you wouldn't even get close enough to do it, and even if you did, can you honestly say that you could murder someone in cold blood, no matter how much they deserve it?"

I want to answer yes. My rage and anger tell me that I could, but somewhere deep down inside, the part of me that longed for a father and was given a monster is telling me I can't. It whispers doubt, and I hate it.

"I can't tell you how to feel, or even what to do, but I will tell you this. No matter how bleak things look right now, you have a chance to be happy. I see how those boys look at you. I see perhaps what you can't, and I know that every single one of them will protect you, even from yourself. Don't force any of them to make a bad decision to save you from doing the same. If I understand you like I think I do, then I know you wouldn't want a life sentence for any of them, just as much as none of them wish that for you. You've already made the right choice by letting them in. Don't push them away now to protect them because you'll only hurt everyone, yourself included, in the long run."

"What am I supposed to do? This is my responsibility, he's my *father,"* I hush out bitterly, hating to acknowledge that fact out loud.

"Whether you like it or not, we are the adults here and we'll do everything in our power to make this right. I know it's hard for you, but I'm asking you to trust us. *Please*."

Louisa pats my hand then stands, leaving me to absorb her words and fight my internal struggle to do the exact opposite of what she's just said. Can I really trust these people who are no more than strangers? In the past I've done that and got screwed over. I trusted my mum when she told me she was sober, only to lose her to heroin. I trusted my teachers who said they wanted to help, then didn't. I trusted social workers who said they'd got my best interests at heart but put my baby brothers in a different foster home than me.

Every time I've had a little hope, it's been dashed like lazy graffiti across a wall ruining my faith in the world. Louisa seems sincere enough, they all do. But that doesn't change anything.

I've been wrong before.

And what about my boys? Because they are *my* boys now. I've let them in and in doing so they're in danger. The King has taken Pink because of me, because he knows how much she means to me. He'll hurt them too, and I can't allow that.

See, the question isn't really about letting them in, loving them even, because honestly I'm already there. The real question here is, when I'm finally face to face with my father, will I be able to end his life?

Only time will tell.

SEVEN

T he journey back to Oceanside feels like it takes an eternity. Cal is driving, and the rest of us wait restlessly to arrive. I'm seated at the back of the minibus watching the view pass by in a blur as we head down the motorway. Sonny is up front talking in hushed tones with Cal. Ford has his eyes shut as though he's sleeping, but I can tell by the tense way he holds himself that he's not. Eastern and Camden are sitting on opposite sides of the bus, occasionally glancing up at each other. There's some kind of unspoken conversation going on between them and despite our tentative pact, the air is fraught with tension. I pull at the frayed hem of my hoody, the little piece of black cotton getting longer and longer as I mull over how the fuck we're going to make it through the next few weeks.

The Freed brothers have returned to London with Louisa and Grim, determined to help us, promising regular updates on what they find out. They made me swear not to do anything stupid, and whilst I agreed to wait for the King's instructions I made no promises of my own.

Mr Carmichael, Kate and Frank have headed back to the academy in another vehicle, needing to keep up the pretence that Kate was taken to A&E for treatment of dehydration caused by gastric flu that she caught from Pink. Tomorrow morning, Mr Carmichael will be announcing Pink's departure to another unit similar to Ruby's to cover up the fact that she's been fucking kidnapped and to keep the rumour mill under wraps. But I'm pretty sure there'll be a few kids who know *exactly* where she is, Monk's wolves to be precise and probably Bram and Red. I have every intention of beating the shit out of them until they tell me, and if they don't, I'll have fun doing it anyway.

"Well, it looks like it's going to be a long night. This is a fucking joke," Cal says, after we've been sitting in traffic for a solid hour. What should have been an hour and a half journey door-to-door has turned into a long arse nightmare given the twenty-mile tailback that we're stuck in. "I need to stop for petrol as soon as we can get out of this traffic jam. I suggest you take the time to regroup before we get back into the grounds of the academy," Cal says, glancing in the rear-view mirror and looking directly at me. I know what he isn't saying. He isn't saying that I, specifically, need to get my head straight. That I, specifically, need to stick to the game plan. Easier said than done when I, *specifically*, have a fucking deranged father.

Yeah, the sarcasm is strong today.

When we pull into the gas station an hour later, I bolt down the aisle of the minibus and jump out first heading straight for the toilet. I walk through the small shop, passing a row of sweets and crisps and some oddly placed fluffy toys. Without a second thought, I grab a pink unicorn with a rainbow horn and shove it up my hoody before pushing open the door to the toilet to do my business. Ten minutes later I'm back outside climbing into the bus. Ford is the only one still sitting inside when I arrive back, the rest of them are either taking a piss or grabbing snacks.

"What have you got there?" Ford asks, turning to face me as I pull out the stupid unicorn from beneath my hoody. His grey-green eyes flick from my face to the pink unicorn and back again.

"If I'd known the way to your heart was buying fluffy toys I might've got you one earlier."

"I didn't buy it," I respond dully. "I stole it... for Pink." My gaze meets his and I bite down on my lip forcing the tears back.

"Don't do that," Ford says, getting up to come sit next to me. He's so tall that he has to duck so he doesn't hit his head on the bus roof.

"Do what?"

"Let your emotions get the better of you," he says, sitting down next to me.

"I'm not..."

"You are." He grabs the toy from me and places it on the seat next to him before lifting my chin. "Look at me, Asia." He searches my face, fierceness making his eyes darken. "You *can* do this."

"Can I? How the fuck can I go back to Oceanside and pretend that my whole fucking world isn't falling apart? How can I face everyone knowing what I know and pretend that I don't want to fucking kill the wolves for helping Monk, because you know it was them, right?" I shake my head, forcing his hand away. "How can you look at Bram and Red and not want to fucking murder them for siding with Monk? Because you know that they've had something to do with this too, don't you?"

Ford sighs. "You have to rein it in, Asia. You have to be smart."

"Don't tell me to be smart when all I want to do is give those bastard cunts hell for helping Monk escape with Pink."

"I do too. You know I do. But jumping them isn't going to help her, or any of us in the long run."

"But you're a fighter, Ford. You live and breathe violence. That's who you are. Don't you dare force me to be someone I'm not."

"You're angry right now and for good reason, but you need to get a hold of yourself."

"I'm not sure I can," I say honestly. I'm strung tight. So tight that the slightest thing will set me off. One dirty look, one word out of their mouths and I'm going to lose my shit. I know it. I also know deep down that if I do, things will get worse for Pink and Camden's mum. It's only now that I truly understand the position Camden was in before. It must've torn him apart not being able to act when all he wanted to do was murder that cunt, Monk. My *brother*.

"You can. I'll help you."

"How?"

"Tonight, you and I are going to the Tower."

"We can't go to the Tower, Ford. It's off-fucking-limits."

"It was. Things are different now. I've squared it with Cal. So long as he knows where we are, it's cool. The guy's alright. He gets it."

"And the others?" I say, glancing out of the window as they pile out of the gas station, arms loaded with junk food.

"They're not invited. Tonight it's just you and me, Asia. I'll swing by at midnight," he retorts with a scowl.

I'm not sure whether I should be happy about that or not.

We arrive back at Oceanside a few minutes past eleven, four long hours after we left the farmhouse. I'm tired and fucking cranky and I'm certain that most of the tossers are watching us from their rooms. Fucking bunch of curtain twitchers. I scowl the whole time we offload, purposely avoiding conversation with any of my boys and only schooling my features into a more reasonable state when Cal hands me my overnight bag.

"You okay?" he asks me.

"No, I'm not," I bite out, my gaze lifting to the window of Monk's room. Empty now that the bastard has kidnapped my best friend. Cal nods tightly, following my gaze.

"Asia, are you coming?" Sonny asks, drawing my attention back to him. Camden has already entered the building. Ford too. Eastern hovers nearby.

"Yeah," I mutter, following him into the annex.

When we hit the stairs, Eastern grabs my hand, holding me back. Sonny reaches the door to our floor then he turns to see where we are, frowning when he notices how agitated I look.

"Asia?"

"I just need a minute with her, okay?" Eastern asks, not letting me go.

Sonny looks at me, waiting. "It's fine, Sonny. See you in the morning."

A muscle ticks in his jaw. "See you then," he responds tightly. He doesn't smile like he usually does, and I have to swallow down the urge to call him back. We've not spoken a word to one another since Louisa sent him away from the kitchen this afternoon and though it's only been a short amount of time, it feels a lot longer. I already miss the easy way we are with each other.

"Come here, Asia," Eastern says the second the door clicks shut on the landing above us. He holds me close, pressing his cool lips against my cheek. I stiffen in his arms, not because I don't want his attention or affection, but because I'm desperate for it.

Despite that, I pull away and step out of his arms.

"I can't right now," I respond quietly before turning on my feet and taking the stairs two at a time. If I let him love me like he did this morning, I might never want to leave his arms again.

Rat-a-tat-tat.

True to his word, Ford knocks on my door a few minutes past midnight, just an hour after we arrived back at Oceanside. Sighing, I decide that keeping Ford waiting is probably a mistake, so I swing my

BEA PAIGE

legs over the side of my bed and open the door. He walks in without an invitation.

"You ready?" he asks me, leaning against the wardrobe as he looks me up and down, his eyebrow cocking at what I'm wearing.

"That depends on what I'm supposed to be ready for?" I retort, folding my arms across my chest.

"Nothing you can't handle," he answers cryptically.

Pulling on my black beanie hat, I zip up my cerise fleece-lined hoodie over my tight orange tank and slip my DM's over my black leggings then follow Ford. When we reach the door leading to the carpark, Cal steps out of his room and stops us.

"Be back before dawn. Don't make me come looking for you. Got it?" he warns.

"Got it," Ford responds, resting his hand on my lower back, his fingers curling into my hoody, sensing my need to bolt. I feel skittish, out of sorts. I have the sudden urge to run and never fucking come back.

"You've got the mobile phone I gave you in case there's an emergency?" Cal asks Ford.

"Yeah."

"Okay, good. I'm going out on a limb here tonight. You've been given a little more freedom given your predicament."

"And you think that's wise because?" I can't help but ask.

"Because I'm fully aware that keeping you guys on a short leash will make the situation worse. The rest of these kids here need some boundaries but I'm trusting you both not to fuck this up. Besides, you're not going alone."

"What?!" Ford exclaims. "That wasn't part of the deal."

Behind us, Frank steps out of his room. I scowl.

"Frank will follow you to the Tower, he'll stand guard whilst you do what you need to do. It's this or nothing," Cal says, daring Ford to object.

"Fine," Ford relents, looking pissed off but not pushing his luck.

Cal gives Ford an intense look but must decide that he trusts him because then he turns to me and says, "Ford told me you need to get your head straight. I hope what he has planned will help you to do that. Be safe."

I nod my head then shake out of Ford's grasp and start jogging towards the gap in the fence.

"Asia, wait up," Ford calls behind me.

When I don't listen and duck through the gap, running full speed the second I'm in the woods, Ford curses under his breath. I'm fully aware that he could catch up with me and stop me if he chose to, but instead he lets me run like a wild creature intent on escaping. Thing is, I'm not running from Ford, I'm running from everything else.

My father. My brother. Our situation.

It takes me just fifteen minutes to hit the beach and I'm not even a little out of breath. Ford arrives shortly after and Frank a little after that. He keeps his distance. Adrenaline and a caustic anger inside my chest, fuelling me. Ford pulls up beside me, panting a little.

"Feeling a little better?" he asks, staring out to sea when I glance at him.

"Not really," I respond.

"Didn't think so."

He catches my gaze, the sea breeze buffeting us both. His dark blonde hair whips against his sharp cheekbones, lashing against his skin. When his gaze flicks to my mouth, I feel the electricity between us spark, but somehow it just makes me anxious.

"Are you going to fuck me, is that why we're here?" I ask, not caring how crass that sounds or if Frank can hear.

I'm more than positive that's why Ford wants me here and right now I'm not sure how I feel about that. It isn't because I don't want to sleep with him. I do. It's just, I'm fucked up in the head tonight. I'm angry. Sex right now wouldn't be a good idea.

"Like Eastern did this morning?" he asks.

"Yeah, we had sex... and?"

"And nothing," he shrugs. "If that's what you wanted, who the fuck am I to judge?"

"It was what I *needed*."

Ford regards me. "Yeah, I get that."

It's true. Eastern had given me some peace in his arms and I love him for it. He allowed me to break and held me whilst I did. "But now..." I blurt out, then slam my mouth shut. How can I explain how I feel? Right now I'm fucking angry. It's like cancer. I can feel it eating away at me, chewing at my gut, gnawing at my bones, breaking me apart. Killing me slowly.

"Now you need to deal with the anger, yes?"

"Yes."

Looking over his shoulder Ford spots Frank and says, "We're going in the Tower, don't fucking come in. We'll be done in an hour."

Then without waiting for a response, Ford grabs my hand and pulls me towards the Tower. It looms in the near distance, behind it an overly large moon hangs like a pendant in the midnight-blue sky, lighting our way. The ocean is wild, crashing against the shore with white crested foam as we half-jog, half-walk across the pebbles. Ford pushes open the metal door and we step into the darkness.

"Wait a second," he orders, dropping my hand. I can hear him fumble in the darkness for a while before a stark bright light flicks on. It illuminates the space enough for us to move about without falling into the pit.

"Where has everything gone?" I ask. The space is empty, bar a couple chairs pushed against the staircase on the other side of the circular room and a cardboard box in the centre.

"Since we stopped coming, the place has been abandoned. The local kids probably nicked the decks and all but one of the lights. Don't really give a shit, honestly." Ford shrugs, unbothered.

"So what now?" I ask him. I'm fully aware of the challenge in my voice, the almost dangerous invitation. If he attempted to kiss me, I'm not sure whether he would get a punch instead of a kiss. Maybe he'd get both. Yeah, he'd probably get both.

"Asia, don't look at me like that," he warns.

"Like what, Ford?" I push.

"Like you want me to hurt as much as you're hurting. Like you want to fuck the life out of me, and whilst I'm not averse to angry sex, I'm not about to fuck you when you're in this state of mind."

"So why are we here then?"

"To deal with that anger tearing you apart. I told you, you need to get your head straight."

He walks towards the cardboard box in the centre of the floor and crouches down, fishing inside. With his back to me I'm able to admire the width of his shoulders, and the dip of his waist. At some point between walking inside the Tower and turning on the light, Ford managed to remove his jumper. I appreciate his fighter physique. It's distracting, though not enough to shake this feeling inside. I'm not sure anything will.

"Fucking might be the answer..." I say lazily, not recognising my voice. It sounds off, distant. Harsh.

"Not tonight, tonight we fight..." he responds, standing with two pairs of boxing gloves dangling from his hands. He chucks one pair at me. I catch them.

"And we needed to come to the Tower to spar because...?"

"Because we don't need any interruptions. I don't need one of the guys breaking our session up because they're trying to protect you from getting hurt."

"And what about Frank?"

"Frank won't come in here, and if he does, I might just knock him out." He shrugs.

"You brought me here to hurt me?" I ask, tipping my head to the side watching him as he pulls on his gloves.

"If you pay attention. If you *focus* your mind, you'll be fine."

"And if I don't?" I ask, stripping off my hoodie and pulling on my gloves.

"Then I guess you get hurt?"

EIGHT

Ford circles me, bouncing on the balls of his feet as he moves. He brings his fist-covered gloves up in front of his face in a defensive position and I watch his biceps flex as he throws some light punches into the space between us.

I remain still, my feet heavy, glued to the floor. For some unknown reason my gloves suddenly feel like two blocks of cement as my arms hang by my side. The anger still eats away at me, but I don't have the energy to fight. I don't have the energy to do anything but stand here and watch Ford move stealthily around me. Maybe fucking was the better option after all.

"Don't do that, Asia. Put your fists up and protect your face," Ford commands, punching the air, moving closer this time. The loose strands of hair around my head lift up as the force of his movements oscillates the air between us. He keeps bouncing on the balls of his feet, every punch he throws getting closer, until one actually meets my shoulder forcing it backwards with a loud thwack, making me stumble. It hurts.

Motherfucker.

His dark gaze meets mine, his eyes narrowing. Then he throws another punch, hitting me on my other shoulder. The power behind it has me reeling backwards.

And that's all it takes.

A nuclear bomb of rage detonates inside my chest, ripping violently out of me in a loud scream. I launch at Ford, my fists flying. I don't think, I just feel. I feel every single drop of anger as it bursts forth like a volcano exploding.

I don't see Ford.

I see Monk. I imagine the King.

And I lose my shit.

I fucking lose it.

Thwack. Thwack. Thwack. TWHACK.

Some of my punches hit their mark, some don't. Either way, I don't care.

I want to kill. I want to rip the world apart with my bare hands.

I feel raw, open, like my heart has beaten its way free from inside my chest, every rib bent backwards, my chest cracked open, blood, muscle and bone torn free and my insides on display for anyone to see.

But it doesn't stop me.

I avoid a few hits, I take more. But I don't *feel* them. I don't feel anything other than the rage.

"Come on, Asia. Is that all you've got?!" Ford shouts, angering me further. I hit him square on the jaw, knocking his head backwards.

But it doesn't stop him from coming back for more, forcing me backwards as he throws punch after punch.

"Let. It. Out!" he roars, and I realise he doesn't just mean the anger. He wants me to spill all the deepest, most secret parts inside of me. The disappointment, the despair, the pain.

"Shout at me, scream, fucking rage, Asia. Let. It. Out!"

As he stalks towards me, the words come. Words long held inside.

With every punch I throw, with every punch I feel them burst free from my lips in a cacophony of pain.

"You. Took. Pink. You. Set. Monk. On. Me. You. Abandoned. Us. You. Killed. My. Mum," I scream, my chest heaving as I plant my feet firmly on the ground.

Sweat slides down my spine, down my face, between my breasts as I wait for him to make his next move. Inside I'm a frenzy, a fucking whirlwind of emotion but I remain still.

I am the storm and the storm is *me*.

Ford stops before me. He's sweating too, his hair plastered to his head and his t-shirt stuck to his chest. He rakes his gaze over me, and I'm vaguely aware of that same electricity that always seems to spark between us crackle and snap.

"Now funnel that pain, that rage, Asia. Draw it back inside you and feed off of it. Let it *fuel* you. Let it *focus* you so you can face the enemy with a clear head. Do not let it ruin you. When you feel as though you're near to the breaking point again, you find me. You fight *me*. I will take the excess that you can't contain," he says fiercely, ripping his gloves off and doing the same to mine. He grabs me by the shoulder as I shake violently in his arms.

"He fucking took her from me!" I shout and I'm not just talking about Pink, I'm talking about my mum because even though she might've stabbed that needle in her arm, he was the one who killed her by abusing her love. I know that. The King broke my mum and in turn he broke me.

"Eastern will hold you when you need to break but *I* will show you how to remain strong. Go to him to fall apart, then come to me when you need to be put back together again. Understand?"

My legs buckle and I fall hard onto my knees, my hands press into the dusty concrete floor as my head falls forward, sweat dripping from my nose.

"Do you understand, Asia?" he asks, dropping before me and forcing my shoulders back. Forcing me to look at him as he kneels before me.

"I understand," I mutter.

"I didn't hear you!"

"I understand," I repeat, louder this time.

"Not good enough. Who will give you strength?" he presses, gritting his teeth. His eyes ablaze with determination, with fire and fury and fucking passion. I see it.

"You," I pant.

"WHO, ASIA?!" he roars.

"YOU WILL!" I bellow back.

"Good. Now you're ready to face those bastards," he says fiercely, his fingers digging into my upper arms. "Get back up on your feet, Asia. Get back on your feet and rule that anger, don't you dare let it fucking rule you!" Ford's hands run down my arms, sliding over my slick skin. He stands, pulling me up with him. "We're done here tonight."

"We are?" I ask, licking my lips. Suddenly my own desire for Ford replaces the rage I feel with a different kind of all-encompassing need. My gaze strips him naked, my fingers itch to do the same. My clit pulses remembering the way his tongue felt pressed against it, his fingers deep inside of me.

"We are."

He drops his hands away and picks up the boxing gloves, placing them back in the cardboard box then strides across the room and pulls on his hoodie roughly, messing up his hair. By the time he looks at me again, I'm torn between wanting to jump his bones and shout at him for denying me what I know he wants just as much as me. The fucking bulge in his pants is a dead giveaway.

"You don't want to fuck me…?"

My voice catches in my throat and in two strides he's yanking me roughly against his chest.

"Oh, I want to, Asia. I want to so bad I'm having a tough time controlling myself," he admits, his hot breath whispering against my mouth. His close proximity sends shivers down my spine as the ache between my leg throbs. I shuffle on my feet, pressing my thighs together to try and alleviate the agony.

"Then why aren't you?" I counter, swallowing hard when he brushes his lips against mine.

"Because you're not ready for me yet. Not yet..." he grinds out, swiping his tongue against my lips once before backing away and shoving his hands in his pockets.

I smile evilly, feeling a rush of power at his obvious arousal. "Maybe it's you that's not ready for me?" I counter, swiping my fingers over my chest making sure I cup my breasts through my vest top. His eyes darken, his pupils enlarging as he watches me roll my nipples. It feels good to tease him. I feel... *powerful*. More so than when I was throwing punches.

"You've no idea who you're dealing with, Asia," he says darkly.

"No?" I tip my head to the side, the tip of my tongue sliding out from between my lips, wetting them before sucking my lip ring inside my mouth. "Pretty sure you showed me who you are when your tongue was buried inside my pussy last night and your fists were bruising my skin just now."

"Not nearly," he smirks, widening his legs. I watch as his hand slides beneath the waistband of his joggers, clutching his cock beneath them. I see the bulbous head peek out from beneath the material. A rush of heat colours my cheeks and pools between my legs as I eye the tip of his cock. Something glints in the harsh light as his hips thrust forward. His dick is pierced.

Fuck, that's sexy.

"You *want* to fuck me…" I observe, my own fingers trailing downwards with purpose. I want his façade to crack wide enough for me to see inside his soul, even if it's only for a little while.

"Yes, I want to fuck you…" he agrees. "But I won't." He chuckles darkly, letting go of his cock and adjusting himself. He rolls his shoulders, loosening up the tension he holds there.

My hand slips lower, ignoring the fact he's turning me down. "You don't want to slide inside of me? You don't want to fill me up, fuck me until you lose your mind?" I ask him, my heart beating wildly in my chest as my fingers seek out that tiny bundle of nerves between my legs. I've no idea where this person has come from. I'm not normally so forward, so unashamedly *dirty*, but with Ford he brings out that feral side of me. The one that can flip between rage and desire just with one hot gaze from his grey-green eyes. The pad of my finger finds my clit, pressing with just enough pressure to make my hips jerk.

Ford chokes back a growl. His body wavering on his feet that are stuck firmly in place. "Not today," he says flippantly.

If it wasn't for the brief flicker of indecision in his eyes I would've been hurt. Only I see what he's doing. In that moment, I understand him. Ford wants me to see he's controlled in all things. He wants to show me that I can count on his unwavering strength when I feel so out of my head with emotions. I get it now. I fall apart with Eastern. I build myself back up with him.

"Okay," I respond just as flippantly, removing my hand from between my legs.

"Okay?" he swallows hard.

"Yeah, I'll find another way to deal with my… needs."

Straightening my spine, I turn away from him and walk towards the exit, feeling ten times stronger than I did this morning. When I reach the heavy metal door, Ford catches up with me and grabs my wrist, yanking me around to face him. He slams me against the door, his eyes flashing with possession.

"I'm controlled in all things, Asia. That's who I am. That's how I need to be to survive. It's how I've always been, but there's something you must know about me."

"And what's that?"

"My control wanes when I'm with you. Be careful, Asia, I fuck like I fight, with a single-minded determination to win."

"Win what?" I hush out.

Ford drops my wrist, stepping away from me. "Maybe next time we're alone together you'll find that out."

"Is that so? Maybe you won't get another chance, ever think of that, Ford?"

He laughs, giving me one of his rare smiles that makes my heart ache and my pussy clench with need. "You and I both know that our time will come and when we do... *come* together, I mean, be prepared to lose your fucking mind."

"God, you're cocky," I mutter, but as we head back to Oceanside I can't help but wonder what it would be like to lose to Ford, mind, body and soul.

NINE

The next morning I knock on Kate's door a few minutes before we're due to head down to breakfast. She greets me with a painful smile.

"Ready to face them?" I ask.

"Not particularly."

I laugh darkly. "Me neither, but we're going to anyway. Get your game face on, Kate, and let's show these motherfuckers we can't be broken."

"I'm not sure I can. I was thinking that I'd just stay in my room today. I am supposed to be sick after all," she responds, pushing against the door, trying to shut me out.

"Fuck that! You're not hiding away like some frightened little girl," I growl, forcing myself into her room and slamming the door behind me. She flinches and for the briefest of moments I feel guilty. Thing is, like Ford did for me last night, I'm giving her what she needs, not what she wants.

"I'm scared for Pink, aren't you?" she blurts out.

"Of course I am. I'm scared to death about what those bastards will do to her, might have already done to her. Don't think I haven't agonised over the fact that if we make, if *I* make one wrong move, she's dead. I get it. But you don't get to hide away, Kate."

"How can we face those bastards... How can we look at Bram and Red, at Monk's wolves knowing that they probably had something to do with her kidnapping?"

"Because we have to. We don't really have a choice."

"I don't want to look at any of them. I don't want to sit in the same canteen, the same class. I don't want to see them laughing and joking as if nothing's happened. I. Don't. Want. To."

"You have to." I sigh heavily, flipping my hair over my shoulder.

"I can't!"

"You know what, Kate. Fuck this! They might've won this battle, but they haven't won the fucking war. We do not show weakness or fear, not to them. So grab your shit and come with me. *Got it*?!" I grit my teeth and hope that my form of tough love works.

"I'm not a fighter like you, Asia."

"Oh, yes, you are. You survived your brother's death, didn't you?"

"You call this surviving?" she bites back.

"Yeah, actually I do. Some people let their past rule them, twist them into something ugly, selfish, *weak*. You haven't done that, and that takes strength. It takes balls, Kate, to live when all you want to do is curl up and die."

"Maybe..." she concedes.

"Not maybe. It does. I hate those arseholes as much as you do, but hiding away in here will only put a target on your head."

"They think I have gastric flu..."

I roll my eyes. "Mr Carmichael might try to convince them that's true, but do you think any of those arseholes will believe that? Come on. Monk ain't here. Pink is missing and you returned with Mr Carmichael and Frank last night not long after us. Even if most of the kids here don't know what happened exactly, it's not going to take long for them to suspect that something big has gone down. If you insist on hiding away in your room, what's left of the HH crew will target you next just for shits and giggles. Don't forget what Monk and his wolves did to me the first week I arrived here. You give them one inch and they'll take a fucking mile."

"They already have…" her voice trails off as she winces, rubbing at her arm.

My eyes narrow. "What's wrong?"

"Nothing." She turns away from me, reaching for a jumper on her bed.

"Kate, what's wrong with your arm?" I repeat. When she doesn't answer I step towards her, and grab her wrist pulling up the sleeve. She has a purple bruise wrapped around her forearm in the exact same shape as a four-finger grip. My eyes narrow when I meet her gaze. "Who did this?"

She snatches her arm away, pulling the sleeve down sharply. "Red."

"That fucking bitch! When did this happen? Why?" I demand.

"The same night Pink was taken. I was going back to Pink's room because I was worried about her. Red cornered me, accused me of *looking* at Bram, warned me off him."

"What? You're not interested in that dickhead!"

"That was my exact response. When I tried to walk away she grabbed me, gave me a slap." Kate sighs. "I should've gone to see Pink, instead I went back to my room and fucking cried. Maybe if I had grown some balls, Pink would still be here now." Kate flops down onto her bed, holding her head in her hands.

"She was fucking in on it," I seethe. "Her, Bram, the rest of Monk's crew. You can bet your arse they were in on it. Keep you out of the way makes it easier for Monk to kidnap her."

"Yeah, I've been thinking the same thing too."

"Those motherfuckers deserve to get the shit beaten out of them."

"They do, but what can we do, they've got the upper hand?"

"No way! You might be a target because of your association with me, but I'll be fucked if I let them hurt you too. You need to make a stand."

Kate wrinkles her nose. "Make a stand?"

"Yeah," I respond, my thoughts veering off in another direction.

"I can tell this will involve me in something I'm not at all comfortable with, right?" Kate groans, giving me a suspicious look.

"There's only one language they understand. *Violence*."

"Jesus, Asia. We can't just have a brawl. Mr Carmichael has laid down the law."

I scoff. "Yeah, and much fucking use that's been. But that's beside the point. Let's use the tools they've given us to our advantage."

"What do you have in mind?"

"I'll ask Cal to set up a *sparring session* in his ring," I say, finger quoting the words, because when I get in the ring with any one of those bastards, I'm not going to be sparring, that's for damn sure. "No one said we couldn't settle a few scores in the ring. That's what it was set up for, right?"

"You're forgetting one important thing, Asia... I really *can't* fight."

"Don't think I didn't notice how hard you pummelled Camden that day we were placed in our groups. I saw the fight in you then. Ford can train you. I'll train *with* you. We all will."

"You already know how to fight," she laughs, rolling her eyes, and I see a little of the old Kate come back.

"And so do you," I remind her.

She thinks for a moment, her dark brows drawing together. "Fine, but I want that bitch Red. She's had it coming for some time now," she says, that spark within her lighting up with her own need for vengeance. I just need to stoke the flames and keep the fire within her alight. Sometimes needing revenge can eat a person alive; sometimes it's exactly what they *need* to keep them fighting. Maybe for me it's the former, but for Kate, I'm hoping it's the latter.

"That's settled then. We train and then we challenge those arseholes to a fight. Shame we can't have the same rules as the Tower, but at least doing this will show you're not an easy target. How does that sound?"

"Like I've lost my fucking mind."

"But you'll do it?"

She narrows her eyes, throws back her shoulders and straightens her spine. "Yeah, I'll do it," she agrees.

I grin, grasping her arm. I always knew Kate was a badass bitch underneath it all. You don't live through the horror of losing someone you loved in fucked up circumstances without having a core of granite. She's tougher than she gives herself credit for.

When we reach the glass doors to the outside, I'm not at all surprised to find my boys waiting for us. Camden is talking in hushed tones with Eastern, Sonny is perched on the low wall, his foot tapping in agitation and Ford has schooled his features into a neutral state, like always. We lurk for a moment, watching them.

"They really are here for you, aren't they?" Kate murmurs, her voice laced with awe and a little bit of sadness. I know why. The person she'd loved had abandoned her when she needed him the most. That must hurt.

"Si's an idiot for not doing the same for you," I say, squeezing her arm in a show of sisterhood. "If you ever get the chance to see him again, I reckon you need to give him shit, and if you don't, then I sure as fuck will."

"I doubt he'll be returning home anytime soon, but thanks for having my back." She gives me a shaky smile then presses her mouth in a line, holding onto the emotion I can see brimming in her eyes.

"For now, I'll just live vicariously through you. Four guys eh, how's that going for you?" Her eyes twinkle a little in mischief, only to be shut down quickly with guilt.

I sigh. You know that feeling when someone dies and you're really fucking sad, but something makes you smile out of the blue making you feel guilty as fuck. Well, this is what that feels like. Only Pink isn't dead, and we have no fucking idea how to save her.

"Sucks doesn't it, this limbo we're in?" I say instead of everything else I'm thinking.

"It must suck more for Pink…"

"Yeah. It must." We lock eyes, and I hug her tight. "Come on, let's show these bastards what we're made of. Let *that* get back to Monk and the King. Perhaps they'll think twice about their next move."

I push open the door and we step out into the brisk cold air.

"Morning, Asia, Kate. Ready to face the enemy?" Ford asks, standing as we emerge. It's a simple enough question but given what happened last night, filled with meaning. Our eyes lock and just for a second Ford lets me glimpse the heart of him. I expect to see darkness, only it isn't as bleak as he makes out, in fact what I see is like a cool pool of water in a scorching hot desert. A pool I'd happily drown in.

"Well?" he insists.

My gaze flicks between my boys, resting on each of them in turn. Every single one of us has a label we've either had to live up to or try to shake free from. The gang leader, the thief, the best friend, the fighter and *me*… the King's fucking daughter. We've all had to navigate our way in a world that doesn't want us to survive but somehow, despite it all, we're still here. We're still fucking fighting.

"Yeah, I'm ready," I declare, walking out into the courtyard and towards the battlefield.

TEN

T he second we step into the dining hall, people stop talking and a hushed quiet settles over the space. Camden and I enter first. He places his hand around my waist, gripping me tightly when I stiffen at the sound of Bram's distinct laughter. Second to Monk's, it's my most hated sound.

"He's pushing his fucking luck," I grit out, my teeth grinding in anger as I glare at the prick. Bram winks the moment my gaze meets his.

"He can push all he likes, Asia, but that motherfucker is going down just like the rest of them," Ford retorts, stepping up beside us. He takes my hand in his and we walk towards our usual spot in the canteen that they've brazenly taken up residence in.

"Move!" Camden snarls as we reach our table. We're gone a couple days and they think they can take our spot? Idiots.

"You gonna make me, *boss*?" Bram snarls, his eyes feral, teeth bared. Beside him Red grins nastily and Monk's wolves snicker. I hate every single one of them with a passion that I desperately want to unleash. My resolve to stay calm wanes.

"No, *I* am," Ford counters, leaning over and grabbing Bram by the throat. He lifts him easily out of his seat and shoves him backwards. Bram stumbles over the upturned chair, falling on his arse. Red gasps, rushing to his side. She glares at us all as the rest of my boys flank me, and Monk's wolves stand readying themselves for a fight. If it wasn't obvious before, it is now. There's a clear divide. Camden is no more their leader than I am part of the HH crew. Like I give a shit anyway. I was never one of them and Camden doesn't need those arseholes in his life. Red fusses over Bram, but like the complete arsehole that he is, he pushes her away and jumps to his feet, getting in Ford's face.

"You'll pay for that."

"I'd like to see you fucking try." Ford grins, a dangerous smile carving across his face as he grips Bram's throat once more and shoves his face close. "You chose the wrong fucking side, *brother*."

"Pretty sure I made the right choice, given the circumstances," Bram retorts, a nasty smirk making him even more ugly than he already is.

"What the fuck do you know?" Camden steps in, his voice deadly and barbed with violence.

Bram flicks his gaze to Camden, looking him up and down like he's some goddamn godfather and *we* should be afraid of *him*. "Everything," he grins.

Prick.

"Hold that thought," Eastern snarls under his breath, his hand coming up to Ford's wrist. "We have company."

Ford drops his hand and shoves Bram away as Mr Carmichael, Cal, Frank and Buddy step into the dining hall, their attention fixated on us all. The shithead Bram has the gall to point his finger directly at me. "I have a message for you, *bitch*," he hushes out, his lips curling back over his teeth.

"And what might that be?" I snarl back. I feel Camden stiffen beside me whilst Ford vibrates with a violent energy. Around us the air snaps with a feral hunger darkening the growing tension in the room into something far more dangerous, something explosive. Bram grins, enjoying my anger. He fucking *knows*.

"Spit it out, dickhead," Camden growls through gritted teeth.

Bram's smile is nothing short of malicious. "Pink is just a watered-down version of red. Weak, timid and easily tainted. I suggest you watch your goddamn step or that pretty little colour might just stain a little darker."

Time stills.

The tick-tock of the dining hall clock suddenly pounds loudly in my ears. Each second that passes like a long drawn out minute. Blood rushes like an angry, poisonous torrent in my veins. All that pent-up rage starts to unfurl. I know I'm losing my shit despite the effort Ford put in last night to help me contain it, but not reacting is harder than I thought. Camden must have inhuman control, given what he's been put through over the years.

"Asia," Ford warns, knowing I'm on the path of no return and trying to bring me back from the brink.

"That's it, Asia, listen to this *bad boy* here," Bram spits, knowing what those words mean. Knowing those words are imprinted on Ford's skin as a constant reminder of who his parents were and the child he once was.

I lose it.

"You bastard!" I shout, launching myself at him. Only my fists don't meet his face because I'm being hauled backwards, one strong arm wrapped around my waist, the other still encased in plaster, hanging by his side.

"Not here," Sonny growls into my ear, pulling me away from the bastard who's laughing now, Red and the wolves joining in. He hauls me away whilst the whole dining hall watches with interest. Even if they don't know what happened to Pink, it wouldn't have gone unnoticed that Monk is no longer a resident at Oceanside. It doesn't take a genius to work out that some kind of shit has gone down involving them both. How the hell Mr Carmichael is going to explain this fucking mess away is beyond me, but I don't get chance to find out.

"Outside, now!" Cal snaps, giving Sonny a look before I'm yanked out of the dining hall by my arm and he strides over to deal with the warring crews who are now facing up to each other with violent intent.

"Let me fucking go," I shout, snatching my arm away as we step out onto the gravel drive in the front of the building, rounding on him. I push against Sonny's chest, trying to shove him out of the way so I can go back inside and murder Bram.

"Don't be fucking stupid, Asia. Jesus Christ, I thought Ford sorted out your fucking rage last night! I can see you're still too worked up to keep a cool head when taunted. Which they're going to do *a lot* by the way."

"Damn it, Sonny, get the fuck out of my way!"

"I just saved your arse in there. You could be a little more grateful," Sonny retorts without a shred of humour in his voice. Something about that makes me even madder. Where has the happy-go-lucky, flirtatious boy gone? I twist on my feet in the opposite direction of the building and stride off, only vaguely aware that Sonny still follows despite my ugly attitude towards him.

"Asia, stop!" he shouts out.

"No!"

"Fuck sake," Sonny snaps, grabbing me from behind. He wraps his good arm around my waist and pulls me against his chest, holding me against him. "Bram is just another pawn in the King's game, you know that, right? He's pushing you, goading you through that little prick. You're playing right into his hands, Asia."

"Don't you think I know that?!" I shout back, turning to face him.

"Don't you think I know that I'm being used in some grand fucking plan? I hate not knowing. I hate not feeling in control. I want to fucking kill someone and if it ends up being Bram then so fucking be it!"

Sonny grips my jaw in his hand, forcing me to face him. "Look at me, Asia. We'll get through this. We'll find a way."

"How? How will we? I feel so fucking useless."

Sonny's gaze softens along with his grip. He doesn't respond with words, instead he leans forward and presses his mouth against mine and kisses me, obliterating any thoughts of murder with a sure stroke of his tongue. In the moment, it's exactly what I need. It's enough to stay my hand, to replace the rage with something else.

"I've got your back, Asia. I'll be there to save you from yourself until the time comes when you can do it on your own," he says against my lips. I can feel him trembling, or perhaps that's me?

I nod my head, forcing myself to breathe, to be calm. "I know you do," I sigh.

"Good, because I'm not going to let you do anything stupid. Think of me as the angel on your shoulder." He grins, showing me those dimples I've become accustomed to.

"More like the devil with kisses like that," I mutter when he follows up his grin with a naughty wink.

"Maybe I'm a bit of both," he shrugs, dropping his hands from my face and wrapping an arm around my waist. "Either way, I got you."

And I know that he truly does.

WHEN IT HITS the end of the school day, I take off to the gym wanting to avoid the dining hall and needing to release some pent-up energy.

When I arrive, I'm surprised to find Ford there already with Kate and Cal. They turn to look at me when I enter the room.

"Looks like you could do with a session in the ring," Cal remarks knowingly, holding out a pair of boxing gloves.

"Yeah, looks like I could," I snip back, snatching them from his hands and pulling them on aggressively.

"Mr Carmichael has informed the other students about Pink's and Monk's move to another unit," Cal says, watching me carefully.

"And how did that go down? Pretty sure they all know it's bullshit."

"Perhaps, but that's not important. What's important is that we carry on as usual. The last thing we need is the authorities sniffing around this place because if that happens, Oceanside will be shut down quicker than Ford can throat grab Bram. Nice move by the way," he says, winking at Ford.

"Do you approve?" Ford asks, giving Cal a confused look.

"Off the record, that little shit deserved a beating, but as a member of staff here I have to maintain the appearance that I'm neutral and keep the peace."

"He knows about Pink," I state.

"Yes, so I've been told. Looks like Bram will need to spend some quality time with Mr Burnside. Let's see if he can draw some information out of him."

I scoff. "Unlikely. The only way he's gonna spill is if one of us makes him. But given violence is off the table right now, I think a session in the ring with those arseholes is warranted at the very least, don't you?" I ask, pinning my gaze on Cal and daring him to deny me.

"I do, actually. Kate explained what you have planned. I think a controlled fight in the ring is exactly what we need right now. This is why I'm here, after all," he shrugs.

"When?" I ask, wanting to know how soon I can kick Bram's arse, albeit in a *controlled* manner. Yeah, like that's going to happen.

"In a few weeks? Kate needs to train, and we need to distract everyone enough so that the Freed brothers and Grim can keep digging without worrying about what's happening here. I'm off campus the second week of March with one of the other groups for their scheduled weekend away so fitting it in before then would be good. Reckon we can get you fighting fit by then, Kate?"

She brushes his question aside. "You're going off campus?" Kate questions, before I can. "Is that wise with everything that's going on?"

"Yes and no. I've no doubt that the King has something up his sleeve that none of us are able to predict right now, but not going away with these kids is as much a giveaway to why I'm here than it is if I make some excuse and stay. Don't worry, we've put some safety measures in place to ensure that no one else is getting kidnapped," he responds, though in all honesty by the look on his face he's about as convinced by those plans as we are.

Ford frowns. "What safety measures?"

"Well, aside from getting more assistance from a few more of my friends, cameras are going up next week, video recording equipment, alarms, etc. This place is going to be rigged up like Fort Knox. No one is going to be able to take a shit without me knowing about it."

"Well, that's just fucking peachy," I complain, glancing at Ford. I'm betting he's thinking the same thing as me. There'll be no more trips to the Tower now. He should've fucked me last night when he had the chance.

"It is what it is. Believe me, I know how much your freedom means to you all, but last night can't happen again. This keeps you all a little safer."

Ford rolls his eyes. "If the King wants to raze this place to the ground and kidnap every kid at Oceanside, nothing and no one will stop him, you do know that, right?"

"Yeah, I know that, but right now this is all we've got."

ELEVEN

I t takes me a few days to calm down. Throughout, my boys stick by my side, taking it in turns to make sure I don't do something stupid like stabbing a bread knife through Bram's eye.

I hate being a liability, but that's what I am right now. One wrong move and things can go horribly wrong for Pink and Camden's mum.

By Friday's Art lesson, I've bottled my simmering rage enough to not want to break the face of anyone who so much as looks at me the wrong way. Regardless, I'm in no mood to sit in a class with Monk's wolves, or should I say Bram's, seeing as they're now following *his* orders, so it's just as well Ms Moore has agreed to let us do some research for our end of term projects in the library.

"Be back by the end of the lesson. I expect to see your sketch pads filled with ideas from all the books you'll be looking at," she says as we leave the room.

Sonny gives her one of his best dimpled smiles. "Sure, Miss."

Of course, none of us will be seeking any inspiration from long dead artists or returning before the lesson is over. I mean, what's she going to do, give us a fucking detention?

The fact of the matter is, that this is just an excuse to get away from

Monk's wolves and a few turncoats from Ford's crew. I love art, but so does half the goddamn school and most of the wankers we want to avoid happen to share our art class on Wednesday afternoons. Since Ford chucked out Bram and Red, No Name crew has lost more of its members. Some have followed the pair, and those that were left behind are keeping their heads down and sticking with the group Mr Burnside has put them in. I'm not sure how Ford feels about it all, but if he's affected at all by their abandonment then he's doing a good job at not showing it. Like always, he keeps his feelings well under wraps.

"Thank fuck for that," Camden remarks as we push open the door to the library a couple of minutes later. "Not sure I would've lasted much longer without pummelling Dagger's smug face."

"Yeah, I hear ya," Sonny agrees, acknowledging the librarian with a curt nod as he leads us to the furthest corner of the library. I get the impression that he comes here quite a lot given how easily he traverses the vast space and shows us a hideaway that gives a little bit of privacy. Not that we need it, given the library is empty apart from us. We take a seat on a grey sectional surrounded on three sides by bookshelves. Getting out my sketchpad so at least it looks like I'm doing some work should a teacher happen to find us, I sit, blowing out a long steady breath.

"It's been intense since we got back," Sonny says, stating the obvious. He swipes a hand through his hair then leans his head back and closes his eyes. He looks tired, strung tight. We all do.

"Tell me about it," I agree, glancing over at Camden. He meets my gaze, giving me a guarded look. "What?"

He lifts his feet onto the low table in front of us and crosses his arms across his chest. "We've heard nothing. This ain't looking good."

"But you said we need to wait it out. You said that was the best way forward!" I say, my voice rising enough for Sonny to snap his eyes open.

"Hey, keep your voices down. We can't afford for anyone to hear what we're discussing," Sonny reminds us both.

"The King has never left it more than a couple of days to send a message and I've called Mum's phone repeatedly, and she's not answering. I've never had a problem getting hold of her before." Camden explains, lowering his voice. "I'm not gonna lie, I'm worried. Something doesn't feel right."

"It's not even been a week yet. He's toying with you both. He wants you so scared that you'd do anything the minute he asks. The Freeds, Grim, they would've called by now if they'd found out anything new. Just hold your nerve, okay?" Sonny says, looking between us both.

Camden frowns. "That's easier said than done, they're not threatening the people you love."

"You're kidding, right? I happen to care about Pink too, not to mention my foster family. I don't want to see them hurt."

"You really trust them, don't you?"

"Yeah, I do. They're good people. Well, the Freeds and Louisa are. I don't know Grim well enough to know whether she is or isn't."

"She's your family, isn't she? Like a fourth cousin, twice removed?" Camden asks, not able to keep the sarcasm out of his voice.

Sonny doesn't try to correct him, he just shrugs. "Ford is closer to her. I keep my distance from Grim and her club."

"You don't like her?" I ask, my interest piqued.

"It's not that I don't like her. She's never done anything to me, it's just she walks in the same circles as the King and you don't get acquaintances like that if you're an angel without a past full of bad decisions."

"So, you *don't* trust her then?" Camden presses.

"I trust Ford and Hud, and they trust her… but that doesn't mean to say I want to hang out with her anytime soon."

"I thought that'd be your thing?" I ask. "Fighting without any rules or regulations."

"That's precisely *why* I stay away. Despite Ford's notoriety, he still has perfect self-control. I don't. If I got into a ring with no rules, I might kill a man."

Camden whistles, looking at Sonny with new eyes. "So you're not just some pretty, dimpled, arsehole joker then," he muses.

Sonny looks at me with a smile in his eyes. "Some say I'm the devil dressed up as an angel..."

"Pretty sure that's a line from a song," I respond, trying to hide the smile in my voice. Sonny always manages to lighten the mood. I appreciate that about him.

"The point is, I know my limits and fighting in Grim's club is one of them. Seeing the people I care about getting hurt is another." He gives me a look and I'm reminded of our kiss and his promise to have my back. Sonny has shown me repeatedly that he does, indeed, have my back and something tells me that he always will. When I first met him I never would've pinned him as selfless. Selfish maybe, but not selfless. I couldn't have been more wrong.

"Speaking of being hurt... how's the arm?" I ask Sonny, my eyes flicking to the cast.

"A pain in the fucking neck," he responds, rolling his eyes. "The sooner I get this off the better. Only another week or so and it's coming off. I'm telling you, getting an itch under this bitch is torture. I've already lost my comb down it trying to scratch one."

Camden raises his eyebrows but doesn't say anything sarcastic like I expect, instead he pulls out his mobile phone and flicks it on, studying the screen.

"Still nothing?"

"Still nothing," he confirms with a frustrated growl.

"Camden, you know the King better than anyone. What do you think he has planned? What should I expect?"

"The unexpected..."

"What does that mean?"

"It means he'll have something planned that you'd never have even considered. You don't get to be where he is, feared like he is, without being clever and a lot fucking twisted."

"Great," I mutter.

"He's calculated, cold. He thrives off control and keeps those he owns under his thumb." Camden looks at me and grimaces. "You're his daughter, and in his mind that means he owns you regardless that he's never once made an effort to be in your life before now."

"But *why* now? Why pop up at this point? What can he possibly gain from this aside from trying to get control over me?"

Camden gives Sonny a look, one that tells me that they might have already had this discussion without me. "What, what are you thinking?"

Camden checks his phone again then scoots closer, perching on the low table in front of me. He takes my hands in his warm, large ones.

"What?" I insist, trying to seek out the truth of his thoughts from his gaze. As usual though, I'm struck with just how beautiful he is. Beautiful and distracting. I blink, forcing my thoughts out of the gutter and into the present.

"Sonny and I have been talking. I have a theory..."

"And?"

"I think this is more personal than just getting control over you."

"What could be more personal than that?"

"Look, Asia, I know the King, and there's no way he wouldn't have known about your existence. Maybe in the early days, after you were born, he would've questioned whether he was your father, but once he decided you were his, what was stopping him from coming into your life earlier? He *chose* to stay away before but now he's staking his claim."

"Yeah, like you said, to control me."

"No, he could've done that at any point before or after your mum died. This is something different. I'm sure of it."

"So what you're actually saying is all those years I longed for a father, he was right there, watching to see whether I was worthy to be his daughter or, more to the point, useful in some way?"

"Asia, the King is not a man with a heart. He doesn't love. So don't feel betrayed that he never sought you out. Be thankful you had seventeen years without him in your life," Camden whispers in hushed tones.

I don't respond. I can't. It hurts too much.

Sonny shifts closer and puts his arm around my shoulder. "I'm sorry he wasn't the father you hoped for," he says.

It's the first time any of my boys have acknowledged my disappointment. They've all been concerned about how my anger and fear is affecting me, but not my disappointment. Somehow, that's way more painful given all the years I've put my father on a pedestal. Hoping for the best and being given the worst is a bitter pill to swallow.

"Me too, Sonny. Me fucking too," I retort, my thoughts spinning off into a depressing cycle.

"I could really use a joint," Sonny blurts out after the silence gets too big.

"Yeah, so could I," I agree, needing something to take the edge off. Normally I could give or take Mary-J but tuning out for a bit might help me to manage this whole fucked up situation.

Camden puts his phone away and looks between us both. "Might be able to help on that front," he says, tucking his hand inside his jacket and pulling out a small bag of marijuana. "This is the last of it. I reckon I've at least enough for one last joint. Come on," he says, getting up and heading towards the fire door.

"Isn't that alarmed?"

"Not according to Sonny," Camden says with a shrug.

"I've crept out of this door loads of times and never tripped anything," Sonny explains.

Of course he has. The guy is a living breathing Spiderman in the flesh. Pretty sure he's scaled most of the walls in this place and found all the ways in and out of this building.

I pack up my sketchpad and follow them. Fortunately for us, the fire exit stairs lead down to the side of the main building that isn't used or overlooked by any of the classrooms or offices. It's bitterly cold, and I start to regret ever agreeing to head outside, but before long the effects of the joint take hold and my teeth are no longer chattering after a few drags. I just wish the effect would last a lot longer because a chill in my bones seems to have set in and I wonder if I'll ever feel warm again.

TWELVE

"Just the three I've been looking for," Mr Burnside says as we walk past his office an hour after we ditched Miss Moore's Art class.

"Yeah? Well, here we are, Doc. Are you gonna give us a detention or a telling off, because neither will have much of an impact," Camden quips, his eyes a little glazed.

Sonny snickers and I hold in a laugh that bubbles up my throat like champagne in a bottle, threatening to break free. Jesus, I've not felt this high since I tried my first joint when I was fourteen. I spent the night laughing at the most ridiculous things with Eastern, then spent the morning throwing up all my guts. It was the best and the worst night of my young life and one I didn't repeat again for quite a long time after.

"Just get inside." Mr Burnside sighs, standing to one side as we file past him into his office.

"What's up?" Sonny asks, plonking himself down on one of the armchairs opposite Mr Burnside's desk. Camden sits in the other seat, then motions for me to sit on his lap.

"That's not very gentlemanly," I complain, feigning annoyance that both of my guys hadn't waited to see if I wanted a seat. I really don't care either way, but it's good fun winding them up.

"What? I *am* being gentlemanly. Come sit on my lap, it's much more comfortable," Camden says, smirking. His topaz eyes light with mirth and even in my slightly inebriated state, I can appreciate that this is probably the first time I've seen him smile since I read Monk's note.

"Hey, my lap is waaaaay more comfortable than his," Sonny responds, patting his leg. "You know you wanna…"

"Don't make me choose," I respond, pretending to think really, really hard as I tap my chin and look between them both.

"Asia, take my chair," Mr Burnside butts in, spoiling our fun.

"Now there's a real gentleman. Thanks," I say, grinning widely as I make myself comfortable in his seat.

"So, what's up?" Sonny asks, turning his attention to Mr Burnside who is still frowning at us all. Oops, I think we've pissed him off.

"You skipped class."

"What's the big deal? None of us were really in the mood to play teacher's pet today. Besides, it was either skipping class or headbutting Dagger or one of Bram's goons. I think we made a good decision," Camden says with a shrug.

"A good decision would've been to excuse yourselves to come and see me, Cal, or Mr Carmichael, not get high on an *illegal* substance."

Camden rolls his eyes. "It's called Marijuana. You can say it, you know."

"I know what it's called, Camden. I also know that getting high isn't going to do you any favours. Right now, you all need to keep your heads clear. You of all people should know that."

"Yeah, well, maybe I'm over the fucking stress of all this. Maybe we're all done with waiting for shit to happen. Maybe, Mr Burnside, we're trying not to lose our fucking minds!" Camden shouts, losing his shit now. Really, it was only a matter of time.

"Cam, man, it ain't Mr Burnside's fault," Sonny says, sitting up in his chair.

"I don't really give a shit. If he wants to poke a wounded animal then he can't expect not to get bit."

"Is that how you see yourself, Camden?" Mr Burnside asks, looking at him intently. "Do you want to talk about how you feel?"

Camden screws his face up and bites out a laugh. "Really? You wanna do your mumbo jumbo therapy bullshit on me now? Do you ever fucking let up?"

Mr Burnside laughs. "No, I don't. Helping people to heal is as important to me as your mum is to you. I won't ever stop trying to do that, like you won't ever stop loving her."

"It was just a goddamn joint. What's the big deal?"

"I get it, Camden. You need to dull the pain. What you're going through, what you're *all* going through is tough and I won't stop trying to give you an outlet to share some of the burden. But I need you to cut that shit out and focus," Mr Burnside says. It's the first time I've heard him swear. It kinda suits him.

"No, you *don't* fucking get it," Camden seethes, his anger spilling out through clenched teeth.

"Cam…" Sonny starts, sobering up pretty quick when he realises we're on dangerous ground.

Camden lifts his hand, cutting Sonny off. "This is bullshit. It's been almost a week since Monk took Pink. Bram and his goons are provoking us every fucking chance they get. Pink is no closer to being found and despite all the fucking theories of where she *might* be, no one has confirmed anything!" he pants, standing. "And I can't get hold of my mum. I can't fucking reach her!"

I get up, traversing the table and stand before Camden, sliding my arms around his waist. It's all I can think of to do because words won't help, and promises won't heal open wounds that run as deep as ours. After a beat, he wraps his arms around my back, holding me close.

"Fuck, I'm sorry," Camden says after a minute. The apology isn't for Mr Burnside but for me. "I need to get my head together."

"You've nothing to apologise for, Camden. Why shouldn't you feel like this? You've been in this position a lot longer than any of us and you've kept your head throughout. That takes a lot of strength," I say, then lift my head up and stand on my tiptoes to press a reassuring kiss against his lips. "But you can afford to break every now and then," I quietly remind him.

"I have to be strong for you, Asia. I need to be because what if...." He looks at me with steely resolve, his beautiful eyes swimming with emotion. There's no need to finish his sentence because I hear what he doesn't say. I hear the words that will tear me apart should he voice them.

What if they're already dead...

"Don't talk like that," I whisper, clutching his face between my palms. "I refuse to believe either are dead. I fucking refuse."

"If he kills my mum..."

"No. Don't. Don't you dare think that."

"...I might not survive it, Asia. I'm afraid I'll lose my fucking mind."

"You are one of the strongest people I know." *You'll survive anything...* Those are words I can't voice out loud because it will only confirm in his head the worst possible scenario.

Mr Burnside coughs, drawing our attention back into the room and breaking the connection we share. "Talking helps. I know you don't believe in therapy, Camden. You're not alone in that belief, but at least talk to each other. Share what you're feeling. If I'm beginning to understand the King, then dividing and conquering is part of his repertoire. Don't let him get between you. When you have each other, you have a lot more than you think."

"That's easier said than done, Doc," Sonny says, looking between us all. He looks pale, the amusement and brief happiness we shared now gone. "We've all spent the best part of our lives trusting no one but ourselves."

"But things are changing. Despite the burden you all carry, I see you evolving into wonderful young adults. Finding people you trust, that you call home when you've been through what you have, is rare. Believe in that, believe in each other, and trust that we are doing all we can to find them," Mr Burnside says.

Sonny nods, getting to his feet. "Has there been any more news?"

Mr Burnside shakes his head. "I understand that Grim is still waiting to hear back from the guy she sent to spy on the King. Other than that, her girls at the Spa have their ear to the ground and will call with any news, even if it seems trivial. The Freed brothers are calling in some favours and trying to gather as much intelligence about the King and his various businesses as possible to see if there's an angle we've missed. Right now, as hard as it is, this is a waiting game."

"No shit," Camden snaps, gritting his teeth.

Mr Burnside looks between us, then seems to make up his mind about something. "I know the rec room is off limits right now whilst it's getting fixed up after the fire, but you guys could use a distraction that is neither illegal or bad for your health, am I right?"

"There's only one thing that could distract me and I'm not sure it's on the cards…" Sonny says, side-eying me with a devilish smirk.

I roll my eyes to hide the fact that my stomach turns to butterflies. "What do you have in mind, Mr Burnside? Because I'll take anything right now."

"Anything?" Sonny smirks.

"Thirsty much?" Camden mutters under his breath, hauling me closer to his side in a show of ownership.

"I'm fucking parched actually," Sonny quips back, pulling a smirk from Camden's lips.

"Yeah, you and me both."

"Jeez, you two have hands, you might want to use them," I banter back, pulling a snort of mirth from Mr Burnside.

"There's a projector in the library. I could arrange a movie night this weekend. You could order some pizzas in. I could grab some popcorn for you all. What do you think?"

"A movie night with pizza and popcorn? I'd say you're trying too hard, Mr Burnside. We're not fucking twelve," Camden scoffs, shaking his head.

Honestly, a movie night sounds amazing but it doesn't feel right, not without Pink. Why should we do anything remotely fun when she's suffering?

"I dunno, maybe Camden's right." I sigh feeling disappointed, then immediately guilty for feeling that way. Pink doesn't get a goddamn movie evening does she? Nausea rises up my throat as I think about what she must be going through.

Mr Burnside winces. "Perhaps not. It was just an idea."

"Hey, ignore them. A movie night would be good." Sonny says.

When I grimace, torn between wanting to do something any normal teenager gets to do and feeling guilty for even wanting it, Sonny gives me a sympathetic look.

"I know it isn't easy, Asia, but what the fuck else can we do right now? You need to take your mind off everything. Give yourself a break. You need it. None of us can help Pink if we're all fucked in the head."

"I don't know. It doesn't feel right."

Sonny ignores me and addresses Mr Burnside. "Are we talking

about everyone? I'm not sure any of us are going to be able to chill if Bram and his crew are there too. We'd end up fucking killing each other and I'm pretty sure you don't want a brawl on your hands," Sonny says.

"Yes, probably not the best idea. Tell you what, I'll set it up so you can all watch a movie in your groups. I can schedule in slots all day. You're supposed to be spending all your social time together anyway, so that works. I'll clear it with Mr Carmichael first and let you know. Does that sound like a plan you could agree to?"

"I suppose," Camden mutters.

"Cam, you're actually cool with this?" I question.

"Sonny's right. We could all do with the distraction."

"Okay, good, that's settled then. Any movie preferences?"

"Nah, just surprise us," Sonny says.

Camden's eyebrows pull together in a frown. "Just no chick-flicks."

"Okay, Camden. No chick-flicks. Got it."

"Except maybe for Dirty Dancing…" I suggest.

"Don't even think about it, Doc," Camden warns, and I can't help but smile a little.

THIRTEEN

Saturday evening we all pile into the library. We're the last group of the day and, admittedly, it has felt good to have something to look forward to. A space has been cleared in the middle of the room where a few sectional seats have been moved together to form a semi-circle and a bunch of cushions have been scattered across the floor in front of them. Hanging from the ceiling is a projector screen hooked up to a laptop that's set on a table over to the side.

Mr Burnside waves us into the room from his spot behind the computer screen, the delicious smell of warm pizza and popcorn permeating the air. Despite Camden shooting Mr Burnside's idea down yesterday, he's the one who seems the most impressed.

"Not exactly how I usually spend my Saturday nights, Doc, but this ain't bad," he admits.

"I'm glad you approve, though I'm having trouble getting the damn movie to start. It's been fine all day." He frowns, clicking on the mouse as he tries to figure out what's wrong.

Camden rolls his eyes. "Well, that's just fucking typical."

"Ah no, wait! It's all good," Mr Burnside says, grinning and snatching up a remote control from the desk. "Just press the red button to turn off the lights and then the green button when you're ready to play the movie."

Camden grabs the remote from Mr Burnside and takes a seat on the sectional. "Cheers, Doc," he says. "I hope it's a good one."

"You're welcome, and I think you'll enjoy this movie. Frank will be checking in regularly to make sure everything's good," he says before leaving us to it.

"What pizzas do we have?" Eastern asks, completely distracted by the food. He shoves Sonny out of the way as he opens the lid to one of the pizza boxes placed on a table to the right of the seating area. "Ham and pineapple, my favourite." He snatches up a slice and hoovers down half of it in one mouthful.

Sonny pulls a face. "Eww, fruit has no business being on pizza…"

"As long as there's pepperoni I ain't complaining," Camden pipes up, looking over at the pizza boxes.

"Got you covered," Sonny mumbles, shoving a slice into his face and bringing the box over. Camden takes it from his hands, flipping the lid open. "These are mine," he states, picking up a slice. I raise my eyebrow at him. "Of course, I'm willing to share with you, Asia."

"You'd better." I sit down next to him, grabbing a piece.

Ford shakes his head and sits on the floor by my feet. "Bunch of gannets," he mutters.

"Aren't you hungry?" I ask him around a mouthful of pizza.

"Not for pizza, no," he retorts, glancing over his shoulder at me, his lips twitching in a half smile.

"Smooth, Ford, smooth," Sonny laughs, dropping beside him on the floor with a steaming margherita pizza balanced on his cast.

"Hey, leave some for me," Kate complains, elbowing Eastern and grabbing the last pizza box from the table. She makes herself comfortable on the sectional to the left of us. Separating herself a little from me and the boys.

"You can scoot in closer. It's a better view of the screen from here," I say.

She raises her eyebrows. "Nah, I'm good. I already feel like a spare part as it is. I don't want to get in the way…"

"Shut-up, you're a part of our crew, get in," Eastern says, dropping beside me and patting the seat next to him. It's a completely platonic gesture, and I adore him for it. Kate gives us both a small smile and scoots closer.

After we're all settled, Camden presses the red button as instructed and the library falls into darkness, then hits the green button and the film starts to play. When a familiar song starts playing and the opening credits appear I choke out a laugh. Mr Burnside is a goddamn legend.

"You've got to be fucking kidding me," Camden grumbles.

"What the fuck is this shit?" Ford complains, and Kate's mouth drops open in shock before she bursts out laughing.

"Don't tell me you've never seen this movie? Where have you been hiding, under a bloody rock? Everyone's seen this movie at least once in their life."

"No, I haven't. What's *Dirty Dancing*, some kind of porno?" Ford responds, and we all crease up laughing.

"Oh my God, Ford, you're fucking priceless," Eastern laughs, leaning over and shoving his head playfully.

"What's so funny… are they *dancing*?" he says watching the credits roll.

Laughter peels about the room once more, but when Jennifer Grey's voiceover starts Camden tells us all to shut the fuck up making me grin from ear to ear. This is the *perfect* choice of film in my opinion, and clearly one of Camden's favourites despite how much he protests otherwise.

"CAN someone tell me what the fuck I just watched?" Ford says, a little disgusted, but I can see the twinkle in his eye and the flush on his cheeks. He liked it too.

"That, Ford, was Patrick Swayze at his finest. Sexy. As. Fuck," I say, with a chuckle.

Ford grunts, scowling.

"Hey, don't worry, bro, the guy's dead," Sonny says, slapping Ford on the back and giving me a wink over his shoulder.

"Urgh, don't remind me," I respond, placing my hand over my heart dramatically.

Camden snorts. "Admittedly he can move, but no one's got moves like me," he says with a cheeky grin.

"Oh yeah?"

"Yeah." He jumps up, stepping over Ford and Sonny, crooking his finger at me just like Johnny does to Baby at the end of the movie. Behind him the credits are rolling and the music is still playing.

"Who, me?" I tease, pointing to my chest.

"*Seriously?*" Ford groans, pulling himself up onto the sectional and getting out of Camden's way as he kicks aside all the cushions to clear a space.

"What are you doing, Asia?" Eastern laughs. I can feel the heat of his gaze as I get up and walk towards Camden, swinging my hips just like Baby does in the movie.

"Looks like you need to up your game." Kate chuckles.

When I reach Camden, he pulls me towards him and wraps an arm around my back, sliding his hand over my arse and cupping the back of my thigh, hooking my right leg up over his hip.

"Hey, *bae-by*. Wanna dance?" he murmurs, a twinkle in his eye. A smile pulls up his lips as he lowers his head, brushing his mouth against my own.

"Not a fan of the movie, hmm?" I respond, grinning stupidly.

"Hmm, I'm a fan of foreplay and if Patrick Swayze gets my girl all hot under the collar, then I'm down with that." He grins then bends his knees and moves against me, imitating some of the sexier moves from the movie.

Sonny whistles as Camden grasps my arse and grinds his hips against mine. I go with it, feeling a little giddy as his strong arms guide me. The rest of my boys watch with fire in their eyes. Looks like they're enjoying the show. When Camden searches for my lips and starts kissing me unapologetically in front of everyone, I have to remind myself that Kate is still in the room and doesn't need to see this. Pushing him back gently, I laugh a little.

"Woah, Camden. I think you're in need of a cold shower," I say, smiling as I press one last kiss against his mouth.

"I'd prefer a warm one with you in it…" he grins. Leaning in close, he brushes his mouth against my ear. "How about it, bae…?"

"What the actual *fuck*?!" Eastern suddenly shouts, making me jump and Camden snap his head around.

I'm about to shut Eastern's jealousy down when I realise he's not actually looking at us, but behind us both at the projector screen. Camden stiffens as the colour drains from Kate, Ford and Sonny's face. We both turn to see what they're looking at.

"Motherfucker!" Camden grinds out, his arm tightening around me. "*Pink*?"

We all watch in stunned silence as a video begins playing. Pink is sitting on a bare mattress in a brightly lit room, her legs crossed, a determined look on her face as she stares directly into the camera. She doesn't appear to be hurt and as far as I can tell there are no bruises on her body, though I've no idea if there are any hidden beneath her clothes. I push that thought away, concentrating instead on what I can see.

"How is this possible...?" Ford questions, stepping up beside me, his fingers automatically reaching for mine. Any answer I might have is cut off when Pink starts to speak.

"Asia, I have a message from the King," she begins, swallowing hard. Her gaze flicks to someone beyond the camera, someone we can't see. Then the camera pans closer to something Pink is holding in her hands. A newspaper. She lifts it up. It's dated today.

"I'm okay." I hear her say, stressing the *'I'm'*. That slight nuance has Camden tensing beside me. He hasn't been able to get hold of his mum in days. Is Pink trying to tell us something? I can't see the expression on her face to see if she is or not, given the camera is still pointed at the newspaper. I sway on my feet with relief, with worry. She's alive. Thank God, she's alive. But what about Camden's mum?

"Fucking Christ," Camden swears under his breath.

"Oh, God," Kate cries, but I can't bring myself to look at her.

My heart fucking hammers in my chest as my mouth goes dry. We all wait in hushed silence, no one daring to breathe let alone mutter another word, as we wait for what comes next.

The screen flickers as the camera pans back out. Two men dressed all in black, wearing black masks over their faces walk towards Pink. They're big, burly, and their body language lacks any kind of sympathy towards her. Anger bubbles inside my chest as one of them-the shorter of the two with red hair-grasps her arm and pulls her roughly off the bed. We see a brief glimpse of her body, and her back view as she's manhandled out of the shot. Then the screen goes black.

"What the ever-loving fuck!" Sonny exclaims, but I shush him because something tells me this isn't the end of the video.

When white letters begin to appear on the screen shortly after, jumbled and out of order, I'm forced to hold my breath as they move about forming a sentence.

TOMORROW, 9PM. THE PIER, HASTINGS – COME ALONE, ASIA. TELL ANYONE, SHE DIES.

MY HEART PLUMMETS.

FOURTEEN

"Camden, stop it! Let him go!" I shout, tugging at his arm but he has a vice-like grip on Mr Burnside's throat that I can't shift him no matter how hard I try.

"Let the man go!" Cal shoves the door to Mr Burnside's office open. It practically falls off its hinges with the force of his entrance.

Sonny steps in front of him, forcing Cal back with one hand on his chest as Eastern grasps him from behind, holding him back. "No, Cal. Stay the fuck back!"

"Sonny?" he questions, looking between us all like we've all lost our minds. Maybe we have. "What the hell is going on in here!? Frank is fucking out cold upstairs."

Frank tried to stop us. He'd seen the murderous look in my boys' eyes but one well-placed punch from Ford and Frank was knocked out cold. If I hadn't been so fucking terrified of what Camden was about to do, I might've been impressed.

"I'll tell you what's going on, Doc here is a fucking traitor!" Camden spits, tightening his grip around Mr Burnside's throat. His face is starting to go purple, spittle forming around his mouth as he struggles for breath. "Get into our heads, make us trust you, then you fuck us over, is that it? Where's my goddamn mum! Where is Pink?!"

"Camden, stop, please! You're killing him!" I continue. "Just let him go. He didn't do this! *Please*," I beg, because no matter how impossible this seems right now, I know Mr Burnside and he wouldn't have set this up. There's no way. He's one of the good guys.

"Then who the fuck did?" Camden snaps, loosening his hold just enough so that Mr Burnside can breathe.

"Whatever… you think… I've… done…" Mr Burnside chokes out, taking in ragged breaths between every word, "I… haven't…"

"You're a fucking liar!"

"Let my husband go, Camden!" Mr Carmichael growls as he rushes into the room. Behind him, Frank leans against the door frame, rubbing his temple, looking more than a little dazed.

Ford steps in front of our principal. "Don't come any closer. I don't want to hurt you, but I will."

"Get out of my way," Mr Carmichael says, his voice low, controlled as they face off.

"That would be a no," Ford retorts, squaring his shoulders.

Something changes in Mr Carmichael. I see it as he takes a step closer to Ford. He's no longer the principal of this school, he's a man who's ready to tear Ford apart to get to the man he loves. If I don't do something right now, this is all going to shit.

"This is madness. Fucking madness!" I shout, trying to get their attention.

"No, Asia, what's madness is that we trusted these arseholes," Camden snarls, his whole body vibrating with a simmering, bubbling, boiling rage.

"You *can* trust us. Just tell me what's happened." Cal tries to break free from Eastern's hold, but between him and Sonny he's not going anywhere. Sonny bares his teeth, and it breaks my fucking heart. One twisted, fucked up message from the King and we're ready to throw down with the people who care about us.

"Everyone stop! JUST STOP!" I scream. "There's no way Mr Burnside's involved. Just think about it!" Camden flinches, and I know that there's a part of him that wants to believe that's true. "Please, Camden, let him go so we can talk."

I'm not beyond pleading, not when it comes to the people I care about making a huge fucking mistake. Somehow, someway, my words register and Camden drops his hand, taking a step away from Mr Burnside who stumbles backwards onto his chair, gasping for air. Mr Carmichael rushes to his side and kneels before him, concern for his husband and anger fighting for control as he glares at us all.

"Jesus fuck, Camden! What the hell is going on?" he asks, his eyes wide with horror as he runs his hand up and down Mr Burnside's arms. "Just breathe, love. Just breathe," he soothes.

"This arsehole gave us a very special movie tonight..." Camden sneers. His fists are clenched at his side and I know it's taking a monumental effort not to launch himself at Mr Burnside once more.

"What are you talking about?" he asks, looking between us all. "Disliking his choice in movie warrants fucking strangulation, does it?!" His eyes narrow at Camden and for the briefest of moments, I see the man he might have been once upon a time. A dangerous man ready to kill for the ones he loves.

"No, not the movie, *after*..." I stumble over my words, pressing a hand against Camden's chest in an attempt to remind him of his sanity, because he's a hairsbreadth from doing something he'll never be able to return from.

"After?" Mr Burnside looks at me in confusion, hurt a rash across his face.

"*Pink.* There was a recording of her. It played after the movie ended," I rush out, not thinking about the warning in the message, just wanting everyone to stop.

"Explain," Cal says, drilling me with his gaze.

"Asia got a message from the King delivered by Pink. Looks like Mr Burnside here added a little extra footage to the viewing," Ford says. There's a quiet kind of anger emanating from him that is just as powerful as Camden's, just way more controlled.

"*Wh-what*?" Mr Burnside rasps, his gaze flicking between us all in panic. "I had nothing... That's impossible!"

"Impossible or not, we just fucking watched it," Eastern says.

"Pink was in a room, being filmed. She held up a newspaper with today's date. She said she was okay..." Kate explains quietly, confirming what we'd seen with our own eyes.

Mr Burnside shakes his head. "I had nothing to do with that. I swear to you."

I want to believe him. I think he's a good man, and yet...

"If not you, then who?" Sonny asks, scraping a hand through his hair.

"I uploaded the movies onto the computer myself... It makes no sense, none. There was nothing like that on the PC this morning..." He hesitates, looking at Mr Carmichael, then at Cal and Frank.

"What?" I ask.

"Unless..."

"What group went before these guys?" Cal asks, following the same train of thought as Mr Burnside.

We fall silent, realisation hitting us all at the same time.

"*Bram*," Ford grinds out.

"That little prick!" Camden turns on his heel and rushes towards the door, but Cal steps in front of him, shaking his head.

"Stop! Beating the shit out of Bram isn't going to help. Let us deal with this," he warns.

"What? Like you've dealt with everything else? Fuck that! I'm going to kill the little bastard, but not before I find out where they're keeping Pink and my mum! Every day that passes they're in more danger and you're doing NOTHING!" he shouts, all restraint gone.

"We're doing everything we can," Cal insists, calmly.

"Bullshit!" Camden tries to shove past Cal, but I reach for him.

"No, wait!" My fingers dig into his biceps, squeezing hard enough to bruise. "You saw what the message said. You know how this works, Camden. You know better than anyone."

Why didn't we think! *Stupid. Stupid. Stupid.*

"*Tell anyone, she dies…*" Kate hushes out.

Seeing her like that, so fucking brave and unreachable had flipped a switch in all of us. My fear has ramped up to full power, a thousand volts pummelling my insides, flaying them. That fear is what made my feet follow Camden and what, eventually, made me see sense and not react. But Camden's resolve to keep himself in check went out the fucking window the second the video stopped.

"Fuuuccckkkk!" Camden roars, slamming his fist against the wall, denting the plasterboard.

"We are so fucking screwed!" Sonny blurts out, pacing up and down. His agitation makes me feel so much worse. But he's right, we are. We're beyond screwed.

"They'll kill her." My voice cracks. Eastern reaches for me, hauling me into his side. He brushes his lips against my hair, trying in his own way to comfort me.

After a beat, Mr Carmichael gets to his feet, a dark look spreading across his face like ink in water. "What. Did. The. Message. Say?"

No one answers.

"Look, we can watch the footage ourselves, but you can save us all time by telling us right now," Cal says, looking between us all. When no one says a word, he continues. "We *all* knew this would happen. The King has played his hand. Now we have to play ours. Tell us."

Pressing my eyes shut briefly to hold back the sting of tears, I meet Cal's gaze.

"Looks like my father wants to meet me at last," I say.

FIFTEEN

"**Y**ou ready, Asia?" Cal asks me the following evening as he checks the wires attached to my chest one last time. He fiddles with the recording equipment, making sure it's working properly before nodding.

I lower my t-shirt, then pull on my hoody, zipping it up.

"Yeah, I'm ready," I lie, feeling far from it. I'm fucking scared. So scared of this going tits-up. The King said to go alone, and whilst that's what it'll look like on the surface, Cal isn't stupid enough to actually let that happen. He's called in more favours and I'll be watched by a man and a woman posing as a couple on a night out at the pier. I've studied a photo of them for the last hour. They look like they're in their mid-thirties and not vaguely capable of stepping in, should I need them to. Then again, looks can be deceiving. Perhaps that's a good thing, the King won't suspect them.

"Jan and Doug are well-versed in this kind of thing. Both have been bodyguards for some very high-profile celebrities and members of the government. You can count on them. If the King tries anything, they'll step in."

"They'd fucking better," Sonny warns as he enters the room, closing the door behind him.

"It's risky," I repeat for the hundredth time. We all know that if the King suspects anything, then Pink is dead. But I have a plan of my own. One that no one is aware of, not even my boys.

A plan I've agonised over.

"If anything happens to Asia…" Sonny chews on his lip, holding back the threat that's on the tip of his tongue. He's torn between worrying about me and his loyalty towards his foster family.

"Yeah, I know, mate," Cal responds, sighing heavily. "But we've got this covered. Trust me."

And he does, trust him, I mean. Sonny believes in Cal, in his foster family. It's why he's here, after all. Of all my boys, he was the only one I could stand being with me here in Cal's office as he checks and rechecks the recording equipment.

"What are the others doing?" I ask Sonny, trying to distract us both from the fact that in half an hour I'll be meeting the King face-to-face.

My *father*.

My *enemy*.

"They're flipping the fuck out. You know how they feel about all of this."

"Yeah, I know…"

Last night we had a huge argument over my decision to follow through on the King's orders. Agreeing to Cal's suggestion was the only compromise they were willing to listen to but even then they hate the idea of me going to meet the King. They're scared for me, I get that. But if we're to understand what the King wants then I have to go through with this. I don't have a choice.

They *must* understand that.

They have to.

"Right, you're good to go. Let's go over the plan one last time. Tell me the rules," Cal demands, fixing me with a determined stare.

"I stay where there's plenty of people. I remain calm. I do not, under any circumstances, go anywhere with him and I give Doug and Jan the agreed signal should I feel in danger and they'll intervene," I respond, reeling off everything we've discussed.

"And what's the signal?"

"I cross my arms over my chest."

Cal nods. "Good. Then let's get you in the car."

Slinging my rucksack over my shoulder, I'm more than ready to get this over and done with. Outside a black cab awaits, the engine running. Sonny draws me against him for a quick hug. "Don't take any risks, okay?"

"Okay," I respond, knowing I'm going to do exactly that because that's what I do. I risk everything for the ones I love. Climbing into the cab, I slam the door shut, and roll down the window.

"See you soon, okay?" Sonny says.

I nod, unable to make him a promise I won't be able to fulfil.

"Wait!"

Behind him, Eastern, Camden and Ford run out of the building. Eastern practically rugby tackles Sonny out of the way and leans into the car, grasping my face in his.

"Be safe, promise me!" he growls, pressing a quick, harsh kiss against my lips before releasing me.

"I…"

Camden shoves him aside.

"Get out of the car, Asia," he says, his fear a hot poker against my skin.

"I can't do that," I respond quietly, shaking my head.

"God-fucking-damn-it, Asia!" he snarls, but he doesn't try to fight Ford off when he gently urges him to one side.

Ford stares at me for a moment then swallows hard. He places his fingers over the edge of the window frame. "Don't be rash. Think with your head and not with your heart. Above all else, come back to us."

"I'll try not to mess this up," I respond, my stomach turning over.

Fifteen minutes later, the car is pulling up outside the main entrance to the pier. If I wasn't so preoccupied with thoughts of murder, I might've appreciated the twinkling lights and the delicious smell of candy floss and grilled burgers.

"That'll be eight pounds," the cabbie says, looking at me in the rear view mirror.

"Here," I say, handing over a ten-pound note.

"Let me get your change."

"Don't worry about it."

"Thanks, love. Enjoy your night."

I don't respond. How can I? I feel sick. Sick to my stomach that tonight I'll be meeting my father for the first and last time. You see, Cal's plan might be to gather information, but my plan is to kill the King. In my rucksack is a knife and I intend on driving it into his heart.

Taking a deep breath, I pull my beanie hat low over my head and walk towards the entrance to the pier. The place is busy, loud. A cacophony of noise. Kids run around screeching with delight, dragging their parents from one stall to another. Teenagers hang out in groups smoking cigarettes and drinking from cans. I'm pretty sure I recognise a few of them from the Tower. Couples walk hand in hand, laughing and muttering sweet nothings to each other.

Everyone seems happy and completely oblivious to my hammering heart and the sweat that slides in a river down my back.

The sound of a balloon popping has me swearing and stumbling into a couple of teenagers who look at me like I'm about to mug them for money. Their fear and judgement have me sneering at them.

"Boo!"

They run off screaming, then burst into laughter when they realise I'm not following them. Ugh, I hate people.

Pressed up against the side of a candy floss stall I force myself to look around, to take notice of my surroundings and the revellers milling about. I'm struck by a father with his child, a little girl no older than seven or eight. She's holding onto his hand and peering up at him adoringly, so utterly in love. When he looks down at her she beams at him, and his smile reflects her own.

Sighing, I push off against the stall and wander away from the crowd towards the end of the pier. The message never said where exactly to meet, so I end up at the furthest point on the pier figuring that if I'm going to commit murder, I'm going to have to do it someplace that's away from the main crowd. I don't make eye-contact with anyone. I don't even try to see which of the couples on the pier might be Doug and Jan. What's the point? My plan doesn't include them anyway.

The further I walk away from the main thoroughfare the darker it gets, and apart from some teenagers snogging in a secluded corner, completely oblivious to the world around them, there's no one about but me.

Good. I don't need any witnesses to see what I'm about to do.

When I reach the end of the pier, the noise of the revellers is blotted out by the high wind, crashing waves and the rapid beat of my heart. Dipping my hand into my rucksack, I feel for the smooth handle of the knife I stole from the kitchen earlier this morning. My fingers curl around the cold metal as I tuck it up the sleeve of my coat.

I'm shivering with a mixture of cold and deep-rooted fear.

I will myself to calm down, to breathe.

I can do this.

I have to.

Pressing my eyes shut, I give myself a moment to centre myself and empty my head of all the swimming thoughts that could so easily drown me as much as the frothing, angry sea below.

When I open my eyes again and peer out into the darkness, I feel like I'm standing on the edge of the world and I know that I'm moments away from losing my soul entirely.

Then I wait, the freezing cold ocean spray biting at my skin.

I don't have to wait for long.

"I see you're braver than I gave you credit for," a male voice says from behind me. I stiffen, my fingers grasping hold of the knife still stuffed up inside my coat sleeve, but I don't turn around. I don't have to because the King steps up beside me and places his forearms on the wooden rail.

My heart fucking pounds so loudly I think I might pass out. Instead, I turn to face the man who was responsible for my mum's death. For a few long seconds all I can do is stare into the face of my father. He has dark hair and olive skin like me, but that's where the resemblance ends because there's a darkness in his eyes that is cruel and unyielding, and just as black as his irises. Camden was right when he said the King can't love. This man before me is nothing more than a stranger with a cold heart and blood on his hands. No amount of expensive clothes he's wearing can cover up that fact.

"I'm surprised you came. I thought you'd have too much of your mother in you. She was weak. You, however, aren't. I like that."

"Where's Pink?" I ask, ignoring his attempt to bait me with talk of my mum.

"She's where she needs to be."

The sound of laughter suddenly rings loud in my ears and the teenagers who were making out in a darkened corner walk right by us. They're not Jan and Doug and I don't know if that makes me feel relieved or not, given what I came here to do. The King's calculating gaze slips towards the couple before he returns his attention to me.

"Teenagers are pathetic creatures, ruled by their hormones and ideals. They do stupid, irresponsible things because they're not adult enough to make grown-up decisions," he says, a dark smile pulling up his lips. I don't say anything in response because I guess there's a point to this. "Like Camden, for example. He turned your head, just like his mother turned mine. What did it do for you, Asia? Was it those beautiful eyes he inherited from his mother? Or was it the fact he was as broken as she is? I can't say I'm happy about your choice in men, but I do understand it. His sister was just as alluring too, pity I didn't have a chance to get to know her better. She would've made a perfect replacement for her mother when I tire of her."

"*Fuck you!*" I snap, realising too late that swearing at the King isn't the smartest move I've made, then again, what difference does it make? By the end of our conversation either he'll be dead, or I will.

His grin turns into a scowl. "Monk was right, you're a feisty one. Quite the mouth on you."

"And Monk's an arsehole."

He shrugs his shoulders. "Yes, he is, but he's also very malleable, gullible too. He's good for only one thing…"

"And what's that?" I ask, falling into his trap.

"Hurting people…"

I stiffen. My mouth goes dry and I can't seem to form any words.

"Don't worry, your little friend is bruise-free… *for now*," he adds.

A moment passes where I want to launch myself at him and cut him good, but I'm not a fool. He's taunting me, pushing me. I refuse to let him. I'm not going to get this opportunity again and I need to make sure I time this right.

"What do you want?" I say, allowing the hate in my voice to seep through. He needs to know how much I hate him and how far I'm willing to go to keep as calm as he is. There's strength in remaining calm even when you're faced with someone who's doing everything to push you to react. Ford was right about that.

"What do you want?" I repeat.

"So many things, Asia, but only one that really counts…" he tips his head to the side and studies my face.

"And what's that?"

"My Kingdom."

"What?" *His Kingdom?*

But he ignores my question and raises his hand. I flinch when the cool leather of his glove presses against my cheek. "I can see why Monk hates you so much. You are more Bennett than he is. You have a fire in your soul that cannot be faked and the need for revenge that will make you spill blood. You're strong," he says, sounding impressed. "It's a pity you're a bastard child. I would have enjoyed teaching you the family business."

"I'm *not* a Bennett," I spit. "I'm Asia Chen!"

The King drops his hand and laughs. The sound is all too similar to Monk's and it makes my skin crawl. My hand tightens around the tip of the blade. I feel the sharp edge dig into my skin, but I don't care. As soon as I'm able, I'm going to fucking slice his neck open.

"You're *my* daughter, Asia, and as such you carry our name. That makes you my property." His voice lowers, as he dips his head so that he's at eye level with me. I can feel the warmth of his breath against my face, and I try not to flinch as he stares right into my fucking soul, picking me apart with every second that passes. My hands shake as I allow the blade to slide slowly lower until my fingers are grasped tightly around the handle.

Shutting down every last emotion, I ready myself.

"What. Do. You. Want?" I say for the third time, not willing to fall for his mind games.

A slow smile carves across his face. "I told you, *my* Kingdom… And you, child, are going to make sure I get it, once and for all."

"I don't understand."

"One life in exchange for another, that's all I ask."

"What?!" I blurt out.

"You want your friend back, then you'll have to do something for me first. Ever killed a person, Asia?"

All the blood drains from my body. I swear to God, I can feel it seeping from my feet into the wooden boards below us. "You want me to *murder* someone?"

"Oh, it's not so hard when you've got a big enough incentive," he responds, laughing.

My mouth pops open in shock, but his smile fades as his eyes flick to something or someone behind me. He rears back suddenly, stepping away from me, and I realise that I might just have missed my chance to kill the bastard. He glances again at something over my shoulder then back at me, his eyes narrowing as his lips draw back over his teeth.

"That was a stupid thing to do, Asia, but not unexpected. You think I wouldn't know you'd talk? You're just a child playing games in a grown-up world."

"What are you talking about?" I ask, even though I know without looking that Jan and Doug have made themselves known. I didn't give them the signal, so why the fuck are they approaching us? Then I remember, I've already broken one rule. Cal must've given them instructions to step in should I move the goalposts.

So fucking stupid! I could've had him. I could've ended this.

"If I give you an instruction, I expect you to follow it to the letter. You'll learn that soon enough. Alas, our time together is now over."

"No!" I shout, my resolve to stay calm evaporating with his threat. He takes a dozen more steps backwards, his hand sliding against the wooden rail as though searching for something. Then I see it, a gate built into the railings that opens onto some stairs leading down towards the sea. The sudden roar of a boat engine comes to life and with it, all hope of saving my friend is gone.

"Wait!" I say. "Take me. My life for Pink's."

He laughs again, opening the gate and stepping onto the platform. "No. I have plans for you, Asia, which involve you staying exactly where you are."

"You kill her, then I don't do shit!" I shout, not caring now. My anger bubbles to the surface until my body shakes with it.

"There are more ways than one to skin a cat. Don't forget, I know everything about you. How are your little brothers, by the way?" he smirks, and my blood runs cold.

"You wouldn't."

"In a heartbeat," he sneers, his gaze flashing to my hand holding the knife. A sinister smile spreads like wildfire across his face.

"No! Don't! I'll do anything." *Not my baby brothers. Not them. Please, God, no.*

"Family's are a bind, aren't they?" he muses. "Loving them makes you weak. I'm not a weak man," he responds. The implication isn't lost on me. He doesn't love and therefore he has no weaknesses and nothing to lose, not like me. "Wait for my instructions. Oh, and next time we meet I advise you not to bring a knife."

With that, he spins on his heel and disappears into the darkness as though he was never really here.

SIXTEEN

"What does he mean '*he wants his Kingdom*?'" Eastern asks me for what seems like the tenth time since I returned. I've been pacing up and down in Cal's office for the last hour unable to do anything but flip between worry and incendiary rage; I feel it rippling beneath my skin, scorching me from the inside out.

"I don't fucking know, and I don't care!" I shout, wringing my hands in front of me. "He threatened my brothers, Eastern. He'll fucking kill them."

"No, he won't get the chance. Your brothers are already being moved to a safe house as we speak."

"Where? How? I want to speak with them. Now!"

"As soon as they're settled, I'll make sure that happens."

"They *were* settled, Cal. As much as it killed me that they were moved so far away from me, they were happy, and now they have to be moved again because of the King and his fucking threats."

"I know it's not ideal, Asia, but they will adapt…"

I raise my hand, cutting him off. "They shouldn't have to adapt.

Isn't it enough that they lost their mum, that our family was torn apart?"

"It is, and I'm so sorry this had to happen."

"I should've killed him when I had the chance!"

"And get sent to prison for murder? No, Asia, where would your brothers be then?"

"*Safe*, they'd be safe!"

Cal sighs heavily. I know he's doing his best but that doesn't make any of this bullshit easier to swallow. "Tomorrow, we'll call your brothers, okay? You can speak to them and put your mind at rest a little."

I nod sharply. "Tomorrow then."

"Okay, good."

"So what now?" Ford asks, like Camden he's been quiet up until now.

"I've just sent the recording of Asia's conversation with the King to Hud and Grim. Now that we have his family name it might open some more avenues we hadn't been able to access before. That's a *good* thing."

"And what about Pink, my mum?" Camden asks. He barely looks at me and I can't tell what he's thinking, feeling. He's shut down completely, not giving anything away.

Cal puffs out his cheeks. "We've removed another target and made sure Sebastian and George are safe, so the King still needs to keep them both alive in order for Asia to do what he wants. That's *something* at least."

"And what does he expect Asia to do exactly? Because as far as I'm aware, he's already King of his fucking kingdom." Sonny says with agitation.

"Perhaps not. We're missing something vital," Cal insists, "And that's what we need to find out."

"Could it be to do with Santiago? Maybe the King is referring to him?" Eastern suggests.

"The King specifically said he wanted *'one life in exchange for another'*... I'm not sure killing his business partner is part of the plan. Then again, this is the King we're talking about. I wouldn't put it past him," Camden speculates.

"So he wants me to kill Santiago, is that what you're suggesting? How the fuck am I supposed to do that?" *I couldn't even kill the King when I had the opportunity,* I think to myself.

"Killing Santiago is an impossibility. Hudson has been trying for years to find a way to get close enough to do that, but he's heavily guarded, not to mention fucking elusive. There's no way you could, Asia. Not that we'd let you, even if there was the tiniest of chances," Cal says.

"What then?" I insist.

"Maybe he meant me?" Camden looks at me with a haunted expression. "I'm no longer useful to him, after all."

"No way. No fucking way," I reply, not willing to even consider that as a possibility.

"No, that's not it either, because if he didn't have any use for you anymore, both you and your mum would be dead by now," Ford says with brutal honesty.

"How do you know she isn't already?" Camden argues.

"Because he wouldn't have wasted the opportunity to tell Asia. He *knows* you're together. If he'd killed your mum then you can bet your arse he would've taken great pleasure in telling her, knowing it would get back to you." Ford clasps Camden's shoulder, squeezing gently. "She's not dead," he states with such conviction that it's easy to believe him.

Camden scrapes a hand over his face and grits his teeth. "You're right. Fuck, man, this is doing my head in."

"Leave this with me, we'll do some more digging. As difficult as this might be, you all need to keep your heads down and carry on as usual," Cal insists.

"By keeping our heads down, you mean we don't get to fuck up Bram and his bunch of goons even though they really deserve it?" Eastern mocks, scowling.

"That's out of the question. No brawling outside of the ring. Concentrate on your fight coming up. The last thing any of us needs is this place getting shut down because the students are killing each other in the halls."

"Fine. No brawling," Eastern agrees, though he looks far from happy about it.

"Come on, all of you need to get some sleep, it's been a long day. There's nothing more that can be done now. Tomorrow the tech team will arrive, and Oceanside will be secured. There will be no more kidnapping on my watch or any fucking secret messages being uploaded without me being alerted," Cal promises.

"Cal, can I ask a favour?" I ask after a beat.

"That depends on what it is?" he replies, looking at me intently.

"I don't want to sleep alone tonight." I sigh heavily, fully aware that all my boys are watching me, and although my voice is steady, there's no denying how vulnerable I feel.

Cal nods, eyeing me carefully. "I get that. Do what you need to do."

"Thanks," I hush out, wondering which of my boys will step forward, or how we're even going to broach the subject of who will stay with me tonight. I know what I don't want… an argument.

Cal squeezes my shoulder then walks from his office, leaving me to try and figure out how to approach this without hurting anyone's feelings. My gaze happens to meet Sonny's first and he gives me a gentle smile.

"Who do you need, Asia?" he asks me softly.

I look between them, trying to decide. In the end I can't, because how can I choose between four boys I care about? It terrifies me, the depth of my feelings for each of them, because it just gives the King more ammunition and more ways to hurt me, to hurt us.

"All of you," I say gently.

"Then all of us you shall have."

BY THE TIME I'm dressed in my comfy pyjamas, washed my face, cleaned my teeth and stepped out of my en-suite bathroom, it's well past midnight.

"Feeling a little better?" Eastern asks me. He gets up from his spot on the floor, stepping over Sonny.

"Honestly, no," I admit. "I'm just really tired."

Tired of being afraid.

Tired of being strong.

Tired of watching my back.

Tired of worrying about the people I love.

Tired of being a whiny bitch.

Tired. Tired. Tired.

So. Fucking. Tired.

Eastern folds me into his arms, holding me close. I breathe him in, pressing my nose against the bare skin of his chest, just allowing myself his comfort. Eventually I pull away, dead on my feet. Exhaustion ripples over me in waves, and it's all I can do to keep standing.

"Come on, Asia, lie down. You look beat," Sonny says, patting the empty space beside him. Like before, when Ford and Sonny slept with me in this room, there are several duvet covers laid across the floor, pillows piled high. Frankly, I'm not sure how we're all going to fit but I don't have the brain cells or the energy to figure it out right now. Everything is fuzzy. Off kilter.

"Thanks," I mutter, flicking my gaze to Camden who's watching me closely from my bed. He too is bare-chested, wearing a pair of low-slung joggers, and whilst I appreciate his physique, my mojo has well and truly left the building.

"Hey, I didn't say you looked ugly, because that's not possible with you. You're fucking gorgeous."

"I wasn't fishing for a compliment, Sonny," I retort, lying down beside him.

"I know that, but can't a man tell his girl that she's beautiful?"

"Sure he can, and thanks, I appreciate it." I lean over and kiss him gently on his lips. He lets out a sigh, his eyelids fluttering shut as I press my mouth against his, but he doesn't try to deepen the kiss. He understands that tonight, what I need most is the oblivion of sleep.

I need to be still. I need to rest whilst the whole world falls into chaos around me so that I'm ready to fight another day.

"What you did was reckless, Asia," Camden suddenly blurts out. I turn my head to look at him, his eyes flash with danger like a tsunami in the Caribbean Sea. "Taking a knife with you... What the fuck were you thinking?"

I sigh, sitting up. Drawing my legs to my chest, I wrap my arms around them. "I thought I could end this..."

"It was fucking stupid," he admonishes, angry now.

"The only stupid thing I did was hesitating," I argue back. Our gazes lock, both of us unwilling to back down. I'm fully aware that by not killing the King I've made our whole situation a lot worse. Who knows what he'll do now?

"It's done. There's no point in arguing over it now," Eastern points out.

"We all agreed Asia doesn't need his blood on her hands," Camden retorts.

"I never agreed to anything," I interject.

Ford narrows his eyes at me, before addressing Camden once more. "I hate the fact that Asia risked her life tonight, but I understand why she did. Point is, can you honestly say if you had the opportunity to kill the bastard that you wouldn't have taken it?"

Camden grunts in response, not willing to acknowledge that he would've taken the risk too.

"We can all agree it was reckless and stupid, but right now Asia doesn't need us dissecting her bad decisions. What she needs is sleep," Eastern says, laying down beside me. He reaches for me, urging me to lie back down. Part of me feels annoyed at them for calling me out on what I'd attempted to do, the other part appreciates their concern. But most of me just feels stupid.

I should've killed the fucking bastard.

I didn't and now I'm going to have to live with the consequences.

"Come on, Asia. You need to sleep," Eastern urges me, his fingers caressing my back in warm circles.

"Okay," I sigh, laying back down whilst Ford hovers by the door.

"Are you going to stand there all night?" I ask him, sleep pulling at my last reserves of energy.

"As much as I want to stay, there isn't much room left," he says, smiling a little to soften the blow.

"Shut up, Ford. You might be some big arse fighter in the ring, but there's room enough for you." Sonny shifts over and pats the space he's made between us. He's so thoughtful, generous with his compassion and it makes my heart ache at how lucky I am and how much I have to lose. Ford raises an eyebrow surprised, I guess, at Sonny's generosity.

"Don't give me that look. We're all friends here."

Sonny's right, we are. Never more so than now. Tonight has proven that.

Thing is, these boys are more than my friends. They're my family, my anchor, and my home. Still Ford hesitates.

"Stop being a martyr, Ford, and lie the fuck down," Camden snaps, watching us all from the bed. "If you don't like the floor, you could always bunk up with me?" he adds after a beat. There's the slight glimmer of humour in his eyes and that in and of itself is something to be grateful for, given everything Camden's going through.

"Who said you get the bed anyway?" Ford asks.

"Hey, someone had to. Besides, I tend to get a little territorial when it comes to Asia, and if I'm lying next to her, none of you jackarses will be able to get close enough to get a look in," he says, making direct eye contact with me. "Especially after tonight, when I both want to punish Asia for taking such a huge risk and fuck her until she can't see straight."

My face heats at his tone and his words. Any other night I might've taken Camden up on the challenge and thoroughly enjoyed it, but tonight sex is the last thing on my mind. I just want peace and that can only happen in the form of sleep.

"Fuck her until she can't see straight. Arrogant much?" Sonny snorts, then clamps his mouth shut when Camden glares at him.

"Shut the fuck up, Sonny, or I'll change my mind and take your damn place."

"Guys, no arguing," I mutter, avoiding the absolute conviction in Camden's eyes and allowing my body to relax as sleep beckons.

"Hey, we're just joking around. Go to sleep, Asia," Sonny whispers.

Only when Ford settles beside me, his fingers sliding across my hips, and Eastern wraps an arm about my waist do I finally let out a long, contented sigh and fall into a deep, dreamless sleep.

SEVENTEEN

By the end of the following week Cal is true to his word and Oceanside is rigged up with all sorts of equipment. Cameras blink from the corner of every room and corridor, filming all our movements. Motion lights have been placed around the site, preventing anyone from getting in or out without being lit up like a fucking Christmas tree, and video recording equipment has been set up in one of the downstairs rooms. They've even hired two guys whose only responsibility is to sit and watch those livestreams for any untoward behaviour and more importantly, to capture any arseholes who want to send us another message from the King.

Cal has also brought in four more guards who watch over us all, creepy and silent. The fact of the matter is this place is as good as any prison now and I'm feeling the strain, not to mention the weight of Pink's abduction. It's been almost two weeks since she was taken and a week since I spoke with my father on the pier.

This has just been another long week of silence. My father sure knows how to fuck with our heads. The only thing that is keeping me going is my fight in the ring with Bram next Sunday. We might have to wear boxing gloves, but I'm still intent on inflicting some serious fucking damage. Even Kate has begun to thirst for her time in the ring with Red.

"I can't wait to see that bitch's face when I send her flying on her arse," Kate puffs as she bounces on her feet, jabbing the pads Eastern is holding up. We're back in the gym again, pretty much commandeering the space.

When she misses the pad and smashes her glove-covered fist into Eastern's shoulder instead, both of their mouths pop open, Kate's in apology and Eastern's in surprised pain.

"Sorry."

"Ow, fuck!"

Kate snorts with laughter, then Eastern joins in. One minute they're sparring and the next practically rolling around with mirth.

"Bloody hell, Kate, you're getting good at this," Eastern says after they've both calmed down a bit. Pretty sure that laughing hysterically for five minutes is more of a sign of how on edge they're feeling rather than Eastern's surprise at how hard Kate can punch.

"I know, right? Thanks to you all helping me train, I'm a lot stronger."

"Red ain't gonna know what hit her," Camden says, as he steps into the gym with Sonny in tow.

The door slams shut behind them. "Where's Ford?" I ask. He hasn't missed a training session with us and is usually here before we all arrive.

"Nice to see you too," Sonny deadpans, then gives me a wink so I know he's only joking and not really bothered by my need to see Ford. He stretches out his arm that is finally free from the cast. A quick visit to the hospital a couple of days ago and he's fighting fit.

Camden frowns. Of the four boys he seems to be the one struggling the most with sharing. Whilst we've spent more time with each other, it's been in a group. Camden and I haven't been alone together at all, and we both miss that. He's more himself when he's alone with me. In a group he tends to maintain his gang leader role, even though we don't really have a leader in our crew. I guess it's hard to change being a certain way when that's how you've always been viewed.

"I haven't seen him all day. Pretty sure he's skipped most of the lessons. Thought he was hanging with you?" Camden responds, and I realise the frown isn't from jealousy but from concern.

"Do we need to worry?" Kate asks, doing exactly that.

"Nah, with the number of cameras strung up around this place and the fucking guards Cal's got roaming the halls, it's unlikely anything has happened. Besides, Ford can take care of himself, right?" Eastern proclaims, looking for reassurance.

Sonny side-eyes Eastern, a grin dimpling his cheeks. "Anyone would think you cared."

Eastern shrugs. "He's a mate, of course I care."

"Well, that's good to know," Ford says, stepping into the gym.

"Where the fuck have you been?" Camden snaps.

Ford rolls his eyes. "Calm the fuck down, Cam, I'm no dog on a leash."

"Never said you were," he mutters, turning his back on Ford and grabbing a pair of boxing gloves, chucking them to Sonny. "Pair up with me," he orders.

Sonny laughs. "You're so fucking bossy, Cam, but now that I'm all fixed up I'll happily smack the shit out of you if that's what you need to deal with your pent-up sexual frustration."

"Yeah, like that's gonna happen anytime soon, *Dimples*. Besides, I ain't sexually frustrated," he retorts, glancing at me with lust-filled eyes that tell me otherwise.

Sonny snorts. "Yeah, and the Pope ain't Catholic."

I watch them both with a light heart. Seeing them rib each other without any menace behind it is a good feeling. We've come a long way, that's for sure.

"Looks like those two are in love," Ford remarks dryly.

They step into the ring and start sparring. Sonny doesn't hold back even with his newly fixed arm. I'm pretty sure he shouldn't be sparring at all, but Sonny won't be told, he goes at Camden full-force. I would say they were evenly matched in terms of skill and dexterity. It would be a close call in a real fight, that's for sure.

"Come on then, Kate, let's get back to it," Eastern says, holding the pads back up. Kate wastes no time in slamming her fists against them. She's getting good.

"Proper bunch of fighters we got here," Ford says, watching them all closely.

"Yeah, thanks to you."

"I only helped to hone what they've already got. Those muppets don't have a chance. Speaking of which…" Ford pulls me to the corner of the room and fishes out his mobile phone from his pocket. "I got a message from Grim earlier today."

"And?"

"And Ma Silva has confirmed her hunch. The King has been spotted at his home on the island a few days after you met with him. She doesn't know whether Pink and Camden's mum are there but in all likelihood they are, given what we know about him…"

My throat constricts, that edginess I've been feeling rising to the surface. It's hard to keep myself in check when I know Pink is being held prisoner. Vengeance is a very real need right now, and something that's building with every passing day. Guilt too, given I had the chance to kill him and blew it.

"So, what now?" I know what I want to do. I want to get out of this place and go rescue them. Fuck what everyone said. Ford swipes a hand over his face, concern creasing his brow.

"We stick to the plan. Grim's gonna talk to Hudson today and they're gonna send someone in to do a proper recon. We need to be absolutely certain he's keeping them there."

"And if he is?"

"Then I reckon at some point soon, shit's going to go down. But for now we…"

"…*Wait*? I'm so sick of hearing that, Ford."

"Yeah, me too. But there's no getting out of this place, not without triggering some kind of alarm."

"Damn Cal and his goddamn Fort Knox shit."

"I know it's difficult and I know you're struggling to keep your emotions under wraps, Asia, but I'm asking you to sit tight. Take a leaf out of Camden's book, he's the master at this."

I glance over at Camden who has just thrown a mean left hook at Sonny, catching him on the jaw. Sonny grins, bouncing backwards and ducking away from his next punch. His grin only seems to fuel Camden's anger more as he starts pummelling Sonny with punch after punch, until both are panting with exertion.

"Yeah, looks like it," I reply sarcastically.

"But you'll keep your shit together until we hear more?" Ford presses, his fingers gripping hold of my arm in a gesture that is somehow both comforting and domineering.

"I'll try, though I might need some help," I admit, tensing with the stress. "This waiting is bullshit. The worst fucking torture."

The fact of the matter is, I've no idea when the King will contact me next, or even how, given Cal has everything under surveillance. Not to mention the fact mentally I'm losing my shit. I can't even look in the mirror anymore without seeing *him*.

He regards me for a long moment, then nods. "I'll come to your room after curfew."

"My room isn't really big enough to spar in."

He ignores my comment. "Leave your door unlocked, I'll be there just past eleven."

"And the cameras?"

He shrugs. "I don't give a fuck. Besides, I'm pretty sure if I ask Cal nicely enough, he'll make sure those nosy arse tossers turn a blind eye so I can come see my girl."

"Your girl?"

"Our girl," he corrects himself.

"*Our girl…* I like the sound of that."

"Yeah, me too."

EIGHTEEN

As promised, Ford enters my room just past curfew. He slips inside silently, padding over to my bed. The light is turned off and I'm curled up on my side facing away from him when he slips under the duvet behind me. I'm wide awake, taut with apprehension. I've no idea why I'm lying in the dark under my duvet instead of waiting for him with the light on.

Hiding maybe... yeah, that's what I'm doing.

I'm fucking hiding like a five-year-old who thinks that their duvet is some kind of invisible blanket that can protect them from the world and all the bad people in it, which is ironic, really, given I'm dressed in very little knowing Ford would come.

I both want him here and don't.

I'm such a fucking temptress... Not.

"Hey, sleeping beauty," he says, his voice a low rumble as he presses his body against mine. His fingertips graze over my hip, sending electric currents over my skin despite my messed-up thoughts. I swallow hard.

"I'm not sleeping."

He laughs. "Yeah, no one this tense could be accused of sleeping. What's up?"

"Everything..."

"Stupid question," he mutters in my ear.

I lay in his arms, trying to calm the anxious thud of my heart and failing miserably. I'm getting that weird itchy feeling again, like I want to shred my skin, peel it back and leave it like a piece of discarded clothing on the floor. Despite my attraction to Ford, I feel off.

"Maybe you should go, Ford. I'm not..." I suck in a ragged breath that makes me shudder. "I'm not feeling like myself. I don't feel right in my own skin..." My voice trails off at how fucked up that sounds and I consider the fact that maybe it's Eastern that I need right now and not Ford.

"What do you need, Asia?" he asks me, as though reading my mind.

"I don't know." *That's a lie. I do know.*

I need to be Asia Chen. The girl who doesn't give a fuck, who'd rain hell on anyone who screws with her. I need to get back to the girl I was before *him*. Before the King became my father. I don't want to be this... this weak half person who doesn't know who the fuck she is, who despises the skin she's in, who failed to kill her dad. I *hate* it.

I hate *me*.

"Turn around, Asia. Listen to my voice. Don't think, just do as I ask. Okay?" Ford says, forcing those horrible thoughts out of my head momentarily as his voice commands my attention.

Turning, I wrap my arms around his back and press my nose into the crook of his neck, breathing him in deeply. "You smell good," I blurt out. *Like cloves and leather.* Warm and enticing.

"So do you..." he replies, his mouth whispering against my skin.

We lie together, holding on to one another. Just being still. After a while he shifts, pulling back slightly. "I'm going to turn the light on now."

"Alright…" I'm almost disappointed that he hasn't tried to initiate sex. That's what I figured would happen, in all honesty. Then again, I thought that the night we went to the Tower and he surprised me then too. Ford untangles himself from my arms and climbs out of bed. A couple seconds later the room is flooded with a soft golden glow from my table lamp. Ford stares at me, or at least at my head poking out from under the duvet cover.

What the fuck must I look like? Ford frowns, a look of indecision crossing his face.

"What?" I whisper.

"This isn't you. This isn't the girl who beat Monk to a pulp, who doesn't take any crap from anyone, who fights back. Where is that girl hiding?"

I sigh heavily. "Maybe you should go get Eastern…"

"No, not today," Ford snaps, shaking his head.

This was such a bad fucking idea. Ford doesn't do vulnerable. I'm making a fool of myself in front of him. The stupid thing is, I've dressed to seduce Ford, and yet I'm acting like some pussy hiding beneath the duvet cover. Talk about mixed fucking signals. My head is all over the place. I haven't been able to stop thinking about Pink, about Camden's mum. Knowing where she is and not being able to help her is a far worse torture than not knowing a damn thing.

Everything is upside down and inside out.

I want to hide from the world and pretend that none of this is happening. I want Ford to fuck me into oblivion. I want to shred my skin in a frenzy. I want to beat someone to a pulp. I want to fucking cry.

I'm so screwed up.

"Sit up," Ford orders, the tone of his voice brooking no argument.

I do as he says, allowing the duvet to slip lower revealing my sheer tank top. It's pretty much see-through. My nipples peak with the sudden cold. Ford's gaze darkens.

"You're not wearing a bra," he comments, stating the obvious as he looks at me from beneath a flop of dirty blonde hair, my sheer top leaving nothing to the imagination.

"You noticed?" I laugh, and it sounds more broken than I care to admit.

"With you, I notice *everything*." He cocks his head to the side, his gaze zeroing in on the tattoo that sits between my breasts and over my heart. "You never did tell me what that tattoo means, what any of them mean, for that matter."

"It's not important."

"Of course it is. I want to know everything there is to know about you. All of it. Every last secret."

"And If I don't want to share?"

"Then I guess I'll have to find a way to persuade you." He shrugs, moving closer.

I bite my lip, my core clenching at the look of fire in his eyes that he shuts down just as quickly as it appeared.

"I thought you'd come here to distract me, not talk. I kinda dressed for the occasion," I say half-heartedly, pushing away the covers to reveal a pair of scanty lace knickers in a colour not dissimilar to his eyes. And by distract, I mean fuck. Because fucking is a sure-fire way of taking me out of my head, *isn't it?*

"Stand up," he orders, that beautiful hint of a smile dropping, replaced instead by a look of sheer concentration. His gaze rakes over every inch of my skin as I stand before him. But he doesn't try to touch me. He just stares for five long minutes, pacing around me, scorching my skin with his hot stare. "Take off your top, Asia," he commands, the deep cadence of his voice like a hot sun burning my skin.

"What if I don't want to?"

"Then I'd say you were trying to poke the beast. Either that, or you're a tease. Are you a tease, Asia?" Ford says, stepping close. The words are cruel, but he says them so gently that they come out as a caress. Ford rakes his gaze over me as he waits for my response, and I get the feeling that being loved by Ford is just like his left hook, powerful enough to floor you.

"What if I don't want to... fuck you, I mean?"

Even though his grey-green eyes flash with challenge, his words are calm, unemotional. "Remove your top, Asia."

I don't.

Ford's gaze darkens, but again his voice shows no emotion. "I won't ask again."

My arms hang loosely at my side as I stand before him, willing him to act. Somehow this has become as much about me getting Ford to crack as it is Ford trying to get me out of my head. I guess it's working somewhat because right now all I can think about is how far I need to push Ford until he lets go of some of that self-control and fucks me until we're both nothing more than a collection of broken pieces scattered across my bedroom floor.

"I always win, Asia," Ford murmurs as he runs his finger along the collar of my vest top. He leans in close and just when I think he's about to kiss me, he rips my vest from down the middle, exposing me completely. I draw in a surprised breath, my heart pounding just behind the tattoo that Ford is staring at so intently now. He leans forward, his gaze following the movement his finger makes tracing the outline. The fact his attention is focused solely on my ink and not my breasts is sexy as fuck. I know he wants me, that's obvious by the strain of his cock against his jogging pants, but he surprises me by not being a typical man who can't be in front of a pair of exposed tits without salivating over them or trying to grope them.

"You've been hurt a lot, Asia," he mutters as he presses the flat of his hand against my tattoo. My heart speeds up at his touch, my nipples peaking to painful points as though they are trying to get his attention. I'm suddenly desperate for him to take them in his mouth, but he doesn't.

"This tattoo is an outward display of how disappointed you are with those who've let you down, who've never valued you enough, who've *hurt* you... All that pain is like a dagger to the heart, am I right?" he asks, lifting his gaze to meet mine. His dirty blonde hair is a messy flop that I'm dying to run my hands through.

"Am I right, Asia?" he persists.

I pinch my mouth shut, not willing to agree or disagree.

"You've bled. You *still* bleed, more so now than ever."

We stare at each other. My mouth pops open ready to admit how close he is to the truth, then he does something that has me choking back those words. He licks my tattoo.

He fucking licks it.

He runs his tongue upwards from the sharp point of the blade to the tip of the handle and my heart fucking thunders.

"You were willing to pierce your father's heart to save us all. Doing what you did took guts, no matter how I feel about you putting yourself in danger like that."

"But I failed... I'm a failure..."

"You, Asia, are far from that. You're fucking incredible," Ford responds, kissing my tattoo.

He lowers his body and kneels before, his hands trailing over my waist and hips until he's in line with my throbbing core. Despite my inner turmoil and self-loathing, my body is very aware of how close he is to the spot I want him to touch the most.

"And this," he says, his fingers feathering over my barbed wire tattoo wrapped around my thigh, "This is a warning for others not to get too close. You've kept people at a distance for a long time. You don't let people in easily for fear of them carving another scar in your heart... yes?"

He doesn't wait for me to agree, instead he leans forward and runs his nose along my tattoo, and up, up, up until he reaches the delicate spot between my legs, the tip pressing against my mound. He breathes in deeply, making a kind of humming noise. My knees almost buckle at the sheer fucking animalistic nature of his actions. Ford grips my hips, sliding his tongue once over my lace-covered pussy, then stands.

"The dove," he says, moving behind me, "Represents everything you long for. Freedom from your past, from the memories that haunt you. Freedom from the disappointment, the pain. But more than that, it's *hope*, Asia. It's new horizons, and a peaceful future," he says, his fingers kneading the knots forming in my shoulders. He steps closer, his body flush against mine as he massages my neck and the base of my skull. I can feel just how much he wants me as his cock presses into my lower back.

"Am I wrong?"

"They're just tattoos, Ford. They don't mean anything other than decoration, and even if they did, it doesn't change a thing. I'm still the King's daughter. I'm still Monk's sister. Pink and Camden's mum are still in danger and I still feel fucking helpless in this skin," I admit.

"They *do* mean something," he says, stepping in front of me once more. "You were born unmarked. A blank fucking slate, Asia. You've tattooed your skin how you see fit because this skin you wear is *yours,* so stop thinking it's any different now you know who your father is. There isn't one part of you that belongs to the King. You aren't his. Understand?"

"And yet you were marked by your parents... none of those scars you wear are a choice you made." My voice trails off as I reach up and pull at the collar of his t-shirt, my fingertip running over the tattoo on his collar bone. "So what does that mean for you, huh? They marked you permanently with that tattoo, with these scars. The King might not have scarred me on the outside, but believe me Ford, I have just as many scars on the inside. We can't get away from the fact that I'm still his daughter and you're *still* their fucking son, no matter how much we both wish it wasn't true," I respond, panting. The look in his eyes has me swallowing hard. It was a cruel thing to say, and I regret it immediately.

Ford steps back from my sharp words and rips off his t-shirt, removing his joggers and pants too until he stands before me naked. His eyes narrow, emotion flashing across his face. Anger, passion, determination lights up his features, shining through the controlled exterior. The façade is cracking.

"I am *not* their son," he snaps, staring at me with the same look he gave me in the Tower. "And you are *not* his daughter!"

"Ford, I'm sorry. I shouldn't…"

"No, you listen to me right the fuck now," he pants interrupting me, his nostrils flaring as the crack widens, a crevice forming. "I embrace these scars. I embrace these two words, not because my parents pinned me down and scored them into my skin but because I survived *them*. These are my battle scars and they are a reminder that I fought, and fucking won. I'm still here, Asia. I'm still fucking standing. I could've had this tattoo removed, I haven't. Why? Because I accept what was and I accept what is. I *am* a Bad Boy. Just like I'm a fighter, a lover, a friend… Just like I'm *yours,* but most of all I'm *me*, scars and all. They may have made me, given me fucking life, but I am no more their son than you are the King's daughter."

"Ford…"

"Look at me," Ford says, holding his arms out wide, the muscles tensing and flexing. "I'm battle-worn and goddamn weary. Some days I can barely fucking breathe because of all the shit I've had to live through. But I do. I fucking do and you will too. You are not your father's daughter. This skin you wear, it's yours. So fucking own it!" he shouts, his voice rising with passion.

For a split second we just stare at one another. The emotion cracking and snapping between us. Then like two magnets, we are pulled together by an unknown force and the whole world implodes, just like I knew it would.

Ford cracks open and I fall right in.

NINETEEN

We step towards each other simultaneously, Ford grasping my cheeks in his rough palms before smashing his lips against mine. He kisses me hard, his tongue slicing through my lips and silencing the whimpers that bubble up my throat, forcing me back towards the bed with the sheer violence of his kiss. I stumble, my breath snatched from me as I fall roughly onto the mattress. If I expected a moment of reprieve, Ford doesn't give me one. There's no slow approach like Eastern, savouring every part of me as he rises slowly up my body. No, Ford attacks with one goal in mind: to win. He rips off my knickers with one hand, the elastic snapping against my skin.

"Fuck!" I exclaim. My complaint is swallowed by another oxygen-stealing kiss. He doesn't allow me a moment to catch my breath.

Now that I've cracked him open he's unleashing himself onto me. There are no whispered words of love from Ford. He acts. This is his own form of conversation, and he's determined to make me listen.

Grabbing hold of my hips, Ford yanks my pussy to his mouth, plunging his tongue deep inside of me until I'm seeing more than stars, until I'm seeing the whole fucking galaxy.

His mouth, his tongue, his lips burn my skin, firing me up until I come hard and fast like a shooting star ripping through the pitch black of night. As my head falls back, Ford rears upwards, grabs his joggers from the floor and pulls out a condom from the pocket. I watch him with half-mast eyes and panting breaths as he tears the packet and slides the condom over the thick length of his cock.

Even then, he acts quickly, not giving me more than a few moments to catch my breath as he moves over me boxing my body in with his.

"Who are you?" he demands, the tip of his cock pressed against my entrance as he stares down at me, into my fucking soul.

"Asia," I pant, breaths shattering from my parted lips.

"No! Who the fuck are you?" he demands, slipping his cock an inch inside of me. He's big, I feel the burn despite the slickness between my thighs.

"Asia!" I repeat, louder this time.

Ford grips my face tightly. There's no softness with him tonight. He doesn't hurt me, but he doesn't hold back either and I like that. I *need* that. He's firm, opposed to gentle, and the complete antithesis of Eastern. He's the fight, not the flight, and everything I knew I needed but didn't know how to ask for.

He's my strength and I cling onto him with all my might.

"Say it again! Fucking say it again!"

"ASIA! I'm Asia!" I shout, the cry on my lips drowned out only by the fierceness of Ford's kiss and the devastating thrust of his hips.

"That's it. This is who you are, fucking own it!" he growls, slamming his cock into me with one hard thrust, filling me up to the hilt. He covers my cry with his mouth, swallowing the passion and the pain, devouring it and filling me up so completely that tears prick at the corners of my eyes.

Ford fucks me.

He fucks me hard, fast, with power and aggression, grasping my wrists and forcing my arms up above my head. We slide against one another, slick with sweat. Muscles bunch and tense as we both battle. He grinds into me, and I wrap my legs tight around his hips, forcing him to do his worst, to split me apart like an atom, so I can be formed into something new, something unbreakable. Something *strong*.

"Don't you dare forget who you are, got it?!"

"Yes," I whimper, his bruising assault making me wet, making me implode.

"The King will never own you. You are Asia Chen, and you are powerful. You are beautiful. And you are your own person. *Not* his," he grinds out, teeth gritted.

His words flip a switch inside me and in one swift move I thrust upwards, forcing Ford onto his back, straddling him this time. I bring my hands down on his pecs, my nails digging in as I find purchase. Ford's fingers grasp hold of my hips, bruising me as I rock against him, tilting my hips and sliding up and down, fucking him just as much as he's fucking me. Deep inside I can feel his cock-piercing rubbing against that tender spot inside, heightening my pleasure further.

"Ford, fuck!" I exclaim.

"That's it, Asia. Claim *me*," he growls, sliding his arm around my back, supporting me as he sits up and I'm straddling his lap. He gives me a devious grin then clamps his mouth over my breast and sucks hard. Tipping my head back, I let out a wild cry, not caring who might hear. I don't give a shit. There's something to be said about letting go completely and utterly, and here I am doing just that. I'm letting go of everything that's hurt me, could hurt me, and replacing it with something else…

Strength.

As my orgasm expands like a seething, boiling blaze in my stomach, so too does my need to fight. It grows with every thrust and every bruising kiss. I pull Ford's head back, yanking his hair in my fist until he's looking up at me.

"Thank you," I whisper, staring into the swirling pits of Ford's gaze and seeing my mirror image reflected back. He's the hurricane and I'm the fucking storm. Both of us are scarred by our parents, both of us have taken on a new identity, shredding the one we were born with, and both of us fight every damn day to maintain it.

Together we're dangerous, powerful, and when we come together, downright devastating. He gives me a rare smile, rocking me with its beauty. "I told you I'd win."

"Win what?" I hush out, my body trembling.

"Your heart, Asia," he responds, placing the flat of his hand against the tattoo inked between my breasts. And just like that, I concede the damn fight just like he knew I would.

The thing is, losing to Ford isn't really losing, not when we've shared such a beautiful, heart shattering orgasm and he's given me the strength I need to fight another day.

WHEN THE SUN rises the next morning, I awake curled up in Ford's arms, my head pressed against his chest. I shift in his hold and he rolls over, still very much asleep. The duvet cover slips lower, and I find myself staring at his back and the couple of dozen burn scars that are scattered over his skin. The pain his parents inflicted makes me want to hurt someone for him, makes me want to *love* him with everything I have just to blot out the hell he went through.

Love. I feel it deep inside. I love this boy too. So much.

The King was wrong. So fucking wrong. Love doesn't make you weak. It makes you strong.

He survived his parents and so will I.

So what if the King's my dad? So fucking what?

I'm still Asia Chen.

Pressing a gentle kiss against his shoulder blade I slip out of bed and enter the bathroom. Last night something special happened between us and whilst Ford never expressed how he felt out loud, I heard him loud and clear. I hope he heard me too.

Turning on the shower, I wait a moment for the water to heat up before climbing under the warm spray, relaxing as it cascades over my skin. Because I'm up early, I take my time cleaning myself, washing my hair with my favourite coconut shampoo that reminds me of Camden. I wonder how he's feeling and resolve to spend some time alone with him today. It's been difficult juggling everything and spending time with each of my boys. Camden and Sonny have been neglected somewhat and they deserve my attention just as much as Eastern and Ford.

Ten minutes after I step into the shower, I climb out of it, feeling refreshed and ready to face the world. Wrapping a towel around my body I quickly rough dry my hair then open the bathroom door, trying not to make too much noise as I hunt for some underwear.

"Morning," Ford says sleepily, sitting up in bed. I watch him in the grey light of a foggy morning as he leans over and flips on the lamp.

"Good morning, did you sleep well?" I ask, towelling off my body and pulling on my underwear.

Ford's gaze rakes over me lazily, heating me up.

"It would be even better if you got over here and kissed me."

I suck in my lip ring, wanting to kiss him but knowing if I do we might never leave this room and make breakfast in time. "As much as I really want to do that, you need to get out of that bed. You've got five minutes to get decent. Besides, I'm hungry."

Ford pulls back the covers and swings his legs out of bed. He's still totally naked and has a raging hard on. His dick bobs as he moves, like it has a mind of its own.

"Don't look at me like that," I warn, trying to remain stern, but failing miserably when he smiles like he's just won the damn lottery. My stomach flips and my heart clenches.

"Like what?" he asks, stepping towards me.

"Like you want to start something again. I've just had a shower."

He laughs loudly, shaking his head at my lame response. "All the more reason to eat you for breakfast."

I giggle, loving this teasing side of him. It's cute. "Seriously, Ford, we haven't got time," I mutter as he steps closer, leaning in to press a searing kiss against my shoulder.

"It's Saturday, it's not like we have lessons to go to. Besides, the way I'm feeling I can make this quick," he murmurs against my skin, his lips trailing up my neck as he nibbles on my earlobe.

My eyes press shut and my body shudders at the sheer force of his presence. Ford is dangerous, deadly and addicting. I like it. No, I *love* it.

"I didn't take you for a five-minute wonder." I grin as he laughs into my neck, biting gently at the tender skin there.

"You're right, I'm not," he replies, grasping my cheeks in his hands and planting a swift kiss against my lips. "With you, I want all the time in the world to screw you until you come."

My cheeks flush with arousal and I sway into him as he steps back, a playful look on his face.

"Is that a promise?"

"A promise implies there's a chance I might not perform my duties and you know better than anyone that I always follow through, especially when it comes to you, Asia." He grins and my heart nearly implodes.

"Get dressed," I laugh, shaking my head at this new playful version of Ford.

Five minutes later we're heading to our table, thankfully this time it isn't occupied by Bram and his crew of bastards. We're still all divided up into the groups Mr Burnside put us in, but whereas I happen to like my group, given it's made up of the people I care most about, others aren't so lucky. Most people look miserable, except for Bram, Red and Monk's wolves who just look smug, like they think they own the world. Fucking dicks. Tomorrow they're going to learn a very hard lesson right at the end of our fists.

Bram snarls at me, and I mouth a *'fuck you'* before dragging my gaze away from their table. I refuse to give them any more of my attention. I've got more important people to give that to, specifically my boys and Kate.

When we reach our table, Camden, Eastern and Sonny greet us with different levels of acknowledgement. Sonny grins, winking. Eastern's smile is a little guarded as his gaze flicks between us both, and Camden just nods, barely meeting my gaze. I swallow, the high I felt waking up in Ford's arms dissipating somewhat. Reality hovers a few feet away just waiting to fuck shit up. If they hadn't heard us last night then it must be pretty obvious now that we slept together.

"Where's Kate?" I ask, avoiding the elephant in the room that is me spending the night with Ford.

"Getting breakfast," Eastern answers, nodding towards the self-service station.

Kate is loading her plate with her usual breakfast food just as Red sidles up beside her. I watch as that bitch leans over and knocks the glass of juice off her tray. It hits the floor with a loud smash.

"Bitch!" I exclaim, jerking towards them.

"I'll handle this," Ford growls, striding off towards the two before I can.

"Leave it, Asia," Camden says, shifting along the bench so I can sit down next to him. "Red doesn't have balls big enough to do any real harm." He sighs, looking and sounding a little jaded. He seems tired of the constant battle just like I've been these past few days. I get it.

"She's my friend."

"She's *our* friend and Ford will back her up, should she need it," he retorts. "You need to choose your battles. Besides, Kate's getting better at handling her own," he continues.

He's right, because when I look back over at Kate, she's standing up to Red. Ford doesn't step in, he simply stands by her side as she says something under her breath to Red. The bitch's face goes scarlet. I can't help but feel proud.

Sonny chuckles, watching them face off. "Red is gonna get a beating," he says, delight lighting his baby blues. "Can't wait to see that happen."

"Yeah, I think she just might," I respond, sitting down. I've never felt prouder. Kate is proving to be exactly as I thought. She's a badass under all those neat clothes and perfect hair.

Eastern slides me a plate filled with eggs and bacon as well as a cup of tea. "Figured you'd need this," he says.

There's an air of acceptance in his gaze, and I know him well enough to know that he's okay with me and Ford sleeping together, even if it must sting a little.

"Thanks, I'm starving."

"I bet. Working up an appetite can do that to a person," Sonny winks, drawing a blush of heat and an awkward smile from me. Trust him to tease.

By the time Kate takes a seat with Ford, I'm already halfway through eating my breakfast. The food settles my stomach a bit and the act of eating gives me a distraction from all the unspoken words between us. It's pretty obvious they all know what went down between me and Ford last night, and I've no real idea how to handle it. They all knew what they were getting into with me and I'm not ashamed of sleeping with Eastern or Ford. Not in the slightest. I just wish it wasn't so... awkward. Given Camden's permanent scowl, I can guess he's not exactly happy, but he isn't ripping Ford a new one, so that's progress I suppose.

"Last night, before he came to your room, Ford filled us in on the phone call from Grim. Looks like her hunch was right," Camden says after a while, glancing at Ford.

I watch as their eyes meet and swallow hard at the look that passes between them. I really don't need them to get into one over who's the alpha male. I know it must be difficult, but they all knew what the deal was when I told them I wanted them all. They're just going to have to figure their shit out.

"What?" Ford asks, cocking a brow at Camden, daring him to start a fight.

"Absolutely nothing," Camden responds.

Kate rolls her eyes, shaking her head in bemusement, but it's Sonny who steps in to cool the rising tension with a few home truths.

"Camden, if you've got something to say to Ford, then say it now. Otherwise, concentrate on how you can be the man Asia needs rather than worrying about what the rest of us are doing for her. You agreed to this relationship as much as we have. So suck it up."

Eastern leans over and spears my last piece of bacon with his fork. "Yeah, I agree with Sonny. You need to figure your shit out, Camden, because Asia needs each of us. Jealousy has no place here. Though, admittedly, I'm finding it a challenge too," he says, giving me a half smile.

Camden mutters something indistinguishable under his breath, then lets out a long sigh. "I *am* cool with it. I'm just not used to sharing. It's gonna take a while."

"Should I go?" Kate asks after a beat. "I mean, as much as I find this whole conversation riveting, I really don't want to know all the finer details about how you are going to work out a banging timetable."

"Kate!" I exclaim, trying to hold in a laugh.

"What? If Pink were here, you bet your arse that's something she would've said."

"But she ain't and that's the real fucking issue, right?" Ford reminds us. "Let's concentrate on that and not how Asia chooses to spend her time, because we all knew what we were getting into when we agreed to Asia's terms and I refuse to apologise for making her happy. Got it?"

"Yeah, got it," Camden concedes.

"At least we know where Pink and Cam's mum are being kept. We can call that a win," Eastern says, steering the conversation back to where it should be.

Camden grunts. "The only win we should be happy with is when my mum and Pink are safe, and those cunts are ten feet under the ground."

"Or in prison," Sonny adds, still peddling the idea that putting the King and Monk behind bars is the better, safer option.

Camden and I exchange looks and I know exactly what he's thinking. Their deaths will be the only option we're happy with.

TWENTY

By the time the fight rolls around the following Sunday, all six of us are simmering with the need for blood. Kate and I have spent most of Saturday and all morning Sunday training with my boys. We've barely rested and my muscles ache with overuse, but it only serves to remind us why we're doing this.

Revenge.

We might not be bare-knuckle fighting in the Tower with no limitations, but the need to cause real harm is no less powerful just because we're wearing padded gloves. Eastern is speaking in a low voice with Kate, giving her last-minute pointers whilst I glare at Bram, eyeballing him across the room. He gives me a slow smile that spreads like a disease across his face as he raises his hand and slides a finger across his throat.

I laugh. As if that's going to scare me.

He's surrounded by his goons like Monk was that night in the Tower. But just like then, they won't be able to help him when he's in the ring face-to-face with me. The worst kind of bullies are the ones who hide behind their crew. On their own, they're never quite as powerful or fearless as they thought.

And that's the difference between me and him.

I don't need my boys to fight my battles. I'm more than capable of settling scores without them. Yes, they give me strength and support, but I don't *need* it to fight like Bram does. Without them he's nothing. You see, his power isn't real. It's built on shaky fountains formed from a crew whose loyalty is borrowed. The second Monk reclaims his throne, those kids will turn their backs on him, too afraid of a bigger, badder wolf who can inflict far more damage than Bram ever could.

"You good, Asia?" Ford asks me, interrupting my thoughts.

"Yeah," I respond, grateful for him. "But I'll be better once I beat the shit out of Bram."

The other night, Ford reminded me of my *own* strength. He forced me to look deep inside myself, to take ownership of who I am, who I've always been. The King might've tried to screw with my head by brandishing my own identity crisis as a weapon all on its own. He might have made me feel like someone I didn't recognise. But in the end, Ford was right, this skin I'm in is *mine*, not the King's, no matter how much he threatens me with his ownership.

I'm Asia Chen, and I'm a fighter. Always have been, always will be.

That knowledge alone is what I'll hold onto when I face Bram in the ring, when I face anyone, for that matter. Because just like the sea is an inevitable wave that chips away at the shore, turning stone into sand, I know I will face Monk and the King again. They'll keep coming back for me. They'll keep finding ways to pull me apart, weaken me, but next time I'll remain solid no matter how much they try to dissolve my strength with threats to the ones I love. At least, I hope so.

"Keep a level head at all times. Hone that anger into a powerful punch," Ford advises.

I can feel the warmth of his hands as he rests them on my hips, moving close behind me. His body heat seeps through his chest and into my back and I feel some of the anxiety that always comes before a fight, dissipate.

"Oh, I intend to. Bram will rue the day he fucked with us."

I can hear Ford's faint laughter before he leans in and whispers in my ear. "Pretty hair colour. Goes well with the outfit."

"I thought so too."

Last night I dyed my hair a hot pink in homage to my friend, a shade darker than my fuchsia leggings and vest top. It wasn't intentional, but when I pulled out my various packets of hair dye I brought with me, pink was the colour I chose. It seems fitting that a piece of what represents Pink is here today, because my fight with Bram is as much for her as it is for me, and I'm not letting anyone forget it.

When Cal calls an end to the current fight between Dagger and a kid who I've seen about but don't really know, my body begins to hum with adrenaline. A natural high that courses through my veins, readying me for the fight.

"Kate's up next, Asia. You need to focus your mind right now. Be the calm *before* the storm, okay?" Ford says.

"Okay." It takes a mammoth effort to remain calm when inside me the storm rages.

"See that boy there, his name's Josh. He's sixteen, one of the youngest kids here," Ford begins, trying to distract me.

"What did he do?" I ask.

"Multiple arrests for carrying illegal weapons. It's doubtful he used them in any criminal activity, more likely he was paid as a mule between one gang leader to another."

"Right," I say. To look at him, you'd be forgiven for mistaking him as a good little choirboy with all that golden hair and pretty dark eyes, and not a weapons mule. Not that it matters here. The only weapons we have are our fists, and the sharp slice of harsh words. This kid Josh is no more than a choirboy without them. We watch as Dagger leaves the ring with a cocky swagger, high-fiving Bram the second he's slipped through the ropes. The gloating is beyond irritating.

"What's the beef between Dagger and Josh?"

"Not entirely sure. Maybe an old score to settle, maybe a new one. Either way, it doesn't really concern us. I only give a shit about my crew, you, Kate and the lads," he admits.

"And No Name, what about them?"

Ford doesn't answer for a while. Eventually he sighs, and I can hear the disappointment in it. "No Name crew was a means to an end. Aside from Sonny, loyalty is a gift none of them saw fit to give. That's the only valuable lesson I've learnt coming to Oceanside."

"The only one?"

"No, not the only one…" His voice trails off, but he doesn't share.

I'm about to press further but Cal climbs into the ring, his presence demanding silence.

"Next up is Red and Kate. In the ring, fighters."

Beside me Kate is bouncing with nerves and a restless kind of energy. I glance at her, meeting her gaze. There's something I see in her eyes that's never been there before; acceptance. She knows that after this fight things will never be the same for her again.

Kate's instincts have kicked in. This is her way of showing the world that she isn't some prissy, stuck-up bitch without a backbone like everyone assumes, but a fighter.

A *badass*.

By the looks of it, Red already thinks she's won given the way she climbs into the ring then leans over the ropes and plays tonsil tennis with Bram. She's so cocky and at ease as she pulls on her gloves, winking at her crew. They all cheer, making howling noises and punching the air with their fists in a pathetic attempt at intimidation.

But Red has underestimated Kate. Pretty soon she'll realise just how much.

"Go get her, girl," I say, reaching over and squeezing her arm.

She grunts in response, focusing on Red and clearing her head of all thought.

Ford reaches for her and squeezes her shoulder. "Keep your eye on the prize, Kate. Ignore the intimidation tactics."

"Yeah, and show her how it's done," Eastern says as he holds the top and middle ropes apart, making room for her to duck through. The pride in his voice is unmistakable as she climbs into the ring.

Both Camden and Sonny shout encouragement. All of us are behind her one hundred percent.

Eastern ducks between the ropes after Kate, fixing her head gear. Bram does the same for Red. Then they're ready.

"Same rules apply," Cal begins, reeling off the rules once more. "Punch above the belt. No strikes to the kidneys or to the back of your opponent's head or neck. Do not use the ropes as leverage. Do not strike your opponent when they're down. A knockout is a clear win. Got it?"

"Got it," they both respond, before Eastern and Bram place teeth guards in their mouths and the pair is ready to fight.

Kate turns to face me, lifting her gloved fist to her head, she taps twice then winks, and I just know she's going to win.

TWENTY-ONE

The loud thud of Red falling to the floor has Bram and his crew roaring in anger.

Kate knocked Red out. She did it, she won just like I knew she would.

Cal bends down, checking on Red just as Bram climbs into the ring and drops to his knees beside her. It's the first time I've seen him show an ounce of care towards her, and I watch as he leans over, studying his face. Only I was wrong, he's not displaying concern.

"Get up, bitch!" he snarls, grabbing her by the arm. She groans, her eye's fluttering open.

What the fuck?! I shouldn't be surprised by his reaction but I am. It only serves to fuel my anger, and when he yanks at her again, Cal snaps into action. Behind me Ford stiffens. He was friends with this idiot once.

"Bram! Back the hell off," Cal snaps, glaring at him whilst Red groans.

"She's my fucking girl." Bram stands. He's seething with anger at Red, at Kate, at us, at *me*. I can feel his hate from all the way across the room.

"Then treat her with some respect!"

Kate looks a little shell-shocked as Cal helps Red to her feet. I can see all the anger and rage she held before the fight drain away, replaced with sympathy for a girl who despises her, who despises us. That's the difference between Kate and Red. Kate feels regret for hurting someone, no matter how much they might deserve it.

"Are you okay?" Kate asks her gently, shaking off her gloves and handing them to Eastern who's standing behind her. She looks between Red and Bram, making her mind up about their relationship. Like me, Kate recognises a battered girlfriend. She recognises a woman whose self-esteem is so low that even such obvious cruelty from her boyfriend doesn't change how she views their relationship. She'll take all the nastiness just for the few glimpses of love. Thing is, whatever glimpses he might show her, that isn't love, that's possession, obsession. It's hate dressed up in fake love. No one who hurts another person the way he does could ever call it love.

It's not.

Red locks eyes with Kate and for a moment I can see a begrudging respect, a whisper of appreciation before it's locked down the second she senses Bram step closer. His fingers curl around her upper arm as he leans over and whispers something in her ear. The expression on her face changes instantly.

"Fuck you, bitch!" she snarls at Kate, spitting at her feet. I watch the glob of saliva and blood hit the floor by Kate's shoe.

Kate grits her jaw, nodding once. "You chose the wrong side," she says softly, before stepping away from them both and out of the ring. Kate pulls off her protective head gear and within a few steps has pulled me into her arms.

"Fuck that bastard up. Make him pay."

I grip hold of her tightly, knowing that she doesn't just want me to hurt Bram for turning his back on Ford or the fact that he helped Monk take my sketches. Or for kidnapping Pink. She's also talking about Red and the fact he treats her so badly.

"I will. I'll make him pay," I respond.

When I climb into the ring five minutes later, Ford following me, a hush falls around the room. There are no jeers, no catcalls or nasty comments. Instead, a dark energy fills the room. On the street this kind of atmosphere would lead to one thing and one thing only... gang warfare. No matter who wins, the other side will retaliate and the hate will continue. A vicious cycle with no end.

This is the quiet before the storm, and I'm not talking about my imminent fight with Bram. He's just one obstacle in a long line of them, until we're faced with our real enemy. The King.

That fight is looming, and it's one I intend on winning.

For now, this is just another battle amongst many.

"Like I've said before, Bram's weakness is his right shoulder. Target as many punches there, okay?" Ford says under his breath, giving me one last piece of advice before stepping out of the ring.

"Got it."

"Don't hold back," Camden grinds out from his position behind the ropes.

"I won't."

Turning on my heel, I face Bram, but not before I look at every single person in the HH crew. My gaze lands on them all. On Dagger, and Monk's wolves. On Red who can't quite meet my eyes. I glare at Diamond and Emerald who've stuck with Monk, maybe through fear, maybe jealousy, it doesn't really matter. They turned their back on Camden, afraid of the big bad wolf that is the King.

"I'm over here, bitch," Bram snarls.

I smile, holding his gaze for long seconds. "So you are."

Cal steps forward, rattling off the same rules he's done five times previously. The second he steps back, I attack.

My right fist meets Bram's shoulder with a loud smack. Then my left follows up with a hit to his temple. Both throw Bram off balance but he bounces back, countering my attack with slick punches of his own. I dodge some. Others meet their marks and my teeth rattle in my head at the power behind his punches. I can already feel bruises forming in the spots Bram has managed to reach. Tomorrow I'm going to hurt, but for now I push the pain away and focus on beating his arse.

He smiles evilly at me after a particularly nasty punch that has Cal separating us for a minute. But I refuse to let him see anything other than my determination to win. I wink back, drawing a snarl from his lips. When Cal steps back once more, Bram ups his game, attacking with even more aggression.

"You think you can win, bitch? You have no fucking idea who you're dealing with," he taunts me, throwing punch after punch and making me work hard to get away from him.

"Don't flatter yourself, Bram," I growl back but he just sneers.

Granted, he's a better fighter than Monk was, far more powerful, but I'm not surprised. Ford already warned me about his abilities. They were friends for a long time. They fought together on the street and trained together in Grim's fight club. He's a good fighter but he has another weakness, other than his right shoulder: *pride*. Bram underestimates me despite witnessing what I did to Monk. You see, pride makes him stupid and that's how I'm going to win. Sweat pours down my back as we both go all out. I keep my fists up, ducking and dodging punch after punch and throwing just as many.

Bouncing on my toes, I drop my defence a little, allowing him to get two good punches in. I don't have to feign the pain after his fist meets my arm then the side of my head, but I can take it. His crew roar with excitement, believing he's got the upper hand as I stumble backwards.

"That's it, bitch, don't fuck with me," he jeers, rolling his shoulders and grinning at his crew.

He's so fucking stupid.

"That really hurt," I respond with a pretend whine, clutching my shoulder. I glance over at Ford who gives me a tiny smile. He knows exactly what I'm up to.

"Hear that everyone? Asia's hurt. Finally met your match, yeah?"

Just like I predicted, Bram drops his defensive stance so that he can preen like a peacock.

It's the chance I've been waiting for. Launching forward, I throw another punch to his weak shoulder then strike his chin with a powerful uppercut funnelling every single ounce of anger from my stomach, up my arm and through my clenched fist. Bram's head snaps back violently.

That's all it takes to win the fight.

He hits the deck with a loud bang, but I can't hear his groans of pain over the cheers of my crew.

"You were fucking amazing, Asia," Sonny says an hour later as we all chill out in the newly decorated rec room. Friends is playing in the background, but none of us are really watching it.

"So was Kate. Did you see how incredible she was?" I retort, grinning with pride for my girl.

Kate smiles softly. "I had some great teachers. Without you guys it'd be me nursing a sore head and not Red…" She sighs, picking at a loose thread on her jumper.

"What's up?" I ask, getting up off Sonny's lap and dropping onto the sofa next to her.

"Winning felt good in the moment…"

"But not anymore?"

Kate looks across at me, shrugging. "I've never really been a violent person but when I hit Red, it felt good knowing that I was hurting her for what she did. Then when she was on the floor and I saw how Bram treated her, I felt... pity."

"I get it." And I really do. Violence is a necessity where I come from and not just the kind of violence between one person to another, but violence people inflict on themselves. There are so many women in Red's position, in Ruby's. I mean, not all men are violent towards their partners, and sometimes it's the women who are violent, but there is a high proportion. It's fucking depressing, honestly.

When I look at my boys I'm filled with a sick sense of dread. Right now, my father is our biggest obstacle. If we defeat him, then we'll have so many more to face. Leaving Oceanside and returning to our old lives will be an impossibility. Where will we go? Will *we* go anywhere together at all? I want to believe that this bond we share, that I feel growing stronger every day, will be enough. Yet, I've lived the harsh reality of life and I know nothing is as simple as that. There's so much we need to discuss, but that's a conversation I can't face right now.

One obstacle at a time.

"Do you think Pink's okay?" Kate asks me after a while, filling the increasing silence. I'm fully aware that my boys have lost interest in the television and are listening in on our conversation.

"It depends on how you define okay," I respond, breathing out a long shaky breath.

Kate searches my face. "Do you believe the King when he said they hadn't hurt Pink?" she asks me bluntly.

"There are different ways to hurt someone that don't involve physical marks. So, no. I don't believe him."

Kate swallows hard, her eyes glistening with unshed tears. "She doesn't have much time, does she?"

I shake my head. "Honestly I don't know, but my gut tells me she doesn't."

Kate falls silent and the air thickens with tension. For the past week we've been concentrating on today's fight, using it as a way to distract ourselves whilst waiting for more news. We know where Pink and Camden's mum are, and despite that, they're still held captive and I'm getting sick of waiting for the King to make his next move. I've never been one to sit back and wait for the fight to come to me.

"Cal, Hud, Grim, they're doing everything they can, Asia," Sonny says.

I know that he believes in them, but chances are by the time they figure out how to get Pink and Camden's mum out, they'll already be dead.

"I know they are, but…"

"…But it's not enough," Camden finishes for me.

We all look at one another, feeling the exact same way. A storm is coming, one that is going to devastate us all.

TWENTY-TWO

Another few days pass where we hear nothing. We go to class, train in the gym and avoid any further confrontation with Bram and his goons. It isn't easy remaining level-headed and calm. I still get moments where I oscillate between worrying over Pink and Camden's mum and needing to beat the shit out of Bram or anyone who looks at me wrong, frankly.

Today's no different.

It's Wednesday morning and I'm sitting in Art class trying to concentrate on my project when Mr Burnside walks into the room. I've barely spoken to him these past couple of weeks, attending my therapy sessions but not really partaking. What's the point? There are bigger things going on in my life than how my mother's death has affected me. I'm done talking about her. I'm done with trying to analyse why I'm feeling the way I am.

It's fucking obvious. Mr Burnside knows about everything that's going on, with my faith in the 'adults' sorting out this mess waning.

Nothing is getting done.

We know where they are. Grim has at least kept her side of the bargain and has sent some dude named Malakai to scope out the King's hideaway, and whilst neither Pink nor Camden's mum have been spotted, the King has, and we all know where he is, so are they.

I'm itching to just break out of Oceanside and go there myself, but I promised Louisa and the Freed brothers that I would let them handle this. Besides, getting out of this prison isn't something we'll be able to do successfully, given the place is rigged to the hilt. I'm positive that's why we've not had any more trouble from Bram and his crew. Well, that and the fact I beat the shit out of him, even if it was in a controlled environment.

I miss the days of sneaking out to the Tower to settle scores the street way. I would've loved to break his fucking nose.

"What does he want?" Camden asks under his breath as we both watch Mr Burnside talking quietly with our art teacher. He keeps flicking his gaze over to us.

"No idea," I shrug, feigning nonchalance when I feel anything but.

"Looks like we're about to find out," Sonny remarks, throwing his pencil on the table and giving up trying to work as Miss Moore strides towards us. All of us are losing the will to do anything, even the things we love. It's hard to carry on as usual when there's a goddamn guillotine hanging over our heads. The fucking King is ruling us, no matter what we try to do.

"You three, Mr Burnside would like to speak with you. Pack up your stuff and head out. I'll see you next lesson," Miss Moore says, a smile covering the annoyance in her eyes.

"Why?" Camden asks, looking between her and Mr Burnside who is waiting by the door. The rest of the class is watching closely. Dagger seems very interested all of a sudden.

"Something about an impromptu group therapy session that can't wait, apparently," Miss Moore explains, her smile dropping. "Why Mr Burnside feels the need to interrupt my class and your learning is beyond me," she adds under her breath.

"Fucking perfect. Just what we need, more goddamn therapy," I say loudly, making sure Dagger can hear, because I can tell by Mr Burnside's face that this has nothing to do with therapy and more to do with our predicament. They must have more news.

Grabbing our stuff we head out of the classroom and follow Mr Burnside.

"Wanna tell us what this is about, Doc?" Sonny asks, as he flashes a concerned look at me.

"As soon as we get to somewhere more private, yes," Mr Burnside responds, shutting down any further discussion.

Instead of taking us to his office, Mr Burnside leads us outside and across the sports field towards the outhouse that Ford, Sonny and I trained in last term. When he pushes open the door, Eastern and Ford are waiting inside with Mr Carmichael and Cal.

"What the fuck's going on?" Camden asks, cutting the tension with a knife.

Ford and Eastern look troubled. Eastern moves towards me, taking my hand in his and squeezing it gently. I know that look he gives me. I've seen it before. Something's wrong, something's really, really wrong.

"Eastern?" I question.

Mr Burnside shuts the door behind us and walks over to Mr Carmichael, giving him a reassuring squeeze on the arm and a gentle kiss on the lips. I've never seen them be affectionate towards each other in public before and it makes me nervous. What the fuck is Mr Carmichael going to say?

"Well?" Camden presses. He's strung tight, so tight that the muscles in his jaw are bouncing with agitation.

"Half an hour ago, Cal received a call from Hudson. We've got some bad news..." his voice trails off as my heart thunders inside my chest. But when Mr Carmichael looks directly at Camden with a sadness that's unbearable, my heart turns to stone.

Please no, not his mum.

"What bad news?" Camden bites out, his voice laced with danger.

Eastern grips my hand tighter.

"I'm sorry, Camden. I'm really, really sorry."

"What fucking bad news, Carmichael!" Camden shouts.

Ford steps closer, placing a hand on Camden's arm but he shakes it off. "Tell me now or so help me…!"

"A body was found of a middle-aged woman. She was wearing a necklace with two diamond hearts…" Mr Carmichael says, his voice sombre. Like Camden, I hear the words but can't quite comprehend them.

No! Not his mum.

"Wait, what are you saying to me?"

"Your mum's dead, Camden…" Mr Carmichael says, the heavy weight of sadness slumping his shoulders.

Time stills. I can't breathe. I can't move. I can only look on helplessly as realisation dawns on Camden's face. *No. God, no!*

"Wh-what?" he stammers, disbelief and shock the only reaction he's capable of having right now. Eastern's grip tightens on my hand, but I barely register his bone-crushing hold. "Say that again…"

Cal steps forward, resting his hand gently on Camden's shoulder. "We need you to go to London with Mr Burnside to identify the body. Hudson has sent a car. It should arrive within the hour."

"How do you know it's her? It might not be her…" he rambles, shaking his head, not wanting to believe what he's hearing. I watch in horror, my feet stuck to the ground, unable to move as Camden begins to unravel before me.

One thought enters my head… *This is my fault.*

I took a knife with the intent to kill my father and this is the King's retaliation.

"This is my fault," I hush out so quietly that I don't think anyone heard me.

"Her dental records match the body found. I'm sorry," Mr Carmichael continues.

"No," he breathes out, wobbling on his feet. He takes a stumbling step forward. "No, you're wrong. Mum isn't dead." But there's no conviction in his words, just a bottomless sadness that opens up beneath him. All the colour drains from his face, filling the void beneath his feet.

"No," I repeat, echoing his words, my knees giving way too. Eastern hauls me into his side, and I find myself hanging on to him for dear life.

"I'm sorry," Mr Carmichael repeats, reaching for Camden.

"It isn't true. You're fucking lying!" Camden spits, shaking his hand off. Tears brim, hovering on his lashes as he begs Cal and Mr Carmichael with his eyes. My fucking heart breaks, seeing him switch between disbelief and desperation.

"I'm sorry, son," Cal says.

Sorry.

Sorry.

Sorry.

Their apologies fall from their lips like the tears that drip from Camden's eyes. I watch them track a path over his flawless skin, feeling numb.

I should *do* something.

You've done enough already, a dark little voice inside my head retorts.

Bile rises up my throat and I'm forced to gulp it down, to swallow the guilt and the pain because that's the least I deserve.

I did this.

"I wish I could tell you it isn't true, Camden, but I can't," Cal says.

"NO! It's not her. I don't fucking believe it," Camden shouts, swiping at his face.

Cal glances at Mr Carmichael who nods. "The body was found yesterday on the banks of the River Thames. Hudson only called us today after the autopsy had taken place. He wanted to be absolutely certain."

"What the fuck?" Sonny hushes out, anger blazing across his features. "You kept this from us!"

"Hudson had to be sure, Sonny, but to be one hundred percent certain we need Camden to identify her body."

For a moment Camden just stares at Cal blinking, not able to take in anything more. Like the rest of us, he doesn't move, he doesn't speak, he doesn't say a word. The room fills with a deathly silence, the kind of silence that only occurs the moment before a bomb's about to detonate, ending life as we know it.

We all wait for the explosion.

Then it comes rushing in, blowing us all to smithereens.

A keening, soul-breaking, heart-tearing, life-ending sound rips out of Camden's throat. None of us are immune to the pain that explodes out of Camden, tearing him apart as he roars, falling forward into Cal's arms. His legs buckle, his knees hitting the floor with a loud smack. Such a beautiful, strong, brave man reduced to a desperate boy calling for his mum.

And it's all *my* fault.

Mine.

"I'm so sorry," Cal mutters, crouching down in front of him as Camden moans over and over again.

But Camden doesn't hear him. He's drowning. The cracks within the depths of his soul fissure, widening and splitting apart with his grief. His distress is deafening. The keening noise he's making has tears rolling down all our cheeks. Nothing is worse than this.

Nothing.

The King has killed his mum.

My actions killed his mum.

"Cam," Ford whispers, dropping to his knees on the floor beside him. He wraps his arms around Camden's shoulders and pulls him tight against his chest, rocking him gently. Camden reaches for him blindly, their pasts forgotten as he holds on tight.

"Shhh," Ford whispers as a tidal wave of pain rushes from Camden, threatening to drown us all.

My gaze meets Ford's and I can see his strength waning. His eyes glimmer and I know he's on the verge of breaking too. Something tells me if that happens he may never recover. Their pain forces me into action, and despite all the guilt I feel, I move towards them. Eastern lets me go, too shocked to do anything but stare at the carnage.

I drop to my knees and wrap my arms around Camden. "I've got him," I say to Ford, easing him out of his hold and cupping his head against my chest.

"She's dead," he moans, his sobs filling the room, his tears wet against my skin as I rock him in my arms and press my trembling lips against his forehead.

"Mum's dead."

What can I possibly say? There are no words that will heal his pain. A million apologies won't bring her back and nothing I can say will make this better.

"I'm alone. I have no one left," he mumbles.

Ford shuffles back, his face draining of colour. Out of the corner of my eye I see Sonny crouch down beside him, resting his hand on his shoulder. Eastern steps closer, kneeling beside me, one hand warm on my back, the other resting on Camden. He gives us his support whilst I try my best to comfort Camden. I want to absorb all his pain, take it from him because it's the least I deserve.

I'll never be able to make this right. His pain is mine to shoulder forevermore. I was so fucking foolish. So stupid. What made me think I could get away with trying to murder the King without any repercussions?

This is on me and as that realisation truly takes root around my heart, a coldness settles beneath my skin, manifesting physically as I begin to tremble.

"I have no one," Camden repeats, delirious in his pain.

"You're wrong, you have us," I whisper, but he's oblivious to everything around him. I'm betting he has no idea that it's me holding him, only that someone is. Selfishly, I grip hold of him tightly, trying to absorb some of his warmth because the moment the fog clears I know he'll come to the same conclusion as me.

I'm responsible for his mum's death.

TWENTY-THREE

J ust over an hour later I watch Camden, Mr Burnside and Ford climb into the car Hudson sent. It leaves from the service entrance of the academy grounds kicking up dust and gravel as it pulls away.

"I'm glad Cal persuaded Mr Carmichael to let Ford go as well. He needed someone with him," Sonny says as I stand like a cold, stone statue next to him.

I murmur my agreement, not able to voice my response. There's so much I want to say but none of the words will form on my lips. I can still feel Camden's grief tattooed against my skin, imprinted there for all eternity. After he was spent, Camden climbed to his feet and did everything he was told robotically. Not once did he look at me.

"Come on, we should go inside." But my feet are glued to the ground as Sonny attempts to guide me back over the field towards the main building.

"You're freezing, Asia. There's no point standing out here any longer. Carmichael said we could take the afternoon off lessons. You're coming back to my room," Sonny orders, taking charge.

"I need to call my brothers first and Eastern should call Tracy," I say eventually, on autopilot. My gaze flicks to Eastern who's talking to Cal and Mr Carmichael. Feeling my stare, he looks over, giving me a pained look. He's worried about his mum too.

"That's a good idea," Sonny cajoles, sliding his hand into mine, relieved that I'm finally moving at last.

As we head into the building a sombre feeling settles over us all. It's almost time for lunch but I'm not feeling hungry. In fact, the very thought of food makes me want to hurl up my breakfast. I just want to curl up into a ball and hide from the world, from my actions and the consequences of them. This constant battle of trying to remain strong is taking its toll, but I force myself to straighten my back and take back what little control I have. Calling my brothers is the first step towards that.

"Mr Carmichael," I say, pulling my hand free from Sonny's hold and catching up with him.

"I'd like to make a call to my brothers. I need to check in on them."

Mr Carmichael nods tightly. "Sure, use my office. Eastern is going to call his mum too."

When we reach his office, Cal rests his hand on my arm. "I want to reassure you that your brothers are safe."

Sonny remains by my side, looking between us. A nervous kind of energy fills the air. He thinks I'm going to lose my cool and take it out on Cal. I'm not. I feel empty. Cold.

Frozen.

I grit my teeth, forcing my mouth to move. "I can't lose them…"

I leave that statement hanging in the air, not able to even allow myself to think the worse. I attempt to follow Mr Carmichael into his office with Eastern, but Cal steps in front of us both. He gives us a look that has my nerves prickling.

"What?" Sonny demands.

"I want you to come to my office after you've finished. We need to talk."

"And we can't do that now?" Sonny asks for me, his gaze flitting between us both.

Cal shakes his head, scraping a hand over his face. He looks like shit, but then again none of us can be accused of looking anything but. Seeing Camden fall apart like that was hard on all of us. "Make your calls then come see me, okay?" he requests, not giving us the opportunity to respond as he strides away.

"What can he possibly need to talk about that can't be said in front of Mr Carmichael?" I ask.

"I'm not sure," Sonny replies, his forehead creasing in a frown. "But I'm going to find out."

Sonny reaches for me and pulls me in for a quick hug before jogging after Cal. I have the urge to follow, but when Eastern steps back out into the hall motioning for me to come, my feet move towards him instead. Pushing away the bad feeling in my chest, I head into Mr Carmichael's office to make that call.

"HOW ARE YOUR BROTHERS DOING?" Mr Carmichael asks, re-entering his office after giving us a moment to ring our families in peace.

I laugh hollowly, the sound unfamiliar, and when the words follow I wince at how they sound too. Robotic, stiff, without life.

"Sebastian said he found a conch shell and can hear the sea every time he lifts it to his ear... He also said that if he listens very carefully, he can hear mum singing his favourite lullaby." My voice cracks and Eastern leans over, grabbing my hand.

Mr Carmichael smiles gently, a range of emotions flicking behind his eyes, but he remains stoic. "I'm sorry they're being affected by all of this." He sighs, taking a seat behind his desk.

"Yeah, me too. Me fucking too," I mutter, making a promise to myself that when this is all over I'm never going to let them out of my sight again. I'm going to fight tooth and nail to get my brothers back.

"And how's your mum, Eastern?"

"Fine," Eastern responds, coughing to clear his throat. "Mum's more concerned about us. Though to be honest, I haven't really told her the full extent of what's going on. She's better off not knowing. Braydon needs to be her priority." He looks at me then and gives me a shaky smile. "He says hello, by the way, and wanted to know what colour your hair is now. When I told him it was pink he said he bet you look beautiful."

"Sweet boy," I whisper, my heart twisting inside my chest. Braydon has always been such a kind, thoughtful, happy kid. So full of humour and courage. He's never sad and never ever complains about his disability. He could show us all a thing or two about strength and living in the moment.

"Good, I'm glad they're... okay," Mr Carmichael says, then winces when I glare at him. There's that word again.

Okay.

We're *not* okay.

"No one's o-*fucking*-kay," I stress, allowing the sudden bitter anger to fill me up. Allowing the flame of it to burn at the ice encasing my heart.

It feels good to be angry. Anger is better than pain and apathy. It's better than soul-numbing guilt. I fuel it, projecting my self-hate and anger onto Mr Carmichael. The seconds stretch into minutes as I just sit staring at him. I wait for him to say something, *anything* to make this better, to make this a dream and not stark reality. But he doesn't.

Eastern watches on in awkward silence. I don't know what I really expected. Every adult besides Tracy has only ever let me down. Mr Carmichael is no different.

"Thanks for letting us call home," Eastern says when the silence gets too heavy. He makes a move to stand but Mr Carmichael holds his hand up.

"Wait a minute, will you?" he says, shaking his head as though snapping out of whatever thoughts that had caused him to shut down so epically.

Eastern sits back down. "What?"

"I know this hasn't been easy on you all..."

"No shit," I spit, wanting to fight, wanting to let out all this bitterness and guilt inside of me. It needs an outlet before it tears me apart.

"I had a call from Crown yesterday. Of course, I didn't tell him what's going on, only that you're working on finding out as much as you can. I managed to get him off your back and not come here to check up on you until we can sort this out..."

"Off *our* backs?" I laugh bitterly. "More like get him off *your* back. What do you think he would do if he knew about Pink, huh? This place would be shut down."

"We're not telling him about Pink because we're protecting her, remember?"

"Protecting her? No one's doing a damn thing as far as I can fucking tell!"

He sighs, pressing his thumb and forefinger against his eyes before finally looking over at me. "We haven't had a chance to talk about how you feel about the King being your father..." he says, conveniently changing the subject.

I scoff, acid filling my veins with bitterness. "You want to talk about that monster now, after what he did...?" *Because of me*, I don't add. That thought hits me like a sucker punch and I have to stifle the groan trying to escape my lips.

"You need to talk about it, Asia. Tell me how you feel," he insists.

"How the fuck do you *think* I feel?"

"Disappointed?" he asks me, nailing it. I'm angry too. Gutted. Heartbroken. The disappointment is the worst. Not that it matters now. I've no right to garner sympathy, not after what I've done.

"You would be too if you were related to that bastard."

"He's not great father material, no," Mr Carmichael agrees, wincing.

"He's not my father, he never fucking will be."

"And Monk? How about him…"

My head snaps up, my nostrils flaring. "Don't mention his name," I seethe and this time Mr Carmichael flinches.

"Perhaps this is a conversation you need to have with Mr Burnside."

"What, you mean a conversation where we discuss how I'm not the daughter of a Chinese Emperor like my mum had peddled all these years, but the daughter of some twisted psychopath?"

"Asia…" Mr Carmichael begins, but I don't want to listen to his meaningless words or bullshit, so I cut him off.

"Did you know that Monk was the King's son?" I ask suddenly, narrowing my gaze.

Mr Carmichael leans forward on his desk, that same dark look I've seen a few times before flashing across his eyes before he hides it with a grim smile.

"I'm going to be straight with you, Asia. I did know Monk was linked to some pretty heavy crime families given the long list of criminal acts he was involved in and all the information provided in his personal file, but I *didn't* know he was the King's son until you did. If I had, perhaps things would've gone differently."

"Yeah, right," I retort.

"I was in prison for fourteen years, most of Monk's life, and before that I left the area I grew up in to try and escape from a future I wanted no part of. I didn't know the King had a child," he retorts, a little too defensively for my liking.

"But recently you had your suspicions?" I press, not able to back down from my hunch because I'm betting Mr Carmichael knows far more than he's letting on. No one lives the life we do and can step away from it all so easily. He knew people, probably still does. The past has a way of catching up with you eventually, I should know.

"Does it matter now? I can't change what's happened," he sighs.

"No, I guess it doesn't change what's happened, but I will tell you something for free, it sure as fuck changes my opinion of you, Mr Carmichael."

"Why?" he has the audacity to ask.

"Because you had a hunch, a gut instinct, and you didn't fucking act on it. If you thought Monk had something to do with the King, you could've saved us all the fucking heartache. You could've thrown *him* under the bus instead of us. Instead, you allowed me to take that deal with Crown. You allowed me to sacrifice my friendship with Eastern to see whether Camden was worth fucking saving, and now we're in this mess because you weren't brave enough to trust your gut and dig a little deeper."

"That's not what I intended..."

I hold my hand up, anger coursing through my blood. I need someone to blame and frankly, Mr Carmichael is as good as anyone.

"Camden's mum is *dead*. She's fucking dead!" I shout, my fingers clenching into fists. "My father is the damn King. Pink is still his fucking prisoner, and somehow we've still got to get Crown off our backs all while stuck in this damn fucking prison and *now* you admit to having your suspicions about Monk!?!" My voice rises with every word. I hold onto my anger with both hands, needing to feel anything other than fear. Needing to fight back, even in just a small way.

"I know I haven't been there for you as much as I should've been." He sighs heavily, a lancing pain ripping over his features. "I've only ever wanted to help kids like you, like *I* once was, to have a better life. To give you opportunities. *Hope.* I wanted to show you that you don't have to be defined by your past, by your..." He clamps his mouth shut, cutting his own sentence short.

Eastern laughs bitterly. "With the King's threat hanging over us all, how the fuck can we have hope?"

"I promise you this will work out," Mr Carmichael says.

I stand abruptly, my chair scraping noisily over the wooden floor. "Promises don't mean shit. Nothing you can say will bring Camden's mum back. Today he broke, and you, Mr Carmichael, are partly responsible for that. You knew something was off about Monk and you didn't fucking act! Every action has a reaction. Every decision made, every choice, a consequence, *remember*?"

"You're right," he says, after a long drawn out silence filled with angry words and distrust. "I am responsible and I'm sorry..."

"Fuck you! Fuck your apologies and fuck your promises. The only way this is over is when the King's dead, and unless you're the one to pull the fucking trigger, I have no damn time for you."

This time Mr Carmichael doesn't try to stop us when we leave.

TWENTY-FOUR

C al is talking quietly to Sonny when Eastern and I enter his office. My anger hasn't dissipated, in fact it seems to be growing with every passing minute, and I'm well aware I'm on the verge of either losing my shit entirely and ripping into the closest person near me or crying an ocean of tears. Neither of which will help Camden.

"Come in, take a seat," Cal says.

Sonny is chewing on his lip, looking worried.

"I'm guessing what you're about to say is going to be bad, am I right?" I ask, readying myself for whatever fucked up news Cal has.

"It's not great, no," Cal responds, motioning for Eastern to shut the door.

"So what is it? Spill," Eastern demands. He hauls his chair close to mine and wraps an arm around my shoulder, sensing I'm not going to like what Cal's about to say. I lean into him, my mind and body needing contact.

"There was a note found with the body," he begins, his eyes flicking to mine. Next to me, Eastern stiffens.

"What note?" I ask.

"A note from the King addressed to someone called *'the Black Sheep'*. At first we thought it was some sick, twisted note meant for Camden but after re-reading it, we decided that it was aimed at someone else."

"Wait, what are you talking about? Does Camden know about the note? Mr Carmichael never mentioned anything when we were with him just now," I ramble, my confused thoughts spilling from my lips in a rush.

Cal turns away from me, and selects an email on his PC, opening it up. Attached is a photograph of a handwritten note sealed in plastic. The shot focuses on the note, but it doesn't take a genius to see what's blurred in the background: a woman's naked body. Camden's mum. My hand rises to my mouth as I gulp down the acidic rush of puke, but there's no stopping the torrent as I rush for the wastepaper basket and throw up.

"Jesus fucking Christ, Cal!" Eastern snarls, getting up to rub my back whilst my stomach empties. Cal gives me an apologetic look as I sit back down then hands me a bottle of water.

"You okay?"

"No," I mutter, washing away the taste of bile with a swig of water but reading the note regardless.

To *the Black Sheep,*

Let this be a reminder. There's no escaping no matter how far you run, or where you hide. The past is your present and your future.

You'll never be free of me. There's only one way out.

I'll see you in Hell.

The King.

"You don't think this note was meant for Camden? It was attached to his mum, after all," I say, swallowing down another mouthful of bile. It burns my throat, reminding me of my part in all of this. My eyes burn with tears, but I know if I let them fall they may never stop.

"At first, we did. But Camden has never hidden from the King, he's never run. Every step of the way, that boy has done the King's bidding to save his mum. This note, it wasn't meant for Camden."

"Who then?"

"Well, if that isn't the fifty-million-dollar question..." Cal clicks the email closed, turning to face me. "When he spoke to you, the King gave you a name: *Bennett*. At first we believed it was a red herring. Just another dead end he'd sent us down."

"But you don't think that anymore?" Sonny asks, leaning his elbows on his knees and perching his chin on his hands.

Cal shakes his head. "Bennett is a fairly popular surname, but after a bit of digging we linked it to a man who rubbed shoulders with the Kray twins back in the 50's and 60's. A very powerful man indeed."

"Who?"

"A man called Montgomery Bennett. He was known as the King of the East End."

"Fuck," Eastern hushes out. "He actually told the truth?"

"Yes, but that isn't the most interesting part. The Bennett family tree ends with Montgomery. There are no records of *any* children that follow. None."

I frown, confused. "So my father isn't related to Montgomery, then? Are you saying he's a fraud?"

"No. I want you to take a look at something for me," Cal says, turning back to his computer. He clicks on another file attached to the same email that held the photo of the note. "Hudson sent me this email shortly after he called about Camden's mum. Grim did some digging. She knows a lot of people. Her lead took her to a manor house in Cornwall where a woman called Fran works as a housekeeper for a very wealthy family. Her real name is Avery Bennett. She's

Montgomery Bennett's surviving daughter and she was the one who provided us with this photograph."

My attention is drawn back to the computer screen and my mouth drops open in shock. There in front of me is a beautiful young blonde woman standing next to a man who looks exactly like my father. The resemblance is uncanny.

"He looks just like the King," I say.

"Yes. This photo proves his relation and his lineage. Your father is indeed Montgomery Bennett's grandson."

"Why all the secrecy then?" Sonny asks.

"Something made Montgomery Bennett protect his family line. All living heirs were forced to change their name, to go into hiding. The Bennett family fell off the face of the Earth, the true heirs to the original King of the East End, a highly guarded secret. Until now."

"Explain," Eastern snaps, looking as confused as I feel.

"The King is well known in the criminal underworld today because of his name and the legacy behind it, but very few people have actually seen the King's face or any of the Bennett family, for that matter. Oftentimes he will send another person into a meeting pretending to be him. As we're beginning to understand, only a handful of business partners know his true identity. Even Grim has never met him, though his name precedes him, of course."

"Camden knows his identity," Eastern points out.

"Yes, and now so does Asia. I'm guessing the fact that the King abusing Camden's mum was a big enough incentive for him to keep quiet, don't you think?" Cal suggests.

Sonny swipes a hand through his hair. "Fucking hell, Cal. How is Camden going to survive this? His mum's dead despite everything he's tried to do to keep her safe."

"We'll help Camden get through this any way we can, but right now the question we really should be asking is why the King chose this moment to come out of hiding? Why reveal his family name if not for a purpose?"

"Because he *wanted* me to know my family name, it wasn't a slip of the tongue," I say before Cal can.

Cal nods his head, looking at each of us in turn. "The King doesn't do anything without a reason..."

"What are you getting at?" Sonny asks, frustrated.

"The King has been watching and waiting for his moment to act. He used Camden's mum to pass on this latest message as a show of power, yes, but also because he knew that note wrapped around her neck would make its way back here. He asked to see you, Asia, so that he could drop the family name knowing you would return to Oceanside and share this information with the only person here that he wanted to hear it. This is a personal vendetta the King has against someone from his past..."

"The Black Sheep?" I ask, a rash of goosebumps scattering over my skin.

"Yes, exactly."

"So, who are we talking about?" Eastern asks, looking more confused, not less.

But here's the thing. I'm no longer confused. I know exactly what Cal is hinting at.

"I know who my father wants me to kill in order to save Pink's life." I look at the three men before me, the blood draining from my face. "The Black Sheep is Mr Carmichael."

TWENTY-FIVE

Back in my room I fill Kate in about Camden's mum and what we discussed in Cal's office. The fucking guillotine has fallen and we're all bleeding from the cut. None of us have come out unscathed. We all feel the deep wounds forming, the biting sting of them that no plaster or medicine will heel. Pain, disappointment, betrayal. I feel it all and if it's fucking me up inside, the same must be true for my friends.

"How did Camden take the news?" she asks quietly, then winces because she knows how stupid that question sounds.

"Like someone had carved his beating heart right out of his chest and crushed it in their palms," I respond, absentmindedly putting my own hand over the heart tattoo that's etched into my skin, rubbing at the ache I feel there. A huge part of me wants to see Camden, to look into his eyes and seek out my place there. Another part, a much bigger part, is afraid. Afraid that he'll never look at me the same way again, that I'll see only hate in those topaz depths.

"Oh, God. This is so messed up," Kate adds, voicing what we're all thinking. "What's going to happen now?" When I don't answer, when I *can't* answer, Kate reaches for me. "You blame yourself, don't you?"

"Who else is there to blame when all is said and done? Camden's mum is dead because I was stupid enough to try and kill the King and not go through with it. I had my chance, Kate, and I blew it. The King has sent us all a very clear message. Fuck with him, and he'll murder the ones we love."

"You can't think that way, Asia. Camden's mum has been the King's punching bag for years now, it was only ever a matter of time before he took her life," Eastern says, trying his best to soothe my guilt.

"Maybe, maybe not. Either way, it doesn't change the fact she's dead and that Camden has to live with the knowledge his mum was murdered then dumped like a piece of trash just so he could send a message to all of us... to the *Black Sheep*."

I spit Mr Carmichael's nickname out, the betrayal I feel making its mark on my soul. He lied to me, to all of us. I hate him just as much as the King, more so perhaps given Carmichael pretended to be someone he's not. I might have blood on my hands, but so does he. As soon as I left Cal's office I wanted to confront Mr Carmichael, but in the end was persuaded to return to my room, to take stock, to decide what the fuck we're going to do now.

We all fall silent as the reality of our situation sinks in. It doesn't matter that none of us ever met Camden's mum. It doesn't matter that she's no relation to us. We're not like the King or Monk, every single one of us is hurting because we care about Camden. When one of us bleeds, so do the rest of us.

Eventually, Kate is the one to break the silence.

"So, let me get this straight, Mr Carmichael's the Black Sheep and he's the one the King wants you to kill in exchange for Pink's life?" she asks.

"It looks that way," Sonny agrees. "We all know Carmichael has a shady past. He's been open enough about what he did to get put into prison, and why. They must've known each other before, him and the King."

"Do you think he was part of the King's crew before he went to prison?"

"He must've been, Kate. Once the King has claimed you as his own, there's no leaving. Death is the only way out… This place here, it's all a fucking pipe dream," Eastern mutters, then looks at me with a pained look in his eyes.

"So why didn't Cal show the note to Carmichael then?" she persists.

"Isn't it obvious?" I ask. "He doesn't trust him now any more than the rest of us do."

"What about Grim? She hangs out in those circles. She's met Mr Carmichael now too. Why didn't she recognise him?" Kate asks.

"Grim's only in her mid-twenties. Mr Carmichael is in his mid-forties. He's been in prison for most of her life, why would she recognise him?" Sonny replies.

"Yeah, I see your point," she agrees. "But where does that leave us? Where does that leave Pink? Because I know you're not capable of killing Mr Carmichael," Kate continues, looking at me. I refuse to meet her eyes.

"Not that he doesn't deserve it," Eastern mutters darkly and I have to agree.

Mr Carmichael has lied to all of us. He's watched us battle against our predicament knowing all along that the King was closing in. Did he know that he was the real target? Did he throw us all under the bus to save his arse, to buy him time? Maybe he did it to draw the King out. Maybe he knew all along I was the King's daughter and he lied to me about that too.

All I know is that he used us, they all have.

And I'm done with it. I'm done being a pawn in someone else's game. Monk, the King, Mr Carmichael, Crown, they all have their own agenda. Every single one of them are using us to get what they want.

I will not allow Pink to be another victim. I'd rather die first.

"Well, what do we do now?" Kate presses, and I see her own thoughts whirring in her mind about how we move forward from this point.

"We have one choice, and one choice only..." I begin, hauling in a steadying breath and steeling myself for their response.

"And what's that, Asia?" Sonny asks, eyeing me carefully.

"We take the matter into our own hands."

"How?" Eastern asks. I expected him to try and persuade me to stick to the plan, to wait it out and rely on the 'adults' to get us out of this mess. Instead, the determined set of his jaw and the matching gleam in his eye tells me a whole different story. Eastern is done playing this game too. It's time to act.

"By escaping Oceanside and getting our friend back."

Sonny swipes his hand through his hair and starts pacing up and down. "Even if we wanted to do what you suggest, Asia, there's no getting out of Oceanside without tripping some kind of alarm. This place is rigged."

Kate grins, her smile would be infectious in better circumstances. "What?" I ask her.

"Are you forgetting who you've got on your side?" She points to her chest, rolling her eyes when no one answers. "I'm the genius hacker, remember? If anyone can get you out of this place, I can. You just need to get hold of a laptop for me and I can do the rest."

I lock eyes with Kate. "You sure you're up for this?"

"I've never been more certain. Pink is my friend too." Her eyes well with tears but she shuts that shit down, refusing to let them fall.

"Okay then, we need to get you a computer." I turn to Sonny, my little thief. "Think you could do the honours? I'm pretty sure your lock picking skills are exactly what we need."

He stops pacing and chews on his bottom lip as he thinks about it. "On one condition," he eventually says.

"And what's that?" I ask.

"That no matter what, you don't resort to murder."

"Well, that all depends on who you think I'm murdering..." I joke, but it goes down like a lead balloon.

"No one. You're not murdering anyone."

I grit my teeth, my lips pressing into a hard line. "Even if doing so means saving Pink's life and all of yours?"

"Asia..." he warns, watching me carefully.

I'm not sure what he expects from me, honestly, because if it boils down to it and this plan to rescue Pink doesn't work out and I'm forced to kill Mr Carmichael to free Pink, or the King to free us all, then that's what I must do. If there's a way to save us without having to do that, then I'll take that path every time, of course I will, but I won't rule murder out just so that my boys can look at me the same way.

"Promise me, Asia," he pleads.

I look him dead in the eye and do the only thing I can, I lie.

"I promise."

It's hard to tell if he believes me or not, either way he nods his head, seemingly satisfied.

"Then I'm in. I'll deal with the fallout with my foster family once this is over," he says, gritting his jaw.

A flash of worry crosses his face before he hides it with a fake grin that hurts my heart. Sometimes I find it hard to look at him, he's that beautiful, even if his smile is fake. Ignoring the flush creeping up my skin, I give him the opportunity to back out. Out of all of us, Sonny has the purest heart and despite me referring to him as the devil all those weeks ago, he is very much the angel wrapped up in a devilish exterior.

Beneath the bravado and the innuendo is a boy who cares too much. What's the saying '*the harder we love, the harder we fall?*'

"I know you've got a good thing going with the Freed brothers and I don't want to fuck that up. Seriously, Sonny, I wouldn't think any less of you if you didn't want to get involved in this."

"They're good people, I can't deny that, but Pink's my friend too. There's no chance in hell I'm sitting this out. Every day they hesitate is another day she's closer to ending up like Camden's mum. We get her out and then *they* can deal with the King."

"Then we're agreed. As soon as Camden and Ford are back, we make a solid plan and we go get Pink, yes?"

Nodding their heads in agreement, the three of them start discussing the beginnings of a plan whilst I reach for a cigarette from the pack on my desk. My hands are shaking so badly that I have to turn my back to them, so they don't see that it takes me a few attempts to light the damn thing. When I finally draw in a deep lungful, I hold the burning smoke in my lungs and stare at my reflection in the window. I look like a ghost, my silhouette bleak against the night sky.

"Want to talk about it, Asia?" Kate asks, stepping up beside me.

I shake my head. "There's nothing much left to say," I respond as she slides her arm around my back and leans her head on my shoulder.

"We'll get Pink back without you having to lose your soul," she says, her voice filled with certainty even though everything else about her is screaming the exact opposite. She's putting on a brave face. I've known her long enough to realise that.

"We will," I say firmly, all the while knowing that if our plan to rescue Pink fails, losing my soul will be the least of my worries.

TWENTY-SIX

I've been staring at the red flashing light of my digital clock for the past hour. Sleep evades me yet again, but how can I sleep knowing what I have to do? All I can feel is Camden's grief, every tear shed, every soul-tearing cry. All I can see is the King's face, his dark black eyes as they regard me. All I can hear are the words he spoke.

"One life in exchange for another, that's all I ask..."

Pink's life for Mr Carmichael's.

I've spent the last hour going over all my past conversations with Mr Carmichael and my head is spinning. Is he really the Black Sheep? Yes, his past is pitted with bad choices, but

maybe we're wrong and the Black Sheep is someone else who works here. Maybe it's just another way for the King to fuck with our heads, to make us distrust one another.

I know I'm clutching at straws but talking about killing someone and actually going through with it are two very different things. I know that. It's easy to say you're capable of murder, but not so easy to slide that knife into someone's flesh or fire that gun and watch the bullet shatter blood and bone. That takes something else entirely. You have to be a little dead inside to commit such an act or maybe that just happens after.

"Ever killed a person, Asia?"

I had been willing, ready to kill the King. Yet, I didn't. I can tell myself over and over it was because the timing wasn't right, or he wasn't close enough but when I really, honestly think about why I didn't slice the King's throat when I had the opportunity, the only answer I can come up with is because I was *afraid*.

Afraid to kill the King.

Afraid to kill my father.

Afraid of the person I'd become if I did.

Afraid of losing the girl I am.

Afraid to lose my family, my boys.

So fucking afraid.

"Fuck!" I snap, my hand curling into a fist as I slam it against the mattress over and over again. "Fuck! Fuck! Fuck!"

Why didn't I do it? Camden's mum would be alive now. We'd be safe.

My eyes are squeezed shut as I try to regain control over myself, but my tears find their way out from between my lashes. I let them fall, promising myself once I'm spent that I won't allow myself this moment of weakness again. That tomorrow, I'll be strong again. I'll be the fierce Asia everyone expects and not some little girl scared to take a life even if it is to save her friend. Turning over onto my stomach I scream my grief and rage into the pillow, allowing it to muffle my pain and soak up my tears. I'm too distracted by my own heart bleeding its pain away that I don't hear my bedroom door open then shut with a gentle click.

Only when I'm spent, and my sobs have died down enough to not drown out all other sounds, do I sense someone else in my room with me. Slowly, I push upwards, swinging my legs out of bed and turn to face the opposite wall.

"What are you doing here?"

Sonny is sitting on the floor, his legs drawn up and his arms folded over his knees, watching me. There's a deep sadness that emanates from him, reflecting my own.

"You're really willing to do it, aren't you?" he asks me, his voice soft, low and achingly sad. "You're willing to kill Carmichael if this plan fails."

"Yes," I respond, knowing I have to find the courage to do it.

"Then it can't fail," he responds tightly.

Sonny pushes up off the floor and approaches me. His steps are heavy, his shoulders slumping. Gone is the boy who loved to tease me, to flirt. Gone is the boy whose dimples flip my stomach upside down. Before me is someone I don't recognise. Someone dark, someone who, if only I took the time to look hard enough, has always been there hiding just beneath the boyish grin.

Sonny sits down on the bed next to me, sliding his hands between his thighs to stop them from shaking. His eyes are downcast, his head drooping between his shoulders as his hair falls forward. Looking at him like this, my stomach flip-flops for a different reason.

"What is it, Sonny?" I ask. We're all upset about Camden's mum, but this is so much more than that.

"Killing someone changes a person. You can never get back what's lost," Sonny whispers.

"I appreciate your concern, I do… but it doesn't change a thing. I will do anything to protect the ones I love."

Sonny lifts his head, looking at me. His eyes are darker than I've ever seen them, more midnight blue in this light. Haunting somehow. He lifts his hand, cupping my cheek. They feel cool against my skin, unfamiliar.

"Do you know why I like to fuck, Asia?"

The question throws me, and I flinch at the cold leaching into my skin. This isn't him. This isn't the warm Sonny I've come to know. Dread tracks a trail down my spine, freezing my insides further.

"No, why?" I whisper, my mouth parting a little as he leans in closer, his free hand sliding up the bare skin of my arm.

"Because it helps me to forget what I did..." His cold thumb presses against my bottom lip, parting my mouth before his hand falls away.

"What did you do?"

Sonny looks away as a coldness folds over us both. I swear to God it's as though we've suddenly stepped into a freezer. My jaw begins to chatter, and I have to grit my teeth together to stop the noise from filling the silence with my fear.

"When I was fourteen and my dad was in prison, my mum decided that she needed another man to warm her bed. She brought this guy back to our house. They were drunk, high. Out of their damn minds. When I heard them fucking, I tried to block out the noise. But when she started screaming..."

"Sonny, you don't have to go on," I say, feeling my stomach turn. I know where this is going. I know how this story ends.

"I went into mum's room. He had his hands wrapped around her throat, her lip was bleeding, her eyes bugging out of her head. The next thing I knew I was standing over this man. His head was caved in and I was holding a baseball bat in my hand. I remember blood sliding from the wood onto the floor. Mum was screaming."

"Sonny." I reach for him, but he flinches away.

"I killed him, Asia. I killed a man. I didn't think, I just acted out of instinct..."

"To protect your mum. You did it out of love," I say, gripping his hand and pulling it to my lips, pressing a kiss against his cool skin.

"It doesn't matter why I did it, only that I did," he responds, his gaze weary. "I started fighting not long after. I fought people with a crazed kind of anger that was only soothed when my opponent hit back. I sought out the pain to blot out what I did. I was angry all the time. I had this beast inside of me that wanted to hurt people as much as I was hurting. Then later I managed to contain that anger and funnel it into something I believed was less damaging. Sex. Only that hurt me in a different way because I didn't fuck to be close to someone I loved, I fucked to get out of my head. Taking a life changed me, Asia, and it *will* change you."

"I'm sorry, Sonny, for what you've been through." His pain is like a million tiny nicks from a knife, splitting open my skin. I bleed for him, for the boy he was.

"What happened after?"

"Mum took the blame. Six months into her sentence she slit her wrists with a pair of scissors stolen from a beauty therapy class she took as part of her rehabilitation in prison."

My hand flies to my mouth as I stifle the cry that tries to burst from my lips. When his gaze meets mine again, it's all I can do not to shed the tears that are threatening to fall.

"I sought out other ways to dull the pain. I became a thief, I stole things. I fucked and I fought, and until I met you, I thought that was all I could do. But you gave me a different purpose, Asia. You gave me a reason to smile, to laugh, to want a life beyond the pain."

"Sonny, I don't know what to say…"

I'm so fucking grateful that he felt comfortable enough to share his past with me, to trust me enough to give up this part of him. But will it change my mind when all is said and done?

If I'm faced with the King again and had the opportunity to kill him, would I walk away? If I had to choose between Pink's freedom and Mr Carmichael's life, could I honestly say that I wouldn't even try to save my friend?

"There isn't anything you can say. I just wanted you to understand why I feel so strongly about this." He stands, walking towards the door but I go after him and grab his hand.

"Don't go, please," I say softly. "I can't lose you too."

He turns to face me, stepping close enough that I can feel his body heat seep through my skin. "I said that I'd always have your back, Asia, and I will. *Always*," he says fiercely. "I'll be there to catch you when you fall, but I need something from you too."

"What do you need...?" I respond, pushing back the flop of dirty blonde hair as he looks down at me.

"To feel..." he says, and my heart aches that little bit more.

TWENTY-SEVEN

Leaning into Sonny, I breathe in his scent of musk and lemon. I so badly want to kiss him, to show him how much I care, but I don't want to be another person he sleeps with to dull the pain. Connecting with Sonny has to be more than just mindless, thoughtless fucking.

It seems important somehow that I give him what he needs, not what he or I want. We might feel the same way, I might want to lose myself in him for a little while, but deep down I know that if I fuck Sonny tonight it would be a mistake.

He's just opened his heart to me and given up his deepest, darkest secret and now he's left raw. Helping him to heal is going to take more than a quick fuck. Not that I'm suggesting Sonny would be quick, actually, I think he'd probably take all the time in the world given what I know about him, but that's beside the point.

Without initiating anything, I let Sonny hold me for as long as he needs. When I feel his arms loosen, I step away from his warmth and take his hand guiding him to sit on the floor opposite me. He looks a little confused but doesn't question what I'm doing. Honestly, I'm not even sure I know what I'm doing. I'm figuring this out as I go along.

"Well, this is new…" he begins, trying to lighten the heavy mood that has settled over us both.

"No talking," I respond, pressing my finger against his lips.

Sonny looks bemused, but he snaps his mouth shut, and crosses his legs in front of him, waiting for my next move.

Sleeping with Eastern had been easy, the most natural thing in the world. Two best friends coming together, a beautiful inevitability. With Ford it was different, he got beneath my skin and tore apart all my self-doubt and self-loathing. He made me stronger with every crushing kiss, with every searing caress. He built me back up.

This time the tables have turned, this time it's Sonny who needs something from me, something *more*. Sex isn't the only way to show someone you care.

"I want you to look at me, Sonny. Lay your hands on your thighs and just breathe."

I expect him to crack a joke, to show me those dimples that melt my heart, but he doesn't. He's deadly serious when he stares deep into my eyes and inhales oxygen as though he's a drowning man.

"That's it, breathe in through your nose and out through your mouth," I say gently.

After a beat he follows my instructions, and with every breath in and every exhale out, I can see the tension leave Sonny's body. The muscles in his face relax and his shoulders lower as we continue to look at one another. I see questions in his eyes, vulnerability, but also trust.

He doesn't know what's happening, or where this is leading, if it's leading to anything at all, but he trusts me enough to follow my lead.

"Just concentrate on breathing steadily. With the oxygen that you draw into your lungs, think of only the positive things in your life, no matter how few that may seem right now," I add with a wry grin.

"Then when you breathe out, let go of all the things that are eating you up inside."

Sonny's chest expands as he inhales a deep breath. When he exhales some more of the tension releases.

I learned this technique from one of my foster parents. She was a Yoga instructor, very spiritual. I spent a lot of time trying not to laugh when she was trying to teach me how to meditate. Mindfulness, she called it. At the time, I thought it was a crock of shit. Now, I see it might have its place.

"Keep breathing steady, keep your eyes fixed on me," I whisper, moving position so that I'm sitting on my haunches in front of him. Careful not to move too suddenly, I rest my hands on his making sure to breathe in time with him.

For long minutes I stay just like that, my hands warming his. I make no move to initiate anything more, concentrating instead on connecting with Sonny in a deeper way because that's what he needs right now. Apart from the breathing technique I picked up from my foster parent, I never really paid much attention. After another five minutes, I start massaging the backs of Sonny's hands. I'm acting on instinct, pure and simple.

I watch his eyelids droop, his long lashes fluttering against his skin as my fingers move up his forearms. As I make tiny circular motions over the firm muscles of his biceps, a deep sigh falls from his lips. When I reach his shoulders, I rest my hands there, feeling the warmth begin to emanate from his skin through his t-shirt.

He takes a deep breath in.

I take a long breath out.

With every breath he inhales, I exhale, and we settle into a steady, calming rhythm. Slowly I move my hand lower, placing it over the eagle tattoo that I know sits within the centre of his chest, inked above his heart. It stutters a little, picking up speed as my fingers press against him, only to find a steady beat when I lift his hand and place it over my heart too.

With every minute that passes, the cold ebbs away and an intense warmth spreads out from beneath our hands as my own eyes drift shut. I'm not sure how long we remain like that, but eventually I become increasingly aware of Sonny's gaze on me. It's so intense that I'm almost afraid to open my eyes. Then I remember who this boy is and what he means to me and I refuse to shy away from whatever I'll see in his eyes. I expect pain, fear, pity, sadness... even desire but when my gaze meets his, all I see is *hope*.

Hope for a better future. Hope for something more.

When Sonny looks at me, he doesn't see a broken girl from a broken home, fighting to survive in a world that's doing everything to destroy her. He sees a future, a life together.

And it does something to me.

Inside my chest something vital takes hold of my heart. It blooms outwards growing stronger, rushing through my veins with every beat of my battered heart. Sonny doesn't make a move closer, he simply stares whilst this feeling takes hold. His gaze traces over my face, moving from my eyes to the tip of my nose, over my cheeks until it lands on my lips. His pupils widen as he takes in another deep breath and with it, my own heart stutters. An energy ripples over my skin, scattering goosebumps over every inch of me, and when Sonny's fingers grab hold of my shirt and he pulls me towards him, I don't fight it.

"I was wondering if you had an extra heart, Asia, because mine was just stolen..." Sonny says, a lopsided grin pulling up his lips as he showcases those beautiful dimples. The line is so fucking corny, and I'm pretty sure he's nicked it off the internet somewhere, but it doesn't matter because I've fallen for it. Hook, line and sinker.

"You're the thief, Sonny, I should be asking you the exact same thing…" I whisper, as he pulls me closer, grazing his lips against mine.

"Touché."

Sonny runs the tip of his nose along the bridge of mine then peppers gentle, sweet kisses against my forehead and cheeks, smiling all the while.

"That's right, I'm a thief and I'm here to steal your heart…" He chuckles, laughing at another corny line.

"You're poetic, you know that, right?" I ask him, smiling to myself as he trails his lips over my chin. When he tips my head to the side and gently nibbles my earlobe, I lose my ability to speak at all.

"I don't need the stars to light my way when I've got the universe right in front of me."

A laugh bubbles up my throat and bursts free from my lips at the awful line. "They're getting worse," I say, shaking my head with mirth.

"I'm getting distracted," he retorts, pulling back and biting on his lip. He looks up at me from under his flop of hair. This time there's no mistaking the desire in his eyes. "What's a man got to do to get you into bed?"

"Do those lines usually work for you?" I ask, tipping my head to the side.

He chuckles. "Pretty much, yeah…"

Shaking my head I get to my feet, pulling him up.

"Smooth, Sonny, real smooth."

Climbing onto my bed, I make room for him beside me under the duvet. I'm still wearing my tracksuit bottoms and t-shirt, causing Sonny to frown.

"Is this your way of seducing me, Asia? Because I'm more than happy to strip you naked," he says, a gleam in his eyes.

"You wanted me to get into bed, so here I am."

"That's not what I meant…"

"I know that." I smile gently, cupping his face in my palm once he's settled down beside me.

"But you're not going to sleep with me, are you?"

"I'm going to sleep with you, Sonny. I'm just not going to *sleep* with you. At least, not tonight."

It's not out of spite, or cruelty. I want to connect with him that way, just not tonight, not after everything that's happened today. He might not like my decision in the moment, but he'll thank me for it in the morning.

He smirks, puffing out his cheeks. "I guess that's not a definite no."

"It's not a no at all. It's just not tonight."

"Why?"

"Because now isn't the right time."

"It feels like the right time to me..." he counters, trying to hide his disappointment and failing miserably. "You slept with Eastern and Ford..."

I sigh, "This isn't a competition, or a race, Sonny."

"Sorry, that was a shit thing to say. Guess I'm a little envious, after all."

"Don't be... If it's any consolation, I really, really want to sleep with you. I'd just rather start the next step of our relationship on a new day that isn't shrouded with death and sadness. Does that make sense?"

"Yeah, it does." he responds, tucking one arm beneath his head and resting his hand between us. Leaning over, he brushes his lips against mine. "Until tomorrow then."

"Until tomorrow... Oh, and Sonny,"

"Yes?"

"You don't have to steal my heart when it's already yours to keep."

"Now who's full of corny lines?" he grins, then tenderly brushes aside a strand of hair that's fallen across my cheek. "Goodnight, Asia."

"Goodnight, Sonny," I murmur, threading my fingers with his.

After a few minutes our breathing synchronises and we both fall into a deep, peaceful sleep.

TWENTY-EIGHT

When I awake just before dawn, Sonny is lying next to me still fast asleep. Shifting closer, I rest my head close to his and just stare at him like a proper little creeper whilst his soft breaths feather against my skin. The long fronds of his eyelashes rest against his tanned skin, and his plump lips are a perfect cupid's bow that I am desperate to kiss. Despite the three-day old stubble and the smattering of hair which peeks up from behind the low v of his t-shirt, he seems so much younger than his seventeen years. Cocooned in sleep where reality is nothing more than a dream, Sonny is peaceful, and I can see the boy he once was before life dealt its blow.

We've all had to grow up fast living the way we have. It saddens me that all the normal things that teenagers get to do are something that we've all missed out on and if we survive what's coming, I hope that we get a chance to rectify that.

Brushing back Sonny's hair, I press a gentle kiss against his forehead, making a silent vow to always grasp happiness when I can find it because in life, there are never any guarantees.

Yesterday showed me that in stark colour. It had been intense, a rollercoaster ride that had left us all feeling churned up and whilst sleep has helped a little to calm my fraying nerves, I know that from the moment we leave this room things will only get worse.

I want to believe that things will work out the way they're supposed to, that maybe they'll even get better. I want to believe that Camden will still want me, that Mr Carmichael isn't a traitor, and that we'll rescue Pink without anyone getting hurt, but I know that's a pipe dream. Reality is so much harder when you've spent your whole life living right in the thick, messy sludge that's life for kids like us. I can't pretend like some other kids might. I never lived a closeted life, wrapped up in cotton wool by parents who wanted to protect me from all the danger that lurks around every corner. I don't have parents who'll fight my battles for me, who can act as a buffer from the big bad world, especially not since my surviving parent *is* the villain who has no problem in making my life a living hell. My only consolation is that right now I can grasp at something good before we have to wade back in and fight. Seize the day and all that. There's still time, even if it is only an hour or so before we have to face the day.

Being very careful not to wake Sonny, I slip out of bed and head into the bathroom to wash up. When I look in the mirror, I see someone unrecognisable. I see a girl who is trying everything she can to stay brave and strong, but is fraying at the edges. Fighting is a part of who I am, I admit, but that doesn't mean to say that I'm immune to feeling weak. I'm only human after all, and right now this human wants to connect. I want to seal that bond between me and Sonny once and for all. Making a decision, I strip myself free from my clothes and take in a deep shuddering breath.

When I head back into the bedroom with clean teeth and a building desire, Sonny is waiting for me. If he's surprised by my nakedness, he doesn't show it. He simply pulls back the covers without saying a word and I climb into bed, laying my body over his in a bold move.

"Is this where we make love?" Sonny asks, his voice quavering.

"Yes," I respond simply, pressing my body against his and loving the feel of his arousal against my core. "Because when all is said and done, love makes the world go around, right?"

"Are you saying you love me...?" Sonny bites down on his lip, a nervous gesture that belies the confidence of his hands as they smooth over my back and grasp my arse, guiding my hips against his.

"Does that thought scare you?"

"No... it doesn't scare me at all. How could it, when I have you?"

My heart swells inside my chest and my core begs for release as I move myself slowly against him. He's still wearing his joggers and whilst I enjoy the friction, that's something I need to rectify. Pressing a gentle kiss against his lips, I push upwards so that I can remove his t-shirt. Next his joggers and shorts come off and within seconds my slick, needy core is pressed up against the hard ridge of his cock.

"Stay with me," I say, gently, rocking my hips as I straddle him.

"I am with you," he responds, his fingertips running up my arms and down over my breasts.

I bite down on the moan that's just dying to release from my lips and clasp his hands, forcing him to pause for a second. "Last night you said you had sex to forget. I need you to stay with me in this moment, can you do that?"

Sonny tips his head to the side, the long strands of his hair falling over his forehead.

"I've longed for this moment for a while now, Asia. There's nothing on Earth that would stop me from being present," he replies sincerely, and with that statement I let go of his hands so he can cup my face and pull me down for a kiss that obliterates my heart. You see, when someone kisses you like you're the very oxygen they need to breathe, it's easy to give up something precious. So when Sonny moulds me against him, his tongue sweeping into my mouth, I hand Sonny my heart willingly and in turn he gives his to me.

For long minutes we just kiss, allowing ourselves the freedom to taste one another, to explore these feelings that bloom within us both. His hands roam every inch of my skin with a gentleness that makes my heart race and my eyes fill with unexpected tears. Tenderness isn't something I'm used to, and the way Sonny kisses me is reverent. He worships me with his lips, cracking me open and diving in. I have to pull back briefly to centre myself, to stop my heart from flying free from my chest.

"Do you want me to stop?" Sonny asks me, his lips plump and as bruised as mine.

"No, I don't want you to stop..." I want him inside me, but I'm also aware that I've never felt more vulnerable. Not because I think he's going to hurt me, but because I can feel *everything*.

"But?" he asks gently, guiding me back down onto the bed so that he's the one above me. He rests his forearms either side of my head whilst he settles between my legs. I can feel the tip of his cock kiss my entrance, and warmth spreads low in my belly.

"I didn't plan this. I didn't think past wanting you..." I admit, hoping he gets my meaning. I don't have a condom.

He bites his bottom lip, a frown creasing his forehead. "Believe it or not, neither did I." He sighs, pulling away. I know how much he wants me. I want him too, so bad that I can't breathe, but neither of us need an unplanned pregnancy to add to the mix.

"Shit, I'm normally better at this," he says with a wry grin.

"You *are* good at this." I heave a sigh, then feeling a little reckless add, "I trust you to pull out when the time comes."

Sonny shakes his head. "As much as I want to go bareback with you. I won't risk it. Just give me a sec okay," he says, pressing a gentle kiss against my mouth before quickly shoving on his clothes and leaving the room.

He's back before I've even had a chance to recover the frantic beat of my heart.

Stripping off, he holds up a condom packet and within seconds has slid it over his still engorged cock. Yet when he climbs above me, he doesn't slide inside me immediately, instead he lowers his lips to my swollen core and kisses me there with as much passion and feeling as he did my mouth. I reach for him, jutting my hips upwards as he grips my hips and sucks and licks at my folds. When stars finally obliterate my vision and I press my eyes closed in ecstasy, Sonny slides inside of me.

For all his bravado and flippant dirty talk, he's a giving lover. Underneath that cad exterior is a deep thinker, a willing participant in this beautiful moment. True to his word, Sonny makes love to me. This isn't fucking, this is everything I never imagined and so much more. I feel loved, adored, venerated and when Sonny finally comes inside of me, his forehead pressed against mine and his gaze boring deep into my soul, I know that whatever happens this connection we share will never, ever be broken.

An hour or so later in the breakfast hall, Eastern and Kate greet us both with grim smiles, not because I spent the night with Sonny, but because Camden and Ford are yet to return. A sinking feeling sits heavy in my stomach. All the lightness and warmth of this morning is quickly swallowed by fear and worry.

"Should we be concerned?" I ask Eastern.

He scrapes a hand over his face. "They've been gone one night. I imagine there was stuff that needed to be done. Paperwork to file for the death, that kind of thing."

"Eastern's right, don't fret just yet," Kate reassures me but when I look over at Bram and his crew, they seem far more preoccupied with our hushed conversation than their own breakfast.

"What the fuck are you looking at?" I snap, narrowing my gaze at Bram. He's still sporting a bruised eye from our fight in the ring and it matches the one Red has courtesy of Kate.

"Oh nothing, just the end of an era is all..." he says, grinning wickedly.

I move to stand, but Mr Carmichael enters the dining hall just at that moment followed by Cal. Neither look happy. When I meet Cal's gaze, my body tensing as Mr Carmichael walks by, he shakes his head, urging me with his eyes not to do something stupid.

I sit, biting my tongue.

God only knows I want to rip into our lying piece of shit principal, but keeping what we know on the downlow is more important, especially since we're planning on breaking out of this place just as soon as we square it up with Camden and Ford. The last thing we need is their eyes on us.

"What do you think Bram meant by that?" I whisper quietly, glancing over at their group. He's still watching us and I'm not going to lie, the smug look on his face has me worried.

"The prick will take any opportunity to wind us up, just ignore him," Sonny responds, reaching for my hand. He grips it tightly, his fingers twining with mine.

When Mr Carmichael reaches the self-service station he coughs loudly, drawing our attention to him. "Good morning..." he begins, then he catches my eye and falters. My gaze drops to his hands which are squeezing the edge of the counter so hard that the whites of his knuckles show. When I look back up, understanding dawns on me. He knows about the note.

"As of this morning, I have handed in my resignation..."

"Fuck," Eastern says, his gaze flicking to mine as the room explodes into chatter.

Bram and his crew start whooping like it's the best news they've had all year, others sit in stunned silence.

"Due to unforeseen circumstances, I have made the very difficult decision to stand down as Principal of Oceanside Academy. I'll be seeing out the end of this week whilst the owners of the school seek a suitable replacement." He takes a deep breath, not bothering to respond to the jibes that have picked up around the hall. It's like he's given up, and that angers me more.

"By the end of the week? He's running. He's fucking running!" I hiss under my breath.

My first thought is blind outrage. How dare he walk away? How dare he take the coward's way out and leave us to face the King on our own? My second feeling is panic. If he leaves, what will happen to Pink? The King will kill her as surely as he killed Camden's mum.

"No!" My body begins to tremble with suppressed rage, and I have to grit my teeth hard to prevent myself from calling him out. "That fucking coward!" I spit.

"Easy, Asia," Sonny warns when some of the kids sitting at the tables closest to us turn to look at me.

"I'm sorry, but this is the only way," Mr Carmichael says, directing his apology to me.

Sorry? There's that word again.

Is he sorry for lying to us? Is he sorry he's running? Is he sorry that our future is even bleaker now? Is he sorry that for a while I fucking trusted him?

Sorry, sorry, sorry.

Fucking sorry.

Mr Carmichael approaches our table and I find my hand tightening around the knife I'm still holding. I could do it now. I could take his life just like the King wants me to do. I could end this all.

Right. Fucking. Now.

Standing abruptly, I face Mr Carmichael. Sonny stands with me, his hand flat against my thigh, holding me back.

"I'd like a word, Asia," he says, his gaze flicking to my hand holding the knife. He presses his mouth into a hard line.

"Drop it, Asia," Eastern hushes out through clenched teeth. He reaches over and plucks the knife from between my fingers and the tightness around Mr Carmichael's eyes relaxes a little. Ignoring the fact that everyone's eyes are on us, I sneer.

"How about I give you two, Mr Carmichael...? Fuck. You!"

Shrugging out of Sonny's hold, I push past Mr Carmichael roughly and race from the dining hall, not giving a shit about what anyone thinks. It's pretty obvious half the damn school knows about my predicament. I'm vaguely aware of Bram's laughter and Eastern calling my name.

I just run.

Picking up speed, I race through the halls and out into the gardens beyond, blindly running. I shove past Frank when he tries to stop me, then punch one of the other bodyguards when he grabs my arm. I don't care that I'm breaking any rules. I don't care about anything other than putting as much distance between me and the people within Oceanside who are determined to fuck me over.

When I finally stop, I find myself on the edges of the small cove where Camden revealed he was Bling. Rushing towards the shore, I welcome the cold wet spray then scream. I scream until my lungs burn and my voice becomes hoarse.

My head is spinning. I don't know up from down, left from fucking right. I'm angry Mr Carmichael's running, angry he's abandoning us knowing what he knows, and yet a part of me is glad because if he isn't here, I don't have to kill him...

But if I don't, Pink's fucking dead.

She's *dead*.

He's just signed her death warrant.

As I look out towards the tumultuous sea, it occurs to me that I could end all this fear, this pain and disappointment right now. I could walk into the waves and let the ocean take me.

I won't have to fight anymore.

My feet step into the water of their own accord before I've even had time to truly contemplate what I'm doing...

TWENTY-NINE

"**W**hat do you think you're doing?" a familiar voice asks me.

It sounds like Camden, but it can't be him because he hasn't returned from London, so I keep walking into the waves, my body moving on its own accord. I feel disjointed somehow... cast adrift. I don't feel the icy-cold water as it laps at my knees. There's no conscious thought at all as I move further into the ocean, my thighs wet now.

"I said, what the fuck do you think you're doing?!"

An arm wraps around my waist tightly, yanking me backwards. A second later I'm pulled from the waves, lifted up in a strong pair of arms.

"Get off me!" I shout, tears that I hadn't realised had fallen blurring my vision.

"No! You don't get to leave me too!" a fierce voice says.

"Camden?" I ask, knowing it's him but having to blink away the tears to see if it's true.

"You bet your arse it's me," he retorts, striding over the pebbles and shoving me against the boulder that his sister's image is painted upon. "What the fuck do you think you're doing?"

"It's all fucking over," I respond, trying to push against him. Only then do I notice Ford, Sonny and Eastern standing close by, but I can't risk looking in their eyes knowing I'd only see disappointment and anger.

I fucking ran.

I'm a *coward*, just like Mr Carmichael.

Pain comes rushing in, slamming into my stomach hard enough to make me double over. I throw up, the acid burning my throat as I empty myself all over the glossy, wet pebbles.

"This is not how we do things, Asia. You don't fucking get to check out because shit has gotten hard. You don't get to fucking leave us because you can't see a way out of this mess. You're stronger than this *god-fucking-damn* it!" Camden roars, not giving me a chance to right myself enough to face his wrath.

"Camden, go easy," Eastern says, stepping closer.

"Don't tell me to go easy. Did you not see what Asia was about to do? I can't fucking believe it!" he retorts, his rage ripping through me, tearing me to shreds.

"Leave her alone. You don't understand what's happened!" Eastern shouts back, stepping between us both, protecting me like he always has. I can't believe I was even contemplating leaving him, *them*. The shame I feel is all-encompassing, and it takes everything I have to keep standing upright.

Camden's nostrils flare as he draws in a breath. "I know what fucking happened, Eastern! The King killed my mum and I spent all day yesterday trying to piece myself back together, so I can stay strong, only to return here and find Asia trying to drown herself!"

"I wasn't…" I say feebly. *Was I?*

"She wasn't…" Eastern repeats, glancing at me with horror.

"Are you fucking stupid?" Camden growls, pointing at me. "No one takes a swim in the middle of fucking winter."

"I know Asia. I know she'd never leave the ones she loves. It was a *mistake*," Eastern says, fiercely, reaching for me. I grab his hand, forcing myself to be strong. Standing on shaking legs, I face all my boys. Sonny and Ford have been quiet, watching this all unfold. I hadn't meant it... I just wanted everything to stop, just for a moment.

"I'm sorry. I just wanted to escape..." I say, feeling like a fucking hypocrite, feeling as weak as my apology. Camden has every right to be angry, they all do. I know I would be if the roles were reversed. "I lost my head..."

"An escape would be going to the fucking cinema, reading a book, *fucking*, Asia. Not taking a walk on the bottom of the goddamn ocean," Camden retorts angrily.

"It was all too much..." I admit.

"When has it not been too fucking much? This is how it is for us."

I hate that he's right, that every day is a fucking fight. Anger bubbles inside me. Not at Camden but at the world, at the unfairness of it all.

"Your mum was murdered because of *me*, Camden," I shout, unable to stop the torrent of guilt from escaping.

"No!" he points his finger at me, his lip trembling. "No. The *King* killed my mum. The fucking King. You do not take the blame for that. No fucking way. Is that what all this is about? I don't blame you, Asia."

And even though his words should be a comfort, they're not.

"Don't you get it, Camden? Pink is going to die because Carmichael is going to run like the fucking coward he is. Crown will return soon, and I'll have no information to give him, sending you and Eastern on a one-way ticket back to prison. Oh, wait, but not before the King decides to kill us all first! I think all of that tops the fucking mountainous shit of hell we've all been through combined," I yell back. We're both panting now and like the sand being washed away by the waves, I feel like my grip on everything is running through my fingers. How can I hold this all together when I can't even keep myself intact?

Camden grits his jaw, nodding. "There she is. There's my girl," he responds, meeting my gaze as relief floods his features. "I need you to be strong, Asia. Don't fucking break. Please don't fucking break."

"Camden…" I plead, because inside my heart does break. For him. For me. "I'm sorry," I whisper, using that word again. That word that is meaningless when all is said and done.

And just like that, his shoulders sag and a hand comes up to cover his face. "I thought you were going to leave me too," he says, his voice crumbling, cracking, the crevice I saw opening yesterday widening.

Dropping Eastern's hand I go to him, pulling Camden into my arms realising something fundamental as I hold his trembling body in my arms. I'm not going anywhere. "It was a mistake, a moment of weakness. I swear to you all, I'm not leaving," I add fiercely, gripping hold of Camden as tightly as he's holding onto me. "Not now, not ever."

"I know that Asia, we *know* that," Eastern says, stepping up behind me and wrapping his arms around my waist. He presses his forehead into the crook of my neck and lets out a long shaky sigh. Sonny and Ford, silent all this time, seem to come around and step close too. Sonny blinks back his shock and wraps his arm around Camden's and Eastern's back on one side whilst Ford flanks the other. They both dip their heads low, hugging us all. We stay like this for a couple of minutes, not saying a word but saying so much. We're no longer five lonely, distrusting people. Now we're a team, a family, one worth fighting for, even if that means fighting the monsters we harbour within ourselves just as much as the ones without.

BACK IN MY ROOM, with clean, dry clothes on, I sit on my bed still reeling. Surrounding me are my boys and Kate. Everyone is up to speed with the latest news and we've gathered together to try and take back some control, to cement our plan.

"Carmichael is leaving tomorrow, so we have to act fast," Ford says, breaking the silence. "It's time we made our move."

"What are you suggesting we do?" Sonny asks, pacing up and down. Of the four boys, he's wearing his agitation on his sleeve. When I glance over at him, he gives me a tight smile and I know that he's finding it hard not to question me about what I almost did. How could we go from making love, our bodies giving true promises to one another one minute and me almost drowning myself the next? I don't have the answers, but I do know that shame still lingers in every pore.

Ford exchanges a look with Camden, a determined set to his jaw. "During dinner tonight Camden and I are going to start a fight. We're going to draw everyone's attention away whilst Sonny steals a laptop for Kate."

"Okay, and where do I come in?" Eastern asks. "Because I sure as fuck ain't going to sit out the chance to lay one on Bram or one of his goons."

"I need you to deal with those arseholes in the spy room. I don't give a shit what you do, but I need their eyes off the cameras. We can handle the rest," Camden chimes in.

Spy room? Are we on the set of Mission Impossible now? I almost laugh, then realise that this *is* mission fucking impossible. Are we really going to be able to pull this off? Then I remember who we are: wily fuckers for the most part *and* determined. Failure isn't an option.

"Okay, I can do that," Eastern agrees.

"Good. Once Sonny's got the laptop, Kate can do her magic," Ford continues, giving her a tiny smile. She grins back, nodding.

"What do you need?" she asks.

"All the cameras out, the floodlights to the sports field off and the back gate into the grounds unlocked. The guards do their rounds on the hour every hour. But between two and two-fifteen am they change shifts. We'll have about fifteen minutes to get the hell out of dodge."

"What then?" I ask. "Even if we manage to get out of the grounds, we're on foot. It won't take them long to pick us up."

"I have transportation arranged," Ford says, flashing me a look.

"You do?"

"Yeah. Grim is on the same wavelength as us. She's sending a car," Ford explains. He glances at Camden, there's more to this than either are letting on right now.

Sonny stops pacing. "She is? And what about the Freed brothers, do *they* know she's helping?"

Ford shakes his head. "When she heard about Camden's mum, she lost her shit. Grim came to see us at the hotel last night whilst Burnside was distracted chatting to Carmichael on the phone. She might be a friend of Hudson's, but she understands our world better than anyone, been immersed in it for a lot longer. She understands what's at stake. So, no, she hasn't told them. We can trust her."

"Fuck!" Sonny grinds out.

"Look, Sonny, I know how you feel about your foster family but there's no way in hell they'd allow us to do this. There's no time left. We have to act now, or Pink is dead, and I know you don't want Asia killing Carmichael any more than I do," Camden grinds out, glancing at me. "Keeping her soul intact is important to me."

"To all of us," Ford adds.

Sonny holds his hands out, shaking them like he's trying to expend some of that restless energy. I watch in fascination as his fingers curl into fists and stretch out again.

"Let me get this straight," he says, looking pointedly at Camden. "You and Ford start a fight at dinner tonight whilst Eastern distracts the security team so that I can steal the laptop, then later Kate shuts down the cameras and we make our escape on foot before getting picked up in a car provided by Grim, yes?"

"That's about the gist of it, yeah," Camden confirms.

"And you think this is going to work?"

Camden's gaze zeros in on Sonny, his topaz eyes mutable like the Mediterranean Sea. Peaceful and enticing one minute, dangerous and tumultuous the next. "It has to. Pink isn't going to die, that much I do know. Can we count on you, Sonny?"

He takes in a deep, shuddering breath, then looks at me. "Yeah, you can count on me. I've got your back," he replies.

No one doubts he has, we're a family now.

SOMEHOW WE ALL make it to our separate classes without tearing someone apart. Better still, I made it to Sally's physiotherapy class without detouring to Mr Carmichael's office and ripping him a new one... or murdering him. Believe me, the thought crossed my mind a thousand times already today and it's not even noon.

Motherfucking bastard.

Fifteen minutes into my lesson with Sally, I realise that she's staring at me with concern and I can feel the deep groove between my eyebrows grow cavernous with the fixed scowl on my face.

"Asia," Sally begins, placing the textbook she'd been holding onto the table in front of her. "Do you want to tell me what's going on in your head, because you've sat for the last five minutes staring out of the window looking like you're about to combust or implode. Neither of which are likely to be pretty, or healthy for that matter."

Or commit murder, I think. Which is definitely not pretty or healthy, particularly for the one getting murdered. "I've got a lot on my mind," I say instead.

She frowns, her pretty eyes concerned. "Is this to do with the news about Mr Carmichael leaving? I have to say, I was shocked when he told us in our staff briefing this morning..." She gets up from behind her desk then perches on the corner of mine. "He's a good man, has done an awful lot for all the kids who've passed through here, but it seems like some personal issues have gotten in the way. I'm gutted, honestly."

"Good man?" I ask, snorting with derision. "Yeah, and I'm Mother Teresa."

Sally crosses her arms over her chest, defensive all of a sudden over the precious Mr Carmichael. Bet she doesn't know he's the fucking Black Sheep and his cowardice means my friend will die. I bet he didn't share *that* piece of information in their morning meeting. I expect her to sing his praises, or at least try to persuade me why she thinks he's so bloody wonderful. She doesn't.

"Nobody's perfect, Asia. We all have our crosses to bear. Mr Carmichael has quite a few."

My head snaps up and my foot stops jiggling with anxiety when I look at her. "What the fuck do you know?" I demand.

Sally sighs. "I know that he's never lied about his past mistakes to any of us. I know that he went to prison for almost killing a man, and I also know that he's helped countless kids to change their path so they can have a future outside of crime. He *is* a good man, Asia, no matter what assumptions you've made about him for leaving like he is."

I laugh. I can't help it. I lean back in my chair and let out a belly laugh that somehow doesn't stop even when the tears start to come.

And they come. They fall heavy and fast down my cheeks in an unexpected torrent. Falling apart in front of my boys, my friends, is one thing. Falling apart in front of a stranger is quite another.

"Asia, it's okay," she starts, resting her hand on my shoulder in a vain attempt to soothe me. I shrug her off and stand abruptly.

"Don't. Don't you dare assume I'm crying for that bastard. I'm not. He's a coward. A fucking coward!" I shout.

Sally stands too, her shock at my outburst obvious. She retreats behind her desk and opens her top drawer pulling out a pack of tissues. I watch her, silently reeling. This is bullshit. I shouldn't be crying. What the fuck is wrong with me? Digging deep, I snatch the proffered tissues and blow my nose loudly, then swipe at my eyes until they're dry.

"Want to talk about it?" she asks gently.

"You're taking over Mr Burnside's role now? Perhaps you think you can fix us like he fucking does?" I say unkindly.

"No. I'm just offering you a non-judgemental ear. Whatever it is you're feeling, it needs to come out. I'm no therapist, but I do know that holding on to the things that are causing you pain isn't healthy. You don't need a degree to know that, just life experience and a little bit of empathy."

I look at her for a long time, then nod my head. "You're right, I do need to share what I'm feeling and right now the only person who needs to hear my shit is the man who's causing it."

With that, I turn on my heels and stride from her classroom with the intent to go fuck something up. Specifically, Mr Carmichael's face.

THIRTY

W hen I barge into Mr Carmichael's office, the door almost falling off its hinges from the force of my anger, Sally is behind me apologising on my behalf. I hadn't even realised she'd followed me and frankly I don't even care. She can fuck off if she thinks I'm going back to lessons with her, no matter how nice she seems.

"I'm sorry, Mr Carmichael, Asia is very upset this morning."

"Very upset?" I respond sarcastically. "That's putting it mildly. I'm fucking *murderous*."

Mr Carmichael doesn't even flinch and that only serves to piss me off more. How dare he be so unaffected by my anger, by my threat.

"It's okay, Sally. I wanted to speak with Asia before I left anyway."

I make a kind of strangled noise, a cross between a sneer and a laugh. "I bet you fucking do. This should be good," I respond, crossing my arms and narrowing my eyes at him.

"Are you sure? I could stay if that would help?" Sally offers kindly. That only pisses me off further. On a better day, I might've warmed to her some more. Today is not that day.

"No!" I snap at the same time as Mr Carmichael. Though, his no is peppered with an appreciative, if not withering smile. I mean, really, this guy fucked up someone so bad they were left disabled. I am *not* the biggest monster in this room.

"Okay, if you're sure," she responds, stepping back quietly and closing the door behind her.

Mr Carmichael waits a few more seconds before gently placing the pen he's holding onto the table and turns to face me. "Do you want to sit?" he asks.

"Do I want to fucking sit? No, Carmichael, I want to fucking *kill* you!" I snap, clenching my fists until my nails dig painfully into the palms of my hands.

He just regards me with this maddeningly calm expression that tells me two things. One, he doesn't believe that I would actually kill him, and two, he's been waiting for me to come and see him all morning. He's had time to prepare for my wrath, to control his emotions.

I, however, am brimming with *everything*.

"That would work for the King, I guess," he says eventually. "What are you going to do, Asia, murder me with your bare hands or stab me in the eye with my pen? I think the second option is better, but only if you're quick enough. You might be a good fighter, but I'm a better one. I wasn't always the principal of a school, but you know that already."

His response and his conviction knock the wind out of my sails, and I find myself slamming down into the chair behind me. "At least I would've *tried* to save Pink's life, even if you beat me in a fight. At least I could say I fucking tried. You, you're just a spineless, lying, piece of shit," I snarl, wishing looks could kill because with mine now, he'd be dead a thousand times over and Pink would be free.

"You believe what you need to believe. I know what I am, who I am," he counters.

"Yeah, you're a *baaaaa-baaaaa*," I mock, imitating a sheep. Childish, yes, but right now I don't give a fuck.

"Nice one. It's been a while since someone has had the balls to goad me like that. But you're quite right, I *am* the Black Sheep. I'm the one who tried to get away. But like all things you run from, they catch up with you in the end. You, of all people, should understand that."

"You're not even trying to deny who you are then?"

"The King and I are familiar, yes."

"And?"

"And what? That's my cross to bear."

"Who were you?" I persist. "The King's second hand, his third? Were you part of his inner circle or just some kid who did a few jobs for him like Eastern? Maybe you had a bit more responsibility like Camden?"

"Does it really matter? I was someone I didn't want to be. I tried to get away from that life a long time ago, long before my younger brother was murdered. I've been running ever since."

But that's as far as his explanation goes. Not that I care. The fact is, he was part of the King's crew and like Eastern said, death is the only way to escape. Everyone knows that.

You see, *death* is either a blessed escape or a journey into hell, but dead? Dead is the cold, staring eyes of Camden's mum.

She's dead and Mr Carmichael is very much alive.

"Pink is going to die, isn't she?" I blurt out suddenly. The absolute truth of that statement hits me hard and I double over in pain. My hands cover my face and I have to bite the flesh of my palms to stop myself from screaming.

"Camden's mum was a warning, but she became disposable. All the King's women are, at one point or another. A sad inevitability. Pink still has value," he insists.

"Pink only has value when I have you to bargain with. You leave, she's dead."

Mr Carmichael gets up, traversing his table and stooping before me. It occurs to me that this is a perfect opportunity for me to save my friend. I could kill him. Right now. I could try and do it. Yet, I don't.

I fucking let him talk.

"How do you know the King wants me dead? Did he say specifically he wanted you to kill *me*?"

"You're the Black Sheep. I read the fucking note. It's obvious."

"I guess it is," he says, giving me an intense look.

"*There's only one way out. I'll see you in Hell.*' Does that ring any fucking bells?"

"Yes, sadly, it does."

"Then you must know that you're the one with a target on your back? You must've really pissed him off. Was the person you put in a wheelchair someone close to him?"

"Being close to someone implies feelings are involved. The King doesn't feel, Asia. He has no heart, or if he does it's as black as fucking night." Mr Carmichael stands suddenly, backing off. "I'm sorry I couldn't protect you from him. This is the only way."

"For you, this is the only way for *you*. Well, fuck you, Mr Carmichael! You're a goddam coward and a fucking liar."

He just nods tightly, not disagreeing.

"You told me once that protecting someone who's wronged you isn't brave, it's cowardly. What you're doing now, *that* is cowardly. I should kill you."

"But you won't…"

I flinch as though he's struck me. Of all the things he's said, those three words hurt the most. They cut to the bone because deep down inside I know it's fucking true and that, *that* is why Pink will die because I can't do it.

"Does Mr Burnside know how weak his husband is? Does he know that you'd rather run than stay and fight? Does he know who you *truly* are? Can he see what I see?" I press, spitting out my hate with as much passion as I can muster.

At least this time Mr Carmichael flinches. Isn't that what the King said? According to him, love makes you weak. Anthony is his weakness.

"He knows some things, but not everything. It's safer that way," Mr Carmichael responds tightly. "I've asked Anthony to stay on at Oceanside. He loves his job. He wants to continue to help even when I can't..."

"When you *can't*?" I snort. "Don't you mean when you *won't*?"

Mr Carmichael sits back down, folding his arms across his chest. "Anthony will work with Cal and the staff to keep this place running until they find a suitable replacement," he continues, ignoring my accusation completely.

"And you're letting him stay knowing the King is after you, knowing he could just as easily kidnap Mr Burnside and threaten his life too? Are you fucking kidding me?"

"With all the new security he's much safer here than with me."

"You make me *sick*!" I spit.

"What do you want from me, Asia?"

It's a rhetorical question, and one in which he doesn't expect an answer though I give him one anyway. My eyes narrow into slits as he looks at me with stone cold silence. He's shut down. Closed himself off to any kind of obligation or feeling. Whoever he was before when he took revenge for his brother's death, he sure as fuck ain't him now. I give him one last disdainful look then get up from my seat. When I reach the door I turn to face him, making sure that my gaze trails up his body slowly as I sneer at him.

"From you I want nothing, absolutely nothing."

We don't need him. We don't need any of them.

Tonight *my* crew, *my* family are taking matters into our own hands.

We're going to rescue Pink or die trying.

THIRTY-ONE

My body thrums with anxiety as Ford, Camden, Kate and I sit at the dining table with our food left untouched. Sonny has already feigned illness and as far as everyone is concerned, he's in his room dealing with a sudden onset of 'man-flu'. Eastern is making his way to the surveillance room as we speak, having wolfed down his dinner and then excusing himself to 'check on Sonny' loud enough for everyone to hear.

In front of me Ford looks at his watch, waiting for the long hand to fall on a quarter to the hour. Shit is going down in less than five minutes.

If we fuck this up, Pink is dead.

There's no room for error. Sonny has to get hold of a laptop for Kate and we have to break out of Oceanside tonight and get to Pink. If we manage to pull this off, then the next stop is the palace and facing Monk and the King.

Camden reaches for me, his hand finding my bouncing knee. He rests it against my leg, squeezing gently, forcing me to stop moving. "Breathe, Asia. You're giving yourself away."

"This needs to happen soon," I reply under my breath, noticing how everyone has almost finished their food and are preparing to head out.

On the other side of the dining hall are Bram and his crew. They're laughing loudly at something, seemingly without a care in the world. I grit my jaw.

Ford looks at me, his grey-green eyes filled with determination. "Eastern should be dealing with the surveillance team right about now…" his voice trails off as one of the two guards, who normally watches over us all as we eat, mutters something into his walkie-talkie then runs out of the room. "Looks like it's a go," Ford says, nodding once to Camden who turns to Kate.

"I know you can fight, Kate, but I want you to head out when shit kicks off. I don't need you with a concussion today, okay?"

"You got it," she agrees, looking relieved frankly. I don't blame her. This is going to get nasty and fast. Cal might have managed to make us behave with all the security guards, the cameras and the controlled fights in the ring, but none of that can dampen the bubbling violence that's been caged within us all. This fight was coming. Tomorrow, a week from now. It doesn't matter, it was always going to happen.

"We all have our roles to play. Let's get this done," Camden says, getting to his feet.

He gives me one last lingering look before striding over to Bram's table. His shoulders are taut, his long-sleeved t-shirt tight across the wide expanse of muscle. Despite the pain he must be feeling, he holds his spine straight, his head high and fists clenched. Everything about him right now screams danger. In this moment, whatever he feels inside is pushed down and tucked safely away so that he can be the man they all once feared.

Camden, leader of the Hackney Hackers. Violent, brutal, fearless.

My fallen leader steps up one more time to show everyone just what he's made of.

Ford glances at me, presses his lips into a hard line. "When the time comes, you need to stop him from taking this one step too far. Can you do that?"

"I can do that," I nod tightly, understanding what Ford isn't explicit in saying. Camden is in the frame of mind to commit murder. We can all sense it.

"Thank you." He turns away from me, then hesitates. When he turns back, his eyes flash with emotion. It's so powerful and unexpected that it takes my breath away. "Don't do anything stupid. *We need you…* I need you," he admits, the tiniest bit of vulnerability piercing through the steel core that is Ford.

"I won't," I reassure him, knowing he's talking about this morning and not what's about to go down. The guilt I feel is still raw, but now isn't the time to address it with Ford, with any of my boys. When this is over, we'll talk about it then. That's if we survive what's to come, of course. He reaches for my hand, grasping it in his, the rough skin of his palm warm. He seems to decide something and when his mouth pops open, I wait patiently for whatever he has to say.

"I need you to know something just in case I wasn't clear when we slept together…" He swallows hard, and we're both acutely aware of the tension filling the room. Behind us Camden is talking in barely veiled anger to Bram. Fortunately for us, everyone's attention is on them. "I thought I was incapable of feeling, Asia. I thought I could never love another person after my parents stripped me of my humanity. Now I know I can. That's because of you." His fingers tighten around my hand. "Do you understand me?" he asks.

I want to hear the words, just to be certain, but I know that they're too precious to be shared with others looking on. So, I don't ask him to say them. Instead, I nod my head.

"I do," I respond.

With one last lingering look, Ford spins on his heel and strides over to Camden's side.

"Fuuuuuck!" Kate exclaims, reminding me that she's still sitting at our table behind me. Her expression is a cross between awe and wonder.

"My feelings exactly," I respond, a little breathlessly.

Half a minute later, Camden leans over and grips Bram by the throat.

A second after that the room erupts into chaos.

Fists fly, kids bray in anger, the kitchen staff scream, and the one and only security guard tries and fails to break up the fight.

Like the ripple on a pond, the fight spreads outwards from the centre. All the rules and regulations we've had to live by recently fly out the window as the need to fight spreads. Violence catches on like a flame, leaping from one kid to another. Over the other side of the dining hall Camden is pummelling Bram who is playing dirty, having grabbed a knife from the table and jabbing it towards him. Thank god Camden is used to dirty fighting, because he disarms him quickly enough, the knife clatters to the floor, and Bram receives a powerful punch to his lip for the trouble. Good.

Beside him, Ford is fighting three different kids, all of them Monk's wolves. Dagger appears to be the most evenly matched, although I have no doubt Ford would be able to outfight him if there weren't two other bastards going for him at the same time.

"Fuck, Asia, this is insane," Kate mutters, ducking as a plate comes hurtling towards her. When I whirl around, Diamond, Emerald and Red are smiling evilly. I can see the intent written plainly on their faces. For all of a minute we've avoided the ever-increasing brawl, but now it's reached us, the metaphorical bubble is about to burst.

"Get the fuck out of here, Kate," I demand, shoving her away from me.

"I'll stay and fight." She holds her fists up in front of her face in a defensive stance.

"The fuck you will. You heard what Camden said. GO!" I shout. "I can deal with these bitches."

"Asia…"

"GO!"

She nods once, then runs.

I don't get time to see whether she makes it out of the dining hall because Red's fist is flying towards my face. I spin away, twisting on my foot and turn in a full circle bringing my right fist up. It meets her jaw with a sickening thud. Red wobbles on her feet and I kick out, my foot landing in her stomach, not giving her a moment to recover from the punch.

This isn't some controlled fight in the ring with Cal supervising. We've reverted back to our roots. We're street kids, with street rules, and we fight until one of us can't fight anymore.

Red doubles over, stumbling back into Diamond who happens to be standing behind her.

Emerald, who managed to sidestep in time, snarls. "You evil bitch!"

I laugh, the sound abnormal, unhinged even.

"Me, *evil*? You don't know the half of it," I counter, painfully aware that the King's blood runs through my veins. It's nature vs nurture. I always assumed I am the way I am because I had a shitty mum, a crappy childhood and got into trouble at the drop of a hat. Given my lineage I'm not sure I know the answer anymore.

Emerald hesitates, proving to me that she knows all about my father. But a dark smile pulls up her lips and she comes for me anyway. This tells me something important. Either she's not afraid of the King (which I find highly unlikely) or he's given them all permission to fuck me up. I'm thinking the latter. My hate for him grows to exponential levels.

Fuck him. Fuck him. *Fuck* him!

I glance quickly over at Camden and Ford who are in the thick of a huge brawl. I can't tell if they're winning or not, given there's so many of them. My gaze flicks back to Emerald, my eyes narrowing. "Sure you want to pick a fight with me, bitch?"

"Oh, I've been wanting this for a while now, Asia. You're nothing but a bastard child of a whore," she counters, her lip curling over her pretty white teeth before she punches me hard on my arm.

The punch barely registers beneath my rage at her belittling someone I love.

No one disses my mum.

No. Fucking. One.

I punch her so hard that her two front teeth fly out of her mouth alongside a spurt of crimson blood, ruining that pretty little mouth of hers. She screams, clutching her face as she backs off. Red screams in rage coming for me again. I act fast, not willing to let her get a hit in. Launching forwards, I punch her repeatedly until she's nothing but a quivering heap on the floor. When I turn for Diamond, ready to take her out too, all I see is the back of her chicken-shit arse as she runs from the room and barrels into Cal and Mr Burnside.

For a moment they stand and stare in shock. Behind them, Mr Carmichael enters flanked by two guards. My nostrils flare and my heart thunders inside my chest when I catch his eye.

Around me tables are being turned over, plates and bowls are being used as missiles, smashing against the walls and the floors as we descend into brutal violence.

Fists and feet hit their mark.

Blood splatters mixing with sweat and spit.

Kids grunt and roar.

Teeth gnash and bite.

It's a fucking colossal, violent mess of limbs and arms and *blood*.

In the midst of it all, Mr Carmichael and I stare at one another over the battling crews. He doesn't shout. He doesn't throw curses across the room. He doesn't even move off into the crowd immediately like Cal, Mr Burnside and the rest of the guards who followed them in, do. No, Mr Carmichael stares directly at me and only me. After a beat, respect fills his gaze.

"That's my girl," he mouths.

What the fuck? That's my girl?

I don't get a chance to contemplate what that's supposed to mean, because Ford calling my name has my immediate attention.

"ASIA!" he roars.

Spinning on my feet, I can see Ford struggling to hold Camden back from Bram who is currently backed up against the self-service station holding onto his bicep, blood pouring through the gaps between his fingers.

Towering above him, Ford and Camden are both bleeding from cuts on their faces, bruises already blooming. Camden tries to shake Ford off, but Ford has him in a tight grip. Which is just as well, given the murderous look on Camden's face.

"Asia!" Ford shouts again as Camden struggles in his hold. My attention is drawn to the knife in Camden's hand. It drips crimson blood, stark against the wooden floor.

"Stand up and fight, you motherfucking bastard!" Camden roars, trying to throw Ford off. I see the rage splitting his heart open as he tries to free himself from Ford's grip.

"Fuck!" I shout, snapping into action.

Pushing through the crowd, ducking and diving between the chaos, I reach Camden. Only it isn't him. The Camden I know isn't there within the topaz depths of his eyes. They're empty. Beautiful, but empty. An endless ocean with absolutely no life within it.

"Camden," I hush out, reaching for his hand that's holding the knife. "Camden, drop the knife." I'm fully aware I have my back to Bram, that I'm putting myself in a vulnerable position. It wouldn't take much for him to hurt me. There are enough pieces of broken glass covering the floor that he could use to do some serious damage. But I don't think about that. I only think about Camden and the boy I so desperately need to return to me.

He's panting hard, his face swelling, his lip and eyebrow bleeding, and despite me calling his name, he looks right through me. Behind him Ford grits his teeth, holding Camden's arms back, unable to disarm him without letting Camden go. If he does that, Bram's dead. We both know that.

"Get the knife, Asia," Ford barks out.

I reach for him, ignoring Bram's groans of pain, ignoring the chaos around us. My fingers tremble as they wrap around his wrist. I try to pry his fingers apart, but he's determined and won't drop the damn knife.

"You need to take it from him!"

"I'm trying!" I retort, pulling at Camden's fingers but failing. I know from experience that when this kind of rage takes over, people get almost superhuman strength. I need to resort to desperate measures.

"I'm sorry, Camden," I apologise, before simultaneously digging my thumbnail into the pulse point of Camden's wrist and biting him hard enough on the shoulder to draw blood.

It works.

Camden drops the knife and I kick it away, out of reach.

A second or two later, a loud piercing noise fills the air and we all have to cover our ears for fear that they might actually bleed. It has the desired effect. Everyone stops fighting long enough to protect their eardrums from bursting. When the ringing stops and we can all straighten up, the violent energy has slipped away as quickly as it arrived.

"One more person raising a fist will get tasered!" Cal shouts, nodding to the guards who are now moving about the room, each holding out the offensive weapon. "I've been tasered once in my life and believe me, pissing your pants is the least of your worries."

Cal steps down from the table. In his hands are a megaphone and a smaller, more compact object. It looks like a rape alarm. So that's where the goddamn awful noise was coming from. A rape alarm is piercingly loud at the best of times. Use a megaphone to make that noise louder and eardrums will bleed.

"Just give us one more excuse and 50,000 volts will be pumped into your body," he warns us all. No one moves.

I've never been tasered but that doesn't mean to say I want to risk it. Fuck that. I just hope Sonny had enough time to steal the laptop. When Eastern enters the dining room a minute later with his hands cuffed behind his back by Frank, I hope we've done enough. His eyes widen as he takes in the chaos but like always, he seems to sense me in the mass of people. When he spots us, relief floods his face; he gives me a quick, sharp nod and I know the job is done.

Come hell or high water, we're getting out of Oceanside tonight.

THIRTY-TWO

I don't get to speak with the boys or Kate. One by one, we're taken into Cal's office to be questioned about what happened. I'm the last to be interviewed, and by interviewed I mean grilled, talked down to. The usual.

"What the fuck were you thinking?" Cal asks me, his eyebrows drawn together in a scowl.

"What was *I* thinking?" I roll my eyes, playing dumb, and rub absentmindedly at the bruise blooming on my arm, courtesy of Emerald who managed to get a jab in before I knocked her two front teeth out.

"Yeah. Tell me why you thought it was a good idea to get into a fight?"

"I didn't get into anything. The witches of East Hackney came at *me*," I remind him for what seems like the fiftieth time.

"Red is nursing a sore head and Emerald has lost her front teeth, Asia."

"And what? I should have just stood there and let them fuck me up?"

He sighs, scraping a hand over his face. On his desk his mobile phone lights up with a new message which only makes him scowl.

"What?" I ask, knowing I've no right to pry.

"Nisha, my wife, is a little upset with me," he explains, surprising me.

"Why is that?"

"Because I've taken on the role of interim principal of this school, that's why, and she's not happy about it. I've already been here long enough according to her."

"You're going to be acting principal…?"

"Looks that way, so I could really do with you all not fucking up so much."

"I told you. They came at me."

"And what about Camden? Did Bram start on him because according to the CCTV footage I'm pretty sure Camden grabbing Bram by the throat was the move that started all this bullshit."

"I guess he did, but can you blame him after what happened to his mum? You and I both know that it was only a matter of time before he lost his shit. This is what happens when you don't fucking act!" I respond, my voice rising.

"There's been thousands of pounds worth of damage. Some kids have been seriously hurt today. I don't know if I can prevent the authorities from coming here and shutting this place down," he replies, ignoring the point I'm making.

"You think I give a shit about that? The *only* people I care about here are my boys, Kate and Pink. This place being shut down won't change the fact that Pink is going to die. How are you going to fucking explain *that* away?"

"She's not going to die."

"What, are *you* going to save her?"

Cal presses his mouth into a hard line.

"No, I didn't think so."

"You confronted Mr Carmichael," he says instead.

"Yes, I fucking confronted him. He's running, Cal. Please don't tell me you're okay with that. Maybe you are, given you seem to be doing jack shit to stop him."

Cal leans forward on his desk, ignoring the second text that lights up his mobile phone. He turns it face down. "We're not doing jack shit. *Trust us.*"

"Trust you?" I counter, laughing bitterly. "Trusting you got Camden's mum killed. Trusting you has led to Carmichael walking and *that* means Pink dies. Does that just about sum this pile of steaming shit up?" Cal grits his jaw but doesn't respond. He knows as well as I do that I'm right. "Yeah, that's what I thought. What's another kid's life when all is said and done?" I spit, standing.

He's not given me permission to leave, but he doesn't try to stop me either.

It's probably the smartest decision he's made yet.

I DON'T SLEEP. Instead, I use my time to pack my rucksack and chain smoke twenty cigarettes trying not to mull over what Carmichael mouthed to me in the dining hall when everyone else was busy tearing each other to shreds.

"That's my girl."

Overfamiliar much? Maybe I just misread what he'd said. It's possible, I suppose, given the situation. Besides, we all know who my father is, and it isn't the gay, soon to be ex-principal of Oceanside Academy. Pushing those thoughts away, I check the time on my digital alarm clock situated by my bed. It's 2 am.

With my ear pressed to my bedroom door, I wait for the gentle tap as discussed. It comes at exactly 2.05am. I open the door as quietly as possible. Camden is standing on the threshold. He raises his finger to his swollen lip, and points along the corridor. I peer around the door frame and see the rest of my crew standing at the door that leads to the stairwell downstairs. Swinging my rucksack onto my back, I follow Camden.

When we reach them, Sonny pushes the door open, it creaks slightly, and we all wince from the sound. Kate gives me a scared look, so I try to muster up a reassuring smile. I'm pretty sure it comes out more of a grimace though. She puffs out her cheeks, shoving the stolen laptop into her rucksack and swinging it onto her back.

When Sonny's assured that we're safe to move, he ushers us through the doors. We all file after him. Me first, then Kate, Eastern is followed by Ford with Camden taking up the rear. We take the stairs as quickly and as quietly as we can. When we reach the ground floor, there's only a small stretch of hallway and a back door between freedom and being caught.

"Are you sure all the cameras are out?" Camden asks Kate.

"Not out as that would raise suspicion quicker, just set on a loop. We need to go now before the guards change over and the men in the surveillance room realise the same guards keep walking beneath the cameras over and over again."

Eastern grins, then whispers quietly. "You're pretty fucking impressive, you know that, right?"

Kate smiles. "So I've been told."

Ford holds his hand up, instantly quieting us all. I hear a door open and close then Cal's voice. He's talking to the guards who are about to finish their shift for the night, thanking them for their help today. We wait for a couple of minutes, our backs against the wall as they pass by on the other side of the stairwell door. When we hear the sound of a car pulling away, we make our move.

"We need to go," Camden hisses.

None of us need to be told twice.

Getting out of the annex building is easy but traversing the main building and heading out onto the field leaves us wide open. Running is about the only thing we can do. So we leg it as fast as we can around the side of the building and onto the sports field. Fortunately for us, once we hit the track that circles the field, it's pitch-black. The floodlights that surround the field are out too, thanks to Kate's wicked hacker ability. The sensors don't switch on and we make it over the field without tripping the lights. When this is all over, I need to do something epic to thank her. I'm not sure what, but I'll figure that out because even though I'm fully aware that things might go terribly wrong, I also know that I will do everything I can to make sure we win.

Because losing isn't an option.

When we reach the service entrance and the large wrought iron gates at the back of the grounds, I have a moment of panic when I don't see a car. That panic is short lived when I see the end of a cigarette butt light up just beyond the gates.

"Malakai?" Ford hushes out, peering into the darkness.

"The one and only," a gruff voice responds, then a shadowy shape moves in the darkness. "Hurry up, we haven't got much time."

Eastern tests the gate, it opens with a small click. He high fives Kate and we all pile through.

Out of the darkness Malakai appears, dressed head to foot in black. He's huge, like a proper *brick shit house* big with wide shoulders and thick arms and thighs. He's tall too, at least six foot five and good looking, if you like your men pushing forty.

"Quit staring and get in the damn car," Malakai snaps, scowling at me.

Camden looks at me and narrows his eyes. Jealous much?

"I wasn't," I shrug, trying not to let out a nervous laugh at the ridiculousness of the situation.

Malakai has dark hair and dark eyes and a chin so chiselled I could cut my hand on it. Pretty sure I can see a black tribal tattoo winding up the side of his neck too. I'm impressed. This man oozes danger. I'm not surprised Grim is friends with him. I'm betting he's spent time in Grim's fight club. When Ford nods tightly, and a look passes between them, it's obvious they've met before.

Malakai reaches for something in his jacket pocket and I can feel Sonny tense beside me. When he pulls out a car key and presses a button on the fob causing a car's interior lights to turn on, Sonny visibly relaxes. He's on edge, just like the rest of us.

"Get in the damn car," Malakai repeats.

Ford and Camden scowl, but they're wise enough not to get in an argument with our getaway driver. Better to put up with a bit of attitude than give him a reason to leave without us. So, we all pile into the eight-seater. Ford sits up front next to Malakai, given he's the most familiar with him. Camden, Kate and I take the middle seats whilst Eastern and Sonny sit in the back. As getaway cars go, it's a pretty sweet ride with leather seats and a sleek interior. It's a BMW according to the logo on the steering wheel. This Malakai has money, that's for sure. Either that or he's borrowed the car from Grim and we all know she's loaded. Running an underground fight club is lucrative, it would seem.

"Buckle-up, kids. I need to get you to the boat before the storm hits."

"Storm?"

"Boat?" Camden and Eastern say simultaneously.

I look over my shoulder at Eastern who grimaces. He hates boats, or rather the water boats float upon. A trip on the River Thames when we were ten had him chucking up his guts. Tracy said it was motion sickness, though he's never had a problem with any other form of transportation.

"You've got to be kidding me," Eastern mutters.

"To get across to the island you need to go by boat. There's no road connected to the mainland. But if we don't get to my schooner before the storm is due to hit, we're not going anywhere."

"What's a fucking schooner?" Camden mutters, glancing over at me.

"I don't know," I retort. "Sounds like a fashion label to me."

"A schooner is a *sailboat*. I'm the captain," Malakai explains, putting the car into drive and doing a smooth 180-degree turn.

I snort with laughter. With his silver rings, pierced ear and tattoos, he's a modern-day pirate if ever I saw one and not some posh, clean-shaven captain. "Grim really does know a lot of interesting people," I say under my breath.

"Grim *is* an interesting person," Ford counters, hearing me.

"You all need to shut the hell up so I can concentrate," Malakai snaps as he pulls out from the service road and onto the main one. "Keep your mouths shut and your eyes peeled. Just because we've made it this far doesn't mean we're not being followed. I owe Grim a debt, and she's called it in. If I don't get you on that island then I'm still indebted to her, and I don't like to owe anyone a goddamn thing."

"Then I guess we'll shut the fuck up because we need to get on that island," I retort, meeting Malakai's gaze in the rear-view mirror. He nods his head. Ten minutes later and going 80mph down the motorway it becomes clear we made it out of Oceanside without getting caught.

For now.

THIRTY-THREE

We arrive on the island a little after 5am just as the first tendrils of light are brightening the sky. The crossing was rough and Eastern suffered. In fact, Sonny and Kate didn't fare well either. Me, Ford and Camden, alongside our illustrious captain, have stomachs made of steel, clearly. Though if I'm honest, there's nothing quite like feeling alive when a storm's raging around you. I've always loved a good storm. I was born during one, after all. It's in my blood.

"We were lucky," Malakai shouts over the roaring wind as he secures the boat to the dock. "The storm is set to worsen before it gets better. It'll hang around for at least the next 12 hours. There'll be no crossings to or from the island until tomorrow morning at least. It could move along quicker, or it might stay longer. We'll see.

"Lucky?" Eastern groans, heaving for the hundredth time since we got on the boat a little over an hour ago. "Just get me off this fucking thing."

Reaching for him and trying to steady myself against the raging wind and undulating water beneath us, I help him climb down off the boat. When his feet hit the dock he flat out lies down, groaning. "Fuck me, I am never getting on a boat ever again."

"As soon as I get Princess secure, we'll head off."

"*Princess?*" Sonny mutters, climbing down onto the deck and bending over next to me. "Fucking *hellion* more like." He sucks in a few ragged breaths as I rub his back. Poor guy.

A shaky, pale-skinned Kate is next to disembark, followed by Ford and Camden. I'm pretty sure she would've joined Eastern lying down on the deck if Camden hadn't wrapped an arm around her shoulder and let her lean into him. She kind of stiffens when I look over at them, but I'm not jealous. Not in the slightest. Camden isn't trying to come onto her, he's merely being a friend, *kind.* I give her a gentle smile, before flicking my gaze to Camden. He stares at me with a fire in his eyes that burns bright, so bright that I have to look away. Nope, he's definitely not interested in Kate.

"Are you doing okay?" Sonny asks me, straightening up and twining his fingers with mine. He's not as green as Eastern, but he's not exactly looking at the peak of health either. Frankly, we all look more than a little dishevelled. Ford and Camden are sporting cuts and bruises from the brawl last night and the rest of us are windblown and either green with sea sickness or pale with worry. The only person who is unaffected is Malakai. I don't know him at all, but I know that he was born to live on the sea. There's a kind of wildness about him that matches the storm that whips around us all. I mean, we're all a little wild, but Malakai's wildness is a different kind to my boys. Theirs is born from necessity, fighting to live, to survive. Malakai's, like mine, is ingrained in his very soul, his DNA.

"I'm cold and hungry, but that's nothing," I respond, allowing Sonny to wrap me in his arms and pull me into his chest momentarily. But getting warm and eating aren't really an option right now. We have a friend to rescue. I reluctantly step out of Sonny's arms and approach

Malakai. He's securing the boat, his large hands and fingers surprisingly nimble. He ties off a complicated-looking knot, then straightens.

"Grab that." He points to another length of rope. My hands are stiff with cold and I can barely get a secure hold on the thick girth when Ford bends down beside me and has grabbed the rope, handing it to Malakai who nods his thanks and secures that rope too. I wait until he's finished before I blurt out my most pressing question.

"How do we get to the palace?" I ask.

Wind whips my hair about my face, tiny little lashes pricking at my skin. The harbour is empty bar a couple of fishermen who are giving us strange looks. It's not every day a bunch of ragtag kids like us step onto their dock, I suppose. Above us thunder rumbles so loudly that Kate jumps. She lets out a nervous laugh when a second later lightning rips through the sky. Then the heavens open. Within seconds, we're drenched.

"We're not going there right now," Malakai responds, grabbing a bag from the dock and slinging it on his shoulder. He seems oblivious to the rain and my anger.

"What the fuck do you mean, we're not going there now?" Camden growls.

"Ma Silva is expecting us," Malakai shouts over the roaring wind, water running in rivulets over his face. Kate is desperately trying to tuck her backpack under her coat in a vain attempt to protect the stolen laptop.

"What? No way! We need to get to our friend, right fucking now!"

"Not until tonight you don't," Malakai retorts, looming over me now. I have to crane my head back to look up at him. The guy's a fucking giant. Not that I can see him very clearly, given my hair is now successfully plastered to my face.

"Tonight is hours away. She hasn't got that long. We came here to rescue Pink and that's what we're going to do, with or without your help," I bark, swiping at the wet tendrils covering my face. Malakai gives me a look that tells me he's not a man to mess with. Another time I might've backed off. Not today. "Grim must've told you about the danger she's in? We're not fucking waiting for you to get your shit together."

"Listen, you'll do what the hell *I* say when *I* say it. We have one window of opportunity to get into the King's palace and that isn't happening until 7pm tonight. Got it?"

"That's hours away!" I shout back, blood pumping in my veins as more lightning cracks overhead.

"You think I don't have a plan or a reason for leaving it until then to make our move? I've been doing this shit a long fucking time and I'm telling you, we don't do anything until tonight. The storm will keep anyone from arriving or leaving and according to Ma Silva your friend…"

"Pink," I snap.

"Your friend *Pink* is alive, but she won't stay that way if you and your friends here make any rash decisions. Understand? For the time being you keep your heads down at Ma's place."

Behind me, Ford steps close and rests his hand on my arm. "Listen to Malakai, he knows what he's talking about."

"Does he, or is he just another fucking fool that pretends he does?" I growl back. "I'm kinda done with trusting people."

Malakai raises a brow. "You've got a lot to learn, kid," he says, before striding off along the dock leaving me glaring after him. A lot to learn about what? Him? I have no desire to learn anything about the dude.

By the time we reach Ma Silva's cottage, which is another fifteen minutes' walk in the freezing rain and lashing wind, I'm cold to the very marrow of my bones. I don't think much of the place. The island is depressing at best and goddamn brutal at worst. There are no convenience stores that I've noticed on our torturous walk, barely any streetlights and a lot of fucking cows and fields. Even though dawn is rising, it may as well still be midnight given the ominous, thick black clouds and torrential rain.

Malakai bangs on the door of a large secluded farmhouse set back off the main road by a long winding path. We all stand shivering behind him. My teeth are chattering so hard that I'm pretty sure I'm going to chip a few if we don't get inside the warmth soon. At least, I hope it's fucking warm. The outside of the place looks as dilapidated as the rest of the island. I mean, really, who the fuck wants to live here? It's too cut off from the world and as harsh as the streets of Hackney, just in a different way. The door swings open and I'm surprised to find that Ma Silva isn't some grey, wizened old biddy, but a young woman only a few years older than me I'd guess. I catch the look of surprise on Kate's face between the hood of her coat pulled low over her head and the scarf wrapped around her mouth. She was expecting someone much, much older too.

"Why are *you* here?" is all Malakai says in greeting, if you can call it that. What a rude arsehole.

"Nice to see you too, Malakai," the girl responds, seemingly unbothered by his attitude. She steps wide, opening the door for us. Malakai storms past, practically knocking the poor girl off her feet. But she just smiles.

"Don't mind him, he's an arsehole," she says, grinning when Malakai makes a kind of rumbling, growly noise. Talk about a bear with a sore head.

"Couldn't have put it better myself," Eastern mutters, giving her a weak smile.

"Bad crossing?" she asks as we all pile into the surprisingly warm cottage.

"It was hell," Sonny agrees, pulling off his baseball cap and holding his hand out to shake. "My name's Sonny, thanks for having us here, Ma Silva."

The girl's mouth pops open and she tips her head back and laughs. "Oh my god, I've never, *ever*, been mistaken for my grandmother. Mum maybe, but Grandma? Nope. Priceless." She swipes her hands over her face and grins, her pretty blue eyes flashing with mirth. "I'm *Connie*. If you hadn't already guessed, Ma Silva is my grandmother and right now she's got a headache. This time from a cold and not from the three glasses of port she usually knocks back every night."

Connie closes the front door, successfully shutting out the weather and motions for us all to follow her into a spacious kitchen with an open fire. It has a large, worn-looking wooden dining table in the centre and not much for mod cons, but it's homely. There are shells dotted about everywhere. Large ones, small ones, little pearlescent beauties all glimmering in the firelight. Someone in this house clearly collects them. On the windowsill behind the sink is a large conch shell and my heart squeezes. It reminds me of my little brothers. They'd love it.

As my boys and Kate enter the kitchen, filling up the space, I can't help but notice how Malakai watches Connie from his spot by the kitchen sink. He looks mighty pissed-off, his big, hulking frame and mean glare a little intimidating if I'm being honest. Though she seems oblivious.

"I thought you were on the mainland?" he asks, ignoring us all completely, his attention well and truly focused on the very pretty, very curvy Connie. If I was gay, she'd totally be my type. She's all soft skin, pouty lips, dark wavy hair, deep blue eyes with big tits and arse that's balanced out nicely with a flat tummy and strong muscular legs all encased in a jean and t-shirt combo. She doesn't have a scrap of make-up on and is still incredibly beautiful. Basically she's a sex bomb and the complete and utter opposite to me. I'm wiry, edgy, I suppose. Less curvaceous for sure.

"I caught the last ferry home yesterday evening. Grandma needed me. Like I said, she's feeling a little under the weather. She told me you had to go to Hastings on business. I'm guessing this is the business she was talking about?" she asks, eyeing us all in turn. There's no judgement in her gaze, just curiosity. When she gives us all a warm smile, Malakai scowls at my boys daring them to try and chat her up. Not that they notice his aggression or her beauty, given they're all looking at me.

"What?" I say.

"Your lips, they're blue," Eastern points out, traversing the table and drawing me into his arms, but he's just as cold and wet. We stand there shivering, neither of us having any kind of warmth to give to the other.

"You need to get your clothes *off*," Malakai points out, even though he's looking directly at Connie. Her cheeks flush pink and she snatches her gaze away. What's their deal? Pretty sure he's old enough to be her dad though he certainly isn't looking at her like a father should. "Clothes off," Malakai repeats, this time glaring at me. Connie rolls her eyes, shaking her head.

"What this brute meant to say is, you should go upstairs and change. All of you. I'm pretty sure none of you want to catch pneumonia. There's plenty of room for everyone, just avoid the two rooms at the end of the corridor, they're mine and my Grandma's. I'll serve up some breakfast at 8am, that should give you enough time to get refreshed and warm. There's an en-suite bathroom in the largest room at the top of the stairs and another bathroom second on the right. Help yourself to towels and things..." her voice trails off as we all stare at her like she's grown another head.

"You're just going to let a bunch of strangers enter your house, make themselves comfortable and then cook them breakfast?" Eastern asks incredulously.

"Why wouldn't I?" she shrugs.

"Because you don't know us..." Kate says, her eyebrows pulling together in a frown.

"Well, what can I say? It must be the trusting country bumpkin in me. Either that, or I happen to know Malakai will protect me if any of you get any funny ideas, which you won't, I'm sure." She flashes him a look, and he presses his mouth in a hard line even though his eyes light with possession. Interesting. "We can catch up in a couple hours, okay? Nice to meet you all," she adds, effectively dismissing us.

Malakai coughs, folding his arms across his chest. I can tell he's feeling cold by the slight tremble of his body, but I'm betting he'd never admit to it. Seems like he's the type of dude who has to be all alpha male and domineering. I can even imagine him banging his chest like Tarzan. The thought makes me smirk.

"You okay, Malakai?" Connie asks sweetly, though I see a hint of amusement in her eyes.

"I could do with getting out of these wet clothes too."

Connie nods, eyeing him slowly. "Yes, you could... but, alas, all the rooms are taken. Including *mine*," she adds with a smirk. "You can change in the lounge."

Her dismissal of him has me choking back a laugh, particularly when he looks like he's about to throttle her or maybe... kiss her? I'm not sure, I don't think he is either. She gives him a sweet smile before turning to look at me, winking.

I like her. She's got spunk.

THIRTY-FOUR

W e all pile upstairs. Kate heads further down the hall finding a small box room to get changed in. She stands on the threshold of the room and grimaces.

"Asia might be into sharing…" she laughs awkwardly, her voice trailing off.

"Go ahead," Ford responds, crossing the hallway and pushing open the door to a large room with twin beds. "Us guys can take this room. Asia can have the one with the en-suite."

"No," Camden says, pushing off the wall and swiping a hand over his head. "As much as I like you guys, I need a moment with Asia. I'll share this room with her." He opens the door behind me and walks into the bedroom without a backward glance. He doesn't ask permission or even see if I'm in agreement, he just *does*.

Sonny grins, his beautiful dimples winking at me. "Looks like Camden needs *a moment*," he says chuckling.

"Erm…" I start, looking over my shoulder at Camden who's already pulling off his wet coat and shoes. Well, this isn't awkward much.

Eastern gives me a gentle kiss. "Go get warm," he murmurs against my lips before following Sonny into the bedroom opposite. "I need to lie down anyway. My body still thinks it's on the boat." I watch him as he flops down on one of the twin beds, not even bothering to remove his wet clothes, leaving me standing awkwardly with Ford.

"I..."

"He *needs* you. Go easy on him, okay?" Ford says before entering the bedroom behind Sonny and Eastern, shutting the door with a gentle click.

Well, I guess that's it then. Looks like I'm sharing with Camden.

Along the corridor, Kate peers around her door. She gives me a knowing smile, then whispers, "You might want to be a little quieter this time seeing as there's an old lady sleeping up here. You don't want to be responsible for giving her a heart attack with all the noise."

"Oh, shut up," I retort. If I had something to throw at her, I would.

Entering the room, I can already hear water running and the sound of Camden moving about in the bathroom. There's a trail of wet clothes littering the bedroom floor. I follow them like breadcrumbs, my nerves firing and a sudden onset of guilt making me doubt myself. I know he said he doesn't blame me for his mum's death but that doesn't stop me from feeling responsible.

Dropping my rucksack, and relieving myself of my coat, shoes and socks on the floor, I push open the bathroom door. Despite everything that's happened and everything that's still to come, I know that there are things we need to discuss, and I might not get the chance again. Swallowing my sudden nervousness, I step into the bathroom, shutting the door gently behind me.

Camden is standing completely naked in front of the shower, his hand under the stream of water as he waits for it to heat up. It's a surprisingly large room, and there's a moment when he doesn't realise I'm there. I take the time to soak in all the gloriousness that is this Camden. He's stunning. Strong, powerful, brave, but when he rests his hands against the side of the shower cubicle and drops his head between his shoulders, he's vulnerable. I feel his grief as though it's my own. Swallowing the sudden lump in my throat, I quietly remove my clothes, stripping down completely. If he's willing to bare himself, then I should too.

"Hey," I say gently, padding over to him. He doesn't move, he doesn't look up. He just remains where he is. I reach out to touch him, my hand resting on his shoulder. "Cam…?"

"I'm fucking lost, Asia," he admits, slowly drawing around to face me and even though there are no tears, I feel the heavy weight of his loss. His shoulders sag with it. This moment of reprieve has only given him the opportunity to think and I want to soothe him, heal his hurt. It's a powerful feeling, this need to comfort him.

"Come here."

He walks into my open arms, pressing his forehead onto my shoulder, wincing when his swollen cheek presses against the hollow of my neck.

"I'm so sorry," I whisper against his skin, feeling sick with guilt, with worry, knowing my words are worthless but saying them anyway. My apology tastes bitter on my tongue. Wrong.

Our bodies are pressed up against each other. His skin is as ice cold as mine.

"I don't blame you. *I don't*," he mutters into my hair, his arms tightening around my waist as he draws in a deep breath.

My hands grasp hold of him, my fingers digging into his back. I want to wrap myself around him. I want to climb beneath his skin. I want to take away all of the hurt. I want to share in his pain, ease his burden. Instead, I untangle myself from his hold and pull him under the warm spray of the shower.

There are no words I can say that will stop the pain he's feeling. No words that will bring back his mum, his sister. All I have to share with him is this overwhelming love I feel. Love for a boy whose art I've adored from a distance. Love for this boy who hurt me then healed some of my own pain. The only thing I can give him in return is myself.

He stands before me, allowing the water to run over his skin, allowing me to see right inside the very heart of him as he falls apart a little. He's holding back, I know. Trying to remain strong in the face of such adversity. Even though he doesn't let go entirely, I know that there are depths to his pain that will unravel over time, and I make a pact to shoulder that pain for him. For us both. When it comes, and it will come, I'll be there to bear the brunt of it.

Reaching for the bottle of shower gel, I pour a small amount in my hand then start washing him gently. Starting with his shoulders, I work my fingers over the hard muscle, easing some of the tension there before sliding them down over his pecs. All the while he remains unmoving. He allows me to wash him, to soothe the pain as much as I can. My hands glide over his chest and stomach, each caress peppered with kisses. Tenderness is the only thing I can offer in the moment. I hope it's enough.

"Asia..." his voice breaks when I crouch before him, placing a gentle kiss against his hip bone. I'm aware of his growing erection, and though I want nothing more than to take him in my mouth, I make no attempt to initiate that level of intimacy. His reaction is a physical response to our nakedness and touches, and not necessarily what he can handle mentally right now. I'm not assuming anything. Standing, I swipe away at the water and the tears mingling on his cheeks. My heart hiccups in my chest at the loss he shares and when, eventually, his gaze flicks from my eyes to my mouth and then my breasts, my heart implodes with the desire I see. The need.

"I want you..." He reaches for me, one hand cupping my cheek whilst the other swipes wet tendrils of hair back off my face. "I've waited, but I can't anymore. I want you so much, Asia."

That admission, that hunger, is all it takes to turn the tenderness into something even more powerful. I see it, I *feel* it.

Neither of us voice those three words. For some, they're so easy to share. They fall from other people's lips like a day-to-day greeting, inconsequential almost. *Easy.* But for me, for my boys, they're words that get trapped inside, stuck in our hearts, caged away. You see, when loving someone has only ever let you down, failed you, it's very hard to voice those words for fear that in doing so you open yourself up to a world of pain.

All I can do is show Camden how I feel, just like I did for Eastern, Ford and Sonny.

Camden groans into my mouth, his body pressing against mine as he pushes me up against the tiled wall. I can taste the longing on his lips and the saltiness of his tears on my tongue as I wrap myself around him and kiss him back with everything I have.

The warmth from the spray is no match to the heat rising between us. Camden's kisses become more demanding as his tongue strokes against my own. Between us I can feel his arousal, thick and long, steel encased in satin. Reaching down I wrap my hand around the width of his cock, stroking him. His fingers tighten in my hair as he pulls back slightly to look at me.

"You keep touching me like that, I won't be able to contain myself…"

Of my four boys he's the only one who isn't circumcised and as he grows in my hand, his foreskin rolls back to reveal a cock that is dark purple at the head.

"I don't want you to contain yourself, Camden," I reply, dropping to my knees before him. When I look up at him he's leaning over with his forehead pressed against his arm on the wall. His topaz eyes bore into my soul as he looks down at me, pools of blissful distraction that I want to dive into and never, ever, come up for air. He reaches down, his fingers trailing over my cheek. It's such a gentle gesture and in such stark contrast to his almost violent erection that I hold in my hands.

"What if I let go…"

"Then I'll catch you."

Camden nods, releasing my face, then gently holds the back of my head as I guide his cock into my mouth. He's so large that I can only draw him in a little way but it doesn't seem to bother him, given the groans of pleasure breaking free from his lips. Grabbing his wet arse with one hand I massage his cheek and the hard muscles of his thigh as he gently starts to undulate his hips. My lip ring drags up the underside of his cock, teasing the thick vein there.

"Asia, you'll make me come," he moans, his fingers twining in my hair, gripping harder. He's trying to control himself and when I release his cock for a moment, licking upwards from the base to the tip, I look up at him. Camden has his eyes pressed shut, his bottom lip sucked into his mouth. He looks entirely undone and sexy as hell.

The fact that he's so turned on fuels my own desire and I draw him back into my mouth, sucking and licking. I hollow out my cheeks and when I taste the first drop of his precum I draw him deeper into my mouth, pumping the base of his cock with my fist in time with his heady moans. When his cum spurts in a violent torrent, hitting the back of my throat, my core tightens and my nipples peak at the power I feel, at the intense need of wanting him inside me too. With his chest heaving, Camden's eyes snap open and he reaches for me, lifting me up under my arms. In one quick motion, I'm standing and he's kneeling before me, hooking one of my legs over his shoulder before his beautiful lush lips are between my legs and his tongue is licking at my clit.

"Beautiful Asia. My bae. Our girl," he murmurs against my core.

With my back against the shower wall, and one foot pressed up against the tiles, I grind myself against his mouth, whimpering at the explosion of feeling building between my legs as he fucks me with his tongue.

The sounds he makes as he brings me to orgasm turns me on so much that when he slides two fingers inside me, I let out a loud moan not caring who might hear. I come quickly and hard, collapsing in his arms. Spent.

But he's not done yet.

Lifting me out of the shower, he strides into the bedroom and lays me on the bed. The door to our room is ajar, and he shuts it quickly before rummaging in his rucksack.

Turning on my side, my body feeling languid, I watch him in the semi-darkness as he crouches down and digs about in his bag, his face so serious. When he doesn't find what he wants immediately he swears quietly under his breath.

"Lost something?" I ask with a soft laugh.

His eyes flick up, taking in the length of my body.

"Fuck," he whispers. "I could come just looking at you."

My cheeks flame. "I know how you feel."

A broad smile lights his face, changing his appearance. I see the boy he once was right there in the fleeting joy in his eyes. When he draws his hand out of the rucksack holding a condom packet, that smile becomes entirely different. It's darker, shaded with lust and desire.

"Get over here, Cam," I say huskily, my fingers curling into the bedspread.

Camden rises to his feet, unfurling like a wild orchid in the starlight. He moves towards me, the muscles of his chest and stomach tightening with every step. Rolling onto my back, I push up on my elbows, biting down on my lip ring as I watch him. He leans over me, his hands pressing on the bed on either side of my hips.

"Open up for me, bae," he says, his mouth parting as he pushes his knee between my legs, urging them to widen. I oblige, my heart tripping up, beating loudly and tearing open, all because of the way he looks at me like I'm his saviour, his *hope*. It makes me afraid. Afraid that I might let him down, just like my mother let me down. She loved me in her own way, but it didn't stop her from leaving. What if these feelings I have for Camden, for all my boys, aren't enough?

"Camden... what if this isn't enough?" I repeat out loud.

"Shh," he murmurs, shaking his head. "Don't go to that place, Asia. Don't doubt what we have. Don't fucking do that."

Settling between my legs, Camden urges me to lay back as he presses his body against mine, encasing me in his warmth. A droplet of water slides over his skin and I press my mouth to his chest, capturing it on my tongue. It tastes of him: intoxicating, dangerous, addicting. I want to drink him in, absorb him. I realise that for so long I've been parched just like a lone sapling in the middle of a desert, desperate for nourishment.

These boys, they're my sustenance.

I lick Camden's skin, not stopping until my teeth and tongue graze over his collarbone. Finding the spot where I bit him yesterday in the dining hall, I kiss it gently.

"I shouldn't have bit you so hard," I mutter, but when his mouth finds mine, my apology is devoured by his plump lips and teasing tongue until all logical thought flies out of my head.

Camden undulates his hips, moving over me like a wave. The length of his cock slides over my core, not entering me, just teasing, giving me a taste of what's to come. As we kiss, my hands smooth over his skin, sliding over his back, his arse. Gripping him tightly, I widen my legs, wanting nothing more than for him to slide inside me, willing to take the risk. I adjust myself beneath him, fully aware of what I'm about to do, but Camden rears back, his chest rising and falling heavily as he rips open the foil condom packet.

"One day I'm going to fuck you bareback, but right now that ain't going to happen."

"Fuck," I mutter, my skin heating as I watch him slide the condom over his thick length.

When he leans over, grasping my hips and flipping me over, I let out a cry followed by a whimper as he yanks me onto all fours and buries his face in my core, lapping and licking and gorging on me. It's the most animalistic thing I've ever experienced, raw and dirty. Just when I think I'm going to come he pulls away.

"Lie flat on your stomach, spread your legs," he orders.

I do as he asks, giving up control willingly, knowing that somehow he needs to reclaim some of it. Camden lies on top of me, propped up slightly against my back. He kisses my dove tattoo, and then brushes his lips against my ear. "You know, for you, I'd sacrifice everything…"

I turn my head to the side. "I know. I'd do the same."

Camden presses his lips to my cheek then slides inside of me with one gentle thrust. I suck in a ragged breath as he settles inside me, his forehead pressed into my shoulder. For one long, drawn out minute he remains there, not moving, not doing anything but breathing in my scent as he allows my body to adjust, giving my internal muscles time to relax around his width. Then when I let out a shuddering breath, Camden slowly moves, kissing my bare neck, my cheek, my hair and every part of my skin within reach. His hand slides up and he grasps my throat gently whilst he fucks me from behind. Sliding in and out of me, his warm breath, his kisses, his whispered words of adoration wash over me, but this time instead of drowning, I'm swimming in the depths with him, holding my breath and trusting him to give me the oxygen I so desperately need. Together we let the wave of our mutual orgasm build and when he pulls us both onto our sides, his arms wrapped around me, fucking and spooning me at the same time, that wave of pleasure undulates out from my stomach washing away all doubt, all pain, all disappointment and all *thought*.

And just for a moment we're free.

THIRTY-FIVE

Propping his head up on his hand, Camden gives me an intense look. "Were you really going to leave us?" he asks, half an hour later. We're under the duvet covers, still very much naked and relaxed in each other's company enough to be honest, to open up.

I sigh heavily, knowing this was coming and knowing I have to answer truthfully.

"I didn't think, I acted. It was a stupid thing to do..."

My voice trails off, but I refuse to look away.

"But did you *want* to leave us...?" he persists, his beautiful brows drawing together in a frown.

"I won't lie to you, Camden. There was a brief moment when I wanted everything to go away, the responsibility, the sadness, the fucking pain and disappointment. A moment of weakness, that's all it was."

He nods. "I get it, Asia. There's only so much any of us can take, but you have to know that all of us, me, Eastern, Ford and Sonny, we all want to be there for you. We *need* you. I fucking need you." He leans in to kiss me gently. It's such a heart-warming kiss that I find it difficult to break away, but I need to explain fully how I feel. I owe him that much, given all that he's lost.

"I thought Mr Carmichael was different," I admit. "I believed him when he said he cared. I believed it when he said that he could make a difference to our lives, my life, even when I pretended I didn't. I can handle knowing he's the Black Sheep, what I can't understand is why he lied about it. Why he threw us all under the bus, why he chose to protect himself over protecting us. That hurt. *It hurts.*"

Camden's fingertips feather over my arm, a gentle warmth spreading out from his touch. "I understand..." His voice trails off as he looks at me, trying to decide whether he should tell me something.

"What is it?"

"The King, your father... he meant something to me once. Back when they first started dating, mum didn't know who he was. Neither did I. He was just a charming businessman with lots of cash. I'd trusted him to take care of us, but he was like a cancer, Asia. Before long he weaved his way into our lives. He destroyed our family. He tore us apart. The King killed Mum and now he's trying to destroy you too. I won't allow it. When the time comes, I'll be the one to kill him. *Me*, Asia. I'll do it gladly."

"No!" I protest. "It isn't down to you. He's *my* father, Camden," I say, sitting up and grasping his chin between my fingers, forcing him to look at me.

"And he killed *my* mother. I *need* to do this." His fingers wrap around my hand, gently prying it away. "Please."

There's no point in arguing, I can see nothing that I'll say will change his mind right now. It's all too raw and honestly I'd rather spend this short time together being close, not rowing over a man who doesn't deserve any more of our attention. No matter what Camden believes, it won't be him who kills the King.

"Tell me about your mum, Asia," he asks as I settle back down in his arms.

"There's not much to say," I reply, my fingers drawing circles on his bare chest. His skin is smooth, apart from little tufts of hair peppered across his chest. I like it. I like him... *a lot.*

"What was she like?"

"She was a woman who couldn't cope with this naughty kid always getting kicked out of school. She was someone who couldn't deal with a life lived in poverty, in a shitty, flea-infested flat with barely any food to get us by. She couldn't see beyond her own pain. She ran into the arms of heroin to obliterate all the bad things I did and all the crap we lived amongst. I didn't make her life any easier."

Camden is quiet for a long while, thoughtful. Eventually he speaks. "She was an addict, Asia. That wasn't on you. How can you blame yourself for that?"

"Because I lived up to the person she believed me to be," I continue, not able to stop now that I've started purging my soul. "If I'd worked harder to help her, to be *good*, maybe she'd still be alive today?"

"You were a kid, what could you have done?"

"*More...*"

"Getting her better wasn't on you."

"I was a shitty kid, Cam. Naughty doesn't even describe how bad I was. I did it all to get her attention, to try and force her to be the mum I needed because attention for doing bad things was better than no attention at all... I let her down."

"She let *you* down, not the other way around."

"It doesn't matter now. There's no going back."

"And the graffiti?" he asks on the back of a sad smile.

"My escape, a way to express myself."

He nods, drawing me against his side, holding me close. "Same… It's the only thing in my life that didn't fucking suck."

"Do you miss being Bling?"

"I miss everything about that kid, but he's long gone now…" Camden says. I can hear the bitterness in his voice, and it makes me ache for him, for what he believes he's lost.

"You might believe that's true, but I don't. I've seen that kid you were so many times since we've become friends."

"Friends?" Camden questions, a smile in his voice. "Who would've thought it?"

"Yes, friends."

"Just friends?"

"Not just friends."

He presses his soft lips against my temple. "No, not just friends," he agrees.

I let that admission hang in the air between us, warming our hearts and soothing a little bit of the ache in our souls. We lie together for another hour, only getting dressed when the smell of bacon cooking and a gentle knock at our door draws us out of the bubble we've found ourselves in.

WE ALL GATHER at the kitchen table. Malakai is nowhere to be seen and our host, Connie, seems distracted as she serves up a hearty breakfast of bacon, eggs, sausages, mushrooms and hash browns. She watches us devour the food over the rim of her mug. When her gaze lands on me, a small smile plays about her lips.

"Did you like the sausage?" she asks me, her voice deadpan even though there's a glimmer of amusement in her eyes.

Kate chokes on her hash brown and Ford has to thump her on the back. Sonny and Eastern look at me with varying shades of amusement. Camden, however, is oblivious. The way he's wolfing down his food you'd think he hasn't eaten in a couple days. Then I remember what's been going on and realise that he probably hasn't.

"The sausage was delicious. It's a brand I haven't tasted before, but I'll definitely have seconds…" I smirk, before gulping back a mouthful of tea.

For a split second the whole kitchen is quiet then Connie barks out a laugh and we all join in. It feels good to laugh, even if our brief happiness is just a bandaid for the pain.

"Well, well, well. I hadn't realised I'd started up a youth hostel for the waifs and strays of the world."

Connie grins as an elderly lady in her seventies stands in the doorway in her fluffy dressing gown and slippers, looking at us all. She has long silver hair braided in a plait that hangs over her shoulder, and eyes the same shade as Connie. Her skin, though pale in comparison to Connie's olive tone, is barely wrinkled apart from a few laughter lines around her eyes and mouth. When her hand disappears into her pocket and draws out a packet of cigarettes and a lighter, I immediately warm to her.

"Morning Grandma, how's the cold?" Connie asks her, pouring a large cup of black coffee and traversing the table to give it to her, tutting when she lights up a cigarette.

"They'll kill you, you know," Connie says, retreating to her spot by the sink.

"No child, cigarettes won't be the death of me, but a certain young man might," she winks then and Ford chokes on his coffee. Now it's Kate's turn to thump him on the back.

"Please don't tell me she's shagging Malakai!" Eastern mutters under his breath. Evidently, not quietly enough, given Connie's sudden frown and Ma Silva's laughter.

"I wasn't talking about Kai. That man's a fortress. I'm not sure anyone has the ability to break down his walls," Ma Silva responds, sitting in the empty chair at the head of the table next to me and Camden. "Been like that since he was a kid."

Connie's gaze flicks to mine and her cheeks flush with heat. When she turns her back on us all, washing up a pan at the kitchen sink, I understand what Connie is trying to hide; she and Malakai are, indeed, fucking and she knows full well about the fortress surrounding his heart. If he has a heart, that is. I'm pretty sure he's a cold fish, given my impression so far.

"I understand my godson has been causing trouble again," Ma Silva says, puffing on her cigarette like an old man would his pipe. Her gaze flicks between each of us, finally resting on me.

"You make it sound like he's just had a brawl in a pub on a Friday night. He's a motherfucking murdering bastard," Camden responds darkly. "And he has our friend."

I grab Camden's hand, squeezing it tightly. It's not her fault the King's an arsehole.

Ma Silva takes one last deep drag on her cigarette, then stubs it out in an ashtray that Connie has just put on the table next to her.

"I'm sorry about your mother," she says gently, reaching over to pat Camden on his hand. "I heard what happened and it turns my stomach. There are many things I've turned a blind eye to over the years when it comes to that family, but I will not tolerate cold-blooded murder. This has to stop. You are here because I care about Grim and she cares about you all. That means I'm going to help you rescue your friend."

"Grandma, I don't want you getting hurt," Connie says, frowning.

She waves her hand in the air, dismissing her granddaughter's concern. "I cannot allow this to continue. I'm his godmother and I took a vow to always look out for Grayson."

Grayson? So that's my father's real name.

"And how do you propose to help us? No offense or anything but you're..." Camden begins but Ma Silva holds her hand up.

"I find the word old offensive. I'm mature, *wise*, and as the saying goes: there's life in this old dog yet!"

"That there is," Malakai confirms, stepping into the kitchen. He still has the same clothing on as earlier, though they appear to be dry now. I'm guessing Connie didn't allow him entrance to her room. Good for her.

Malakai greets Ma Silva with a kiss and a hug, and she pats his face like he's her favourite person in the whole world. When he straightens, a look passes between him and Connie. She turns away, gripping the side of the sink as she looks out of the window at the storm raging beyond.

"Connie," Malakai says.

"Malakai," she responds tightly.

What the hell happened between the two when we were upstairs? They certainly haven't been fucking, that's for sure. Malakai stands next to Connie, an innocuous act in itself, but when he grips the sink, I see his pinkie finger feather over hers. She stiffens as though burned, snatching her hand away. I raise my eyebrows, wondering what the fuck is going on between the two of them. The sexual tension is ridiculous. You'd have to blind, deaf and mute not to notice.

"But how *can* you help us?" Ford asks, straight to the point as usual.

"I've overlooked my godson's misdemeanours for far too long and that is *my* sin to carry, but I will not allow him to hurt one more person, especially not a child. I promised his mother that I would save him from himself and I've not done a very good job at it. That is going to change as of today."

Ma Silva folds her hands together and tips her head to the side as she looks at me, not bothering to actually answer Ford's question as she stares intently in my direction.

"Do I have food on my face?" I ask, swiping at my mouth.

"There's a resemblance..." she responds, narrowing her eyes a little. "But you have far more soul in your eyes than he does. The fact that you're here to rescue your friend tells me all I need to know about the kind of person you are. Empathy, *love*, that isn't usually a Bennett trait. Then again, that might not be entirely true because there are some exceptions. Avery being one of them."

"Who's Avery?"

"My best friend and your great-aunt. She lives in Cornwall, working as a housekeeper for a wealthy family that lives there."

"Was that who Grim went to see? The one who provided the photo of Montgomery Bennett?" I ask.

"The one and only. She cut ties with her family a long, long time ago, choosing to lead a different, simpler life with men that made her happy..."

"*Men,* not man?" I question.

"Yes, caused quite the stir back then when she was young. Though I see loving more than one man isn't frowned upon so much these days." She smiles, looking between us all. My cheeks flush.

Ma Silva is perceptive, which smacks me as interesting given she doesn't seem aware that her own granddaughter is fucking a man twice her age. Then again, maybe that's what she wants Connie and Malakai to think. I'm beginning to understand that nothing much gets past this old woman.

"So what's the plan?" Eastern cuts in, resting his knife and fork on his plate. "I'm guessing you have one."

"I do, young man. I'm one of the *only* people the King trusts to enter the Palace. He's invited Connie and me over for dinner tonight to meet his son, Montgomery, named after his grandfather and Avery's father."

"Montgomery?" Camden questions.

"I believe you know him as Monk, am I right?" Ma Silva responds.

"Monk's real name is Montgomery... fucking figures. A dick name for a *dickhead*," Eastern snipes. Ma Silva doesn't correct him.

"We intend on keeping them both occupied whilst you rescue your friend. That is the long and the short of it."

"I'm sorry, what?! Connie is *not* going into that place! Over my fucking dead body!" Malakai shouts, making Kate jump with his sudden outburst. Connie stiffens, not daring to look at him. She keeps her back to us all, but I can see how her shoulders lift with tension. Perhaps even anger. But Ma Silva has no problems facing the brute.

"Since when did *you* have any right to say what Connie does or does not do? The last time I checked, she's her own person and she most certainly does not need a man to make any decisions for her!" Ma Silva snaps.

Interestingly Malakai backs down, but even though he doesn't argue back, I can tell he is not done discussing this, not by a long shot. Connie turns around to face us all, to face Malakai. She takes a deep breath.

"I'm accompanying Grandma because I refuse to let her do this on her own," she responds, glaring at Malakai. He glares back and I swear to God, if we weren't in the room they'd either slap each other or fuck each other right here on the kitchen table.

Maybe they'd do both.

"Jesus, fuck, those two need to get a room," Camden mutters under his breath.

"Nah, this is hot as hell. Nothing like a bit of angry sex to get the blood pumping. Let them carry on, I say," Sonny says quietly, a smirk on his lips.

"You don't need to be there, Connie," Malakai protests.

"See, here's the thing Malakai. I don't sail away when things get tough. I don't leave. I'm going with Grandma because there is no way I'm letting her do this alone. You just *try* to stop me and see what happens," she challenges.

"This isn't a game, Connie. That man is dangerous. His son is no better. What is this dinner about exactly, anyway? Is the King lining you up for Monk, because from what I've heard he likes to beat his lovers into submission." Malakai slams his fist against the counter.

"Why do you care, huh? Green isn't a pretty shade on you, Malakai," Connie snaps back.

Malakai grits his teeth, his glare promising a fight when they don't have an audience. When I stop staring at them both and look at Ma Silva she has a knowing look on her face, a tiny smile playing around her mouth. She definitely knows they're fucking.

"That's settled then. Tonight at 7pm Connie and I shall have dinner with the King, and you'll have a few hours to find your friend, then get the hell off this island," Ma Silva says, giving us all a wide smile. If I didn't know any better, she looks almost excited about the prospect.

"I'm sorry to be the bearer of bad news, but have you seen it outside? Malakai said that the storm is going to continue for hours yet. Even if we manage to get Pink out, we're not getting off this poxy island," Sonny points out.

Ma Silva smiles and raises her eyebrows. "Well, that's where you're wrong. Malakai is the best sailor there is, he'll get you off this island, storm or not."

THIRTY-SIX

At 6pm we gather in the living room. Ma Silva looks relaxed and at ease, her long, black, woollen coat covering up her beige twinset and woollen skirt. Her hair is tied up in a chignon and she's wearing some red lipstick, a little of which bleeds into the fine wrinkles around her mouth.

Kate, myself and the guys are perched on various pieces of furniture, waiting for Connie and Malakai to come and join us. He's been a beast all day, and we've pretty much kept out of his way, spending time in the rooms upstairs or going over our plan for the thousandth time until we all know what we're doing. First, Connie and Ma Silva will arrive at the Palace at a quarter to seven. They will keep the King occupied long enough for Kate to hack into the Palace's security system, allowing us to access the service gate at the north side of the site and enter the building through a window in the cellar. Then we'll follow Ma Silva's directions to the east wing where she believes Pink is being held. Kate will remain in the car, ensuring that if there are any backup security firewalls, she'll be able to take them down too. We take out whoever we need to take out, grab Pink and get out. Killing the King isn't an option according to Malakai.

Whatever.

Because as far as I can see, there's a huge flaw in this plan: Connie and Ma Silva will be left behind and I never, ever leave anyone behind. If the King has any inkling as to what we're doing, then they're as good as dead. Malakai's a clever man, I'm pretty sure he knows that too. Though I suspect he has his own agenda. When he enters the room dressed up like an MI5 agent, I'm certain he does.

"You ready?" Malakai grunts.

Dressed head to toe in black and looking fiercer than ever, Malakai is tooled up with enough weapons to slay a small army. A utility belt holds two sheathed knives, pepper spray, a taser and a fucking gun. Who is this guy?

"Look at all that gear," Camden remarks, eyeing him warily.

"Got any more of those?" Eastern asks, nodding towards his utility belt.

"No. I don't give weapons to kids," he grunts in response, then promptly pulls out a phone, staring intently at the screen as he sends a message to God knows who. Grim perhaps?

"Now I really do feel like we're on the set of Mission Impossible… who the fuck is this guy?" Sonny smirks.

"Your worst fucking nightmare, or your best friend, depending on how you choose to conduct yourself. Don't piss me off and you'll do fine," he adds with a growl.

"Well, that'll shut me up," Sonny mutters, shooting me a wide-eyed look.

"Has Connie seen sense and is staying behind? Because I really don't need another obnoxious kid to look after. She's a liability," he snarls, unkindly.

Ma Silva raises her eyebrows, glaring at Malakai. "Connie is quite a resilient young *woman* as you well know, so I suggest you start treating her with a little more respect or face my wrath," she warns. "Now, you apologise for calling my granddaughter an obnoxious kid."

Malakai scowls but doesn't get to respond as Connie enters the room just at that precise moment.

"Thanks Grandma, but I wouldn't bother. Like you said, Malakai is a fortress, there's no point in trying to make a rude, pig-headed arse with zero manners apologise to anyone."

If our mouths pop open at how hot Connie looks, Malakai's chin is practically on the floor. I'm half expecting his tongue to come rolling out of his mouth just like a cartoon character on the TV. It's hilarious. Connie smiles sweetly at Malakai, her cherry lips glossy and plump.

"Connie, child, you look absolutely stunning," Ma Silva says, her eyes welling.

"You think?" she responds, swiping her hands over the velvety emerald material of her bodycon dress. It has a sweetheart neckline that shows off her voluptuous cleavage and she's wearing knee high boots that hug her calves and ankles as tightly as her dress hugs her skin. I would never assume such a beautiful woman would be insecure, but the way she seeks approval proves that she is.

"That's completely inappropriate. Get changed," Malakai snaps, shaking his head to break himself out of the trance he's so obviously in. "You are not going in there to impress those two arseholes."

Connie frowns, her cherry lips pursing as she glares at him. "You need time and if looking like this helps to keep the King and his son's attention then I don't see what the problem is. I've been told before that beauty has no value in the real world. Perhaps tonight my beauty will come in useful, that *and* my exceptional skills at making small talk interesting," she adds with a glimmer of mischief in her eyes.

"Whoever told you that is a fool, beauty is as much a weapon as intelligence. You just got to know how to use it to your advantage," Ma Silva announces with a smile that suggests a past beauty that lingers still. When her gaze meets Connie, I can't help but notice the small dip of her head and pride light her eyes.

"I think you look stunning," Kate remarks, smiling gently.

"Thank you. I appreciate it."

"Well, if we've all finished fawning over Connie, I suggest we get going. It's going to take a lot more than beauty to pull this off tonight. Try weeks of surveillance and planning," Malakai growls.

Connie turns away, grabbing her coat from a hook on the back of the door. If you weren't looking close enough, you might not have noticed the slight drop of her shoulders and the flicker of hurt in her eyes. I have the sudden urge to tell Malakai what I think of him. What a prick. It's obvious to everyone in the room, bar Malakai, that Connie hasn't dressed up for the King and Monk, but for *him*.

Whoever said that love is blind knew what they were talking about.

TEN MINUTES later we're rolling up to the back entrance of the palace with the car headlights switched off. Rain is still pelting down and I literally have no idea how Malakai can see where he's going, given it's pitch black. The guy must really know this area well, either that or he's fucking insane.

"Kate, you need to do your thing," Malakai says, looking over at her.

She nods, flipping open the laptop, booting it up. Within minutes she's typing away and the black screen is filled with lines and lines of code. Her fingers move quickly across the keyboard as she frowns in concentration.

"Do you know, Kate, if I weren't so crazy about Asia, I might just fancy you a little bit," Sonny says with a laugh. "Nothing like a computer geek to get the blood pumping."

In response Kate lifts her hand, flipping him the middle finger. We all laugh, and that laughter gains momentum as we wait for her to tell us she's cracked the security system.

"Enough!" Malakai snaps, twisting in his seat to face us. He taps on his iPhone watch. "According to Connie, they've arrived and are being led to the dining hall by the butler. When she messages me to say they're all seated together, we move."

"Isn't it a bit risky, her texting you?" Ford asks, leaning forward in his seat so that he's looking over my shoulder from behind. My skin warms at his closeness, and when he brushes a kiss against my neck, I tremble a little.

"She has an iPhone watch too. One quick tap on her wrist and the pre-programmed message is sent."

After another ten minutes of waiting, Malakai's watch lights up. "We're a go," he confirms, a muscle in his jaw feathering as another message pops up on his wrist. "Kate, we good?"

"Piece of cake," she confirms, grinning at us all. "You've got one-hour tops before the security firewalls kick in and the sensors pick you up. You need to be out of here at ten past eight. Any later and we're in trouble."

"That should be more than enough time. Thank you." Malakai pulls down his black ski mask, indicating we should do the same. One by one we follow suit, leaving only our eyes and mouths visible as we pile out of the car. Before heading towards the gate, Malakai leans inside the open door.

"If I send you an SOS, I want you to message this number then get the hell out of here. I'm assuming you can drive?" Malakai asks.

"You assume correctly."

"Good. Drive to the harbour and wait on Princess. Someone will come for you."

Kate nods, her eyes fearful. "Who am I messaging?"

"Backup."

"Do you have backup?" Eastern asks, surprised.

Malakai closes the car door with a gentle click. "A good soldier always has a backup plan. Fortunately for you all, I'm the best of the goddamn best. Now, come on. Let's find your friend."

"Just a minute," Eastern says, facing me. He grips my shoulders. "You could stay with Kate. We can do this on our own. You don't need to come."

"No way. I'm not letting you go in there without me. That's not happening, Eastern."

He grits his teeth, biting down on his response. I know he's afraid for me. I'm afraid too, but I will not back down. I need to prove to them that I have their backs after I let them down so spectacularly the other day. For better *not* worse, I've chosen these boys, these men, and they've chosen me. If one makes a stand then we all do. That's the way it has to be from now on. We're a family by choice and that's what makes us strong.

"Asia, you ready?" Ford asks me, drawing me back into the moment.

I grit my teeth and nod my head, ignoring the bead of sweat that falls down my spine, reminding me of the fear and danger we're all in. "I'm ready."

He glances at the rest of the guys, a determined set to his jaw. "We finish this tonight. No one fucks with our family and gets away with it."

Stepping forward, he holds his arm out, his hand fisted. Eastern doesn't hesitate, he places his palm over Ford's closed fist and grips it tightly, a fierce look passes between them. So much has changed these past few months since I joined Oceanside, and despite the dangerous situation we're in, my heart swells with admiration, with joy at the fierce loyalty they share now.

Next to place his hand into the circle is Camden. His split knuckles are still weeping a little, and beneath the swelling of his face I catch the darkness in his gaze and the need for revenge.

"You up for this, Cam?" Ford asks him, concerned for his friend, because they are friends. We all are. The last few months have brought us closer, bound us together in an unbreakable unit. Camden gives Ford a look that cuts his question dead.

"No motherfucker is going to stop me, and if I should die tonight, I will spend all of eternity making sure that cunt wished he'd never been born."

Ford nods, grimacing. We exchange looks. Both of us are fearful for him. If we survive tonight, it'll take Camden a long time to recover. Perhaps he never will. Either way, we'll be right there by his side ready to catch him when he breaks, and he will break. We all will eventually.

Sonny flicks his gaze to mine and for a moment I can't breathe. He says so much without saying anything at all.

"Sonny?" I question. Being here is hard for him, not because he doesn't want to fight, but because he's afraid of what will happen if he does.

"I'm here. I've got your back. Let's do this," Sonny says just as passionately, placing his own hand over the others. I hope he survives this. I need him to.

"Asia?" Eastern prompts, his gold-flecked brown eyes more tumultuous than I've ever seen them before. I know he wishes I wasn't here. I know he wishes I'd stayed behind. That I was safe. They all do. But this is my family too. This is my fight as much as theirs, more so perhaps.

"This is where I belong. I'm ready," I repeat, cupping their hands between mine and pushing away the pain I feel inside. I grip their hands tightly. "It's time for payback. It's time for retribution."

Around us the air crackles with tension and the humming need for vengeance.

The King might be my father, Monk my brother, but they're *not* my family.

These boys are. No, correction, these *men* are.

And we're here to fight.

Entering the building is surprisingly easy. We slip through a low window into a musty-smelling cellar filled with boxes of junk, long since forgotten by the household. A faint light filters beneath the gap of the door at the top of the wooden stairs, and the space around us is lit up by Malakai's phone. He swipes at the screen enlarging what looks like a floorplan of the building.

"The good news is that it's a fairly straight run to where they're holding Pink…" Malakai says after a beat.

"And the bad news?" Eastern asks, his hand reaching for mine. He squeezes it with reassurance.

"We have to pass the security detail."

Ford glances at me. "How many are we talking about?"

"As far as Ma Silva has been able to calculate, approximately twelve men work for the King here at the Palace. Four covering each of the three floors. Pink is being held in a room on the topmost floor."

"And you know this how?" I ask.

"Callum sent Grim the footage of Pink and in turn she sent it to me. I've watched that film a dozen times over. Pink is being held in a circular room. According to Ma Silva, and backed up by the floorplan, there is only one circular room and it's in the east wing."

"Shame Pink's hair isn't long enough to make a rope. She could've saved us all this trouble," Sonny blurts out, then clamps his mouth shut, grimacing. When he gets nervous he tends to get verbal diarrhoea. "Sorry, not funny."

No one bothers to pull him up on his remark. We're all feeling anxious.

"Let's get this done," Malakai says, pulling the knife free from his utility belt.

Out of the corner of my eye, I see Camden and Eastern retrieve something from their jackets too. Both are holding knives of their own. Pretty sure they've come from Ma Silva's kitchen.

"I said no weapons," Malakai growls, using his knife to point at them both.

"If you think we're going up there without any way to defend ourselves, you need your head fucking tested," Camden retorts, gripping the five-inch knife tighter.

Malakai frowns. "I suppose you three have weapons too?" he asks, looking between us.

"No. We've got our fists. We can fight. Don't need any weapons to do serious harm like these two pussies here," Sonny responds, smirking.

"Shut the fuck up, dimples," Camden says darkly. He's in no mood for jokes today.

Malakai rolls his eyes. "You *all* need to shut the fuck up and follow me. I will deal with any guards we might come across. The *only* time you're going to be using any weapons, including your fists, is if I'm knocked out cold and you're forced to defend yourself. Am I clear?"

"Clear," we all chorus.

When we open the door onto the ground floor, Malakai is soon eating his words because in front of us are half a dozen guards headed up by Monk.

My.

Fucking.

Brother.

THIRTY-SEVEN

"Hello, Asia, glad you could make it," he says, and even though we're all wearing masks, it's not hard to tell I'm the only woman amongst a gang of men.

"Monk," I hush out.

"Montgomery Bennett to you, little sister."

"I am not your damn sister, you piece of shit!" I shout, finding my voice at last.

Monk laughs and the sound grates on my last fucking nerve. "You can protest all you like, but you know as well as I do that the Bennett blood burns through your veins. Nothing quite like abject violence to ease the soul, hmm?"

"Fuck you! I'm *not* a Bennett," I spit, acutely aware of my boys stepping into formation beside me. The air hums with the violence Monk speaks of. But this kind of violence is born from the need to protect, not some sick twisted way to get our rocks off like Monk.

"You don't like the name? You should be grateful to be a part of such a world-renowned crime family, Asia. You know there's a reason my father named me after the most notorious member of the Bennett family," Monk says, an evil smile pulling up his lips. He lifts his hand, crooking his finger. My heart thunders in my chest as Pink is brought forward, held upright by another guard. Her head dangles between her shoulders, her feet dragging across the floor.

"Is this what you came for?" Monk asks, lifting the chin of my friend.

"Pink?" I hush out, sudden nausea rising up my throat. She's barely conscious, her face swollen, her lip split and bleeding. She groans and something inside of me snaps.

"YOU BASTARD!" I scream, rushing forward only to be hauled backwards by strong arms. Ford holds me as I struggle to get to my half-brother. I never wanted to rip someone apart more than I do right this second. I swear to God, I'm going to claw open his stomach with my bare hands and gut him just like he's gutted me with his abuse of my friend.

"Easy, Asia, two of the guards have guns," Ford whispers in my ear.

Monk laughs. "You fucked with the wrong family."

My breath comes in short, sharp breaths. "I *am* family, remember!? Like you said, Bennett blood runs in my veins too. You underestimated me once before and I handed you your arse. Don't doubt me again," I growl, elbowing Ford hard in the diaphragm. He lets me go with a grunt and the next second I'm reaching over grasping for the gun strapped to Malakai's waist, only it's no longer holstered there.

Time slows.

Malakai shoves me aside.

I stumble.

Three shots ring out in quick session.

Bang.

Bang.

BANG.

Pink falls forward, crashing to the floor as the guard holding her falls backwards, a gunshot wound between his eyes, bits of brain, tissue and bone splattering the men behind him. The two other guards holding the guns follow suit.

A heartbeat later all hell breaks loose as time speeds up once more.

"Grab the girl!" Malakai shouts to whoever's listening. The gun he's holding is knocked out of his hand by a well-placed kick from one of the guards. It fires again, the stray bullet piercing a hole in the wall opposite, sending tiny shards of plaster into the air.

Malakai launches himself at the nearest guard, throwing punches as he swerves a razor-edged knife. Eastern, Camden and Ford all pile in, fighting off the other remaining guards, and Sonny, who's nearest to Pink, reaches for her, ducking as Eastern's knife whizzes past his head and hits another guard in the chest. Shock registers in the guard's eyes as he falls to his knees choking on thick, viscous blood before he can even think about drawing his own weapon.

Did Eastern just kill that man? *Fuck.*

I don't have time to even comprehend what that means for him, because my attention is drawn back to my brother as he barks out an order into a communication device strapped around his upper arm. My heart pounds loudly in my ears, everything around me blurring in a broiling mass of violence as my attention zeros in on him. There's no fear in his eyes, just elation. He already thinks he's won, and that worries me way more than what's happening now. An awful thought passes through my head... have we been set up?

I've no time to consider my stray thoughts because I'm dodging one guard's punch and ducking out of the way of another as I scramble over to Sonny and help him drag Pink to the corner of the room. Behind us my boys and Malakai are fighting the remaining guards whilst my brother looks on, one foot already backing out of the door. He's ready to make his escape should his guards lose.

And they're going to lose.

We both know that.

My boys and Malakai, they're fighters, and they're winning this round. But this is just a taste of what's to come. They've been waiting for us.

"How is she?" I lean over Pink's prone body, checking her over with one quick assessing swoop of my eyes and refusing to think past the here and now. She's still wearing the same clothes as she was in the video and her hair is matted and unkempt.

"Concussed at the very least," Sonny responds, pushing a strand of blood-matted hair out of Pink's face. She groans, her eyelids fluttering open, but they are unfocused and bloodshot.

"You're safe now," I murmur, leaning over and pressing a kiss against her forehead. Even that light touch has her moaning in pain.

"We need to get her out of here," Sonny draws her into his arms, ready to stand up with her as soon as the guys have made mincemeat of the guards.

"Be ready to go just as soon as they're done," I order, snatching my head around.

Behind us my boys are still fighting, swiping at the guards with their knives. I watch in horror as one guard jerks forward and slashes Camden across his cheek through his mask. I see blood spurt in a violent splash of red as he roars in pain.

"Camden!" I scream, scrambling on my feet to get to him, but he pushes me back with one hand before swiping at the guard with the other. The guard rears back and brings his leg up in a high arc, knocking the knife from Camden's hold. It flies out of his hand and slides across the room, stopping near my feet. I bend down to pick it up and for a brief moment consider passing it back to him, only I can't get it to him in the midst of such violence.

"Stay back, Asia. I'm okay!" Camden shouts, fighting with

everything he has despite the slash to his face and the blood seeping from his cheek.

Squeezing my fist tight around the handle I get back on my feet, searching for Monk. Just like the chicken-shit he is, I watch him retreat. He gives me one last lingering look, a smile playing about his lips, then runs.

"MONK!" I roar, dodging the guards only to be faced with another who appears from the doorway, pressing a gun to my forehead.

"Don't fucking move," he grinds out.

Time stills, my heartbeat slowing as my ears ring with impending doom. The cold metal bites into my skin as my life flashes in front of my eyes. I close them, pressing back the tears that are desperate to fall.

I don't want to die like this.

I *won't* die like this.

Gritting my teeth, I curl my fingers into fists, my body stiff, ready to throw a punch...

BANG!

When the sound of a gun firing fills my head, I assume death has claimed me. Except conscious thought isn't possible when you're dead, right?

My eyes snap open as the guard falls to his knees half his face blown off, his face fixed in a permanent state of shock. Well, the half that remains. When I reach up to touch the mask covering my face it's seeped with blood. I rip it free, drawing in ragged breaths. Another two more shots ring out and the remaining guards fall to the ground, leaking blood in a river across the floor. All of them dead.

In the doorway stands a man dressed in similar attire to us all, his face covered in a black mask, but I'd recognise those eyes anywhere...

They belong to the *Black Sheep*.

THIRTY-EIGHT

"You need to get to her right now!" Mr Carmichael orders, firing off shots down the hall. He looks directly at Malakai who nods, slipping from the room and running full pelt in the opposite direction of the guards, whilst Mr Carmichael covers his escape. He doesn't question. He doesn't look back. He runs to find the person he cares about most, even if he denies it to himself: Connie.

"What the actual fuck!" Camden exclaims, pulling off his mask and swearing with the sharp sting. His face is covered in blood, a thick slash mark runs from his temple across his cheek. My heart thunders but he doesn't seem to notice the pain, too intent on staring at Mr Carmichael.

"What are you doing here?" Ford asks

"I've no time to explain. Get out of here!" Mr Carmichael shouts, still firing shots from his gun.

Ford helps Sonny lift Pink, whilst I reach for Eastern whose face is drained of colour, his knees buckling in shock. He's looking at the guard who has his kitchen knife sticking out of his chest.

"I killed him…" he whispers, ripping off his face mask and drawing in deep stuttering breaths. "I fucking killed him."

Drawing his face between my palms I squeeze his cheeks just like I used to do when we were kids and he needed someone to drag him out of his fury or his sadness. "Focus, Eastern. You did what you had to do. Now we need to go."

I flash a look at Camden who is now watching Mr Carmichael with narrowed eyes, his balled-up mask pressed against his face. I know what he's thinking, because it's the same as the rest of us. What the fuck is the principal of our school doing here?

"You've less than three minutes before the King reigns hellfire on all of us. I can only hold the rest of his guards off for so long. GET THE FUCK OUT!" Mr Carmichael roars at us.

Gathering Pink in his arms, Sonny heads back down the stairs into the cellar, presumably so he can haul her out of the window and get her to the car waiting beyond. Eastern and Camden follow him, but I linger at the top of the stairs, Ford by my side.

"What about you?" I say to Carmichael as he reloads his gun and fires off a few more rounds.

"I'm here to atone for my family's sins, Asia. Now fucking go!"

We run.

Above us the sounds of gunshots still ring in the air, but I have no time to think about anything other than getting Pink to safety. Ford climbs out of the window first, whilst Camden holds it open so we can slide a half-conscious Pink into his strong arms. Once she's clear of the ledge, we all pile out after her. We don't wait to see if there are any guards left on the grounds, Ford simply scoops Pink into his arms and legs it to the spot where Kate is waiting in the car.

Except when we get there, she's gone.

"Well, if it ain't the Brady Bunch," a voice says, stepping out of the darkness.

My skin crawls, my heart races, my world stops fucking spinning as Monk steps out of the shadows with Kate, a gun pressed to her temple.

"Make one wrong move and she dies," he sneers and Kate whimpers. Her eyes are filled with regret, with acceptance even. She believes she's going to die.

Fuck that.

"You bastard!" Camden growls, his fists clenched to his side as more men step out of the darkness. All of them are tooled up, guns cocked ready to fire. Ma Silva was wrong. The King has far more guards than any of us had anticipated.

We're fighting a losing battle. Monk knows it, and now so do we.

Sonny steps in front of me, his instinct to protect me overriding everything else. "You don't want to do this, Monk. Let us go. You've had your fun."

"Fun?" His laugh is brittle, broken, and like the gathering storm full of destructive intent. He has no intention of letting us go. "The party's just getting started, Sonny, and it looks like you're all the guests of honour. Except for Kate here, she's *mine* to play with now."

We all watch as he buries his nose in Kate's hair and draws in a deep breath. She is shaking so violently that I worry Monk's going to pull the trigger by mistake. I will her with my eyes to calm down.

"What the fuck do you want from us?" Ford grinds out, a still unconscious Pink in his arms.

"If I had my way you'd be dead already, but it seems the King has other plans. He wishes for the pleasure of your company. The King, our father, wants to see his daughter, and where she goes, so do you all, apparently."

"Move!" a nameless man orders us, cocking his gun and jerking his head.

For one crazy moment I consider fighting back. It's what I've always done. Fight. But as the heavens open once more and the sky cracks with thunder, the storm pelting us from all sides, I make the only choice I can, I turn around and start walking towards the Palace knowing that Monk is right; where I go, so to do my boys, even if that is straight into Hell.

WE ENTER A LARGE BALLROOM, at the centre of which is a grand table. The King is sitting at the head, flanked on either side by Ma Silva and Connie. Ma Silva is calm, her emotions carefully controlled. Opposite to her Connie sits shivering in her seat, her teeth chattering loudly. There's no sign of Malakai or Mr Carmichael and my heart plummets. What if they're both already dead? And the King... Well, there's no fear in his eyes. His face is void of emotion. If I didn't know any better I'd assume he was made of granite and rock, not flesh and blood like the rest of us.

When our eyes meet and he smiles that sinister smile of his, I know that today is my last day on Earth. I know without any shadow of a doubt that I'll never get to see my baby brothers again. I'll never get to hold Tracy close and sit with Braydon talking to him about stupid things like how long it takes Eastern to get ready to go out, or how we both prefer Marvel over DC. I can't bear to look at my boys, at Pink or Kate, for fear I will lose all self-control. If there's one thing I do know, the King will never see me cry.

I refuse to give him that power over me.

As we're forced into the room, guns still trained on our backs by the King's guards, he raises a glass of wine before taking a sip.

"Yet again you surprise me, Asia," he says, resting the glass back on the table as he regards me. "Quite a mess you've made this evening."

"Fuck you!" I respond, unable to help myself.

He barks out another laugh, entertained by my reaction. When he turns to Ma Silva and places a hand over hers, I flinch as though he's reached out and slapped me. Not because he's touched her so affectionately, but because she has let him.

"I had no idea, Ma, that my daughter was such a little firecracker."

"She certainly has your blood in her veins," Ma replies calmly, not a hint of fear or disgust in her eyes. She gives him a gentle smile, her other hand lifting to cover his. The exchange sickens me. My God, is she in on this too? Was this all a fucking setup?

"Grandma?" Connie hushes out, surprise registering on her face.

"Ma Silva's loyalty to my family knows no bounds. She brought me you, after all," the King says as he suddenly reaches for Connie's hand and presses a kiss against her knuckles. "Quite the rare beauty."

"Grandma?" Connie repeats, tears falling unbidden from her eyes now.

Ma Silva remains stoic. She doesn't react and my own stomach bottoms out.

What the fuck has she done?

When the King's attention returns to me, I flinch. My heart fucking pounds in my chest, desperate to flee, to protect itself from certain death, but my rib cage keeps it trapped, securing it inside. I daren't look at my boys. Daren't show the King how truly afraid I am, not for me, but for them. My boys. I feel them beside me. I feel their wrath and their rage. I feel their loyalty and their love.

"You, Asia, are quite a rarity."

"How so?" I ask, humouring him. I'm holding onto the hope that Malakai and Mr Carmichael aren't dead, and that somehow they'll save us. It's a childish hope, but it's all I have. Assuming Mr Carmichael is here to save us at all. I still don't understand why he's here. How he got here. I thought he'd run.

"I'm here to atone for my family's sins, Asia. Now fucking go!"

289

Those words echo inside my head, reminding me that there are secrets yet to be uncovered. Were Mr Carmichael's family members involved with the King too? I'm not sure I'll ever find out the answer to that question now.

"The Bennett girls are often vacuous, trifling little things better used for their beauty not their intelligence or fight, and whilst coming here tonight was a stupid decision, I like your tenacity."

"It's taken seventeen years to cultivate, no thanks to you," I respond, unable to ignore the veiled insult. Clearly women are regarded as lesser humans in his eyes. Figures, given how he used and abused Camden's mum, murdering her as a message to us all.

My gaze travels to Ford who is still carrying Pink. She's beginning to come around, her eyes fluttering open. Ford notices, but he refuses to put her down on her feet. Instead, he allows Camden to take her from him and despite the pain he must feel from the wound on his face, he holds Pink gently in his arms.

My heart expands with the love I feel for them all, then shatters when my gaze hits Kate on the other side of the room, and I see the pure, unadulterated fear in her eyes. Fear that turns to disgust as Monk mauls her breast with his meaty hand.

"Get your fucking hands off her!" I shout, every ounce of anger and rage I have pouring from me. Less than a second later, the cold, hard butt of a gun is pressed once again into the back of my head. Eastern grabs my hand, his touch reminding me that I'm not the only person here who has a gun aimed at them.

"Asia, don't," he warns me.

The King laughs.

"You truly are a Bennett, such conviction, such *violence*. I see it shining in your eyes. You are no weakling. I admire that, Asia." He heaves a sigh as though he's actually affected by my outburst, but a stone statue is all he is. There's not one ounce of empathy in his body. The man's a fucking psycho.

"It's a damn shame. I really should've introduced myself a lot earlier. Things could be so different now."

"Different?" I bark out a laugh.

"Yes, Asia. You could've been a part of this family. Alas, you and your friends are going to die tonight. I don't like loose ends."

"I would never have accepted you. You're nothing but a murdering bastard!"

"I take it that you're disappointed I'm your father?"

"That's a fucking understatement. Who wouldn't be disappointed? A man who uses kids to do his dirty work. A man who sells girls, who deals drugs. A man who murders innocent people, who threatens the ones I love. Are you even fucking human?" I sneer, knowing all that I have left are the sting of harsh words. Not that they will make a difference, given my father has no heart to break. I turn to look at Ma Silva, my anger spilling over to her. "And you, you evil fucking witch! How could you do this after everything you said?" I point at Connie, who flinches. "You sold us out and now you're handing over your own granddaughter to the King? Just like that?"

Ma Silva looks at me, a flicker of something in her gaze that makes me believe that everything isn't as it seems, but whatever I saw, she shuts it down quickly.

"Connie will make a wonderful companion and I have no allegiance to you, child."

"Bitch," Sonny snarls under his breath.

"What about Malakai?" I ask, my voice rising. "Does *he* mean nothing to you?" I *saw* the way Ma Silva was with him. There was affection between them. How could I have been so wrong?

"Malakai is a thorn in my side. Connie has had her fun. Now she will fulfil her duties."

"*Grandma!*" Connie shouts. Tears well in her eyes, but Ma Silva refuses to look at her.

"Speaking of which," the King interrupts, looking bored. "Where is that bastard cousin of mine?"

"*Cousin?*" What the fuck?

"Yes, Asia, he's a Bennett too, though he's refused the family name favouring his mother's… In fact, he's not the only other Bennett you've met." The King smiles evilly, but I refuse to be drawn into his games. I refuse to ask who he's talking about even though a part of me needs to know.

"Bring Grayson in!" The King barks out to one of the guards who nods, spinning on his feet and leaving the room.

Grayson? I thought the King was Grayson?

This time Ma Silva flinches. Her gaze flicks to mine, real fear apparent in her eyes. "He's here?" she whispers.

The King laughs as he rounds on her, slapping her so hard around the face that her head snaps violently to the side. Connie cries out, standing abruptly only to be forced back into her seat by a guard that appears behind her.

"Sit the fuck down," the King snarls at her. "The sooner you learn to obey me, the better. Your life may very well depend on it."

"What the fuck is going on?" Eastern whispers under his breath. He's moved in closer, Sonny flanking my other side.

"I've no idea," I hush back, confusion setting in.

Ma Silva rubs at her face and I see the look that passes between her and Connie. It's filled with regret, love, compassion, fear, and I see a tiny glimmer of the old woman I met today in her gaze.

"It'll be okay," she promises her granddaughter, then turns to me with a sorrow-filled gaze, before addressing the King. "This ends now. It's time to stop. I won't see you hurt these children."

The King laughs. "I knew it! You had this all planned out, didn't you, Ma? You think you could fool me? You think I wouldn't see through your act tonight? I knew you wouldn't give up Connie to me. Always so soft-hearted, always helping the waifs and strays. I bet you already care for these kids. Always trying to fix the broken, aren't you?"

Ma Silva nods, straightening her spine. "God knows I tried to help you over the years. None of these children deserve your hatred. What kind of monster are you?"

Her response has me breathing out a sigh of relief, which is ridiculous given the circumstances. She turns to look at me. "I'm sorry, Asia. I was trying to buy us some time."

The King sneers. "Did you honestly believe that I wouldn't notice Malakai scouting this place? You're an old fool," the King spits before turning his wrath to me. "And you, Asia, have brought me the one person I've been chasing for years. Let's see just how much your veins truly run with Bennett blood when you fulfil your part in the bargain and kill the bastard."

"You want me to kill Malakai? *He's* the person you were talking about when you wanted a life for a life?"

The King laughs hollowly. "No, not Malakai, though he too will die tonight. It was *always* the Black Sheep. That is, Mr Carmichael to you."

"Why? Because he killed one of your men for murdering his brother?"

"No, I told you why, because this is *my* kingdom, not his." The King slams his fist against the table making the plates and glasses shake.

"His?"

He ignores my question, anger running his mouth. "*I'm* the rightful heir, not Grayson, not my older brother."

THIRTY-NINE

"What the actual fuck?" Camden spits, his shock nothing in comparison to what I'm feeling. My words are smothered in disbelief as my brain tries to catch up.

Mr Carmichael is the Black Sheep.

The Black Sheep is Grayson Bennett.

Grayson Bennett is the King's older brother and the rightful heir to the Bennett throne.

He's my *uncle*.

He's the true King.

How in the hell didn't I realise?

"BRING HIM IN!" the King roars. Connie visibly blanches, and Ma Silva's head snaps to the door opening in the far corner of the room. Her face crumples as Mr Carmichael walks into the room, a gun pointed to the back of his head by the guard sent out to fetch him. His expression is blank as he holds his arm awkwardly. I notice a stream of blood dripping from his fingers. He's been shot.

"Well, if it isn't the prodigal son returned," the King says, hate pulling his lips up into a snarl.

"Brother," Mr Carmichael responds. "I would say it's good to see you but, of course, that would be a fucking lie and I'm tired of lying." His gaze flits to mine but I am struck dumb, unable to move, let alone blink in response.

"Ah, yes, Monk told me about your new life. A principal of a damn reform school, a bad guy turned good. You couldn't fucking make it up. As soon as Monk described you to me, I knew I'd finally found my long-lost brother... the black sheep of the family. Father would be so disappointed."

"It was all a lie? Everything you said about your brother, about your past, it was all a fucking lie! You're a goddamn *Bennett*?" I choke out, finding my voice, hurting more than I ever thought possible. "How is that even possible? You look nothing like each other." Apart from the eyes... their eyes are the same.

The King throws his head back and laughs. "I've always wondered about that too. I'm pretty sure Grayson here is the product of some illicit affair that our father saw fit to keep secret."

Mr Carmichael, or should I say, Grayson doesn't rise to the bait. Instead, he addresses me directly. "I *never* lied to you about that, Asia. My younger brother *was* murdered in a mistaken identity because your father sent him to kill *me*. Even after I'd abandoned the family name he wouldn't let me walk away."

The King snorts. "Our little brother was always the weakling of the family and no good to anyone. Fucking good riddance."

Mr Carmichael flinches but continues on regardless, ignoring the King, his gaze never once leaving mine. "I did beat a man nearly to death in retribution. I did turn my life around. I did want to make a difference, Asia. I *do* give a shit about you," he insists. "That's why I'm here."

I tip my head back and laugh, bitterness filling the air. "You give a shit so much that you failed to do a damn thing about your fucking brother, even though you of all people know what he's capable of?

Camden's mum is dead! You, Grayson Bennett, are nothing but a coward!" I scream.

"I should've acted earlier. I thought we had time," he repeats earnestly. "I was wrong, and I'm sorry. Nothing I can do will change what's happened, but I refuse to allow you to ruin your life by killing my brother when that is my responsibility and mine alone."

"Kill me?" The King laughs, and his guards join in.

"It's too little, too late," I retort, shaking my head in disgust ignoring them all.

"You're right, I was too late to save Camden's mum and I was too late to step in for Monk, but I refuse to allow my brother to ruin what's left of his bloodline. There's no coming back from murder. I won't let him ruin you, Asia. After the fight you staged yesterday I knew you'd decided to save Pink yourself, so I left Oceanside a few hours before you all did. I waited for you to arrive then I called Malakai and he told me your plan. He's the only one I've kept in contact with over the years. I trust him with my life."

"I'm not ruined. I'm a true Bennett. I am my father's son!" Monk cuts in, taking his anger out on Kate who whimpers under his rough grasp.

Mr Carmichael looks genuinely gutted as his gaze falls on Monk. "You are, indeed, your father's son. No good ever comes from being a Bennett."

The King gives a slow clap of his hands whilst my thoughts reel with everything he's said.

"Quite the speech, Grayson. Only, there's no hiding from who you truly are. Once a Bennett, always a fucking Bennett until death us do part. This speech won't change that fact, *brother*."

The King stalks towards Mr Carmichael, raising his hand. For a moment I think he's going to hit him but when he wraps his hand around the back of Mr Carmichael's head and brings their foreheads together, I'm more shocked by the display of affection. For a heartbeat the two brothers just stare into each other's eyes. Then Mr Carmichael reacts.

"Get your hands off me," he snarls, rearing backwards and headbutting the King who stumbles backwards, laughing.

"Still have that Bennett temper, I see," the King drawls, loosening his tie as though ready to fight. "There's no getting away from it, no matter what name you choose to hide behind."

"I'm not hiding anymore brother. I'm right fucking here."

"Just where I want you," the King retorts, jutting out his chin.

The guard behind Mr Carmichael pushes him forward, the gun pressed into the back of his head. "Sit," he demands.

Mr Carmichael sits down next to Connie as the King takes his place at the head of the table.

"I'd like my daughter to join us," the King says, looking at the guard behind me. I get shoved forward, almost losing my balance. Eastern lunges for the guard and gets a punch in the face for the trouble.

"Sit the fuck down, Asia, or I'll put a bullet in your boyfriend's head!" the King warns when I try to reach for my oldest friend. Tears prick my eyes as the guard aims his gun at Eastern. A heartbroken look passing between us.

"It's okay..." I whisper, knowing it isn't. Knowing this is it. Eastern's whole body is shaking, not through fear but from rage. "I love you so much," I say to him, knowing this may be the only chance I get. I don't allow myself a moment to see his response, instead I move my gaze to Kate, to Ford, then Sonny and finally Camden who's still supporting Pink. She's awake now, trembling against his side, holding on tight.

"I love you all. My boys, my crew, my *family*," I say.

It's the first time I've voiced those three precious words. Right here, in front of my father who has never loved a person in his life, in front of my half-brother Monk who hates as passionately as I love. The thing is, I don't feel weak for loving them like the King said I would. I feel strong.

So. Fucking. Strong.

My entire life I've always believed that words are meaningless. That they're just sentences strung together to create a fairytale, a story. Fakery dressed up into something pretty to soothe and placate. Yet, right here, as my four boys look at me with love in their eyes, I know that words are powerful when spoken from the heart, just like Mr Burnside had said all those months ago.

"I love you," I repeat, straightening my spine, pulling my chin up before turning to face my father. "And you," I spit, pointing an accusatory finger at the man who's responsible for all this heartache and pain. "I *hate* you."

"Sit down," the King commands with a dismissive flick of his hand as the guard pulls out a chair for me. He watches me as I sit at the table next to Ma Silva. My hand rests on the white linen, my fingertips curling around the material, bunching it up. Ma Silva reaches for me, her fingers wrapping around mine. She squeezes tight, an apology right there in her touch. The King notices and sneers.

"Love is a weakness. Hate, violence, anger, they're emotions that are worth something. They are what keep you alive in this world full of fantasy and make believe. Didn't your own mother spin tales about me? Wasn't I a figment of her wild imagination, nothing but a story conjured up for a daughter desperate to know her father?"

"How the fuck do you know that?" I ask.

"Because that's what she told me on the first and last occasion she came to me and begged for money. She was lucky I didn't kill her. Then again, the heroin my dealer supplied her did a fine job of that. So, I guess I did kill her after all, albeit from afar."

The King laughs at the look on my face and I see red. My anger blurs my vision. Grabbing the butter knife, I don't think, I just launch for him across the table only to be yanked back by the guard behind me. The cold metal of his gun digging into my temple.

"Try that again and you're dead," the guard growls.

"Asia, don't let him get to you," Mr Carmichael says calmly, a look I can't interpret flashing in his eyes. My breaths come in short, sharp pants as I try to control myself.

"See, Asia, love makes you weak," the King repeats, his eyes narrowing at his brother.

"Is that the lie you tell yourself these days?" a familiar voice says. *Malakai.*

The King stands. His mouth dropping open as he stares at the huge brute of a man. Except his shock isn't because Malakai has walked into the room without a hair out of place, it's because he's holding hands with a girl no more than four or five years old, a gun aimed at the King's blackened heart.

Who the hell is this? My question is answered half a beat of my troubled heart later.

"Daddy?" the little girl whispers, her huge brown eyes brimming with tears.

"*Daddy?*" I hush out.

The King blanches, his face paling. A flicker of emotion, so miniscule I almost miss it, flashes behind his eyes. "Don't be afraid, Ronnie. Malakai won't hurt you, I *promise*," he assures her vehemently before focusing his attention on Malakai, his eyes narrowing

"You have another child?" I ask, shocked by that brief look of *fear* tracking a path across his features and the fact there's another little girl who belongs to the King.

He snatches his head around, meeting my gaze. "Yes, surprise," he says, waving his hands in the air like some fucking maniac. Behind me

I can hear Camden swear under his breath and mutter his shock too. How did he not know that the King had another child? A heartbeat later, we all find out.

"Veronika was the product of a short affair that I had with a woman before I met your mother, Camden. Another whore who's only worth in this world was to give me Ronnie. When I found out about her birth I made sure I didn't repeat the same mistakes as I did with Asia. So, I took her. She's been our little secret, hasn't she Monk," he adds, staring at his son who just grits his jaw and nods.

"Why didn't mum say anything?" Camden blurts out. It's not a question he expects to get an answer to, but the King seems happy to share regardless.

"Because your mum knew if she did, I'd kill both her and you."

"You're a fucking arsehole!" Camden shouts, earning him a whack from one of the guards. The sound of his breath whooshing from his mouth has my heart stopping and tears pricking my eyes. I blink them away. I will not cry.

Shock renders me speechless as Mr Carmichael stares at his brother with hatred in his eyes. "Grayson, meet your niece," the King says, as though this isn't the most fucked up situation ever.

Mr Carmichael's gaze softens as he looks at the frightened little girl. "Hello, Veronika. It's nice to meet you," he says, before glaring at Malakai, his gaze darkening. "I told you to get her out."

Malakai grits his jaw, looking from Mr Carmichael to Connie. "You have people here you care about and so do I…"

"Malakai, what were you thinking?" Connie hushes out, catching on quickly. It's obvious he's come back for her but at the expense of getting Veronika to safety. "She's just a child."

"All the more reason to make sure both she and you are *safe* from this monster," he responds, picking Veronika up and tucking her into his side.

"You need to get her out of here. Now!" Connie continues, shaking her head and looking in abject horror at Malakai.

"And leave you with him? No," Malakai retorts stubbornly.

Connie turns to look at Ma Silva. "Grandma, did you know about this?"

Ma Silva nods. "Malakai told me about a little girl he'd spotted here. I put two and two together and made him promise me to rescue her too when the time came. I hadn't bargained on them getting caught."

"You fucking conniving old bitch," the King snarls.

Ma Silva ignores him and turns to Mr Carmichael. "Why didn't you come see *me*, Grayson? It's been almost twenty-five years. I promised your mother I would always watch out for you. Maybe we could've gone about this differently."

The King snorts. "Always the favourite. Good old Grayson."

None of us acknowledge his petty jealousy.

"I had to cut ties from everyone, including you. It was the only way to keep you all safe. But like my brother said in his *note*," Mr Carmichael spits, "The past catches up with us all eventually. I couldn't hide anymore. I couldn't see another person hurt at the hands of this family and live with a clear conscience. This morning when Malakai told me about this little one, it only cemented my decision to return here and deal with *him* once and for all."

"How fucking noble of you, Grayson! Always the goddamn hero."

"Enough, you always were a whiny little bitch," Malakai snaps at the King whilst Veronika cries silently in his arms. He pulls back the gun's hammer, his finger putting pressure on the trigger. "This is over."

The guards move in closer, aiming their guns at Malakai instead of my boys.

The King holds his hand up. "Wait!" he snaps.

"Father, you need to end this now. Shoot the bastard!" Monk yells at the guards, clearly not giving a shit about his little sister and the fact she could get caught in the crossfire. He presses the gun into Kate's temple hard enough to make her yelp. "I'll fucking kill this bitch if you don't let Veronika go!"

"Shut the fuck up, Monk," the King responds, snarling. "You won't be shooting anyone until I fucking say so. If *any* of you pull the trigger and risk Ronnie's life, I will strip the skin from your body whilst you're alive and feed it to my fucking dogs! That includes you, Monk!"

"Daddy?" Veronika blurts out, the tears that were welling now spilling down her cheeks.

She looks at him wide-eyed as if the man before her is the monster Malakai accused him of being. I swear to God, the King baulks and I see another flash of humanity in the black depths of his eyes.

"Don't be afraid," he says to her, the knuckles of his fists white as they grip the back of his chair.

But Veronika isn't just afraid, she's *terrified*. The length of her brown hair doesn't hide that fact from her big, brown, soulful eyes. Eyes that are so similar to mine. She sees the guns. She sees Pink covered in bruises and cuts. She sees her older brother holding onto a trembling Kate. She sees *me* and even though she has no idea who I am, there's recognition in her eyes. Aside from the pink hair we are so very alike, it's uncanny. I want to reach for her, soothe her. It's not her fault. None of this is her fault, and even though Malakai is gentle with her, I know he's playing a dangerous game with her life to save all of ours, including hers.

Except the King sees something in Malakai that the rest of us clearly don't and he doesn't try to call Malakai's bluff.

"What do you want?" the King asks, his hand still held up, warning his guards off.

"Your men need to drop their guns. Right the fuck now," Malakai demands, not for one moment taking his eyes off my father.

The King grits his teeth, then nods. "Do it," he demands.

"Father?!" Monk shouts.

"For the last time, Monk, shut the fuck up!" the King snaps.

The guards drop their guns and with one look from Malakai, my boys have grabbed them.

"On your fucking knees!" Malakai shouts.

The guards drop to their knees with guns aimed at them now.

"Give her to me!" the King demands.

Malakai shakes his head, looking directly at Connie. "Come here," he says softly.

"Let the girl go, Malakai," Connie says, her voice cracking.

"Come here. *Now!*" he repeats.

Connie gets up, walking towards him. As soon as she reaches his side, Ronnie holds her hands out to her, recognising that she's a safer bet, but Malakai refuses to let her go knowing as well as I do that if he did, the King would make his move.

"Asia, Ma, Grayson, you too," he orders.

Ma Silva gets up and stands beside Connie. Mr Carmichael remains where he is, his gaze trained on the King. "I'm not here to be saved, Malakai," he says.

"What's that supposed to mean?" Ma Silva asks.

Mr Carmichael doesn't answer, but we all know what he isn't saying. He's here to kill the King, even if that means forfeiting his own life to do it.

"What about Kate?" I ask, snapping my head around, but Camden has already passed Pink to Eastern and is pointing a gun at Monk's head.

"Let her fucking go, prick!" Camden snarls, the congealed blood on his face weeping with fresh blood as he speaks.

The second Monk drops his arm, Camden snatches the gun from his hand and pulls Kate behind him. Only when she's out of harm's way does Camden crash the handle of his gun against Monk's face twice in quick succession. I can hear his nose break from the other side of the room. He drops to his knees, cursing loudly, but Camden doesn't give him a moment's reprieve, instead he hits him again. The third punch knocks him out cold. He steps over Monk's limp frame and strides towards the King, his gun raised, ready to fire.

"Now you're going to pay for killing my mother," he snarls, reaching the King and pressing the gun into the back of his head. The King doesn't even flinch, but Veronika, she screams. The sound pierces the air and shatters my heart.

"I hate you!" she yells at Camden.

Tears pour down her face as she struggles in Malakai's hold, trying desperately to reach her father and I realise something then. No matter how evil, every monster has someone who loves them. Innocence doesn't see the ugliness inside someone's heart until it's too late and by that time the ugliness has either broken their spirit or moulded them into their image. Monk is a carbon copy of his father, but I refuse to allow the King to break Veronika's spirit like he tried to break mine.

"Veronika, is that your name?" I say gently, traversing the table and stepping beside Malakai and my little sister. I hunch lower so that my eyes meet hers. "Sweetheart. Your brother hurt my friend. He did that," I say, pointing at Pink. Her gaze follows my finger and her eyes widen.

"No, he wouldn't," she whispers, her little hands trembling even though she grits her jaw, showing me that despite her age, she's a fighter.

"He's a bad person just like our father," I say, taking her hand and squeezing it gently.

She snatches her hand from mine, anger blazing in her eyes. "NO!" she shouts, that one word hurting me more than I ever believed possible. Her innocence, her blind faith in the King, in Monk, shatters my heart. Today, one or both are going to die, and I know that this little girl will never forgive us, no matter what we do or say.

"Don't listen to her, Ronnie. Don't believe her. She's only trying to make you hate me. You don't hate me, do you, little one?" The King says, his eyes softening. Though when he glances at me I see the calculated look within them. He's manipulating her. He knows exactly what he's doing here. There's no love there. None. Whatever I saw earlier is gone. The man is as cold as we all know him to be.

Veronika shakes her head. "I don't hate you. I love you, Daddy," she says passionately, her little hands reaching for him. Connie covers a sob, folding herself into Ma Silva's hold.

The King grits his jaw. "Until the day you die, right, baby girl?"

"Until the day I die," she whispers back.

The King nods, turning towards Ma Silva despite the fact Camden has a gun pressed against his head. "Make sure Ronnie's taken care of."

Ma Silva nods. "I'll make sure she forgets every single thing about you. That's the only promise I can afford you now."

"I won't forget you, Daddy! I won't!"

"It isn't me I want you to remember, Ronnie. Look around this room. Remember them. Imprint their faces in your memory and when the time is right, you'll have your revenge."

"Enough, you sick bastard," Camden snaps, pulling back the hammer of his gun. "Take the kid out of here, she doesn't need to see this."

Malakai nods, handing Veronika to me. Despite her anger, her fear, she somehow senses that I'm her flesh and blood and holds on tight. Her screams are muffled as I run with her from the room, the sound of a single gunshot following us out.

FORTY

Camden steps out of the police station two weeks later accompanied by Hudson. Alongside me are my boys and the remaining Freed brothers. I run into his arms, almost barrelling him over with the force of my hug.

"*Bae-by,* you need to let me breathe," he laughs, folding me into his arms and hugging me back just as tightly. "It's only been two days!"

"Two days too long," I complain, drawing back only to kiss him passionately, my fingers feathering over the scar on his face. Behind us my boys whoop and whistle, reminding us both that we're on the steps of a police station in a very public place.

"I've missed you all too," he responds, hauling me into his side and fist-bumping Ford, Sonny and Eastern.

"You good?" Ford asks him.

"I am now."

"We were worried for a bit, mate," Eastern says, swiping a hand through his thick hair. It's a little longer than he usually wears it, falling in long curtains to his cheekbones, but instead of making him look younger, he just looks sexier. Plus, it's pretty nice to tug on.

"Hud's lawyers are shit-hot, there was no way he was going down for murder, not with all the evidence stacked against the King and the admission of guilt from Carmichael," Sonny points out.

"That and the fact that Camden *wasn't* actually the one to pull the trigger," Ford adds, grasping Camden on the shoulder, a look passing between them.

"Wait until we're in the car," Hudson admonishes. "It's still going to court, and Camden is a *witness* to the events of that evening, as are all of you."

"Yeah, not the best conversation to have in public," Max agrees.

We all pile into Bryce's eight-seater, settling in for the two-hour journey back to Oceanside. We've been on a hiatus from the academy, staying with the Freed brothers whilst each of us took turns being questioned by Crown with the support of their lawyers. The day after Mr Carmichael's arrest on the island, the Freed brothers turned up ready to murder us. I expected their anger, what I hadn't expected was their concern nor their love and unwavering support.

In the beginning, I'd believed their guilt at not acting sooner had forced them to help us, but pretty soon I realised that wasn't the case. They're good men. The best, actually. We all owe them more than we can ever repay.

"Tired?" Ford asks Camden as Hudson pulls out of the station.

"Fucking exhausted, actually," he replies.

Camden has been questioned twice. This time he's been held in custody longer than the first. Both his and Mr Carmichael's prints were found on the weapon used to shoot a hole in the King's head, and despite Mr Carmichael's confession, Crown has been like a dog with a bone. But with Mr Carmichael's confession there's nowhere he can go with it. For now it's over. Until the court hearing, that is.

"Let's get out of here," Camden says, leaning back in his seat and closing his eyes. I'm betting they've not given him much time to sleep even though he's still classed as a minor in the eyes of the law.

His eighteenth birthday is in a month's time, followed shortly by Ford's then Sonny's. Mine isn't until the end of the year. I'm still the baby of our crew. That's if you don't include Kate and Pink who are both younger than me by a couple months. And we do include them, just not when it comes to the bedroom, because in there they're all mine.

As the car moves through the streets of London, my thoughts stray to Mr Carmichael. Or should I say, Grayson Bennett, the oldest heir of the King crime dynasty. A man who tried, and failed, to extricate himself from his family's legacy of violence, crime and corruption.

Underneath all the mistakes, I do believe he's a good man who was born into a bad family.

He proved how good the night he threw himself at the mercy of the law, admitting full culpability for his brother's murder and taking the flack for everything that happened at Oceanside Academy leading up to that moment. Both his admission of guilt combined with the fact that Grim came up good by gathering enough information on the King's drugs business and sex trafficking ring at the spa in Hastings, has got Crown off our backs.

"Anyone heard from Malakai?" Camden asks after a while.

"No, he's still AWOL," Hudson confirms.

Shortly after Mr Carmichael's arrest, Malakai left the island and Grim retreated back into the underground fight club scene, sending just a single text message to us via Ford.

You did good. Anytime that you need a friend, hit me up.

"What about Connie?" I ask.

"She's getting on with her life, hopefully," Sonny responds. He wasn't keen on Malakai, neither are the rest of my boys.

"Hmm, perhaps." Though I'm not so sure. I saw the way they looked at each other. Their story hasn't ended yet, I'd bet my life on it.

"Connie and Ma Silva have extended an open invite back to their home on the island," Eastern says to Camden, who pops one eye open and gives him an 'I don't fucking think so' look.

Eastern laughs. "Yeah, that was my response too."

Whilst I've talked with Connie a couple of times since that weekend, I've no desire to return to the island either. Maybe one day she'll find the courage to leave her safe haven and come visit us. Either way, I just wish her well. She's another person I'm happy to call a friend, and Malakai sure as fuck doesn't deserve her, that's for sure. If he ever grows some balls and returns to the island to admit that he cares about her, then maybe he'll be able to save their relationship. If he doesn't, that's his loss.

The only sticking point with all of this is Monk and my half-sister Veronika. One of whom claims we're the real masterminds behind his father's murder and the other a child whose trauma has made her mute. She's just a kid who lost her father. A kid who never knew the man he was, only the man he pretended to be. Another child a victim of the King's rule and now living somewhere far away with a foster family. I hope time will dull the pain, will erase her memories. She's young enough to forget.

It's all we can hope for.

"What's the news on Monk?" Sonny asks. With the King dead and Mr Carmichael in prison, he's our biggest threat. Monk is vindictive. He won't let this go. Not ever.

"Still in custody. It's unlikely he'll get bail given his sentencing is next week. Ruby came forward with fresh allegations of rape and abuse over a two-year period," Bryce explains with a heavy sigh.

"Rape?" I hush out, my throat constricting. Despite the nausea I feel at what she's suffered at the hands of my half-brother, I'm also proud of her courage. Ruby has got her revenge after all.

Bryce nods. "I'm afraid so. She's not his first victim either. Several other girls have stepped forward, including Diamond and Emerald."

"I didn't know…"

"Why would you? Those girls weren't your friends, Asia," Camden says with a heavy sigh. "But they were my responsibility."

I squeeze Camden's hand, showing him that despite the implications of his words, I still love him. "You aren't responsible for what happened to them. At least now they've found the strength to step away from the people who've hurt them. Maybe they'll move on, finally."

He nods. "I hope so."

"The way things are looking, Monk will get a long sentence. He won't be released from prison for many, many years to come," Bryce confirms, easing some of my worries. I'm not foolish enough to believe we've seen and heard the last of Monk, but a few years reprieve is more than I could've hoped for. We'll be ready for him when he comes for us, and he will come, mark my words.

"But by that time, we'll all be long gone, right?" Ford says. "We ain't returning to Hackney?"

"Yes. That's the plan," Hudson confirms.

"And what about Santiago? He can't be happy about his *businesses* being shut down," Sonny questions, sarcasm dripping from his mouth.

"Santiago isn't your problem. He's mine," Hudson responds tightly, shutting the conversation down before it has even begun.

"Correction, bro, he's *our* problem," Max reminds him and Bryce nods in agreement, a look passing between them both.

There's more trouble brewing, except this time it's knocking on the Freeds' door, not ours. The only difference is, they have the contacts, the money and the means to take out Santiago. We just had our wits, our courage and sheer bloody mindedness.

"Hey, don't worry," Camden says, noticing my frown. He reaches for my hand, pulling it onto his thigh. I stroke my fingers up and down his leg, soothing us both with the contact as I push all thoughts of

Santiago out of my head. It's been hard enough to survive these last few months, we're not taking on Santiago too.

Camden sighs, the muscles of his face relaxing as we touch, our physical closeness easing one another's heartache. On the other side of me, Eastern leans in close, pressing a kiss against my cheek. Behind me, Ford and Sonny talk quietly until eventually a peaceful quiet descends as we race along the motorway.

Half an hour later Hudson breaks the silence. "Oh, I almost forgot. Cal wanted me to pass on a message."

"Yeah, what's that?" Camden asks, lifting his head off my shoulder.

"He says you all owe him a few stress-free weeks and a bottle of hair dye. The guy's aged about twenty years since taking over the role of acting principal and Nisha isn't happy about having a silver fox as a husband. At least, not this early on."

We laugh but despite the humour give Hudson our word to stay out of trouble. We've all had enough of it to last a lifetime.

OUR FINAL COUPLE of months at Oceanside blur into a series of moments captured in vibrant colour. Memories are made as we become an even tighter-knit group. Each moment documented in my sketchpad, brought to life in acrylic and oil, charcoal and pencil.

Pink and Kate study hard, determined to make the most of their remaining time and I throw myself into my physiotherapy and art lessons, the only two that hold any value to me. By the time our final week rolls around, we're all ready to move on with our lives, including Cal who is handing the baton to my favourite therapist. Starting in September, Mr Burnside will take on the role as principal of Oceanside, determined to carry on Mr Carmichael's legacy whilst his husband remains incarcerated at Her Majesty's pleasure.

"If I can't have a relationship with my husband, then I'll just have to be married to the job. I intend on keeping Oceanside open and fulfilling his dreams," he'd said to me, after we'd exited the courthouse a month ago.

Mr Carmichael had been sentenced to life imprisonment for the murder of the King and even though I'd expected tears from Mr Burnside, what I got was stoic determination and an unwavering faith that his sentence will be cut short.

That determination hasn't faltered, and the only reason he didn't take up the role sooner is because he's been working day and night with the Freed brothers to get my uncle's sentence lessened. It might be a fruitless task to some, but to Mr Burnside and Mr Carmichael, it's a worthwhile one. Maybe it will work. Maybe it won't. Either way it gives them both hope, and that's something no one wants to deny them.

Now, as we all gather in the car park behind the annex building, a group of kids no longer at war, there's a heavy sense of melancholy. Even Bram and Red have given up trying to fuck us over and the remaining kids of the HH crew have disbanded. With the King dead, and Monk put away, Bram isn't strong enough of a leader to keep the crew together. We've not forgiven either of them for the part they both played, but if this whole sorry tale has taught me anything it's this: forgiveness isn't in my nature but moving on is. As long as they don't fuck with us, then we're good.

"Good afternoon," Cal says with a bright smile as he stands beside me.

The day is warm, and the first hints of summer fill the air carrying the smell of the briny sea up the hill and into our lungs. It might seem a strange spot to celebrate the end of our time at Oceanside, but it's fitting. At the start of this term, Mr Carmichael had given me permission to use the back wall of the annex to display my end of year art project entitled *Reject*.

A word that has so many meanings for every single one of us here at Oceanside.

Rejected by society, we're the kids parents warn their children about.

We're the outcasts, the misfits, the delinquents, the dregs of society. We're the reprobates, the criminals, the savages no one saw fit to love and everyone wanted to avoid.

And yet when I look out into the crowd, my hand clutching onto the rope tethered to a piece of material covering the wall, I don't feel like a reject anymore. I don't fit into the mould I've been forced into. I'm not any of those labels.

I'm me. Asia Chen. Artist, friend, lover, sister, partner.

When I spot my boys, a feeling of acceptance fills my heart, warming me from the inside out. Each one of them filling a hole in my heart, plugging up the cracks, fixing me.

When I look at Kate and Pink, two girls I never believed I'd ever be friends with, I know this is just the start of many years of friendship. When I see the Freed brothers and Louisa, I see what my boys and I can become. When I witness Mr Burnside's smile even though he's hurting inside, I see an inner strength that I recognise in myself. And when I look at my baby brothers, I have *hope*. Hope that one day soon they'll be mine again and we can be together once more.

Getting to this point has only cemented my opinion that I've made the right decision with my art because even though society as a whole can reject us kids for what they see at face value, the only opinions that matter come from the family *I've* chosen.

"We're gathered here today to celebrate the end of these students' time at Oceanside. To give them our well wishes and to support them in their future endeavours. Asia is one of our most talented students and she has been given permission to share her art with us and the future students who pass through these halls," Cal continues, winking at me. "So without further ado…"

Grinning, I pull on the rope, basking in the reactions of the people here that I love.

Because Kate, Pink, Camden, Eastern, Sonny, Ford, me. None of us are rejects.

We're *family*.

And that word, above all others, is the one I chose to spray paint across this wall in glorious rainbow colours.

EPILOGUE

Three years later.

"A re you sure those two little buggers haven't had chocolate for breakfast? They're running around the living room like rats on speed," Sonny grouses, a twinkle in his eye as he enters the kitchen. "Pretty sure they'll be climbing up the walls next!"

I laugh, pouring myself another cup of coffee. I need at least two in the morning to keep me going. Having four boyfriends with needs means this woman doesn't get much sleep. That and the fact George has taken to sleepwalking every night, doesn't help either. He might be seven now, but that hasn't stopped his imagination any.

"Nope, just marmite on toast," I reply, peering down the hallway of our tiny house just as George sprints out of the living room, Eastern hot on his tail. Seeing them laughing and playing together warms my heart.

"Hey, watch your step!" I call, as George slides across the wooden floor in his socks almost banging head first into the wall opposite. Fortunately, Camden steps out into the hall from the small study and captures George in his arms.

"Whoa, tiger. Take it easy," he laughs, swinging him up into his arms and over his shoulder as though he weighs nothing. I suppose he doesn't to Camden, who's grown broader and more muscular than the boy I remember at Oceanside.

Striding down the hall, Camden deposits George on the kitchen stool, messing up his hair with his large hand. "You, Georgie, need to calm your socks. Take a seat whilst I whip us up some pancakes."

"Yum!" George fist-pumps the air and grins.

"He's just had three slices of toast. I'm pretty sure he's full," I say, shaking my head.

Camden flashes me a grin that melts my knickers. "*Bae-by,* George is a growing boy and needs to develop those muscles, don't you, Georgie?"

"Yep! Ford said that when I grow up I'm gonna be the best fighter the world has ever seen. He said I'm even better than Sebastian, that *I'm* his favourite."

"Hey, buddy, I do not have a favourite. You're both my little fighters." Ford protests, stepping into the kitchen, his hair all messed up from sleep.

Behind him Sebastian saunters in, copying Ford's every move. He's nine now and grown so tall. I can already see the young man he's going to become in the lazy smile he wears and the twinkle in his deep green eyes that are currently staring at Ford in adoration.

My little brothers love all my men, but Ford is their favourite. His endless patience and devotion to them is beautiful to witness. They each take it in turns to spend time with them both, but Ford actively seeks Sebastian and George out even when it's not his turn. He dotes on them and in turn they worship him.

Eastern steps into the room, clapping his hand onto Ford's shoulder. "Late night?" he asks, looking between us both with a smirk.

He knows as well as the rest of us that Sunday nights are set aside for Ford and me. My cheeks flush at the ache between my legs. Last night was most definitely a late one. Pretty sure we both only got a few hours of sleep. Ordinarily I wouldn't complain, but today I start my new job as a physiotherapist to an ex-ballet dancer up at the beautiful Browlace Manor. I don't want to mess up.

"So who's watching the kids today?" I ask, looking between them all over the rim of my coffee cup.

Eastern glances at Sonny and they grin. "We've got a job at the harbour. We'll be out all day."

"You do? That's great," I reply, accepting a kiss on the cheek from Eastern as he leans over and grabs one of the pancakes Camden has tossed onto a plate.

"But what about the sea sickness?" I ask, knowing that the ocean isn't Eastern or Sonny's favourite place to be.

"We're working on the docks, not out on the ocean, thankfully," Eastern explains.

Ford huffs, plonking himself on another stool. His gaze meets Camden and they both frown.

"What is it?" I ask.

"It just shows what a pretty face can do. No one wants to hire two blokes covered in tats who look like they spend more time causing trouble than earning an honest living."

"I love your tats, and your faces," I respond, rounding the table and wrapping my arms around Ford's naked chest which is now covered in a huge tattoo of four warriors surrounding their queen. You can guess who's the queen. My fingers trail over his skin as I speak. "People who pass judgement so quickly are usually the ones you want to avoid anyway. Something will come up. I have a good feeling."

"Yeah, Asia's right. Fuck 'em," Camden adds, then grimaces when I glare at him. "Sorry... pancake?" He smiles sweetly, and I instantly forgive him for breaking my 'no swearing around the kids' rule. We have a jar filled with coins from all the bloopers.

"Can't, need to go. Wish me luck," I say, checking my watch and groaning at the time.

"Good luck, Bae-by," Camden says, drawing me in for a lingering kiss. When he releases me, I press a quick kiss on the top of George and Sebastian's heads. Then kiss each of my men in turn before waving goodbye.

When I reach the front door, I stop for a moment, smiling as I listen to their loving banter and my little brothers' laughter. We've come such a long way, the five of us, and now that my brothers are mine to keep forever thanks to the Freeds' help, our family is complete.

Opening the front door to our tiny home, I step towards my car, excited for my first day at my new job, knowing somehow that from this moment onwards no matter what troubles might come our way, we have each other to weather the storm.

And that's a gift I never thought I'd have; love, happiness, and a family to call my own.

THE END

FLICK the page for information on Malakai and Connie's love story.

OUT NOW

Who else felt the sexual tension between Malakai and Connie...? You, dear reader? Yeah, me too. I felt the pull of those two so much that I decided to write them their own story. Out now is *Beyond the Horizon* a M/F, age-gap romance that may or may not set your knickers on fire and turn your heart to mush. Get ready for sparks to fly!

Read on for an excerpt of Beyond the Horizon!

Grab it here

He arrived on a warm summer's day...

Malakai Azaiah Dunbar, a loner whose home was the ocean I adored.

I was eighteen, he was thirty-six.

My foolish heart was stolen by a man who refused to accept I existed. A forbidden kiss sending him back into the arms of the ocean.

I was nineteen. He was thirty-seven.

He was changed. Cruel. Abrasive. Until he wasn't and I gave him something precious.

I'm twenty. He's thirty-eight.

He's back but doesn't know I've grown to love him more with every passing year.

Just like the ocean we both adore, Malakai is mysterious, tumultuous, dangerous, and not to be tamed. But this time I'm going to keep him. This time I'm going to make him stay.

**This is a May to December standalone contemporary M/F romance with high heat levels and a love story that might just make you weep.

SNEAK PEEK!

Turn the page for a
Beyond the Horizon
excerpt

IN THE BEGINNING...

Connie

The first time I saw him I had just turned eighteen. I was sitting on my family's private beach humming along to Hozier as it played through the iPod that I carried with me everywhere I went. My toes were dipped in a shallow rockpool, the seawater warmed by the midday sun. I remember so clearly the tiny see-through fish swimming about my bare ankles. I remember the swathe of emerald seaweed gently moving in the current made by my wiggling toes and the smell of briny sea air.

It had been a peaceful summer's day. Idyllic.

The sun had been high and hot, the August rays warming my tanned skin, drawing out a rash of freckles across my cheeks and shoulders and colouring streaks of blonde in my coffee-brown hair. I'd been wearing a dark blue swimsuit with a pair of cut-off denim shorts that showed far too much skin according to Grandma Silva.

"Save something for the imagination, child. Real beauty is a gift that doesn't need to be flaunted," she'd often said to me.

But I was my mother's daughter.

I was free-spirited, headstrong, and far womanlier than I had any right to be at such an age. With a fresh face, cupid bow lips, long dark tresses and eyes as deep blue as the sea I adored so much, I knew I was pretty. People never look too deeply when all they see is a pretty face. My soul, however, belonged to someone who'd lived far longer than my eighteen years and I never let anyone get close enough to see into the depths of me. Maybe that was to do with the fact tragedy had struck my life so young, or maybe I was always born to be that way. Either way, I felt older than I was, even back then.

Perhaps that was why I'd remained behind whilst my friends had visited the mainland in search of fun, wanting nothing more than the hustle and bustle of a busy town or city. My best friends were bored with living on our little island nestled off the coast of Kent, cut off from the world and as backward as a third world country when it came to mod-cons. The only way in or out of the island was by boat and if a bad storm hit no one was going anywhere.

But despite my friends' desire to leave, I'd been happy and content to spend time in my own company writing lyrics and listening to my favourite kind of music, the kind that can move a person, can change them just like the gentle waves that moved against an ever-changing shore.

In my hand I'd clutched my notepad, my pencil scratching against the cream paper, my round cursive filling the pages with lyrics that I'd kept hidden inside my heart. I'd been so engrossed in the words flowing from the pumping organ within my chest that I hadn't noticed the schooner dropping anchor a mile out to sea. I hadn't noticed a lone figure diving into the water, until strong shoulders and powerful strokes came into my peripheral vision and I'd looked up from beneath the shade of my straw hat.

I'd been immediately entranced, so caught off guard by this sudden intrusion to my most sacred place that I'd dropped my notepad into the pool of water at my feet. I hadn't even bothered to try and rescue the waterlogged paper, too intent on trying to get a better view of the mysterious stranger swimming towards my family's private beach, Broken Shores.

The small cove had been named by my great-great-grandmother who'd lost her heart and soul the day her beloved had lost his life to the waves many, many years ago. According to my grandma, the women of our family are cursed when it comes to love. We might be destined to find our soulmate, but we're never allowed to keep them. My grandma believes that where true love is concerned for the women of our family, tragedy always strikes, ripping hearts in two and shredding souls apart.

"Never fall in love, Connie. Keep your heart guarded. Save it from the pain, child."

Just like my great-great-grandmother, Grandma Silva also hated this cove just as much. Grandpa John had died on this beach, a massive heart attack taking him from her at the age of forty-five. So I understood why she'd refused to visit, why she'd hated Broken Shores so much, but I could never hate such crushing beauty. How could I, when it had brought me *him*?

Malakai Azaiah Dunbar.

A bronzed god with rippling muscles and black swirling tattoos that covered his arms and chest in designs that had made my heart ache and my core clench with strange new feelings, awakening something forbidden, something... *dangerous.*

That day he stole my heart without even realising it, but that didn't matter to me because I had given it freely despite my grandma's warning, maybe even because of it. When he'd looked up at me, the dark forest-green of his eyes narrowing on mine, salty seawater running in rivulets over his taut golden skin, I'd known at once that he was my soulmate. I'd known it deep down in the very marrow of my bones even when he'd refused to believe it. Even when he sailed away from it, from me, I still believed.

I *still* do.

I was eighteen that day he walked onto my beach. He was thirty-six.

The expanse of eighteen years kept us apart back then.

But like the terns that nested in the cliff face of Broken Shores, he returned the following summer. He returned the next summer after that too, and with every year that passed, the gap shrank until the only expanse that kept us apart was his schooner sailing beyond the horizon and his refusal to believe in us.

Perhaps I should've heeded my grandma's warning. Perhaps I should've guarded my heart against him. Only I didn't.

I still refuse to do that.

What you're about to read is our love story or perhaps our very own tragedy. I guess that still depends on how it ends...

AUTHOR NOTE

So, there we have it. Asia and her family of *delinquents* got their happy ever after. At one point, I wasn't sure if that was going to happen. These characters really did send me on a merry-go-round. A lot of late nights were had wrangling them and they put up quite a fight.

There's was a story of heartache, pain and disappointment so I knew I had to give them what they deserved; happiness, and a family to call their own. Of the three in the trilogy, this story was the most difficult to write. Letting them go was hard, but I hope to revisit them one day!

But first, Malakai and Connie. If you got this far you would have read the excerpt from Beyond the Horizon. I hope you enjoyed it!

I have to say these two characters just leapt off the page for me. The second I wrote them into Family I knew I had to give them their own tale. Malakai is pig-headed and stubborn, but then so too is Connie. Together they are electric. I'm talking combustion and stars colliding and all that wonderful, crazy, all-encompassing, life-altering love. It's what we all dream of, am I right?

As always, thank you for continuing on this journey with me and my characters. Most days I'm still awed that people actually want to read what I write. So, to you, dear reader, I am indebted.

To be certain that you keep up to date with all my releases and news, please do come and join my Facebook group, *Queen Bea's Hive*, where I'm most active.

Once again, thanks for sticking with me. Here's to plenty more stories to come.

Love, Bea xoxo

ABOUT BEA PAIGE

Bea Paige lives a very secretive life in London... She likes red wine and Haribo sweets (preferably together) and occasionally swings around poles when the mood takes her.

Bea loves to write about love and all the different facets of such a powerful emotion. When she's not writing about love and passion, you'll find her reading about it and ugly crying.

Bea is always writing, and new ideas seem to appear at the most unlikely time, like in the shower or when driving her car.

She has lots more books planned,
so be sure to subscribe to her newsletter:
beapaige.co.uk/newsletter-sign-up

Check Be a out on TikTok:
https://www.tiktok.com/@beapaigeauthor

f facebook.com/BeaPaigeAuthor

instagram.com/beapaigeauthor

pinterest.com/beapaigeauthor

BB bookbub.com/authors/bea-paige

ALSO BY BEA PAIGE

THEIR OBSESSION DUET

The Dancer and The Masks

The Masks and The Dancer

ACADEMY OF STARDOM

(ACADEMY REVERSE HAREM ROMANCE)

#1 Freestyle

#2 Lyrical

#3 Breakers

#4 Finale

ACADEMY OF MISFITS

(ACADEMY REVERSE HAREM ROMANCE)

#1 Delinquent

#2 Reject

#3 Family

FINDING THEIR MUSE

(DARK CONTEMPORARY ROMANCE / REVERSE HAREM)

#1 Steps

#2 Strokes

#3 Strings

#4 Symphony

#5 Finding Their Muse boxset

THE BROTHERS FREED SERIES

(CONTEMPORARY ROMANCE / REVERSE HAREM)

#1 Avalanche of Desire

#2 Storm of Seduction

#3 Dawn of Love

#4 Brothers Freed Boxset

CONTEMPORARY STANDALONES

Beyond the Horizon

THE INFERNAL DESCENT TRILOGY

(CO-WRITTEN WITH SKYE MACKINNON)

#1 Hell's Calling

#2 Hell's Weeping

#3 Hell's Burning

#4 Infernal Descent boxset

Printed in Great Britain
by Amazon

80812000R00194